# AURORA BLAZING

ALSO BY JESSIE MIHALIK

*Polaris Rising*

# AURORA BLAZING

## A NOVEL

## JESSIE MIHALIK

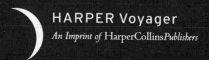

HARPER Voyager
*An Imprint of* HarperCollins*Publishers*

AURORA BLAZING. Copyright © 2019 by Jessie Mihalik. All rights reserved. Printed in the United States of America. No part of this book may be used or reproduced in any manner whatsoever without written permission except in the case of brief quotations embodied in critical articles and reviews. For information, address HarperCollins Publishers, 195 Broadway, New York, NY 10007.

HarperCollins books may be purchased for educational, business, or sales promotional use. For information, please email the Special Markets Department at SPsales@harpercollins.com.

Harper Voyager and design are trademarks of HarperCollins Publishers LLC.

FIRST EDITION

Designed by Paula Russell Szafranski

Library of Congress Cataloging-in-Publication Data has been applied for.

ISBN 978-0-06-280241-5

19 20 21 22 23   LSC   10 9 8 7 6 5 4 3 2 1

*To Dustin, my heart and soul.*

*I love you.*

# ACKNOWLEDGMENTS

My deepest gratitude to the following people who helped make this book possible.

Thanks to my agent extraordinaire, Sarah E. Younger, who always has my back and is a joy to work with. I could not ask for a better agent!

Thanks to my editor, Tessa Woodward, for her excellent editorial advice. She makes my books so much better! And thanks to Elle Keck, Kayleigh Webb, Imani Gary, and the rest of the team at Harper Voyager for their help and support.

Thanks to Victoria Mathews, the copyeditor who found my dropped articles and misplaced words.

Thanks to Patrick Ferguson, Tracy Smith, and Whitney Bates for reading the raw draft, giving me feedback, and understanding when I fall in a deadline hole for two months. You are the best!

Thanks to Ilona and Gordon for their help, support, and guidance.

Thanks to Bree and Donna for shouting about my books all over Twitter. I'm sure many of you found me because of them and I am deeply grateful.

## ACKNOWLEDGMENTS

My utmost love and gratitude to my husband, Dustin, who is my first reader, greatest cheerleader, and dearest friend. Thank you for cooking while I work!

And finally, thanks to you, readers. You took a chance on my debut novel and came back for book two. Your support means everything! Happy reading!

# AURORA BLAZING

# CHAPTER 1

L ady Taylor had bugs in her walls and not the kind with jointed legs and crunchy bodies. The tortured piano in the corner whined out something that vaguely resembled music as I fought the urge to pull out my com and track the signals to their sources. Three different broadcast frequencies meant at least three different agencies were interested in what happened at a Consortium ladies' afternoon tea.

Or perhaps they were just interested in Lady Taylor.

My mind spun down that avenue, looking for motive, before I forcefully reined it in. I had to focus, dammit. If only these events weren't so dreadfully dull.

A nearby conversation caught my attention. I smiled into my teacup as the two girls behind me debated in fierce, heated whispers whether or not I'd killed my husband. They didn't realize the terrible piano music wouldn't hide their discussion.

My youngest sister stiffened at my side as she overheard a particularly exuberant theory. I put a restraining hand on her arm. Catarina's eyes flashed with fury, but I minutely shook my head and she settled down. She glanced behind us, no doubt cataloging the girls' faces for future retribution.

Neither the words nor the speculation bothered me, and indeed, they gave me something to focus on. But my youngest sister had always chafed at the daily viciousness of Consortium life.

A quick glance confirmed the girls were from one of the lower houses. A brunette with straight hair, tan skin, and a face just a touch too narrow for true beauty sat beside a stunning young woman with ebony skin and black curls. We had been introduced at some point, but memory was fluid and mine more than most. I couldn't recall either of their names.

This was likely their first social season—they hadn't yet learned how to subtly skewer an opponent with a smile and a few well-chosen words. Even Catarina could probably send them from the room in tears with little more than a sentence.

Besides, the girls' speculation as to *how* I could've killed Gregory provided some much-needed distraction. The formal sitting room was almost claustrophobically small, with no windows and heavy, ornate furniture. You'd never know we were in the penthouse of a thirty-story building.

The two dozen impeccably dressed, sharp-eyed women seated in little cliques facing the piano only added to the oppressive atmosphere.

"Bianca, why do you let them continue?" Cat asked in an exasperated whisper. I'd been on the receiving end of many exasperated whispers lately.

"What, you don't think I paid Gregory's mistress to get him drunk and push him down the stairs?" I asked, quoting the latest ridiculous suggestion.

Uncertainty flashed across her face as her mask slipped the tiniest bit. "Of course not," she said stoutly. She shot me a sly smile and continued, "You're a von Hasenberg—you'd do it yourself."

That was as close as any of my sisters ever got to asking

me what had really happened. And every time it caused a riot of emotions—fear, anger, relief, love—as I waited to see if *this time* would be the time they would ask.

I set my teacup on its saucer with precise, iron-willed control. The two pieces met without the telltale rattle that would indicate my internal turmoil. The interminable piano piece finally came to an end, saving me from having to respond.

"—was poison—" the curly-haired gossip said into the sudden silence. She choked off the words on a strangled gasp. Out of the corner of my eye, I saw her freeze as every person in the room turned her way. Her black curls trembled as she swallowed nervously. The sharks paused, smelling blood.

"What was that, dear?" Lady Taylor asked with false sweetness. She had a daughter—one who could not play the piano for love or money. If these two were shunned, her daughter would have a better shot at making a good match.

The silence stretched as the girl floundered. The second girl, the brunette, sat stone-still, doing her best to blend in to the furniture.

"She was asking if poison was the best option to remove a particularly stubborn weed," I said smoothly. Lady Taylor's laser gaze swiveled to me, but as the daughter of a High House, I outranked her, and she knew it.

"Is that so?" she asked.

I tipped up my chin a fraction. Ice frosted my tone. "You doubt my word?" When she took a second too long to answer, I stood. Catarina rose with me.

Lady Taylor paled beneath her flawless makeup as all eyes now focused on her. "Of course I didn't mean—"

I would feel sympathetic, except she *had* meant to cause offense. She was conniving, and I'd let her get away with too much for too long because I just didn't care. I'd already done my duty to my House, my position was secure, and I had no one I needed to impress.

But the moment she'd doubted my word, she'd taken it too far, a fact that was just now dawning on her.

"I realized I have somewhere else to be," I said. I turned to the curly-haired gossip. She was as young as I expected, perhaps seventeen or eighteen. "Walk with me," I said.

She rose but kept her head bowed. When the brunette started to rise, too, I shot her a quelling glare. She wilted back into her seat. She hadn't attempted to bail her friend out, so she would have to fend off the sharks on her own.

I linked arms with the curly haired girl and swept her from the room over the protests of Lady Taylor. Catarina kept pace beside me. We didn't speak until we'd cleared the front door.

"My lady, I'm *so* sorry," the girl said miserably as I pulled her along toward the transport platform.

"You should be," Catarina said.

I rolled my eyes. "What is your name?" I asked.

"Lynn Segura, second daughter of House Segura," she said.

House Segura was a small house with modest assets, one of the many lower houses that made up the bulk of the Royal Consortium. "How did you manage an invite to Lady Taylor's tea?" I asked. House Taylor was one of the more powerful lower houses.

"Chloe received an invite and brought me along," she said. At my blank look, she blushed and elaborated, "Chloe Patel, first daughter of House Patel. She is the woman I was with."

That made more sense. House Patel was also a lower house, but they had three eligible sons around the same age as Lady Taylor's daughter. And their interests dovetailed nicely with House Taylor's.

"Are you going to tell my father?" Lynn asked.

We emerged outside into the sun. The transport platform had tall glass panels to block the worst of the wind, but a breeze swirled gently, teasing the hem of my gray dress. Serenity sparkled under the cloudless sky. The only city on Earth and the heart of the Royal Consortium, Serenity was a hive of activity. Transports and ships crisscrossed the sky, glittering like jewels.

For all its flaws, I loved this city.

I let the girl fret in silence while the three of us climbed into the waiting House von Hasenberg transport. Catarina sat facing backward while I sat next to Lynn. I waved the embedded chip in my left arm over the reader. "Take us to Macall's Coffee House," I said. The transport chimed its acceptance, then slid off the thirtieth-floor platform and headed northwest.

The glass panel in the floor showed another transport in House von Hasenberg colors—black and gold—shadowing us from below. Our security detail was a new and unwelcome change, but three weeks ago we'd gone to war with House Rockhurst, so it was deemed a necessary evil.

If the ladies of the House hadn't presented a united front, we would have had armed guards escorting us to tea. As it was, they escorted us to evening events, but only followed us via transport during the day. Serenity was officially neutral ground, but both Father and our director of security were paranoid.

Lynn practically vibrated in her seat, desperate to know if I'd tell her father but smart enough not to ask again. She had potential.

"I am not going to tell anyone," I said. "We are going to enjoy a cup of coffee in public and have a nice chat, then we will part on agreeable terms. The next time I see you, I will make a point of saying hello."

Lynn's eyes narrowed. "Why?" she asked.

"Because your behavior made a boring tea interesting. And because if I do not, Lady Taylor will destroy you."

Lynn flinched as the full implication of her actions hit her. She squared her shoulders and met my eyes. "What can I do to repay you?"

I tilted my head as I regarded her. I'd saved her because I could and because I remembered my own disastrous first season. I hadn't expected anything in return, but I wasn't so hasty as to turn down a debt freely offered, either. She wasn't the first girl I'd saved, and thanks to that, I had eyes in many places.

"You do not *have* to do anything," I said seriously, "but if you ever overhear anything you think I might find interesting, I would be grateful if you would let me know."

She nodded, her eyes bright. "Consider it done."

MACALL'S COFFEE HOUSE OCCUPIED A GROUND-FLOOR corner of a tall office building in Sector Three of the von Hasenberg quarter. Floor-to-ceiling windows wrapped around two sides of the shop, giving those inside a sense of airy lightness.

The café was decorated in cream and brown, with real wood and leather furniture—no plastech dared to breach these walls. The tables and chairs were beautifully mismatched with charming, understated elegance. Someone had put a lot of time and effort into making the design look effortless.

House von Hasenberg retained a table with an ideal location: next to the window and slightly separate from the surrounding tables. All three High Houses retained tables, aware that as much business happened here as on the floor of the Royal Consortium. But because we were in the von Hasenberg quarter, our House had received the best location.

After the waiter left with our orders, I activated the silencer built into the table—another perk. By default, silencers only blocked sound in one direction, so we could still hear the people murmuring around us, but no one could eavesdrop on our conversation.

The silencer prevented any sounds or wireless signals in a two-meter radius from transmitting outside that radius, including voices, coms, or bugs. If someone wanted to know what we were gossiping about, they'd have to read our lips.

Once Lynn realized I really wasn't going to bite, her wit and humor returned. She wasn't quite brave enough to ask me outright if I'd killed my husband, but the same cleverness that made her spout wild theories made chatting with her entertaining. Saving her had been the right move.

We chatted for forty-five minutes before Lynn took her leave. The door had barely closed behind her when Catarina pinned me with a stare. "This is how you know everything about everyone," she said. "You have a legion of spies masquerading as young women."

I sipped my lemonade and said nothing. She was wrong, but she drew the exact conclusion I had intended. Shame slid through my system, soft and sour. I didn't like lying to family, even by omission, but it was the only way to ensure they—and I—stayed safe.

"How many have you saved?" Cat asked.

"I don't keep track. A dozen, maybe. I started when I returned home after Gregory's death." The true number was twenty-seven, and that only counted the people I'd truly helped, not those like Lynn who had just needed a momentary rescue. If I included everyone, the number would be closer to sixty. And I'd started well before Gregory's death.

Our prenup had protected House von Hasenberg's interests, not mine. When my husband died, I inherited nothing. His family wasted no time hustling me out of their lives. Money was far less of an issue than stability and familiarity, so I ran home like the wounded animal I was.

"I can't believe you're running your own spy ring," Catarina said with a laugh. "I bet it drives Ian insane."

I smiled. Ian Bishop was the director of House von Hasenberg security—an inconspicuous title for a far-reaching power. He had his fingers in House intelligence gathering, security forces, and even military maneuvers. He was the most arrogant man I'd ever met, and that was saying something considering I grew up in a High House.

He was also one of the most handsome, but a trained interrogator couldn't force the admission from my lips.

One of my few true pleasures these days was beating Ian to a piece of intelligence. It had turned into something of a competition, and I was currently ahead by two. Or, at least, my shadowy, anonymous online persona was. Ian had no idea I was feeding him information from multiple directions.

"Ian doesn't think the daughter of a High House is capable of anything other than being a trophy wife," I said. "I enjoy proving him wrong."

"I thought Ada would've disabused him of that notion," Catarina said. "He tried to catch her for two years and failed."

My younger sister Ada was exceptional, but even she wasn't *that* good—as head of security for a High House, Ian had nearly infinite resources at his disposal. He'd failed because I'd fed him a constant stream of false information, while giving Ada all the info she needed to stay ahead of him.

I wanted to tell Cat, to let her in on the secret, but one secret led to twenty others, each more dangerous than the last. I held my tongue.

"Oh, I'm supposed to meet Lady Ying in twenty minutes to go shopping. You want to join?" Catarina asked.

I repressed a shudder. Shopping with Catarina was a masochistic endeavor if ever there was one. The girl could spend seven hours in a single store. Seven. Hours.

Luckily for the rest of us, Ying Yamado was always game for a shopping trip. She and Catarina were close friends—as close as the daughters of two High Houses could be, at least.

"I'll pass, thanks. I'd like to make it home before tomorrow," I said.

Catarina rolled her eyes at me. "I'm not *that* bad."

I just raised my eyebrows until she cracked and broke down into giggles.

"Okay, maybe I am. But you're missing out," she said as she stood. She kissed the air next to my cheek and then she was gone. I disabled the silencer, and the communication signals around me rushed in, overwhelming and nauseating.

After all of this time, I should be used to it, but Gregory's gift just kept on giving. He'd been a brilliant scientist and a horrible husband, wrapped together with a morally bankrupt bow. I don't think it ever occurred to him to *not* experiment on me.

Now I could mentally intercept and decrypt wireless signals, whether I wanted to or not, and I had no idea how. Gregory's lab had been destroyed, taking most of his secrets to the grave.

He had tampered with both my brain and my nanobots, the infinitesimal robots in my blood that were supposed to aid healing. Father would dearly love the tech, so much so that he would absolutely approve more experiments on me if he found out about my abilities.

I'd been a test subject for long enough.

So I kept my secrets to myself and became a grieving widow in public. It kept Father from pushing me to remarry—which I would never do—and covered some of my new eccentricities.

I attended teas and lunches and balls when I would've

preferred staying home. But staying home would not let me find other young women who could use my help, so I sucked it up and played the idle aristocrat.

At home, I earned my keep by using my network to track down information for House von Hasenberg. Father didn't know exactly where my information came from, but he knew that if he needed something found, I could find it.

I finished my lemonade and pretended my head didn't feel like it was being stabbed with stilettos. The headaches were worse when I was in an open public space, as my piddly human brain couldn't keep up with all of the information flowing to the implant from my modified nanos.

My com lit up in my mind's eye a second before it vibrated in my handbag. Because I was attuned to it, I knew I'd received a message and what it said without looking at the device itself. Decoding transmissions, even the secure transmissions my com received, was almost comically easy. Whatever else Gregory had been, he truly had been a gifted scientist.

I'd taught myself to tune out most transmissions so they became ignorable background noise. It didn't help with the headaches, but at least I didn't have to constantly hear strangers' messages in my head all day. Now they burbled along like a distant stream in the back of my mind. I could hear individual messages if I focused, but mostly they were white noise.

I was Gregory's fantasy of an ideal wife, forced to listen to everything without being able to respond. I didn't know if he'd planned to add transmission abilities later or if he'd designed it this way as a cosmic joke. If it was the latter, the joke was very much on him. I smiled in grim satisfaction.

I pulled out my com to read and respond the old-fashioned way. The message was from Ian. It was short and to the point. *You were scheduled to return home, not split from your sister.*

*The security detail followed her. Remain where you are until the replacement detail arrives. I have eyes on you until then.*

My smile morphed into a grin as I typed my reply. *I was just leaving. I'll be home before they arrive.*

*STAY PUT.* The reply was so fast, I wondered if he had pre-typed it. I'd hate to think I was so predictable.

I didn't bother with a reply. If he was actually monitoring the cameras, he'd see me leave. Otherwise, he'd certainly notice when my tracker started moving. Either way, I wasn't going to sit around for who knew how long waiting for his security team. My head ached at just the thought.

The coffee shop was close enough that I could walk home, but that was sure to make Ian apoplectic. And while I didn't really think Serenity was unsafe, we *were* at war and some basic safety precautions were prudent.

I ordered a House transport and waited until it arrived before leaving the building. I didn't see Ian's second security detail, so he was sure to be livid. I resisted the urge to tap into our House security cameras to see for myself.

The transport dropped me at the private family entrance without incident. I cleared the new security checkpoint then waved my embedded identity chip over the reader at the door. The reader beeped as it verified that my chip and biometrics matched. The door opened, and I let myself into the ornately carved stone building I'd called home for twenty-one of my twenty-five years.

The heavy stone blocked some of the wireless signals, and I sighed in relief. I stepped out of the entryway and a shadow detached itself from the draperies.

I had a blaster in hand before my brain recognized that I wasn't being attacked by a stranger. No, I was being stalked by Ian Bishop.

I wasn't sure that was an improvement.

# CHAPTER 2

L ady von Hasenberg," Ian said in his precise, clipped accent. Fury etched lines in his handsome face, but his deep voice still slid over my skin like cashmere. "A moment, please."

I'd kept my name during my marriage, one of the benefits of being the daughter of a High House. Instead, Gregory had changed his last name to gain the power of mine. That power felt very flimsy with Ian glaring down at me.

Ian Bishop was tall and lean, with broad shoulders that narrowed to a trim waist. He wore a charcoal three-piece suit with a pale blue shirt and matching tie. I'd never seen him in anything other than a suit or tuxedo, but my imagination was more than willing to try. I'd bet a good deal of money that vast expanses of delicious muscle hid under the layers of fabric.

He was devilishly handsome, with a strong jaw and icy blue eyes. His hair was dark blond, shorter on the sides and longer on top. It was continually tousled, making a woman imagine running her fingers through it to smooth it.

Or maybe that was just me.

I pulled my tattered public persona around me as I returned my blaster to the clutch holster. At a meter sixty-eight,

I was the shortest member of my family by far. I made up for it by wearing towering heels. But even with the added height, Ian still topped me by at least ten centimeters.

While I'd never quite mastered Mother's trick of looking down on everyone regardless of height, I also refused to let him believe that *he* could look down on *me*, so I met his gaze head-on. If eyes were the windows to the soul, then, by all appearances, his was a lonely, desolate place. However, I couldn't shake the feeling that Ian Bishop was more than met the eye.

"Director Bishop, to what do I owe the pleasure?" I asked, all false innocence.

A muscle flexed in his jaw and I could practically see him counting to ten in his head. "You ignored a direct order and put yourself in danger," he said at last.

"No, I ignored a direct *suggestion* and arrived home unscathed." I smiled sweetly. "Was there anything else?"

"Am I the director of security for House von Hasenberg?" Ian asked.

I nodded obligingly.

"And are you part of House von Hasenberg?"

"Last I checked," I said drily.

"So therefore, when I make a *suggestion* concerning your safety, you would be well-advised to *follow it,*" he bit out. "I know it is difficult for you to drag your mind away from gossip and parties long enough to pay attention, but I don't make suggestions for my own health; I do it to keep you safe."

I stiffened and a fleeting expression crossed his face, too fast to identify. My training solidified around me like armor, distancing me from the fury blazing through my system. If he was cold, then I was ice.

I tilted up my chin. "If your security plan is so fragile that a single change causes it to crumble, that is not *my* failure." He started to reply, but I cut him off. "Director Bishop, this has been *delightful,* as usual, but now I must go. So many parties to think about, you know."

It was a mistake to let him know that he'd gotten to me, but I couldn't stop myself. I swept away, the only sign of my anger the staccato beat of my heels against the marble floor.

Anger carried me to my suite before burning out. Ian Bishop wasn't worth the headache. He'd made it abundantly clear that he was not interested years ago. I still cringed when I thought back to my awkward attempts to flirt with him when he had first arrived as a mere bodyguard.

He'd had a plan, one he wasn't going to let an "empty-headed princess" deter him from. Even seven years ago he'd been a real charmer. But what he lacked in charm, he made up for in sheer, pigheaded determination.

In just three years he'd moved from bodyguard to director of security—and no one was quite certain how. The position usually only went to someone with decades of experience, not a kid who, at the time, hadn't even hit twenty-five. Now that he'd entered his late twenties, he was still at least three decades younger than his peers.

I flopped onto my canopy bed and let the curtain fall closed behind me. Custom-designed, the bed acted as an isolation chamber that blocked most wireless signals. The curtains were three layers of a fine metal mesh that connected at the top and bottom to metal embedded in the canopy and under the mattress. The metal cage directed signals around the bed and canceled out the signals in the space inside, leaving me in blissful quiet.

I'd also completely shielded my office on the pretense of security, and the rest of my suite had a smaller amount of shielding hidden behind the paint and plaster. Just because I was a science experiment didn't mean I had to be miserable in my own home.

I sighed in relief as my headache started to subside. Even when I wasn't focusing on a signal, my nanos and brain were decoding it, like a computer running in the background. I hadn't yet found a way to turn it off, but the human body was remarkably adaptable. When I'd first been modified, I couldn't stand unshielded spaces for more than an hour or two without passing out. Today, I'd been out for eight hours and while my head *hurt,* I was still functional.

I had stayed out longer than I'd planned, and I had another event tonight. I had enough time for a nap, but then I'd have to get up and dressed for House Chan's betrothal ball. Their only daughter was marrying a wealthy businessman and rumors indicated she might not be thrilled about her upcoming nuptials. I needed to see if the rumors were true. Plus, I'd already agreed to be House von Hasenberg's ambassador for the event, and House Chan was an ally. If I didn't show, there would be consequences.

There were always consequences.

"Alfred," I said to my suite computer, "wake me up in two hours. Until then, do not disturb me unless it's urgent."

A chime indicated acceptance of the command. With my com in the isolation cage with me, my messages would automatically be routed to my suite computer, allowing the system to wake me if something important came through.

With that final thought, I dropped into sleep with the ease of someone who'd learned to grab sleep whenever possible.

THE GENTLE ALARM BROUGHT ME TO INSTANT AWARE-ness. My headache was gone. I felt good enough that tonight might not be terrible. I stretched and enjoyed the quiet for another minute before I opened the curtain and let in the cacophony of signals.

I dressed with care, aware that I was representing House von Hasenberg tonight. With synthesizers able to turn out faux haute couture in a matter of hours, it became a status symbol to wear gowns made by hand, fashioned from real materials and not their synth equivalents, even though it was difficult to tell the two apart at a glance.

The strapless evening gown I chose was made of purple silk in a shade so dark it appeared black in all but the brightest light. The fitted bodice hugged my chest, while the full skirt hid my heels and made me appear taller. Dresses were the battle armor of choice for Consortium ladies, and this one promised to hold its own.

I swept my long hair up into a complicated twist and pinned it into place with the ease of long practice. My hair was naturally a mousy brown, a shade that did nothing for my fair complexion. I'd endlessly tinkered with the color over the years before settling on my current shade of light brown with subtle blond and red highlights.

Hair done, I considered my makeup options, waving through my presets. Each option overlaid my face in the mirror, showing me a real-time preview of the result, while the individual settings were displayed on the right. The current trend was for gem-encrusted *everything*—eyelids, brows, temples, and even eyelashes—though I didn't know how anyone could stand it.

Luckily, being a von Hasenberg had its perks—I didn't follow trends, I made them.

I picked a simple style of deeply lined, dark smoky eyes and natural lips. I altered the eye shadow color to hint at the purple in my dress. Even so, I'd look positively unadorned compared to most ladies tonight, which would make me stand out. I pressed the application button and closed my eyes. Two seconds later, a beep signaled I was done.

A final check in the mirror confirmed I was as ready as I was going to get. I picked up the clutch that held my blaster. It was an unwritten rule that you could bring weapons to a Consortium event as long as you did it discreetly. Showing up with a long gun slung over one shoulder would be gauche—and would probably get you barred from entry—but five hidden blasters? Totally cool.

I exited my suite to find Ian loitering in the hall outside my door. He straightened as I approached. He'd changed into a black tuxedo, and I had the sinking feeling that I wasn't going to appreciate whatever he was about to say.

"Director Bishop, here to snipe at me again?" I asked.

His calm expression didn't change. It was nearly impossible to bait the man when he wasn't already in a fury, but that didn't mean I ever stopped trying. He brought out the worst in me.

"I am here to escort you to House Chan's ball," he said.

"Where is Edward?" Edward was my normal evening guard. He was a nice young man with an easy attitude and a quick smile—so, basically, the opposite of the man in front of me.

"He is providing additional coverage for Lord Ferdinand tonight," Ian said.

"Of course he is," I muttered. Louder, I continued, "Very well, let's get this over with."

Ian offered me his elbow and butterflies took flight in my stomach. I sternly told them it didn't mean anything, it was just a polite gesture—Edward did the same, usually with a wink and a flourish.

My hand still had the slightest tremble as I took Ian's arm.

I schooled my expression and let him lead me to the waiting House transport. With the war, we were no longer allowed to take public transports. He helped me into the vehicle then followed and sat across from me. He leaned back and the shadows embraced him.

I glanced away before I became entranced by the play of light and dark across his cheekbones. The man was entirely too handsome for my peace of mind. I needed a distraction.

"Have there been active threats against the House here in Serenity?" I asked, meeting his eyes. "Is that why security is tighter tonight?" I hadn't come across anything, but I'd been out of commission for most of the afternoon. If new info had come in today, I wouldn't have seen it.

Ian stared hard at me, but I didn't look away. Finally, he sighed and ran a hand through his hair. "No," he said, "nothing credible. Just a feeling I can't shake."

I nodded. Ian had long since proven he had good instincts.

"Why do you accept a feeling without question but disregard an order made for your safety?"

I shrugged. "I trust your gut. If you had explained yourself this afternoon, I would've listened. I thought you were just being your normal paranoid self. Despite what you think, I am not stupid."

"I never—" He bit off the sentence and took a deep breath. Whatever he meant to say was lost as the transport settled in front of House Chan's building. Ian's mask of indifference slid back into place as if the past few minutes hadn't happened.

Ian climbed out and checked the surroundings before offering me a hand. I took it and allowed him to help me out of the transport. House Chan owned Sector Four of the Khadela quarter and the towering metal-and-glass building in front of us was their headquarters.

When High House Khadela had fallen long ago, the lower

houses had scrambled to claim a piece of the quarter for them-selves, moving in from the outer sectors of the other quarters. Since then the real estate was in constant ownership flux. One could tell how well a lower house was doing by their address and the number of buildings they owned—House Chan was doing *quite* well.

Ian guided me past the guards posted at the door, all of whom were smart enough not to try to demand my invitation. The two-story lobby was dominated by an enormous crystal chandelier that stretched from ceiling to floor, more art than illumination.

The elevators to the upper floors were tucked off to the right, behind another set of burly guards. To the left, wide dou-ble doors were thrown open to the ballroom, allowing a glimpse of the glittering spectacle inside.

I squared my shoulders, lifted my chin, and pasted on my social smile. Showtime.

Without a word, Ian dropped back to hover behind my right shoulder. I swept into the room on a murmur of acknowledg-ment. As I made my way to the hosts, people cleared my path with a quick curtsy or bow. The boldest tried to catch my eye, but most moved aside with bowed heads. Women were swathed in a riot of colors while the men stood as solemn beacons in gray and black.

The hosts' table was on a raised dais in the middle of the back wall. As I approached, Lord and Lady Chan rose, as did their daughter and her betrothed. The daughter swallowed nerv-ously and slipped her hand into her betrothed's. He gave her a gentle squeeze of reassurance, and she summoned a smile.

Perhaps my information was wrong after all.

I inclined my head to the table with a genuine smile. "Lord

and Lady Chan, thank you for inviting me to celebrate your joyous day with you. Father sends his regards and best wishes for a happy union between Lady Elise and Mr. Ruth."

"Lady von Hasenberg, we are honored by your attendance. Please, enjoy the dancing and refreshments," Lord Chan said. He lifted his arm and the string quartet in the corner eased into sound. After a shallow bow to me, he guided his wife to the center of the room to begin the dance. Elise and Mr. Ruth, whose first name I couldn't remember, followed as the guests of honor.

My official duties now over, I relaxed a fraction. The nap had helped and my head barely ached. With the number of signals flying through the room it wouldn't stay that way for long, but for now I could enjoy myself.

I had not danced since Gregory's death, but that did not stop the invitations. Occasionally I longed to join the whirling masses, but as I turned down a leering gentleman old enough to be my grandfather, I remembered why I'd made the decision. I'd declined five more gentlemen and one adventurous lady by the time I made it to the buffet.

"You don't dance anymore?" Ian asked softly.

Only my training prevented me from startling at his voice, so close to my ear. "No," I said.

I picked up a dainty china plate and selected a few hors d'oeuvres. Today I felt well enough to eat, but it wouldn't do for the daughter of a High House to load up a plate, no matter how ravenous she was. Plus, if I snacked all night, I always had something to do with my hands.

"Why not?" he asked.

"You should eat if you are hungry," I said instead of answering. I snagged a glass of champagne from a passing server and expertly balanced both plate and glass as I nibbled. I put my back to a wall and observed the room. Ian stood next to me, eyes scanning the crowd.

"Tell me what you see," I said on impulse. It was a game we'd played a lifetime ago when he was my personal guard.

I didn't expect his eyes to flash to me. "You were worried that Lady Elise was being forced into the match," he said.

I took a measured breath and masked my surprise. How did he know? More important, how *much* did he know?

"I haven't figured out why you care," he continued, "but I have a few guesses. You can rest easy, though. From what I've seen, the two are ridiculously in love."

I glanced to where the two were dancing while smiling and laughing as if the rest of the room didn't exist. "I drew the same conclusion," I said. So why was a rumor of the opposite floating around? I'd have to dig into it.

"Why do you care?" Ian persisted. The man was like a dog with a bone. I'd have to give him something or he'd never drop it.

"Mother was concerned the House would be destabilized if the marriage was unhappy," I lied smoothly. "She sent me to determine if her concern was warranted."

Ian didn't look entirely convinced, but he didn't push for more. Unfortunately, that probably meant he'd be doing digging of his own when he got back to his office. I didn't need Ian Bishop sticking his nose into my business.

"What else do you see?" I asked.

"A lot of people who don't value what they've been given."

I rolled my eyes. "You used to be much better at this game. Getting old?"

When his flashing eyes met my gaze directly, I remembered that it wasn't the best idea to taunt him. He proved me right. "You are unhappy," he said quietly.

I barely kept my mask of nonchalance as the verbal dagger slid home with deadly precision. How did Ian know something not even my siblings had picked up on? Nothing to do but bluff my way through. "Of course," I said lightly, "I lost my husband."

He shook his head, but I was saved from his response when the room seemed to decide I'd had enough time to eat in peace, never mind that I hadn't actually finished my plate.

"Lady Bianca," an older woman I vaguely recognized said, "please allow my daughter to apologize for earlier." She dragged forward the brunette from Lady Taylor's tea. Ah, here were Lady Patel and her daughter Chloe.

Chloe simpered at me. "Lady von Hasenberg, I am *so* sorry for Lynn's behavior earlier. I had no idea she would behave so poorly or I never would've invited her along. I hope you put her in her place."

Keeping my mask in place took an extreme force of will. This chit thought to betray her friend *again*? My smile was not nice—Chloe took an involuntary step back.

House Patel wasn't an ally, but they weren't an enemy, either. I considered my options while Chloe started to look a little ill. A wave of whispers then a ring of silence radiated out from our little group.

Finally, I said, "It seems House Patel has much to learn about loyalty and friendship." I waited just long enough to see her eyes widen and her face pale, then I turned and walked away.

"Was that wise?" Ian asked under the cover of excited voices.

In five minutes, everyone in Serenity would know I'd slighted House Patel. But if House Patel thought to come after me for it, I'd level them. Luckily, Lord Patel was known for his cool head.

"Yes," I said. "And once they calm down, they will realize I could have done so much worse."

The rest of the night passed in fake smiles and polite small talk. Everyone wanted to know what had happened with Lady Chloe, but when it became clear I wouldn't discuss it, they moved on. When my head ached enough that continuing to smile became difficult, I decided it was time to wrap up.

"Ian, please call the transport while I say good-bye to the hosts."

He nodded, touched his earpiece, and murmured to the operator. After a brief good-bye to House Chan, I headed for the door. I was *done.*

"Wait," Ian said, touching my elbow before I could exit the lobby. "The transport is still a minute out."

To distract myself, I let my mind drift to the messages flying through the ether. One communication channel was using a form of cryptography I'd never seen before. Interested despite myself, I began mentally pulling it apart.

I was so immersed in the task that I barely noticed when Ian guided me outside.

# CHAPTER 3

I couldn't consciously explain how I broke encryption. Encrypted data looked like puzzle pieces to my mind's eye and I intrinsically knew how to put them together. When I did, a void revealed the key and the encryption unlocked.

For most encryption, the entire process took seconds. For encryption I'd seen before, I could do it without thought.

This encryption was far trickier.

The puzzle pieces slid around my mental landscape like nothing I'd seen before. Pain spiked behind my left eye but I refused to give up. Finally, finally I pinned the pieces in place and revealed the key. The encryption unlocked, revealing a second layer of encryption, one I knew well because it came from my own House.

The message unlocked.

*Go.*

Why would someone encrypt a one-word message in one of the most complex encryption schemes I'd ever seen? Was it a test?

We were nearly to the transport when the sound of shattering glass broke through my distraction. I didn't have time to look around for the source of the sound before Ian tackled me to the ground and shoved me against the bulk of the transport. He shielded my body with his, completely blocking my view.

I tried to push him aside but it was like trying to move a mountain. "What's going on?"

"Shots fired at Bright. I need an armored transport *now*. Team Two, sweep the area," Ian shouted into his com.

The transport window half a meter over our heads shattered in an explosion of glass.

"Fuck," Ian growled. "We're too exposed."

"I can shoot," I said. "I have a blaster."

He shifted enough to meet my gaze. His eyes blazed with icy blue fury. "You will do no such thing," he said. "You will stay down and let me do my job. I will protect you."

"But—"

"No. End of discussion."

My temper woke, but I was smart enough to follow an order that was meant for my own good. Someone was shooting at me. On *Earth,* supposedly the safest place in the 'verse. The Royal Consortium Defense Force, or RCDF, was the group tasked with maintaining the peace. They must be having a collective aneurysm right now.

If not now, then they would be when Father brought the fury of House von Hasenberg down on them. As patriarch of one of the three High Houses, Albrecht von Hasenberg was one of the most powerful people in the 'verse. When he wasn't happy, heads rolled—sometimes literally.

"Am I the only target? Are my brothers and sisters okay?" I asked.

Ian refused to answer, which sent my worry spinning out of control. I mentally reached for the messages flying through the air, trying to find my family's familiar com signature.

The headache slammed into me with the force of a freighter. I'd overextended myself with the encryption. Black spots danced in my vision, and I had to let the search go or risk passing out. What little food I'd managed to eat soured in my stomach.

"Where is my transport?" Ian yelled. "And where the fuck is RCDF?"

Since I couldn't answer either question, I figured he must be talking to someone on the other end of his com.

Ian popped his head up to look through the shattered transport window. It took all of my willpower not to drag him back to safety. He ducked back down just as another blaster bolt slammed into the door, centimeters from his head.

"Shooter is in the twenty-story building west of House Chan," Ian said. "Top third."

A heavy troop transport settled next to us. The doors opened and fully armored RCDF soldiers streamed out. They hunkered down behind our transport, but no more shots were fired. Perhaps the shooter had fled now that backup had arrived.

"It's about time," Ian snarled. He kept a hand on my shoulder so I couldn't sit up.

"Lady Bianca, are you well?" the soldier closest to me asked.

Only years of strict training kept me from offering my true thoughts on the stupidity of that question. "Catch the shooter and I'll be better," I said.

"We're working on it, my lady," he said.

"Let's get you into the transport," Ian said. "Can you crawl in that dress?"

"I'll make it work," I said.

"Stay low," Ian cautioned, as if he thought I planned to stand and waltz to the vehicle.

I rolled over onto my belly. I tucked my toes, planted my hands, and pushed up just enough for the front of my body to clear the ground. My arms protested but held—barely. I'd only recently started going to the gym again, but I'd rather be shot than admit how out of shape I was to Ian Bishop.

I slid one leg forward, dragging the bottom of my dress up as I did. I reached forward, then pushed off with my leg, like I was climbing a wall. I repeated the motion on the other side and crawled forward on my hands and toes.

My progress was slow but steady. The dress hampered me, and I envied how easily Ian crawled in his tuxedo. To his credit, he didn't try to rush me, he just kept pace beside me.

When we reached the troop transport, Ian pushed himself up into a crouch then picked me up and swung me into the vehicle in one smooth motion. His easy strength stole my breath, but he took my silence as offense.

"You can yell at me later," he said as he climbed inside. "For now, stay on the floor. The windows are reinforced, but the floor is safer." He slammed the transport door closed, then swiped his right arm over the chip reader. "Take us to House von Hasenberg's private entrance."

The transport lifted off. I closed my eyes and didn't try to get up. My head felt like I'd gone several rounds with my old self-defense tutor, and that lady had packed a mean right cross.

"Are you injured?" Ian asked, his voice laced with concern.

"No," I said. It sounded like a lie, mostly because it *was* a lie. I worked on pulling my tattered public mask back on. Once I was certain I could maintain the facade, I opened my eyes and met Ian's gaze. My voice was cool when I asked, "Are my siblings okay?"

Ian glanced away. "As far as I know," he hedged.

"Who?" I demanded as I sat up. My head swam, but I refused to show weakness. When Ian didn't answer, I asked again, my voice knife-sharp.

I had an older brother and sister, a twin brother who was younger by thirteen minutes, and two younger sisters. We were all close despite our parents' attempts to drive us apart. If any of my siblings were hurt, the rest of us would rain hell and damnation on whoever was stupid enough to do it.

"I haven't heard from Lord Ferdinand's team yet," Ian admitted.

Ferdinand was my oldest brother and heir to House von Hasenberg. He had done his best to shield the rest of us from the worst of Father's fury, and although he hadn't always been successful, we adored him for it.

I pulled out my com and checked our sibling group channel. Everyone except Ferdinand and Ada had checked in. Ada was off-planet and wouldn't get the messages for some time, so I wasn't worried about her.

I let the others know I was okay and the channel blew up with questions. No one had heard anything from our oldest brother and worry lurked behind every message.

"I'm assuming you have additional units en route to Ferdinand's location?" I asked Ian.

His jaw tightened. "Yes, Lady von Hasenberg."

The title gave away his irritation with me for questioning his ability to do his job, and I smiled internally.

"Where was Ferdinand tonight?" I asked.

"He had a private dinner scheduled in the Yamado quarter," Ian said.

"With whom?"

"I am not at liberty to say," Ian said. His tone said he wouldn't budge, so I turned my questioning elsewhere.

"Care to explain how someone was able to shoot at me tonight?" I asked.

"I intend to find out," he said with a scowl. "Do you know of anyone who wants you dead?"

I raised an eyebrow. "No, Director Bishop, I can't think of a single soul," I said sweetly. Ask a stupid question . . .

He sighed. "Anyone *in particular*?"

That was a harder question. No one came to mind, but that didn't mean no one wanted me dead. I was the daughter of a High House and suspected of killing my husband. Before that, I'd publicly worked for Father, gathering information on our rivals using whatever means necessary. The list of people who wanted me dead was far longer than the list of people who preferred me alive.

"I haven't had any active threats," I said at last. "And despite what you and Father think, I don't think House Rockhurst is stupid enough to bring the war to Earth."

"You'd be surprised," he said darkly.

I wouldn't, actually. I'd seen the same data he had, and I saw nothing that indicated a Rockhurst attack was imminent. Of course, I hadn't seen anything that indicated *any* attack was likely, so someone was playing their cards very close to their chest.

"Are you sure they weren't shooting at *you*?" I asked. It would make sense because as the head of House security, he would be the first person tracking Ferdinand.

Ian shook his head. "The shooter had a clear shot at me from the time we stepped outside, but he only took the shot when you moved slightly ahead of me. He misjudged your speed and shot in front of you. You were the target."

I swallowed. It wasn't the first time I'd had a close brush with death and it probably wouldn't be the last. But it never got any easier.

The transport landed. Ian waited a second, then slid the door open. House von Hasenberg glowed like the sun. Floodlights turned night into day and soldiers patrolled outside the walls.

"Expecting another attack?" I asked.

"Someone is welcome to try," he growled.

He bent over to pick me up but I stopped him with a hand on his chest. Firm muscle hid under the fine fabric of his suit. He was so close that I could see the darker blue ring around the outside of his irises.

"You cannot carry me," I said, my voice quiet but adamant. "Weakness is a vulnerability. I'd rather not become a target for every moron with a grudge if you don't mind."

He paused for a long second then nodded. "I will assist you out," he said.

Ian stepped out of the transport and then offered me his hand. When I grabbed it, he pulled me out and helped me stand. Vertical, my head rang like a gong. My dress was a little the worse for wear, but it still covered me, so I ignored the damage and pretended all was well. I excelled at pretense.

"Steady?" Ian asked under his breath.

Rather than answering, I inclined my head and dropped his hand. I walked to the door without so much as a wobble, although the effort had cost me. I swiped my arm over the reader and the door unlocked.

Ian pulled the door open for me, and I swept inside. "Contact me as soon as you know anything about Ferdinand," I tossed over my shoulder.

After the door clicked closed, he caught up to me and pulled me to a stop. "You should see a doctor," he said.

*Over my dead body.* And if I had it my way, not even then. I didn't say it aloud, but some of the sentiment must've leaked through in my expression because Ian frowned.

"I am fine," I said. "I will be better when Ferdinand is safe at home, so I suggest you get to it." I sank enough dismissive condescension into that sentence to founder a battle cruiser.

Ian stiffened and his face smoothed into a polite mask. He bowed slightly. "As you wish, Lady von Hasenberg," he said. "Do not leave the House without notifying me." He turned and stalked down the hallway toward his office.

Once he was out of sight, I breathed a silent sigh of relief. Ian could be damned persistent when he set his mind to it, but I'd found that just the right tone would cause him to storm away in a fury. And like it or not, I'd had plenty of practice being a condescending bitch thanks to my status as daughter of a High House.

I headed for the family wing, unsurprised to see guards posted along the hallway and outside my suite. Thanks to some careful nudging on my part, my suite had turned into the gathering spot for sibling meetings. It worked well because these days I was the only sibling who consistently stayed on Earth. Everyone else was usually off on some errand for the House. When they were home, my brothers and sisters had access to come and go from my suite as they pleased. As a bonus, the additional shielding in my room meant it took longer for my headache to worsen.

Catarina and Benedict were waiting for me. Sitting next to each other, no one would guess they were siblings. Catarina had Mother's dark hair and golden skin. Only she and Ada had been lucky enough to take after Mother. The rest of us shared Father's lighter hair and ruddy skin.

Benedict, my twin, jumped to his feet. Even with my heels, Benedict towered over me. I often claimed that he'd stolen all of my height because he was the tallest of all of my brothers and sisters.

"What happened?" he asked. He pulled me into a hug before I could answer.

"Someone shot at me outside House Chan," I murmured into his chest. The reality sank in as I crashed from the adrenaline high. Someone had shot at me. On *Earth*.

A rock settled in the pit of my stomach. This was the first time someone had tried to kill me on Earth. The world shifted as my one sanctuary crumbled to dust.

"Was the shooter caught?" Catarina asked.

Benedict pushed me toward the sofa. "Sit, I'll get you a drink," he said.

I sat. The adrenaline crash had made me shaky and nauseated. "I don't know if the shooter was caught," I said. "Director Bishop ordered RCDF troops to the location, but they were late. Have either of you heard from Ferdinand?"

"No," they said in unison.

"I pinged his com with an emergency message, but he didn't respond," Catarina said.

Worry pressed on my chest. It was unlike our serious older brother to fail to respond to an emergency, no matter what he was doing.

"Do you think it was Rockhurst?" Benedict asked. He handed me a martini and I took a grateful sip.

"Are they that stupid?" Catarina asked. Because she was the baby of the family it was all too easy to forget that she was a von Hasenberg in her own right. A razor-sharp mind hid behind her innocent face.

"I don't think so," I said, "but Director Bishop doesn't agree." I paused for a second, then clarified, "Well, I don't think Lady Rockhurst is that stupid, but who knows about her children."

Richard Rockhurst certainly hadn't shown the best judgment when he had decided to go after Ada. My younger sister was far too clever for him.

"I was under the impression that House Rockhurst went on lockdown after Richard's stunts," Catarina said. "Lady Rockhurst was livid that he lost one of their prototype ships and forced them into premature war."

"I've heard the same," Benedict said. "But holding the von Hasenberg heir could swing the war in their favor if she thought she could get away with it."

"Yes, but if she's caught, then she has to face the RCDF as well as House Yamado and the lower houses," I said. "It's a risky move for potentially little reward. House von Hasenberg has six children. Father is ruthless enough to write one off, even if Ferdinand is his favorite. You know it, I know it, and Lady Rockhurst certainly knows it."

Benedict and Catarina nodded. Father would fight to get Ferdinand back because anything else made the House look weak. But if he decided it was a lost cause, he would cut our brother loose.

The suite door opened and our oldest sister, Hannah, stormed in. Her pale blue gown flattered her complexion but did nothing to hide the thunderclouds in her expression.

She flopped down next to me, stole my martini, and drained the glass. "Sorry I'm late," she said. "I left a dinner party in my honor. Pierre tried to stop me. He is furious," she said with grim satisfaction.

Pierre was Hannah's husband. Much like my own marriage, Father had arranged everything and left Hannah no choice. It was not a happy match. Now she lived to infuriate the man who had bought his way into our House.

"What do we know?" Hannah asked.

Benedict got her up to speed. Unfortunately, it didn't take long because we didn't have much to go on.

"So why Bianca and Ferdinand and not the rest of us?" Hannah asked.

"Perhaps they've heard that Bianca has a legion of spies," Catarina said before I could answer.

Hannah and Benedict turned to me in unison. "Do tell," Hannah drawled.

Once again Cat jumped in before I could speak. She told them about our morning with relish. It wasn't too often that our baby sister got the drop on one of us, so she enjoyed their surprise.

"Had you heard anything about an attack?" Benedict asked.

"No, nothing," I said. I didn't mention the message I had decrypted. That would lead to more questions than I could answer.

No one knew that I could break encryption. Gregory had been as paranoid as he was brilliant, and as far as I could tell, he had kept his research secret. His lab—and our House—had been on a tiny, distant planet that wasn't exactly a tourist destination. His family had long since moved away, but Gregory had kept the family seat because he liked the isolation. And the lack of prying eyes.

It was much more likely that I was a target because someone knew I dealt in information.

"Director Bishop said Ferdinand was in the Yamado quarter at a private dinner. He wouldn't say with whom," I said, "but I intend to find out."

My siblings stayed for a little while longer, then began to trickle out. Hannah was the last to leave. She stopped me before I opened the door for her. Her expression was serious.

"What's up?" I asked.

"If anything happens to Ferdinand," she said slowly, "I plan to abdicate my place in line. I refuse to become heir."

I blinked at her, thrown. If something happened to Ferdinand, and then Hannah abdicated, I would be next in line.

I did not want to be next in line. I barely managed my current responsibilities.

"Why?" I finally managed to ask.

"Pierre," she said shortly. "I refuse to give that bastard any more power, over me or anyone else." Fury darkened her face. "Do you know what he said when I told him about the attack on you and that Ferdinand was missing? He made a joke about how his lot is improving now that he's married to the heir. He's lucky I didn't punch him in front of all of his so-called friends."

She took a deep breath and shook her head. "I have every confidence we'll find Ferdinand, but I wanted you to be prepared, just in case. Please don't tell anyone else."

"Does Ferdinand know?"

"Yes, we've discussed it."

"Do you want me to do something about Pierre?" I asked seriously.

She pulled me into a hug. "No, but I appreciate the offer. I've got it under control."

I thought about her words long after she left.

# CHAPTER 4

'd stayed up late last night looking for any sign of Ferdinand or the attack, but I hadn't found anything. Ferdinand was scheduled to have a late dinner at a small restaurant in the Yamado quarter and he'd reserved the entire restaurant.

He never made it to the appointment, but interestingly enough, Evelyn Rockhurst *had*.

So why were the heirs of two warring Houses meeting in secret?

I'd sent Evelyn an obliquely worded message. Despite the late hour, she had quickly responded with a midmorning time and the location of a tea shop squarely in the middle of the Rockhurst quarter. Warring Houses weren't banned from visiting their enemy's quarter, but it wasn't exactly encouraged, either.

If Rockhurst had orchestrated the attack, I would be walking into a trap.

Still, it was my only lead, and I wouldn't pass up the opportunity. I requested a transport, then set about getting ready. I decided on gray slacks, a black blouse, and a pair of my tallest heels—Evelyn Rockhurst was statuesque and I needed us on an even playing field.

Arming myself would send the wrong message, but going to the meeting defenseless was also a bad idea. I pulled out the heavy silver cuff that concealed the best of House von Hasenberg's shielding technology. This was the newest prototype—it no longer required a paired necklace to function.

I held the cuff to my identity chip for ten seconds, then clasped it around my left wrist. I felt a tiny prick as the embedded DNA tester sampled my blood. A subtle vibration indicated success. The cuff was now authorized until I unclasped it.

In standby mode, the cuff would hold a charge indefinitely. Once active, it was good for up to two hours or eight close-range shots. I wouldn't activate it unless it looked like the meeting was a trap.

I left the suite and headed out the private family entrance. My transport was waiting, as was a security detail in a second vehicle. I waved at them and mentally apologized for the ass-chewing Ian was bound to give them once he figured out what I'd done.

I climbed into the transport and programmed in the destination. As the vehicle lifted off, I sank deeper into my public persona. Evelyn was just as shrewd as her mother, Anne, the matriarch of House Rockhurst. I needed to be on my game.

The transport settled outside the tea shop with nearly ten minutes to spare. The shop was bustling, filled with sharp-eyed men and women who were doing a poor job of disguising their true purpose.

And standing between me and the shop was Ian Bishop. His face was a hard mask of anger, and despite his seemingly casual stance, I could see the tension in his body.

With nothing to do but brazen it out, I exited the transport. "Hello, Director Bishop. I suppose half of those patrons are ours?"

His eyes narrowed. His voice came out low and harsh. "I had to scramble to get people here to protect you when they should be out looking for your brother and that's all you have to say?"

I retreated behind the icy facade of my training, where his words couldn't cut like blades. "I do not remember asking for your help, Director Bishop. I have the situation well in hand. And stay out of my correspondence."

I'd sent the message to Evelyn through my normal House account because I hadn't really thought she would respond. I knew that account was under surveillance, but I had expected Ian to be busy enough with other things to miss the message. I should've known better.

"You are not to go anywhere with Lady Evelyn," Ian said. "Stay in my sight at all times. I have people outside as well. If things go sideways, hit the floor and stay there. I will come to you."

"I do not need your help," I reiterated. "I will speak to Lady Evelyn—*alone*—and find out if she knows anything about Ferdinand's disappearance. Stay out of my way."

I moved to sweep past him, but Ian caught my arm. His grip was gentle, but I could feel the steel strength of his fingers. I stopped abruptly, then cursed myself for the weakness. I refused to meet Ian's gaze and the speculation I knew I'd find there.

"I am trying to keep you safe. Do not do anything reckless, Lady Bianca," Ian said softly.

I glanced up at him. "I am never reckless," I said. These days, it wasn't even a lie, though that hadn't always been the case.

Ian raised his eyebrows but didn't contradict my statement. He leaned in close. "Lady Evelyn is already here," he murmured into my ear. "I don't think a single person in the shop is just a customer, so be careful. I'd prefer not to have a battle in the middle of Serenity."

"I will see what I can do."

Inside the shop, the roomful of people watched me out of the corner of their eyes as I made my way to Evelyn's table. Situated in the middle of the shop, it had a three-meter circle of clear space around it.

Evelyn stood with a polite smile. In her early thirties, with strong features and a slimly muscular build, she favored her father more than her mother, though she had the trademark Rockhurst blond hair and blue eyes. Even with the added height from my heels, she topped me by several centimeters.

Her makeup didn't quite hide the dark circles under her eyes. Her brow was lined with worry, and she looked like she hadn't slept much last night. The question was why.

Evelyn didn't offer a hand to shake. Instead, she waved me to a seat. A silencer already sat on the table and I could tell it was working by the silence in my head. However, it would be remiss of me to trust her technology.

"If you don't mind," I said, as I slipped my own silencer from my purse. At her nod, I clicked it on and placed it on the table. I met her direct stare. "Do you prefer the diplomatic route or shall we cut the bullshit?" I asked pleasantly.

She blinked, but that was the only sign of her surprise. I'd dealt with her a few times and regarded her more highly than her mother, but I didn't have a real feel for her personality. My opening was a test as much as anything.

Evelyn grinned and it seemed far more genuine than the polite smile she'd worn earlier. "Let's cut the bullshit. As far as I know, we didn't attack you, and we don't have Ferdinand," she said.

"And *would* you know if someone in House Rockhurst had orchestrated the attack, even if it was Lady Rockhurst herself?"

"Yes," she said with complete conviction. "I can't speak for every soldier under our command, but no orders came from House leadership."

"Could it have been Richard? Some sort of payback for Ada?" My sister had made a fool of him when she'd stolen his prototype ship. And Richard Rockhurst did not seem like the type to forgive and forget.

Evelyn let a tiny grimace slip through her mask. "Richard thought that he was helping the House avoid war by pursuing Ada. Mother showed him the error of his ways," she said, her voice flat. "He is not in any position to scheme."

Her tone indicated that she didn't agree with whatever Lady Rockhurst had done. I filed away that tidbit of information. There was dissent in the ranks of House Rockhurst.

"You do realize it's highly suspicious that Ferdinand disappeared on the night he was meeting with you, right?" I asked.

She inclined her head. "It is the reason I agreed to meet with you." She paused, then continued, "You are not what I expected, but I suppose I shouldn't be surprised."

"Why were you meeting with Ferdinand?" I asked.

The pause was longer this time. Her eyes seemed to take my measure, but her expression didn't give away anything of her thoughts. I sat patiently, but internally I wanted to shake her and demand answers.

Finally, she reached for her purse. I felt the entire room tense, and I could practically feel Ian's eyes burning a hole in my back. She smiled slyly, then slowly pulled a handheld fabric fan from the bag. She snapped it open and waved it lazily in front of her face, obscuring her mouth.

Whatever she was going to say, she didn't want anyone to be able to read it from her lips.

Very quietly, she asked, "Do you trust your brother?"

"Absolutely," I said.

"More than your father?"

It was my turn to pause, to weigh the impact of a true answer. "Yes," I said at last. I didn't elaborate, but I trusted all of my siblings far, far more than I trusted my father.

"Ferdinand and I have been dating for nearly a year," Evelyn said.

I could hardly believe that my serious, dutiful eldest brother had done something as rebellious as dating the heir of a rival House in secret, but she seemed sincere. I smiled. Good for him.

Evelyn continued, "As you can imagine, the war made things difficult. We hadn't met in weeks. Last night was supposed to be our reunion." She paused again before she said, "And we were going to discuss the best way to end the conflict."

She lobbed that bombshell at me without any warning, so only my training prevented my mouth from dropping open in surprise. "How?"

Evelyn's expression was full of regret. "I'm sorry. I know Ferdinand trusts you, but I cannot, not that far."

I dipped my head in acknowledgment. "Do you have any proof?"

She waved the fan closer to her mouth. "Swear to me that you won't tell your father or my mother," she said. "I don't need an accident in my future on top of everything else."

I propped my elbow on the table, rested my chin on my thumb, and curled my fingers in front of my mouth. "As long as your information proves true, and no other evidence starts pointing back to you, I will not share the information with our parents."

"I will send the file directly to your com. With the silencers, there's less chance it will be intercepted, as long as you are sure your com is secure."

"My com is secure," I said with a faint smile.

She transferred the file and I saved it in a secure quarantine. I would open it later. I was willing to give her the benefit of the doubt, but I didn't trust her completely.

"Find him," she said, "please." She swallowed and her mask slipped a tiny bit. I caught the anguish in her eyes. She was either the universe's best actress or she truly cared for Ferdinand. "I am searching, too, but I must be far more cautious. Still, if you need anything, you now have my secure address. I will do my best."

"Thank you," I said.

"I'm sure you know this, but do not contact me at public events. I'm already putting myself at risk meeting you today."

"Of course," I said. "I appreciate your candor. You are not what I was expecting, either." I stood and inclined my head. "Farewell, Lady Evelyn."

"Farewell and good luck," she said.

I clicked off the silencer and returned it to my purse, then turned for the entrance. Ian scowled from the edge of the cleared three-meter circle, not even attempting to look anything but impatient and intimidating. He silently followed me from the shop.

IAN ESCORTED ME TO MY TRANSPORT. HE WAITED UNTIL we were inside before he questioned me. "Well?"

"She said House Rockhurst isn't responsible, and for now, I believe her."

"Why?" Ian asked.

I shrugged. "Just a feeling," I said. "Have you found any surveillance video from the attack?"

"I've requested assistance from House Yamado. I tracked Lord Ferdinand to the edge of their quarter, but all of the surveillance I've been able to dig up has a ten-minute loop in it."

I blinked at him in surprise. I hadn't caught the looped video when I'd been digging for information. I could blame it on exhaustion, but Ferdinand's life was on the line—I needed to do better. "You think House Yamado is involved?"

"I don't know," he said with a frustrated noise. "I hope they just have a spy in their security team because otherwise it means they are throwing in with House Rockhurst against us."

A war on two fronts would be grueling for House von Hasenberg. The war with House Rockhurst had barely begun to ramp up. So far, both Houses were pouring military resources into the distant, uninhabited Antlia sector because it seemed to be the only place to find alcubium, the rare resource that powered House Rockhurst's new, faster FTL drives. But it was only a matter of time before the war turned bloody.

Our scientists were trying to reverse-engineer the FTL drive in the Rockhurst prototype ship as quickly as possible, but production was still months, if not years, away.

We could only assume that Rockhurst hadn't outfitted their entire fleet with the new drives yet, or they would've tried to wipe us out with hit-and-run tactics we couldn't counter. We outmatched their traditional fleet, but if they added House Yamado to their side, we would be overwhelmed.

"Let me know when they reply," I said. Ian raised an eyebrow. "Please," I tacked on belatedly. "He's my brother."

"It would be better if you stayed out of it," Ian said, "and let me do my job." He sighed and rubbed his face, and it occurred to me that he looked tired. Ian *never* looked tired. I'd seen him work for forty-eight hours straight without a single sleepy blink, but today he looked worn.

"Are you okay?" I asked gently. I couldn't help myself. Ian had the uncanny ability to sneak under my armor, even when he wasn't trying to.

His face smoothed into a pleasant mask, wiping away the hint of vulnerability. "I'm fine," he said.

The sting of rejection was a familiar hurt, but it still stole my breath. Outwardly, I smiled and nodded, as placid as a lake. I glanced out of the window, trying to determine our location. "Are we returning home?" I asked.

"You are," he said.

He looked like he expected me to argue, but I just inclined my head in agreement. I needed to look at the file Evelyn had given me. And at this point, I was far more effective at finding information virtually than by dashing around the city. With Ian working on finding footage of Ferdinand's kidnapping, I could switch to figuring out who could have actually pulled it off. I doubted it was the same group who had ordered it, but one might lead me to the other. Or Ferdinand. I would call that a win, too.

Ian's expression turned serious. "I don't have time to chase you all over Serenity, not if you want Ferdinand found. Every minute you waste is one your brother is missing. Are you going to stay put?"

Anger almost loosened my tongue, but I shoved it down at the last second. "Yes." *Until I have more information. Then I am going to get Ferdinand with or without you.*

Ian still did not look convinced, but I just smiled serenely and let the conversation lapse into silence, already planning where I would start my search. If I wanted someone kidnapped without it tracing back to me, I'd go to the Silva Syndicate. There were a few other options, but the Silva family ran the largest underground crime organization in the 'verse.

And unlike the black market on APD Zero, the Consortium very much wanted to wipe the Syndicate out, mostly because they refused to give the Houses a cut of their profits.

Because they were targeted by the RCDF, the Syndicate leadership was distributed on several enormous spaceships that were constantly on the move. Occasionally the RCDF would get lucky and catch one, but like a hydra, two more would spring up to replace it. I'd visited one of their ships just once, back before my marriage, when I was still doing active assignments for House von Hasenberg. It had taken a lot of very fast talking and massive amounts of money to walk away unscathed.

But they'd also delivered exactly what they'd promised.

I was pulled from my thoughts when our transport settled outside the House von Hasenberg family entrance. Ian gestured for me to stay put as he slid the door open and stepped out. He glanced around at the security personnel in place, then reached in to help me from the transport.

"I know you are plotting something," he said quietly as he escorted me to the entrance. "Do not leave the building without letting me know and taking a full security detail. Do you understand?"

"I plan to spend the day researching Ferdinand's disappearance," I said.

"That didn't answer the question."

"No, it didn't." I smiled as I slipped into the building and left him scowling on the doorstep. One day he would learn that I responded far better to requests than demands, but that day didn't appear to be today.

# CHAPTER 5

On the way to my suite, I checked our sibling group channel, but no one had heard from Ferdinand. Ada had chimed in that she was okay and hadn't been attacked. Everyone was speculating on who could be behind the attacks, but no one had any solid leads and no ransom demands had been made. I wasn't the only one who thought the Syndicate might be involved, though.

Ada had asked her friends Rhys and Veronica to keep their ears open. Rhys was a smuggler and Veronica had been a fence before she fled her home, so both had connections in the shady underbelly of polite society that might come in handy.

I opened my official House account, just in case. Ferdinand wouldn't message me there unless it was his last resort, but I would never forgive myself if he had and I'd ignored it.

My official account had scores of messages, but nothing from Ferdinand. However, Lynn Segura, the young woman I'd chatted with yesterday, had messaged me late last night. I opened her message as I entered my rooms.

Lynn had seen Ferdinand with three other men in Sector Eight of the Yamado quarter while she was on her way to a party last night. By the descriptions, the three men were his bodyguards. She said she hadn't thought anything about it until the news came out that he was missing.

I sent her a response, thanking her. I had no doubt that Ian knew exactly where Ferdinand had been, thanks to the trackers on the transports, but I sent him the time and location anyway. If he was looking for footage, it was another place to look.

I stepped into my study and shut the door behind me. I nearly sighed in relief as the wireless signals winked out. While isolated, only wired devices like the terminal in my desk would be able to make outside connections, but the signal isolation didn't block wireless transfer within the room.

I copied Evelyn's file to a secure partition on my terminal, turned on process scanning, and then opened it. The scan didn't flag anything suspicious. The file was a flat list of messages, and Evelyn had left the message headers intact. I recognized one of Ferdinand's private addresses.

Even with the private address, the messages were obliquely worded, but I was familiar enough with Ferdinand's style to recognize his voice. If this was a fake, then it was an excellent one.

The messages went back months, though some had been redacted to little more than a greeting and closing. It felt strange to poke through my brother's personal correspondence. I had no trouble snooping through strangers' information, but I'd always tried to give my family a bit more privacy.

For now, I would assume that House Rockhurst did not order the attack. So who did that leave?

Unfortunately, the list was a long one.

Ferdinand's kidnapping was a blow to House von Hasenberg, but far from a fatal one. Father would bring the full might of the House down on whoever was stupid enough to do it, and even threats on Ferdinand's life wouldn't be sufficient to stop him.

Someone either had nothing to lose or they thought they'd get away with it, which meant hiring professionals and not leaving any loose ends—such as a kidnapped heir who could escape and point fingers.

I'd been working from the kidnapping angle because I didn't want to contemplate the alternative, but I had to at least consider that this was an assassination. Taking the body would be unusual for an assassination, but not unheard of in the name of absolute secrecy. Still, as long as Ferdinand's death folder remained unreleased, I would work under the assumption that my brother was alive.

I closed Evelyn's file and brought up my highest-level personal firewalls. My connections were normally encrypted, but I added several layers of additional protection, including bouncing the connection through a multitude of servers, both my own and public. Finally, I kicked off a script that made a lot of connections and requests to help hide my real traffic in the noise.

I was about to do a deep dive into the dark part of the Net and I didn't want anyone to be able to follow my trail, in either direction.

I'd been gathering information for years under various anonymous online personas, so I started there. I checked my digital drop boxes one at a time. For each one, I went through the whole procedure again, just with different servers. It was paranoid, but it also kept me safe.

There were a few interesting messages that I flagged for follow-up, but most of the messages I got were worthless—common rumors, wild speculation, or lewd suggestions. My various identities were well known in their circles, and I paid generously for good information.

I saved the most likely account for last. This identity was

known to want Consortium gossip. Almost all gossip was worthless by the time it was sent, so it was a badge of honor in some circles just to have produced a piece of information worth payment.

I had a dozen messages and nearly all of them pertained to the attack on me or Ferdinand's disappearance. I started with the messages about Ferdinand. The first two messages were from unknown contacts and didn't offer anything I didn't already know. The third message was from someone I'd worked with before. It hinted about Ferdinand's dinner with Evelyn, which wasn't public info as far as I knew. I sent them a small payment and a request for more info. They probably didn't know anything more than I did, but double-checking was worth the expense.

None of the other messages about Ferdinand were useful, so I moved on to the messages about the attack on me. Only one message seemed like it might be useful. The sender claimed to have information about the shooter. The contact was one of my regulars, so I went ahead and made the good-faith payment and requested more information.

I posted an oblique request for information about House von Hasenberg and House Rockhurst on a couple of the boards buried deep in the underbelly of the respectable Internet. Making a semipublic request meant I would get a lot of spurious messages, but it also meant anyone with real knowledge would know I was looking.

Unfortunately, my usual passive information gathering hadn't turned up any useful information, at least not yet, so I had to switch to active looking. The risk was higher, but so was the potential reward.

I refreshed my security protections, then stood and pressed a switch on my desk. The lights in the room died and the walls disappeared. WELCOME TO HIVE hovered in front of me, formed by one of the projectors in the room. Below the text, a red virtual CONNECT button glowed softly.

I passed my hand through the button and held for a count of five. It was a safety measure to ensure I didn't connect accidentally. The button winked out, replaced by a bustling projected street in a gleaming virtual city. I rested my fingers on top of my desk as I waited for the initial vertigo to dissipate.

HIVE stood for High Impact Virtual Environment, though few remembered the name was actually an acronym. It was the largest virtual reality zone in the 'verse, and one of a handful of communication protocols allowed to use the FTL communication network. Every few years another new zone popped up to try to derail HIVE's dominance, but so far, none had succeeded, in part because HIVE was backed by the three High Houses.

On the low end, users could enter HIVE with just a set of cheap smart glasses. At the other extreme, some users had dedicated rooms with treadmill floors and force suits that made interacting with the virtual world feel real. Originally designed as a game, HIVE was now used for everything from business to pleasure, though both the Consortium and the syndicates tended to eschew it for more traditional face-to-face meetings—there were fewer hidden eyes in the real world, after all.

Although the Consortium rarely conducted internal business in HIVE, they still wanted everyone to know that the zone flourished because of their benevolence. Each High House owned a prime block of the main street where entering users landed. Users could bank with the Houses, shop for virtual items like synthesizer recipes, or deal with various administrative issues like taxes and fines.

To my left, House von Hasenberg's stone-and-crystal skyscraper defied physics but made for a pretty building. On my main account, I "owned" an entire floor of that building. I used it for the occasional long-distance meeting, but I, too, preferred face-to-face appointments.

Today I was logged in as Fenix, one of my anonymous accounts. This avatar was a tall, busty redhead with matching red cat ears, wearing a black corset and black leather pants, complete with a high, giggly voice. Everyone assumed I was a man in real life, an assumption I protested too loudly and too often.

Avatars had to be approximately human-sized but were otherwise only limited by the user's imagination, so all manner of creatures inhabited HIVE. A blue mermaid wearing a sparkly silver bikini top swam by, despite the fact that we were nowhere near water. Realism was optional in HIVE, and users competed to have the most interesting and unique avatars.

"HIVE," I said, "transport to Nadia's bar."

"Transporting to saved location 172b.217r6.2a2w," a female computer voice responded. The projection flickered then shifted to reveal a narrow brick alley ending in a wall with a single black door. Unlike most locations in HIVE, this alley wasn't connected to the rest of the zone. Only users with the exact address could visit, and the address updated frequently, so random users couldn't just wander in.

I lifted my right hand and held it palm down over the desk, then leaned forward very slightly. The motion trackers in the room captured the position of my hands and the movement of my body. This particular combination meant I wanted to move forward, toward the door.

There were several ways to move in HIVE, but once you got the hang of leaning, it required the least amount of effort. I'd set the hand gesture as a requirement because I tended to move around while I talked and I didn't want my avatar walking into walls in the middle of a conversation.

When the door was right in front of me, projected over my desk, I reached out and pressed on an invisible button, about chest high and left of center. It took a couple of tries before I hit the right location because it was a little more difficult without force gloves to provide tactile feedback. Finally, a click indicated success and the scene changed.

Nadia's bar was dim and smoky, with wood-paneled walls and dark leather furniture. A long mahogany bar ran down the left side of the room. In the middle of the room, groupings of low chairs were separated by generous empty space, ensuring privacy. And Nadia's regulars all had shrouded alcoves along the right side of the room.

I knew something was wrong as soon as the scene loaded. Normally the bar buzzed with muted conversation as information flowed. Today, however, the soft jazz background music was the only sound.

A few users sat in a sullen cluster in the center of the room, shackles around their wrists. I saw a catgirl, a big green *something,* a blue lizard man, and more. They must be new, because experienced users would abandon an avatar as soon as it was clear they couldn't defeat the security measures. Better to lose an account than give the authorities time to track down your real location.

Nadia stood behind the bar, her stunning sable skin set off to perfection by an off-the-shoulder aqua dress. Her avatar looked entirely human, a purposeful choice designed to engender trust. She didn't even glance my way, but thanks to the magic of technology, she whispered in my ear, "House raid. Get out now, if you can."

"I need information," I whispered back.

"I will reopen tomorrow. The new location will be posted in

the usual places. But my regulars will be scared off for a day or two."

"Actually, I was hoping to talk to you."

"If you get free, meet me here in ten," she whispered. An address popped up and I saved it.

She blinked out of existence as a man stepped out of the farthest alcove. I squinted through the hazy air, but, unfortunately, I'd recognize him anywhere. Ian Bishop moved my way in his official avatar. At least now I knew where he got some of his better information. Too bad he couldn't have waited another twenty minutes.

"Who are you?" he asked me.

"Who are *you?*"

"Ian Bishop, House von Hasenberg security." He held out his hand but I made no move to take it. Instead, I held my left hand out, palm down. My avatar didn't move, but it brought up my supplemental menu. I had a feeling I was going to need it sooner than I'd prefer.

The room twisted, glitching as HIVE tried to handle whatever destruction Nadia had kicked off on her way out. She was probably trying to wipe the whole damn bar. My admiration for her went up.

It was odd, looking directly into Ian's eyes. My avatar was the same height as his, and the projectors in the room mapped the projected image to my actual height, so the point of view would be correct. Ian's avatar was as perfect as I would expect from a House representative. He looked exactly like himself.

"Well," I said after a long pause, "I suppose since you've killed the buzz, I'll be on my way. Nice meeting you, security man."

"Not so fast. I have some questions." He raised his right hand and shackles appeared around my wrists, called into existence by the zone admin security scripts. He would also be trying to track my real location. He held out his left hand and the room stabilized slightly, though the edges kept fading away.

I didn't even need my extra scripts for this level of restraint. I laughed and pulled my hands apart. The digital shackles snapped in half and disappeared, defeated by my standard security settings.

Ian's expression flashed to annoyance and I couldn't hide my grin. Before he could try again with something more substantial, I blew him a kiss, then swiped my left hand through the exit script on my supplemental menu.

The projection flickered as the script jumped me through five random locations. It wasn't exactly stock functionality, but I'd spent enough time in HIVE to have found a few tricks. I ended up in what looked like someone's living room. Luckily it was unoccupied and no one questioned my presence.

I checked the location Nadia had sent me. Like the bar, it wasn't in the standard zone map. I'd be going in blind. I'd known Nadia—as far as two highly secretive, anonymous people in a virtual world could know each other—for five years, and she'd never betrayed me. That didn't mean that today wouldn't be the day she would start, but I felt confident enough to risk it.

"HIVE, transport to saved location eight."

"Transporting to saved location 208a.080m3.1q5y," the computer said.

The projection wavered, then solidified into a cozy sitting room with pale peach walls and sleek charcoal furniture. A quick glance around revealed that there were no doors. Nadia sat curled up in an overstuffed chair in front of a roaring fireplace. She gestured at the chair next to her.

I directed my avatar to sit and the projection's perspective shifted again so we were at eye level even though I remained standing in real life.

"You escaped," she said.

"I did. Thank you for the distraction. He was too busy trying to stabilize the room to try anything too serious."

"What information is so important that you'd risk a House raid to get it?"

"Likely the same information that caused the raid in the first place," I said carefully. "I have a client who is very interested in Ferdinand von Hasenberg's disappearance."

She glanced sharply at me. "You're working for House von Hasenberg?"

I didn't have to fake the sly grin. "No."

She relaxed, and I filed that information away. She stared into the fire for a long minute. "I think you should walk away, Fenix. This isn't something you want to poke into. Leave House politics to the Houses. They can take care of themselves."

"I would if I could," I said softly. It came out far more bitterly than I had intended.

Nadia's expression turned hard. "If you need help . . ." She trailed off, leaving the offer open.

"You don't know how much that means to me," I said, "but I am okay. And a job is a job. This isn't the first I time I've stuck my nose where it doesn't belong."

"Ten thousand credits and you forget where you heard anything I tell you," she said. "And don't darken my door for a few weeks while the heat dies down."

It was a ridiculous amount of money, but I wasn't in a position to bargain. I brought up my communication menu and sent a message to myself. It caused my avatar to look distant, as if

I was communicating with an actual client. "Deal," I agreed a few minutes later. "Client insists on half up front, half after you deliver."

Nadia shook her head. "Your client must be stupid or desperate."

"Who says they can't be both?" I asked with a smile. "Do we have an agreement?"

"We will when I see some credits."

I pulled up my menu and transferred five thousand credits to her account. My own account was funded from untraceable currency, preventing anyone from following a paper trail back to my real identity.

Nadia waited until the transfer was completed, then she said, "The rumor is that the Silva Syndicate was paid to knock off Ferdinand, but either the hit payment didn't go through or they got greedy and grabbed him instead. There was a sketchy rumor about a ransom, but the Syndicate is too smart to take on a High House directly. If I had to guess, they're planning to break him for information, or bury him in the deepest hole they can find."

I froze and let the rage burn through my system. When I was sure I could keep my voice neutral, I asked, "How reliable are these rumors?"

"Silva was definitely responsible. The rest is merely speculation. They are playing this one very close and it's only thanks to a few well-connected friends that I know as much as I do."

"Do any of these friends have a line on where I might find one of the Syndicate's ships? Or one of the Silvas?"

Nadia frowned at me. "You are walking a dangerous road, my friend. I hope you know what you are doing."

"So do I."

She inclined her head. "I might know someone who knows something, but that information will be very expensive."

"My client is aware that such information is valuable," I said. To underscore the point, I sent her the second half of her payment.

"I will ask around. If I hear anything, I'll be in touch."

"A pleasure, as always. Stay safe," I said.

"You as well."

I raised my hand in farewell, then transported out to a location just off the main street. I checked my security settings, then ran an additional scan to ensure Nadia hadn't bugged me. Everything came back clean.

I logged out, just to be extra safe, then logged in with the same account. As long as I was here, I needed to check my virtual safe house and ask my contacts there for information, too. Some of them had dealt with Silva in the past.

"HIVE, transport home," I said.

"Transporting to saved location 192z.168b7.1h4m."

Much like Nadia's bar and home, my home was not on the standard HIVE map. I loaded into a completely black space, and any attempt at shedding light would fail. This was the first level of protection.

"I am Fenix. I rose from the ashes. Allow me to enter and find comfort," I said. The passphrase was specific to me and coded to my avatar's voice and cadence.

A silver door appeared. I tapped out my entry pattern, and the scene changed to a cozy living room with a wall of books and soft, plush furniture. Windows looked out into a green forest, with sunbeams dancing through the leaves. It was meant to be as comforting as possible because this was a digital safe space, both for the people I'd already rescued and for those who had decided to stay where they were and support others with shared information.

This network wasn't nearly as broad as my anonymous

contacts, but each person in it was fully vetted and trusted, and many of them held important positions. For some, it was too dangerous to send messages even to anonymous accounts, so we left "physical" messages on a note board. I quickly checked the existing messages but none pertained to the attack and none required my immediate attention.

I reached out and grabbed an empty notecard. A voice prompt came up, and I said, "Ferdinand has reportedly been taken by Silva. I need any information you can find about the attack or the Syndicate. Time is of the essence."

My words were transcribed onto the card. You *could* write in HIVE, but it was slow and messy, so most written text was actually dictated. I added a large red exclamation mark and tacked the note to the board. It wasn't the fastest communication method, but eventually everyone would see it.

I'd done as much as I could, so I logged out of HIVE. The projectors in the room turned off and the lights slowly brightened back to normal.

I sat down and rubbed my forehead. If Nadia's information was correct, then the Syndicate had my brother. I agreed that they wouldn't try to ransom him, which explained why no one had been in contact. And it meant I had a very narrow slice of time to rescue him before they broke him in a way that couldn't be fixed.

With that in mind, I reconnected my secure Internet connection and started looking for information on any of the Silva ships. Because they were all in constant contact, I just needed to find one of them, it didn't matter which. I'd love to find the one with Ferdinand aboard, but the possibility was too small to count on.

I lost track of time until the suite computer broke my concentration. A short, sharp chime sounded three times before falling silent. Because my com was cut off from wireless communication and my terminal was connected to a private network, important messages were routed through my suite computer. I'd just received three emergency messages.

I disconnected from my fruitless search for the Syndicate and reconnected to the House network. The messages were from my siblings, addressed to me directly, and flagged as emergency. That was never a good sign.

The first two, from Hannah and Catarina, urged me to check the news as soon as possible. But it was the third message, from Benedict, that chilled me. He'd kept it short and sweet: *Father plans to put you under house confinement. If you want to flee, go now.*

# CHAPTER 6

I paused just long enough to check the news, then ran for my closet. Someone had done a remarkably good job of painting me as a traitor, one who worked with House Rockhurst to betray Ferdinand and House von Hasenberg.

Even if Father didn't believe the story—and I hoped he wouldn't—he would be furious about my meeting with Evelyn Rockhurst. And despite my preference for electronic sleuthing, eventually I'd run into a lead I'd need to track down the old-fashioned way. I couldn't find Ferdinand if I was locked in my suite.

My hands shook as I stood frozen in my closet. I didn't have time for a breakdown. I shoved a change of clothes and a pair of blasters in a protective case into a tote. I strapped a stun pistol in a holster around my waist and threw on a cloak over my blouse and pants. Finally, I added my purse with the silencer still inside to the tote.

Good enough.

I headed for the door, but it did not open on my approach and the manual open button did nothing. "Alfred, open the suite door."

After a few seconds, the suite computer responded. "Request unavailable. Your suite is locked for your safety. Please remain where you are." The computer didn't have emotions, but I still thought it sounded contrite.

If Ian Bishop thought I'd remain locked in my own damn suite until he could be bothered to come collect me for Father, then he was about to get a rude awakening.

I darted into my study for a pair of smart glasses. They connected to my com and displayed information hands-free. These were a high-end version that featured both hand and eye tracking, allowing me to leave my com in my pocket but still interact with it.

The glasses turned on automatically when I put them on. The standard information overlay—time, location, calendar—came up in my peripheral vision, but I swiped my hands up and the menu appeared front and center.

With no time to waste, I tapped into the House's security system and checked on the cameras outside my suite. The video came up on the bottom half of the glasses. So far, the hallway was clear, but that would change once I overrode the lock. I'd need to move fast, because while I could take down the whole system, doing that while we were at war was unwise.

First and foremost, I needed a ship. I briefly considered stealing *Polaris,* the Rockhurst prototype ship, but I didn't know if it was still space-worthy. For all I knew, the scientists had it in pieces in the hangar. And Ada would kill me if I damaged her baby. She'd grown attached to that ship.

My own ship, *Aurora,* was less than a year old. I'd bought it after Gregory's death. His family had kept my previous ship when I returned to House von Hasenberg. What's mine was his and what's his was his.

House marriages were *the best.*

Luckily, I'd kept the vast majority of my money in numbered accounts he couldn't access or I'd be broke in addition to homeless and shipless.

I shook myself out of my angry thoughts. *Aurora* was one of the nicest personal ships in our fleet. I could probably find and steal Ferdinand's ship if I had to, but I wanted *Aurora*—Ada wasn't the only one attached to her ship.

My ship was in the secondary House hangar. To get to it, I'd have to travel the length of the House, then either skirt around the primary hangar or go through it. The secondary hangar should be less busy, but getting there undetected would be tricky.

Stalling wouldn't make it any easier, so I put the cameras outside my door on a two-minute loop, then unlocked my suite. I raised the hood of my cloak and took a deep breath. Leaving would make me look guilty as hell, but I couldn't just sit around and wait for Ferdinand to turn up dead. Holding that thought close, I stepped out into the hall and locked the door behind me.

For once, my modified nanos came in handy as I monitored the security frequency. A security team was headed my way, but they were still thirty seconds out. I ducked into a dimly lit hidden passage with ten seconds to spare. Adrenaline made me shaky, but I kept moving.

Ian would probably be monitoring these passageways, but the surveillance was spottier and I knew exactly where all of the cameras were and how to avoid them. Ian had been advocating for additional security for these tunnels for years, but Father had resisted. We all assumed that he, too, wanted to be able to slip out of the House unseen.

I pulled the bottom of my cloak up and carefully stepped over the first laser tripwire. Breaking the beam would send a security alert directly to Ian. At the next intersection, I edged along the inside corner, just out of view of the camera. Avoiding security meant I took a meandering route to the hangar.

I kept one eye on the security footage on my smart glasses while also monitoring wireless communications. Because I hadn't answered the door, the security team was debating whether or not to breach my quarters without my permission.

By the time Ian gave the order, I was nearly to the primary hangar. There was a flurry of communication as the team found they couldn't get my door to unlock. Ian's voice took on an annoyed tone that made me smirk, but I couldn't gloat yet. He wasn't the head of security for nothing, and I still had a busy hangar to cross.

My com vibrated and Ian's contact information popped up on the glasses. He was requesting a video connection. I rolled my eyes and swiped his contact information offscreen to decline.

Unfortunately, Ian was nothing if not persistent. He tried again with a voice-only connection. I swiped that one away, too, then blocked him for five minutes. He'd try to track me with my com signal, but I'd made a few modifications that would make that more difficult. It wouldn't fool him for long, but I just needed a few more minutes.

I performed the complicated hand gesture that activated the highly illegal secondary identity chip in my right arm. The secondary chip was a von Hasenberg specialty, allowing multiple identities to be stored on a single chip. Specific identities could be selected by a series of finger movements. It was perfect for covert work because switching identities made a trail much harder to follow. And it was untraceable—even by our own security teams.

As far as I knew, only von Hasenberg family members had these exact chips, but I would be surprised if the other Houses didn't have something similar.

I touched my right thumb and pinky together. The primary chip in my left arm held my real identity, but scanning into the hangar as myself would let Ian know exactly where I was. Scanning in as Isabella Blanc, a high-level House von Hasenberg advisor, wouldn't set off any alarms. At least not right away. As soon as Ian did any digging, the identity would fold, but it wasn't meant for long-term use.

I stopped at the end of the hidden passageway. Opening the final door required a House von Hasenberg ID, complete with House seal, but it was one of the few doors that didn't log access unless it was opened without the proper credentials. It also didn't open from the outside, so once I left the building, I'd be stuck.

I unlocked the door with my primary identity chip and stepped out into the hidden alcove. I'd be completely exposed in the hangar, but the diplomatic seal on my false identity meant the security guard wouldn't look too closely at me. It wasn't unusual for a cloaked figure to be seen coming and going from the hangar—not everyone wanted to shout that they were working with one House over another.

Now I just needed to pop back up on the video surveillance somewhere that wouldn't be too suspicious. I took a twisting path to the hangar entrance. It looked like I couldn't make up my mind which way I wanted to go, but really it was to skirt the cameras. I came back into view as I swiped my right arm over the chip reader.

The door opened and the guard inside waved me through with a brief glance. I didn't envy him the dressing-down he was about to receive. I advanced through the building with a purposeful stride, moving as fast as I dared. A few other people were milling around, giving me a tiny bit of cover.

I hit the exit at the same time that the security team found my suite empty. My head throbbed with splinters of agony as I tried to keep track of the security frequency while filtering out everything else. I gritted my teeth and kept going.

I made it into the secondary hangar without anyone stopping me, but Ian had ordered my ship watched. I stopped in an alcove out of sight of the main landing bay and tapped into the security system.

The video showed *Aurora* was in the first berth. Four men in House von Hasenberg uniforms lingered near the ship's cargo ramp. They weren't even trying to be inconspicuous.

I set off a fire alarm in the storage area on the far side of the hangar. The guards in the video looked at one another. *Come on, come on.* Finally, three of them shrugged and ambled off toward the back of the hangar while the fourth reported it.

I drew the shock pistol from the holster. It had been years since I'd actually needed to shoot someone. I hoped that muscle memory would be enough or this escape would be going nowhere fast.

I was already in motion by the time Ian's voice ordered the men back to their posts. I ran silently toward *Aurora*. The sole remaining guard stood next to the cargo ramp, facing away, toward the alarm. The other guards had not reappeared.

I said a prayer of thanks for small favors, then waited until I was close enough that I couldn't miss. I shot the guard in the back with a silent apology.

He screamed as he fell, but I was already climbing the cargo ramp. I swiped my real identity chip over the control panel and the cargo door slid upward. The other guards shouted a question, but they would be too late.

Once the door was high enough, I ducked inside. "*Aurora,* how many people are onboard?"

"You are the only passenger, Captain," the ship replied.

"That's what I like to hear," I murmured. I used the cargo bay control panel to close and lock the door and retract the ramp. "*Aurora*, take us into orbit." The ship chimed, and I felt the subtle vibration of the engines engaging.

I had to get off the ground before Ian locked the hangar doors or denied me launch clearance. I would worry about a destination once I was free of the building.

Unfortunately, I wasn't fast enough.

"Permission to launch denied," *Aurora* said. "Ground control requests an immediate shutdown."

"Emergency override code F8H07Z4." It was Ferdinand's personal override code. If they hadn't locked it down, it would have priority access to nearly any von Hasenberg system.

I held my breath until the ship said, "Override approved." The engine noise changed as the ship launched.

My com vibrated and Ian's info reappeared on my glasses. The five-minute block had expired. I confirmed *Aurora* was on course for orbit, then accepted the video link as voice-only on my side—I could see him, but he couldn't see me.

If I'd thought I'd seen Ian at his angriest before my meeting with Evelyn, I'd been dead wrong. I'd never seen him as furious as he was right now. His face was set in lines of granite and his eyes blazed with temper. His jaw was clenched so hard I was afraid he'd break his teeth.

It seemingly took him a force of will to open his mouth. "Lady Bianca, return to the ground. *Now*," he gritted out.

"No."

"Every resource I have to waste tracking you is a resource that's not looking for Lord Ferdinand. Is that what you want? Your brother to die because you're being stubborn?"

Adrenaline and fear and anxiety mixed into a potent tempest that pounded through my system. "My brothers and sisters are *everything* to me," I argued, deeply insulted. I pressed my lips together to prevent an angry tirade from spilling out.

There were so many things I could add: how Ferdinand used to take my punishments when I was sick or injured, all the way back to the faint edge of my earliest memories; how Hannah had shown up after Gregory's death and bundled me home without a single question, despite the righteous fury in her eyes at my weak condition; how my siblings were the only people in the 'verse who loved me for *me*.

I would personally storm the gates of hell for any of my brothers or sisters. To claim otherwise was to fundamentally misunderstand me as a person.

Realization dawned. Ian was far too clever to make such a mistake; he was trying to use my love for Ferdinand against me. It would be so easy to underestimate Ian Bishop, to be blinded by his gorgeous features and miss the intelligent, patient predator lurking beneath the surface.

I vowed not to make that mistake.

"You have an interesting way of showing you care," Ian said. Even knowing what he was up to, it was good that he was currently on the ground or I might be tempted to throttle him.

"You don't *have* to track me. You can keep looking for Ferdinand while I do the same."

"You think Lord von Hasenberg is just going to let you gallivant across the universe when it's being implied that you're a traitor? You don't know your father very well."

Actually, I knew Albrecht von Hasenberg better than nearly anyone. He'd want to keep me close to save face, sure, but also because he knew I was the best intelligence officer in the House. He didn't know about my network, but he knew that I could find information no one else could, an invaluable skill to a House with secrets to hide and arms to twist.

And also because he knew I had a trove of information that would likely cripple the Consortium if it got out—which it would if I died and couldn't reset the auto-release timer.

"Just because you tell Father you're searching for me doesn't mean you have to actually search for me. I'm tracking down a lead on Ferdinand. Once I find my brother, I'll return."

"Bianca, I can't protect you if you run," he said, his expression taut and urgent. "Return and give me the lead. We'll find Ferdinand faster if we work together."

"I can take care of myself, and I refuse to be a prisoner in my own house. Instead of hunting me, you should figure out why someone would want to frame me as a traitor. Perhaps they have useful information."

"I already have a team on it. I don't need you to tell me how to run an investigation," he said stiffly.

I almost slipped up and let him know that his heavy-handed raid had scattered one of the best sources of information in HIVE. I clamped my lips on the words at the last second. He didn't know I was Fenix and I preferred keeping it that way.

"In that case, it seems we're at an impasse. If you agree not to search for me, I'll send you any information I find that I won't have time to investigate."

"Albrecht has already demanded your capture. It's the same priority as the search for Ferdinand. I don't have a choice."

"There's always a choice," I murmured.

"Not this time." His voice was flinty.

"I am not returning until I find Ferdinand, so if you want to find me, find him." With that, I ended the connection.

My head pulsed in time with my heart and my blood pressure felt dangerously high. Of all the frustrating men in the world, I had to have Ian Bishop dogging my steps. I groaned. If I'd learned anything during Ada's time on the run, it was that

Ian never gave up. Maybe I'd get lucky and he'd send a team after me, rather than coming himself. And maybe pigs would fly.

At least I wouldn't have to worry about the RCDF. Neither Father nor Ian would want to air our dirty laundry in front of the enforcers of the Consortium. House von Hasenberg would handle my retrieval on its own, which meant that I'd escaped, for now, because the House didn't have anything in orbit capable of capturing *Aurora*.

I headed upstairs to the flight deck. *Aurora* was a relatively small ship with just four levels. The flight deck, captain's quarters, and guest suite were on the top level. Because it was my personal ship, I'd reconfigured the standard layout. Instead of crew quarters, level two held the mess hall and medbay. The crew quarters were moved to level three, and level four included the exercise room and maintenance access.

The cargo bay was at the aft of the ship and spanned two stories from level four up to level three. Right now, it was nearly empty. The ship was kept stocked with essentials, but I'd need supplies if I planned to track down Ferdinand.

And I knew just who to contact for the kind of supplies I needed.

WHEN MY SISTER ADA HAD BEEN BANISHED FROM EARTH, she relocated to Sedition on Alpha Phoenicis Dwarf Zero. APD Zero was a planet-wide black market, and Sedition was its largest city. It was also the first place Ian would look for me, so I couldn't go there directly.

But Ada was also friends with Rhys Sebastian, a well-known smuggler, and Veronica Karim, a former fence. Between the three of them, they could get me anything I needed, no matter how rare or illegal, and Rhys had the ships required to meet me anywhere in known space.

So where could I go that would be convenient for Ada but unlikely to be the first place Ian would look?

I pondered the question as I entered the flight deck. In the center of the room, the captain's chair stood in front of a half-circle console made of sleek glass. The tactical and navigation stations flanked the captain's chair on the left and right, respectively. I'd kept them more for tradition than need; I could control the entire ship from my console.

I slipped into my chair and logged in. The window shutters were closed for launch, but the video screens showed Earth falling away and the darkness of space opening up in front of the ship.

Thanks to its excellent computers, *Aurora* was capable of jumping nearly three thousand light-years at a time on its own, but getting far enough away that Ian couldn't track me down in a matter of hours would require the help of a gate. Gates were giant supercomputers that could plot safe jump points millions of light-years away.

Gates usually operated in sets of two or more. The second gate wasn't required, but if you jumped into deep space with no gate to calculate your return trip, then you'd have to risk jumping back using bad data. No one would voluntarily jump with bad data if it could be avoided.

I owned a small hotel in Atlantia, the fifth-largest city on the popular resort planet of Gamma Carinae Dwarf One. I'd purchased the property through a series of subsidiary and shell companies. The paper trail was so convoluted that it was highly unlikely anyone could ever link the building back to me. GCD One had a nearby gate and a constant stream of traffic—two more ships wouldn't even register.

I plotted a course for Atlantia and routed it through two

gates, just in case Ian managed to talk the RCDF into giving him my first jump coordinates. It added a six-hour cooldown for the FTL drive, but it would take Ada time to gather supplies anyway.

Earth's gate was one of the fastest available, so although I was forty-ninth in the queue, my estimated wait time was only five minutes. I dashed off a quick message to Ada while I waited and encrypted it with our shared secret key: *pegasaurus*. We'd made up the creature as children then promptly forgotten about it until we had needed a secure, hard to guess but easy to remember key.

It was very early morning on APD Zero. I felt a little bad about flagging the message as an emergency because it would cause a ridiculous alarm on her end, but this *was* technically an emergency. Ada could catch up on her beauty sleep later.

*Aurora* chimed as the ship got a jump point from the gate. A few seconds later, the sound of the engine changed as the FTL drive engaged. The screen flickered as the ship switched to auxiliary power, then the engine noise reached a peak and fell silent.

The window shutters retracted. I'd chosen a gate outside a busy space station, but you'd never know it from looking. Even at just fifteen minutes away, the station was a faint light against the inky darkness of deep space. I'd like to visit but that was asking for trouble. If Ian followed me, he would assume the station was my final destination. It was safer for me to stay on *Aurora* and wait out the FTL cooldown, even if sitting on my hands for six hours felt like an eternity.

The main engine restarted and I directed the ship away from the pull of the lights. *Aurora* automatically tracked and avoided the dozens of ships around us. Without a nearby star, visual reconnaissance was worthless. There was, however, a neighboring asteroid field brimming with valuable resources for those brave enough to mine them—hence the station.

The proximity to the gate meant that communication was nearly as fast as on Earth. Ada's message, when it arrived, came with a truly astonishing number of expletives. Ian wasn't her favorite person to begin with and he wasn't winning any more points with this latest stunt. Neither was Father.

She promised to get the supplies I needed and meet me on GCD One in a few hours. Now that I had more time, I sent her the coordinates and access codes she'd need in case she got there first. I also added a few things to my supplies list. I didn't know what I'd be facing, so better to be overprepared than underprepared. Though, knowing Ada, she'd show up with an armory in tow. The real trick would be convincing her to remain behind while I went in search of Silva.

Perhaps what she didn't know wouldn't hurt her.

# CHAPTER 7

I'd spent six hours looking for information on the Syndicate with little success. There were persistent rumors of an upcoming event, but no one had any details to share. The Syndicate's anything-goes events had taken on near-mythical status. They were one night only and the Silva family usually waited until the very last minute to announce a location. The secrecy prevented any undesirables, like the RCDF, from showing up and ruining the atmosphere.

The event could be tomorrow or in two months and only one of those worked for me. For now, I would have to assume it was too far in the future and keep searching for information on their current location.

*Aurora* chimed a one-minute jump warning. The FTL drive was ready and the gate had provided our next jump coordinates. There had been no sign of Ian, but I had received a blistering message from Father ordering me home in no uncertain terms. My response had been a single sentence: *I will return once I find Ferdinand.*

Staying ahead of Ian when I wasn't home to monitor his progress would be a challenge. I would have to keep my head down because I didn't believe for a second that he'd actually stop looking for me, no matter how much sense it made. Ian was tenacious, and I'd made him look incompetent. He'd come after me with a vengeance.

The jump to GCD One was uneventful. The window shutters didn't retract since we'd be entering the atmosphere soon, but on the vid screens the planet sparkled, sapphire, under the blue-white light of GCD.

The main engine restarted and *Aurora* continued on course to Atlantia. My hotel had a private hangar for the penthouse residence, which was one of the reasons I'd bought it. In the last few years I'd sent more than one woman there who had needed an escape, whether temporary or permanent, but it was currently unoccupied.

GCD One was known for its beautiful pink sand beaches and clear turquoise water. The mild light of GCD rarely caused sunburns, allowing visitors to spend more time outside. And the days were longer than Universal Standard Time, the time used on Earth, so time seemed to pass more slowly. The local calendar had only six days in a week, and the tourist board had run a very successful ad campaign about their lack of Mondays.

Atlantia was nestled in a protected cove between a nature preserve and the sea. Many of the wealthy tourists skipped it because of the lack of high-end shopping and dining. I enjoyed the peace and quiet, plus if Consortium types avoided the area, then both I and the women I sent here were less likely to be recognized. Win-win.

"Beginning atmospheric entry," *Aurora* announced.

The ship picked up a subtle vibration as we descended. The compensators muted the worst of the turbulence but they couldn't completely eliminate all of the signs that the ship was essentially slamming into the thickening atmosphere.

*Aurora* descended until I could see the shape of the city. In the far distance, the buildings of Perousa reached for the sky. GCD One's largest city housed over a million full-time residents and nearly as many tourists in the peak season.

Some of my anxiety bled away. Atlantia had always been a sanctuary for me. I didn't visit often, but no bad memories lingered here. Only sun and sea and peace.

On the ground, an unfamiliar ship that could've been *Aurora*'s twin sat in the hangar's second berth. It was in excellent condition. The cargo ramp was down, but the door was closed. No one was visible.

I called Ada's com voice-only. Her contact information showed on my smart glasses along with the connection status. I was 90 percent sure it was her ship, or at least one she'd borrowed, but there was no sense in walking into a trap if it wasn't.

Ada picked up on the second ring. "Are you here?"

"I'm here," I confirmed. "Is this your ship in my hangar?"

"*Jester* belongs to Rhys. Captain Hargrove was kind enough to give us a lift," Ada said, a strange inflection in her voice.

"Should I bail?"

"What? No!" She laughed and lowered her voice. "Scarlett Hargrove and I don't see eye to eye, that's all. You'll understand when you meet her. She's on the ship if you need them to move or something."

"No, the ship is fine where it is. I'll see you in a few minutes. Are you in the penthouse?"

"Yes. I brought Marcus, Rhys, and Veronica. We're admiring the view and raiding your kitchen. I think Veronica has Rhys fixing brunch. Brace yourself."

I laughed and disconnected the call. We were on opposite time schedules but brunch for dinner sounded lovely. Mostly I was just happy I'd get to spend a few hours with Ada, though I'd need to sneak in some sleep or I would be worthless tomorrow.

I'd never met Veronica in person, but I had worked online with her and Rhys when we were trying to dig up information on the Genesis Project. The Genesis Project was a secret Consortium genetic manipulation experiment that had attempted to turn Ada's soul mate, Marcus Loch, into a supersoldier.

The Consortium scientists had been far more successful than they ever could have hoped, right up until the point when Loch had decided to go rogue during the Fornax Rebellion. The Consortium claimed the rest of Loch's squad had died during the mission, but my brief research hinted otherwise. Both Ada and Loch had refused to answer any of my carefully worded fishing attempts, so all I had was guesswork and conjecture.

I unclipped from my seat and exited *Aurora*. I double-checked that the cargo bay door was closed and locked. I didn't need anyone poking around in my ship while I wasn't here.

The penthouse had a private elevator with an entrance right off the hangar. I swiped my identity chip over the panel and the light turned green. Nerves fluttered in my belly as the elevator ascended. The last time I'd seen Ada she had been leaving Earth because Father had banished her. Now I appeared to be following in her footsteps, though I hadn't been officially banished—*yet*.

The elevator opened directly into the foyer. White marble floors anchored pale blue walls. An entry table held a vase with a bouquet of fresh, colorful flowers. They added a floral note to the scent of warm baked dough floating through the air.

The living room had the same dark, delicate furniture I had in my suite at home, but the real draw was the view. Floor-to-ceiling windows framed the balcony, and beyond that were nothing but clear blue water and deep blue skies.

From here, the penthouse felt like it was the only thing for kilometers. Even the number of wireless signals was bearable thanks to some light shielding. My head still throbbed from earlier, but it wasn't getting any worse. Thank goodness for small miracles.

Ada and Loch were on the balcony, leaning against the railing and looking over the sea. Ada's dark hair was tousled from the wind and she had on a pair of black pants and a bright coral shirt. She was smiling up at Loch, who had planted himself beside her. He sported his usual shaved head, dark clothes, and don't-fuck-with-me look, but as I watched, his serious expression broke. He grinned at Ada as she dissolved into laughter.

I moved farther into the room and Loch glanced at me through the open balcony door. He nudged Ada and she spun around. "Bianca!" She hurried inside and pulled me into a hug. "Are you okay?"

"After you left, the neighborhood went to shit," I teased, "but I'm fine. I can't stay long. Director Bishop is searching for me, and I have to find Ferdinand before he catches up to me."

"Do you have any leads?"

"A few."

When I didn't elaborate, Ada rolled her eyes and sighed. "Did you think I would accept that as an answer?"

"It was worth a shot," I said.

"Let's see if Rhys has destroyed the kitchen yet and then you can tell us what you know."

Despite the fact that the penthouse was equipped with a very nice food synthesizer, the kitchen was also kept stocked with essentials even when I wasn't here. I never knew when someone might need a place to stay, and cooking was far more soothing than punching a button. Unused supplies were rotated out to a local food bank before their expirations.

Rhys and Veronica were putting this week's supplies to use. Rhys Sebastian must've started the day perfectly turned out in a navy suit, but he'd taken off the jacket and rolled his sleeves to the elbow. He was carefully stirring something in a large bowl. Rhys was classically handsome with tan skin, close-cropped blond hair, and light eyes.

Next to Rhys, Veronica Karim was supervising his work. Tall and slender, with warm brown skin and long black hair, she was beautiful. If she and Rhys ever decided to have a baby, the universe would probably implode from the cuteness overload. She had on loose charcoal pants and a deep violet blouse. She caught sight of us first.

"Lady Bianca, I hope you don't mind that we're using your kitchen," she said with a smile. Her voice was low and melodious.

"That depends. Do I get to sample whatever you're making?"

She laughed. "Of course."

"In that case, carry on. And it's just Bianca."

Ada held out an arm toward Rhys and Veronica. "Bianca, meet Rhys and Veronica. I know you've worked together before but I don't think you've met in person."

"It's lovely to finally meet you," Veronica said.

"Likewise," I said.

"Sorry, I would greet you properly but if I mess up this strawberry whipped cream I'm afraid Veronica won't let me have any of the shortcake she made, and her food is not to be missed," Rhys said with a charming grin.

I thought I'd grown immune to looks and charm, but Rhys was putting that theory to the test. I wouldn't want him for myself, but he certainly was easy on the eyes.

"The whipped cream comes first," I agreed with a smile.

"How long are you staying?" Ada asked.

"I jumped twice on the way here, so the FTL drive cooldown will take almost twelve hours," I said. "I want to be ready to go by then, but you don't have to stay that long because I'm also going to need to sleep. I'm sorry I woke you all up so early."

Surprisingly, it was Loch who waved off my words. "What happened?" he asked.

I brought them up to speed while Rhys finished the whipped cream and started slicing fruit. By the time I was finished, brunch was ready. We carried the food out to the table on the balcony and sat in the gentle afternoon sun. A light breeze carried the briny scent of the sea and kept the temperature pleasant.

I ate lightly, my stomach queasy thanks to the headache. Rhys hadn't been joking—Veronica was an excellent chef and everything tasted amazing. After eating what I could, I sipped coffee, lost in my thoughts.

Rhys broke the silence. "I haven't heard anything about your brother's disappearance other than what's been reported on the news, but I've got a few people asking questions. If it really is the Syndicate then I might get a lead or two. I've worked with them before."

"Have you heard anything about their upcoming party?" I asked.

Ada turned to me with a dark look. "Don't even think about it," she warned. "They already have Ferdinand. Are you going to serve yourself up on a platter, too?"

"That wasn't my intention, no. I've been on a Silva ship before." Ada blanched, but I kept going. "I know how they operate. They are driven far more by money than politics, and I have no problem buying Ferdinand back if that's what it takes. I just need to track one of them down. Assuming it's soon, the party is the best option."

"It will be a tricky deal to pull off," Veronica said.

"I know, but if I don't try, Ferdinand suffers."

"Marcus and I will come with you," Ada declared.

"No," I disagreed gently. "This is not a case where more people mean more safety. And if things really do go south, I'll need someone who can bail me out. You can't do that if you're locked up with me."

Ada opened her mouth to argue, but Loch beat her to it. "Bianca is right," he said. "One or two people can slip in quietly, but take a team and it looks like an invasion."

They shared a look before Ada sighed in defeat. "Very well. We won't go with you, but we'll be close. And at the first sign of trouble, we'll bring the invasion." Her smile was sharp and just a little bit scary. My little sister had changed in the two years she'd been gone.

"Thank you," I said.

We discussed plans and options until I could barely keep my eyes open, but it all boiled down to one hard truth: if I couldn't find Silva, I wouldn't find Ferdinand. We talked about contacting them electronically, but in the end, we agreed that tipping them off early would be a good way for Ferdinand to get dead and dumped in an unused corner of the universe.

When I yawned for the third time in as many minutes, Ada said, "Go to bed. It's late in Universal and you need sleep. We'll go down to the beach for a while. It's been ages since I was last on GCD One and I want to enjoy the water while I'm here."

"There are plenty of guest rooms, so make yourselves at home. You already found the kitchen and you're welcome to whatever is in it. There's also a synthesizer if you need something I don't have."

"Bianca, we'll be fine. We are all adults. Go to bed."

"Fine, fine," I said with a wave. She might be an adult, but she'd always be my little sister. "Wake me up if any news comes in. Otherwise, I'll see you in six hours."

"Make it seven," Ada demanded.

"Watch it. I have a whole host of baby Ada stories that I've been *dying* to tell someone. Remember the time when you ate—"

Ada clamped her hand over my mouth. "If you tell that story, I will shave your head bald while you sleep."

"Well now I *have* to hear the story," Rhys said.

Ada glared at him before switching her glare back to me. *Bald,* she mouthed succinctly as she removed her hand.

"What did she eat?" Rhys asked.

"If you want to hear the rest of the story, you'll have to ask her. I like my hair as it is." I stood and gathered up my dirty dishes. "Oh, that reminds me. Ask her about her time as a self-barber, too." I dodged away from her playful smack with a laugh.

"So you decided to cut your own hair?" Loch asked, his deep voice rumbling with amusement. "How did that go?"

My work finished, I beat a hasty retreat before Ada could threaten me again. I was glad we got a moment to play, because the crushing worry for Ferdinand was never far away.

I dropped my dishes in the kitchen, then retired to my bedroom. The rest of the suite was open and available to anyone who visited, but my room was kept locked. I swiped my identity chip over the reader and the door clicked open.

The sea-green room was dominated by a large bed with crisp white bedding. The closet and en suite bathroom were off to the left. On the right, a wall of sliding glass panels led out onto a private balcony and offered an uninterrupted view of the water.

I admired the view for a second before I lowered the blackout curtains. I switched on a lamp as the room descended into darkness. Because the days were longer than usual on GCD One, most residences invested in quality blackout shades—it was hard to sleep with the sun shining in your eyes.

The room was a little more shielded than the rest of the penthouse and that, plus the minimal number of signals in this part of Atlantia, meant I could rest in silence. By the time I finally flopped into the bed, it was well after midnight Universal. I was asleep almost before my head hit the pillow.

I AWOKE TO FURIOUS POUNDING ON MY BEDROOM DOOR. "Bianca! Bianca, wake up, dammit! Wake uuupp!"

It took me a second to recognize Ada's voice. "What's going on?" I asked groggily.

Ada apparently hadn't heard me over her own shouting, so the auditory assault continued.

I switched on a lamp and checked my com. It was just after four in the morning Universal Time and midevening local time. I stumbled to the door and wrenched it open. "What?" I demanded.

"Ian is here," Ada said. "Grab your stuff."

I blinked at her and the words bounced off my tired brain. "What do you mean he's here?"

Ada swept past me into the room and began gathering up my clothes and accessories. "He's here, in the building. Loch spotted him entering the main part of the hotel. He must've tracked your ship." She paused. "Or ours. You never know with that sneaky bastard. Here." She thrust yesterday's clothes at me.

I caught them reflexively and started getting dressed. Ian had tracked me with uncanny speed and skill, which meant that Ada was probably correct and he'd bugged my ship.

Sneaky bastard, indeed.

"He must've planted an external hardware beacon that I failed to notice," I said.

Ada nodded. "Rhys has Scarlett's crew checking both ships for trackers. We'll get you sent off clean."

"Doesn't matter. I can't jump for almost six hours. He'll catch me in the air."

"Not if we disable his ship," Ada said with a predatory smile.

"Too risky. Is your ship ready to jump?" She nodded. "If we find a tracker, how do you feel about being a decoy?"

Her smile morphed into a grin. "I *have* felt the need to visit the far reaches of the 'verse lately."

I put on the smart glasses and tapped into my private view of the hotel's security feed. Ian was at the front desk, talking to my hotel manager. The video didn't have audio, but she was shaking her head and holding her hands up in a placating manner. Ian looked annoyed—the manager wouldn't be able to stall him for much longer, but I made a mental note to send her a bonus.

Ada and I hurried down to the private hangar. Someone had barred the doors and Rhys, Loch, and Veronica stood next to two loaded-down sleds covered in tarps. Rhys was talking to an unknown woman. She wore dark clothes that accentuated her long, curly red hair. She would be beautiful if she wasn't so busy scowling at Rhys.

"That's Scarlett Hargrove, *Jester*'s captain," Ada said quietly.

"You don't like her."

Ada exhaled audibly. "She was the one who came and got me after Father banished me. She and Loch had a moment."

I narrowed my eyes at the hulking ex-con at the bottom of *Aurora*'s cargo ramp. I'd warned him about what I would do if he hurt Ada.

"Put away the murder face, Bee," Ada said, reverting to

the childhood nickname she only used when she wanted to get away with something. "They are like family. I realize that now, but at the time I was jealous, and I'm still trying to get over my initial impression. It doesn't help that she treats me like I'm somewhere between invisible and gutter scum."

I swiveled my glare to the woman who dared to treat my sister like scum. "Scarlett Hargrove, you said?" I murmured, mostly to myself.

"Let it go," Ada said. "She and Rhys and Loch are friends. Hurting her would hurt them, so I ignore her. You should, too. Please."

It was the plea that did me in. "Fine," I sighed. "Let's get this stuff loaded while you tell me what you've brought."

As we approached the group, Rhys said, "We found the tracker but haven't removed it yet. What do you want us to do?"

"Bianca needs a few more hours before she can jump," Ada said. "Attach it to *Jester* and we'll play decoy."

Rhys turned to Scarlett. "Have your crew transfer the tracker. Looks like you're stuck with us for a little longer."

"At least it's less likely to damage my ship than your stupid plan," she groused, but affection underlaid her tone.

"Do I even want to know?" Ada asked.

"No," Veronica and Scarlett said at the same time.

I climbed *Aurora*'s cargo ramp and swiped my identity chip over the control panel. The cargo door lifted and I stepped inside. Loch and Ada followed me and the sleds floated along behind them, following their paired beacons.

Loch parked the sleds in the middle of the cargo bay and started sliding the pallets full of crates off onto the floor. Each sled held two pallets and they looked like they weighed a ton. "I would offer to help, but I'm not actually sure I can move one of those," I said.

"Don't worry about it," he said with a grin. "I'm almost done."

"What *is* all of this stuff?" I asked Ada.

"We decided your list was too small, so we added a few things that might come in handy. If you come across anything you don't recognize, send me a message, but it's mostly standard stuff like clothes and weapons, combat armor, boots, secure coms. We tossed in a surveillance drone and a handful of bugs and trackers. Oh, and your favorite chocolate and coffee. My treat."

"Thank you, Ada," I said around the lump in my throat. Ada had been gone for so long that I'd forgotten how well she knew me.

"No worries. Bring Ferdinand home."

"I will."

Rhys and Veronica stepped into the cargo bay. "I have a clean identity ready, if you need one," Rhys said by way of greeting. "I just need to know what name you prefer."

"Anna White," I said. Anna was one of my middle names, so it was easy enough to remember, while being generic enough to be hard to search for.

Rhys typed something on the device he carried, then said, "I need your identity chip."

I touched the thumb and ring finger of my right hand together for a long second before I held out my arm. Rhys slid the device up my arm until a beep indicated it was directly over my secondary identity chip. Thicker than a com, the rectangular device had a *"Property of the Royal Consortium"* label still attached to the side.

"Do I want to know where that chip programmer came from?" I asked.

"I've found it's better if you don't ask," Ada said. "Plausible deniability."

"This identity is only level three—it's all I had available on such short notice. So don't go pissing off the RCDF or the police or you'll have a bad time," Rhys said.

Black market identities typically came in five strengths, ranging from level one to level five. Level one identities would fall apart with even the most cursory glance, but they were also dirt cheap. Level five identities would have your own mother swearing that she'd never met you before.

Level three tended to be a balance between price and performance. The identity included enough background information to pass a midlevel private background check, but if the police started digging, they would spot the inconsistencies.

This chip already contained two level-five identities that I'd used previously. I'd used one while escaping, but I didn't think Ian knew about the other one. I still wouldn't use it unless absolutely necessary.

The chip programmer beeped again and Rhys pulled it away from my arm. "You're good to go," he said.

"Thank you. All of you. For everything."

"Family sticks together," Ada said. She pulled me in for a hug. "Keep in touch or I'll hunt you down."

"I will. And I'll let you know as soon as I find anything."

"Scarlett suggested we launch together," Rhys said. "Once you hit space, go dark and put as much distance as you can between you and Ian."

I waved in farewell as they left to find their own ship, then I went to get ready for launch. I smiled at the thought of Ian's face when he found he'd been chasing Ada.

He really should've just stayed home.

# CHAPTER 8

The launch went off without a hitch. Once we were out of sight of the ground, Captain Hargrove turned her ship toward the gate while I continued on away from it. Clear of the atmosphere, I pushed *Aurora* to max velocity. The more distance I could put between me and Ian, the less likely he would guess we'd swapped the tracker.

Captain Hargrove told me it would be ten minutes before they got a jump point from the gate. I asked to be notified just before they jumped, so I could shut down communications. It wouldn't be very convincing if I was supposedly somewhere else but still receiving calls here.

And I expected Ian to call at any minute.

He did not disappoint. The call came through voice-only and I wondered what he was hiding. I needed to keep him distracted for the next ten minutes, then drop the call in the middle of our conversation. I connected voice-only, too.

"Hello, Ian," I said. "Did you enjoy your vacation?"

"Lady von Hasenberg, you are to return to Earth immediately, by order of your father. Failure to do so will result in criminal charges and the posting of a sizable bounty for your return."

My eyebrows climbed upward. "Going to air dirty laundry in public now, are we? What charges do you think you have?"

"Treason against a High House." He said it without a hint of humor. Yeah, he was still furious with me.

"That will never stick."

"It doesn't matter. It's enough to post a bounty, and Lord von Hasenberg is insistent on your return by any means necessary."

"Why?"

"He didn't say," Ian said, unbending enough that frustration crept into his tone. "Perhaps he fears for your safety."

I couldn't help the dismissive scoff. "Have you seen any pigs winging past your window lately?"

"The reason doesn't matter. He has ordered you home and you must comply or face the consequences."

"Then I will face the consequences."

"Bianca, be reasonable. You won't be able to help Ferdinand if you're locked up in some merc's ship. Return to Earth and I promise I will allow you to assist with the investigation as much as I am able."

"That's not good enough."

"I am trying to compromise," he growled. "I can investigate just as well without your help."

I let the pause stretch as I debated playing my wild card. What the hell, it might not make any difference, but if ever there was a time I needed an edge, it was now.

"Did you know, Ian Noah Bishop, that there is no record of you prior to when you joined House von Hasenberg as a bodyguard? Oh, there are a few false trails, extremely well done, level four at least, but they ultimately lead nowhere. You just appeared one day, a fully formed twenty-one-year-old with no history. Why is that, do you think?"

Dead silence greeted me from Ian's side of the line.

"I am uniquely suited to find Ferdinand," I continued, "but I will be hobbled if I am locked up at home. Persuade Father to let me run with this one."

"I can't," he said, his voice like gravel. "Believe it or not, I tried. He is adamant that you return."

A one-minute warning message arrived for *Jester*'s jump. "Well, then, I guess I'll have to dodge you *and* the mercs. Farewell, Ian."

I disconnected the call and put *Aurora* into deep stealth. All communication ceased and the ship no longer repeated broadcasts or used any sort of signal-emitting technology.

It was a little dangerous to use deep stealth so close to populated space. First, it would limit the amount of information I could gather about the ships around me, so *Aurora*'s navigation computer would have to work harder. And second, it made my ship nearly impossible to track, which meant other ships' navigation computers wouldn't route around me until the last minute. But as long as I stayed vigilant, the danger was minimal.

Without communications, I couldn't check to see if Ian followed through with his threat to put a bounty on me. I had five hours to kill before the FTL drive was ready to jump and nothing to do but watch empty space roll by. I couldn't even catch up on my sleep because I had to keep an eye out for other ships.

It was going to be a long five hours.

I MANAGED TO STAY AWAKE BY DRINKING COPIOUS amounts of synthesizer coffee and pacing. The real coffee Ada had given me would've been wasted on my tired taste buds, and I didn't want to leave the flight deck long enough to find it anyway.

Ian had not shown up and demanded my immediate surrender, so it seemed that he had taken the bait and followed

Ada. I hoped she led him on a merry chase before he figured out she wasn't me.

I routed *Aurora* on a direct course to Delta Tucanae Dwarf Four. DTD Four was a known Syndicate stronghold and general information hub. Secrets were traded like commodities, and because of that, it was also a popular mercenary hangout. If Ian really had posted a bounty on me, I would have to be extremely careful.

I lowered the stealth level enough to allow the ship to request a jump point from the gate. I was twenty-ninth in the queue with an estimated wait time of eight minutes. If my contact on DTD Four came through with information, I'd have to leave my beloved ship behind and start hopping starliners, because the jumps after this one would each require a two-day recharge for the FTL drive—time I didn't have.

It was absolutely clear why Rockhurst was willing to go to war to keep fast FTL technology to themselves. It would be a game changer in more ways than one, and the House who controlled the technology would be unstoppable.

The one-minute warning sounded, and I brought *Aurora* out of stealth. The engine noise changed as the FTL drive engaged, then DTD Four appeared on the vid screens, shrouded in darkness. A solar day on the planet was long enough to be measured in months of Universal Time. I wouldn't be seeing sunlight anytime soon.

I connected to the planet's network and secured a berth in one of the nicer spaceports in Brava, the main city. A nice spaceport had fences, security checkpoints, and armed guards that patrolled constantly. Cheaper spaceports had none of those and a good chance that your ship would be missing pieces when you returned.

Many first-timers left their ships at the orbiting station,

thinking they would be safer than on the planet. They were wrong. Entire ships had vanished from the station without a trace.

While I was on the network, I checked the news. There was no news of a bounty on me, so either Ian had been making idle threats—unlikely—or he still thought he could persuade me to return. When he caught up to Ada he was going to go ballistic. I would worry for her, but she'd spent two years looking out for herself. Plus, with both Rhys and Loch with her, she had plenty of extra protection.

*Aurora* descended smoothly through the atmosphere. The ride got a little choppier as we neared the hangar. Rain lashed the outside cameras, dropping visibility to mere meters. Luckily, the ship's sensors were well equipped to deal with inclement weather and *Aurora* landed gently on the assigned launch pad.

This spaceport could hold a dozen ships spread out in two rows of six. Based on the limited view from the outside cameras, about half of the pads were occupied with ships of varying quality. A couple of newer ships meant *Aurora* wouldn't stand out too much, but some extra protection wouldn't be a bad idea.

Before I could arrange that, however, I had to change clothes. Not only had I been wearing these for two days, but my blouse, slacks, and heels were wildly inappropriate for Brava.

I kept spare clothes and boots onboard, simple clothes in sturdy materials that made me look more like a merc and less like the daughter of a High House. In Brava, it was far better to be unremarkable.

The captain's quarters on *Aurora* included a sitting room, a bedroom with a bathroom en suite, and a study. The sitting room was painted a bright, happy cyan, while the bedroom and study were done in soothing shades of pale green and blue, respectively.

My closet was stocked with pants and shirts in darker

colors. I selected a pair of black pants and a crimson shirt. A heavy pair of boots with thick soles completed the outfit. They wouldn't give me as much height as my heels, but they were far more practical.

I slung a holster around my waist and added a blast pistol on my right hip and a combat knife on my left. The knife was not likely to save me if it came down to that, but in Brava it was better to be prepared for everything. I still wore the shielding cuff I'd put on for my meeting with Evelyn. That meeting felt like a lifetime ago.

I packed extra clothes and toiletries in a small backpack. I could stay on *Aurora,* but if Ian posted a bounty on me, then the mercenaries would tag my ship within a few hours. It was safer to find a shabby hotel that accepted anonymous credits and didn't ask questions.

I debated taking the silencer. It would help if the signals become overwhelming, but none of my other identities had permission to carry one. If I got caught with it, I would have to prove I was Bianca von Hasenberg or face an automatic ten-year sentence. Normally, proving my identity wasn't a big deal, but I was trying to stay under the radar, so I left it in my purse.

I pulled on the backpack and added the final piece of my wardrobe, a waterproof hooded cloak that covered me from head to toe. It would protect against the rain and help to disguise my identity.

I put several hard credit chips into separate internal pouches to protect them from pickpockets, then headed to the cargo bay to look through the supplies Ada had brought for me.

The four pallets were stacked high with individual crates. I removed the straps and pulled the crates free. Each crate had a neat electronic label indicating the contents. It was a far more organized system than Ada normally used, so I bet Veronica or Rhys had helped.

Ada really had outdone herself. She'd gotten everything I requested plus a bunch of useful stuff I hadn't. I grabbed an extra com and a few trackers and bugs. I considered the blast rifle but decided it would be a little too conspicuous, even with the cloak over it. There was a fine line between being armed enough to not be an easy target and being so heavily armed that you obviously carried something valuable.

I checked the outside cameras with my smart glasses. The weather remained terrible, but it was unlikely to change any time soon, so I'd have to deal with it. I closed the front of my cloak and raised the hood. I set an alert to scan the news for any mention of my name. With nothing left to do, I opened the cargo door and stepped into the rainy, midmorning dark.

I TIGHTENED THE TIES ON MY HOOD AS THE WIND TRIED to rip it away. Rain pounded down, overwhelming the hydrophobic coating on the glasses. Water was supposed to slide right off the lenses, but the rain was coming down hard enough that it looked like I was peering through a waterfall.

The cold, wet air smelled of thunderstorms and industrial chemicals. This spaceport was on the edge of the city's ore-processing facilities and other factory complexes. The proximity to the factories was one of the reasons this spaceport was safer than most; company travelers paid well and regularly, but only if their ships remained in one piece.

The wireless signals were moderate in this part of the city. I listened in for a few seconds and didn't find anything out of the ordinary. I zeroed in on the spaceport's signal and heard someone say they were going to check on the new arrival.

A minute later, a security guard emerged from the gloom while I was double-checking *Aurora*'s security protections. The guard wore a full set of combat armor bearing the spaceport's name and logo. When he saw he had my attention, he touched his fingers to his helmet. "Ms. White," he said, his voice tinny through the helmet's speaker, "we have you registered for two weeks."

"Yes. This ship means a great deal to me. I would appreciate it if you kept an extra-close eye on it," I said. I slipped him a credit chip with a thousand credits on it. "I'll double that upon my return to an intact ship."

The chip vanished into a pouch on his belt, and he inclined his head in agreement. He faded back into the darkness. I was still monitoring the wireless signals, and I heard him report that my ship was to receive extra protection.

Ship as safe as I could make it, I let the signal monitoring go before my headache turned blinding. I headed for the exit. A series of large, illuminated signs warned that the spaceport was no longer responsible for your safety once you left the premises. They meant it, too. Spaceport personnel *might* take a potshot at a mugger if they were in range and you'd paid extra protection money, but even that much effort wasn't guaranteed.

The lack of security made ground exits a little dicey. Company representatives were advised to contact their business and wait for an armed transport before exiting.

The hulking, brown-haired armed guard working the exit building raised an eyebrow when my head only came up to his chin. "Have you called a transport?" he asked.

"Not yet."

Surprise and concern lit his face when he realized I was a woman. "You're not going to try to walk, are you? You armed?"

"No and yes," I assured him. "This is not my first visit," I said with more confidence than I actually felt. I used my smart glasses to order a transport. I wasn't stupid enough to try to walk anywhere near the spaceport, even in what passed for morning here.

"If you need a clean place to stay, hit up Jade's. It's in the flower district."

"Thanks." Recommendations in Brava always came with a grain of salt. Likely the person recommending either got some sort of kickback or was sending you into a trap. The flower district was one of the nicest parts of this city, which wasn't saying a whole lot, but it was less likely to be an outright trap. My contact, Peter Guskov, had his storefront on the edge of the district.

I tracked the transport's progress on my smart glasses. The landing pad was on the roof. When it was thirty seconds out, I drew my blaster and kept it visible. I shouldn't need it on the roof, but one never knew for sure.

At the top of the straight staircase, the transport exit consisted of two doors, like an airlock. The outside door wouldn't open unless the inside door was closed and locked. I stepped through the first door and let it close behind me. The lock slammed home. The second door release button glowed green.

The transport settled outside. The roof was lit with floodlights that fought against the dark and rain. Nothing moved. I pushed the door release and the door slid open.

I moved for the transport, staying alert. No one attacked and I breathed a sigh of relief when the transport door locked closed behind me. I searched for Jade's and found it near the middle of the flower district. It was close enough to Guskov's shop that it would probably be safe to walk as long as I was careful.

I selected the address and the transport lifted off. I sighed and leaned my head back against the seat. I was cold and damp, despite the cloak. Welcome to Brava. Ada would have a heart attack when she learned where I was.

The transport stayed fairly close to the ground because most of the buildings were stone and not more than three or four stories tall. The wind made the ride a little bumpier than I'd like, but I arrived in one piece.

Jade's was a small hotel on the corner of one of the main streets and a narrow alley. A bright sign decorated by a carved jade dragon indicated the hotel had vacancies.

I exited the transport and hurried to the door. A bell tinkled overhead when I pulled it open. I stepped into a small but clean lobby. The main desk was off to the left and a couple of chairs on the right clustered around a lit fireplace.

A petite woman with long, straight black hair bustled out of the back room. She smiled at me. "You must be Ms. White," she said. "I am Jade, the owner. Gunther will be pleased that you arrived safely."

So this recommendation was a kickback and not a trap. Probably.

I stomped a few times to knock off the worst of the rain before I dripped all over the dry floor. When I was reasonably dry, I lowered my hood. "Does Gunther work at the spaceport? About this tall?" I asked, holding my hand twenty centimeters over my head.

Her smile grew wider. "Yes, that's my Gunther. He looks fierce but he's a big teddy bear."

I'd have to take her word for it. Gunther looked as if he could pull arms off people without breaking a sweat. "He said you have rooms available?"

"Yes. One hundred credits a night, with a two-night deposit. Breakfast is included." She showed no sign of recognizing me as Lady von Hasenberg.

"I'd like to prepay for a week," I said.

She didn't even blink. "Checkout on the seventh day?" she confirmed.

Because solar days and nights lasted months, most Brava residents were used to thinking in Universal Standard Time. So a day was just twenty-four hours, regardless of whether it was dark or light.

"Yes, please." I hopefully wouldn't be here that long, but Peter Guskov moved at his own pace. If he thought I was trying to rush him, he'd let me cool my heels for a few days just because he could.

Jade held out a chip reader. "Scan here, please."

"I'd prefer to pay with hard credits."

That got me a raised eyebrow, but she didn't protest. She entered the amount on the reader then handed it to me. I inserted a credit chip with a moderate amount of credits. The reader shouldn't report the total available credits back to the vendor, but some vendors were shadier than others.

Jade took the machine back after I removed my credit chip. She handed me an old-fashioned keycard. The fact that she had them handy told me I wasn't the first person to stay here who was reluctant to scan my identity chip. "Your room is on the fourth floor. The lift is out of order; are the stairs going to be a problem? Do you need help with your luggage?" She peeked around the desk, looking for my bags.

"No, thank you, the stairs are fine. I can manage my backpack."

"Breakfast is from six to nine in the dining room." She gestured to a door behind me. "And the stairs are farther down that hall on the right."

I thanked her and headed for the stairs.

# CHAPTER 9

**A**s a young woman, my self-defense tutor had kept me in excellent physical condition, something that I'd taken a bit for granted. After Gregory modified my nanos, I hadn't felt well enough to keep exercising. I'd recently started going to the gym again, but I was nowhere near my normal fitness level, and I felt the four flights of stairs.

I let myself into the room I'd be calling home for the next few days, assuming I could hack it. My head was already lightly throbbing. Tonight would be the first night I voluntarily slept in an unshielded room in four years—since Gregory had first modified my nanos.

I'd nearly died before he'd conceded and deigned to shield my bedroom. I didn't remember much of those early days but apparently I'd gone into seizures any time I was exposed to the minimal amount of signals around our House.

For the first six months after the injection, I'd been too sick to continue working remotely for House von Hasenberg, which had caused Father to start asking questions. I think that, more than anything else, is what changed Gregory's mind. He didn't want Father to steal his research before it was finished.

After my body had begun to adapt, Gregory would occasionally lock me in unshielded rooms to see how I would react. I'd been too weak to fight back, both physically and emotionally. The shame of that failure still burned in my chest.

I shook myself out of my thoughts and glanced around. The room included a small bed, a nightstand with a lamp, a narrow wardrobe, and a window overlooking the alley. It was sparse but clean. Even the tiny attached bathroom had been scrubbed to a sparkling shine. I made a mental note to thank Gunther for the recommendation if I saw him again.

Rain ran down the window, blocking most of the view, but there was no fire escape outside, so I didn't have to worry about midnight visitors. I used my com to search for bugs or trackers in the room. The search came back empty, which was surprising enough that I ran it again, with the same result.

With no extra eyes on the room, or at least none that I could detect, I carefully hid a few of my credit chips in various nonobvious locations. If I got mugged, I didn't want the assailants to have access to all of my hard credits at once. I stashed my backpack in the wardrobe but kept a couple of the trackers and bugs in my pockets. I also kept my weapons and the second com. Walking out unarmed in Brava was just asking for trouble.

I checked on directions to Peter Guskov's shop. He wouldn't actually be there, nothing was ever quite so easy, but I needed to make initial contact in order to set up the real meeting. The shop was a kilometer away on foot, but with the horrible weather, I went ahead and ordered a transport. It was an extravagance that a normal Brava citizen wouldn't have purchased, but Guskov already knew I wasn't a normal Brava citizen.

Going down the stairs was far easier than climbing them. Jade was nowhere to be seen, but my transport waited outside. I pulled up my cloak's hood and stepped out into the downpour. It was nearly noon, yet it remained pitch black. I couldn't live on this planet in the dark for months at a time. Continuous sunlight wouldn't be much better, either.

I entered the address and the transport lifted off. The trip took less than five minutes, but I remained mostly dry and entirely unmugged, so I decided it was a worthwhile expense.

The transport landed outside a shop window filled with various odds and ends. Expensive antiques sat beside cheap plastech knockoffs. One mannequin sported an evening gown, while another was dressed in head-to-toe combat gear.

I pulled on my public persona. Peter Guskov was very particular. He had a process and it required a great deal of patience, especially when the information you wanted was time sensitive. I could not afford to lose my cool.

An armed security guard opened the door for me. "You break, you buy. You steal, I break," he said, his meaning clear even with his heavy accent. "No cloak."

I shed my cloak and hung it in the provided space. "I expect that to be there when I return," I said.

If the guard was surprised that I was a woman, he didn't show it. He nodded.

The shop was empty of other customers, so I perused the shelves slowly, keeping an eye out for the sculpted sapphire bluebird I knew lurked somewhere in one of these piles of junk. The room was chilly without the added benefit of my cloak and I shivered. That, at least, was a solvable problem. I grabbed a black sweater in my size, paid for it, and put it on.

It took me another twenty minutes to locate the bluebird, partially hidden behind a stack of empty energy cartridges. I plucked it from its hiding spot and took it to the cashier, a blond kid in his late teens. Another guard stood a few meters away, a deterrent for anyone who thought they might be able to overpower the kid.

I set the bird on the counter. "How much for this?" I asked.

The cashier smiled and gently picked up the sapphire figure. "Mabel is not for sale; she's our mascot."

I smiled serenely when I really wanted to shake him and demand he get to the point already. But this dance was how Peter protected himself, and for all the kid knew, I really did just want to buy the bird.

I continued spouting the required lines. "I will pay you a fair price. My aunt adores bluebirds and this is the prettiest one I've ever seen."

"I am sorry, madam, but the bird is not for sale." His grin was properly apologetic and charming. "Perhaps something else in the shop has caught your eye?"

"I will look," I said. I'd already spotted the book on military tactics that was the next step of the process, but I made a show of poking around the shop. When I'd worked my way around to the book, I picked it up, flipped through it, then tucked it under my arm.

I waited an additional two minutes, time I silently counted off to keep from rushing, before I moved back toward the cashier. "How much for the book?"

"Oh, what a find! That's a rare edition. It's fifteen hundred credits."

This edition was as rare as the air we were breathing and about as valuable. Guskov had a crate of them in the back. The fee was just another step to ensure I was serious about meeting with him.

"I will take it. Are you sure you aren't willing to sell the bird?"

The cashier rang up my purchase and held out the chip reader. I checked the total, then paid with one of my credit chips.

After the payment went through, the kid said, "Perhaps the owner would be willing to sell for the right price. Write down your name and number and I will ask." He handed me a white paper card and a pen.

I wrote down my real name and the address of my secondary com. I handed the card back to him and he glanced at it, then his eyes widened and he blanched. "My lady—"

"Keep that to yourself, if you don't mind," I said quietly.

"Of course. Sure. Will do." He clamped his mouth shut.

This time my smile was genuine. "Thank you. I will await your call."

I ordered a transport and collected my cloak. My stomach rumbled with hunger. I hadn't eaten anything since last night's dinner.

"Go to Tatiana's," the guard at the door said. "Best food. Good price."

And also likely owned by someone in Guskov's pocket, who would watch me like a hawk and report back. Still, food was food, and if Guskov protected it, at least I didn't have to worry about the other factions jumping me. "Thank you."

In the transport, I searched for Tatiana's and found only one result, a noodle house a few blocks away on the other side of my hotel. It was still in the flower district, so the neighborhood should be safe enough. I set the destination and the transport lifted off.

The lack of sleep was catching up with me. I'd need to work in a nap or I wouldn't be sharp enough to deal with Guskov. And in the absolute best-case scenario, he wouldn't contact me until late tonight, anyway. Speedy this process was not, but it was my best chance of information until Nadia got back to me.

Tatiana's noodle shop had that warm, welcoming vibe that treasured neighborhood gems developed over time. It might be a front, but it was a nice one. Business was brisk enough that no one paid obvious attention to me. I ordered a beer and a bowl of BioBeef noodles.

Synthesizer beef equivalent wasn't quite as good as the real deal, but it was far easier to come by. Even if the shop didn't have a synthesizer in house, they could order BioBeef from a local distributor for approximately 1 percent of the cost of real beef.

I carried my beer to a table in one of the darker corners of the room and lowered my hood. The strong scent of food wrapped around me, causing my stomach to once again complain about its empty state. Some days food smells nauseated me, but today was thankfully not one of them.

A waitress balancing a full tray expertly delivered a bowl of noodles as big as my head without dropping anything. The dish steamed gently and the smell was spicy and salty and divine.

I was nearly a quarter of the way through the meal, an achievement, when my news alert went off. I surreptitiously pulled up the info on my glasses only to lose the rest of my appetite.

Ian had gone through with it.

I was now a wanted woman, though House von Hasenberg was spinning it as a safety issue. They were concerned about my well-being considering the recent attack on me and would pay for information on my whereabouts. I was presumed disoriented and should be detained until a representative of the House could retrieve me.

The atmosphere of the shop hadn't changed at all, but I felt as if I had a spotlight shining on me. Ian Bishop was once again going to ruin my best chance of information with his ham-fisted tactics. It's as if the man lived to frustrate me, even from halfway across the 'verse.

I ordered a transport and tracked its progress. When it was thirty seconds out, I slipped from the table and raised my hood.

I wove through the crowd toward the exit. I was two meters from the door when a man bumped into my left side.

He wrapped an arm around my shoulders. "Keep moving," he said, his voice low.

I drew my blaster under the cover of my cloak, but I continued toward the door. We stepped out into the rain and my transport settled in front of us.

"This yours?" he asked. When I didn't answer he said, "Get in."

I twisted away from him and he let me go. He held his hands up as if approaching a scared animal. "I just want to help you, my lady," he said. He had a striking face, not quite handsome but somehow arresting nonetheless. He was tall and lean and probably pushing forty, but time had treated him well.

"Who are you? Did Guskov send you?"

His eyes darted over my shoulder and I spun, but not fast enough. The stunstick hit like a lightning bolt. I screamed as my body lit up in agony. The implant in my brain erupted in pain so intense I thought my head was exploding.

When darkness rose to swallow me up, I didn't fight the pull.

I CAME TO ON A HARD BENCH. MY HEAD ACHED LIKE someone had stabbed a stiletto into it, multiple times. My brain implant really did not appreciate being hit with a stunstick.

A quick peek around assured me that I was alone in a standard mercenary holding cell. I couldn't quite focus on the wireless signals flying about the room, but I knew I was under surveillance.

I sat up with a groan and did a quick inventory. My right cheek throbbed and when I pressed against it, it felt bruised. Had I hit it when I passed out? I couldn't remember.

The mercs had taken everything I had on me, including my

weapons, coms, and credits. They'd even taken my cloak. I hated the thought of hands riffling through my pockets while I was defenseless. Hell, I hated being defenseless in the first place.

I leaned back against the wall and closed my eyes. I realized that perhaps I hadn't given Ada enough credit. She'd successfully dodged security teams for years. I'd been caught in five minutes, maybe less, and we'd had the same training. She was going to have a field day with this.

That thought brought me up short. Maybe Ada would arrive before Ian? The bounty hadn't said *which* representative of House von Hasenberg had to pick me up, and the mercs wouldn't care as long as they were paid. I crossed my fingers that she saw the news first.

I pieced together my public persona. Before Gregory, becoming outwardly emotionless had been second nature, drilled into me by countless tutors and Consortium events. But while physical pain sharpened some of my siblings, it completely derailed me and made it so much harder to keep my emotions in check.

The cell door opened and the man from earlier entered. In the light, his eyes were pale green and his hair was a light reddish blond. He held out a sealed bottle of water. When I refused to take it, he set it on the bench next to me.

"I'm Rob. Sorry about the cheek," he said. "We didn't expect you to pass out. Your nanos should take care of it in a few hours." A hint of bitterness crept into his tone.

Nanobots had to be designed for each person's DNA and were prohibitively expensive. My modified nanos still healed, but they were slower than most. I'd be sporting a bruised cheek for at least a day.

I raised an eyebrow. "Stunsticks are designed to incapacitate their targets," I said. "You failed to plan for that and I paid the price." He tried to interrupt, but I continued, "How long was I out?"

"Maybe an hour," he said. "We had a doctor check you, just to be sure you were okay. Why did you mention Guskov?"

"He and I have business."

Rob paled. "Were you under his protection?"

My smile was designed to discomfit. "Too late now, don't you think? Have you contacted House von Hasenberg?"

"Yes, they have someone on the way. He should be here in a little while. Do you need anything until then? Would you like to contact Guskov?"

*Freedom and painkillers would be a good start.* I didn't say that, though. "No. And you should be aware that I know *exactly* how many credits I was carrying." I let ice slip into my tone. "I expect them returned to me, along with the rest of my stuff."

He grimaced but didn't argue. Despite my current incarceration, I was still a von Hasenberg. I could make life very unpleasant for him and his team.

"If you need anything else, just ask. We are keeping you in here for your protection. If any of the less scrupulous squads knew you were on-planet, they would try to retrieve you themselves. It would not end well for you."

"You're a saint, Rob," I murmured under my breath.

He grinned. "We all have to eat," he said. "Don't try anything stupid and we'll get you safely back to your House without any further drama." He left, locking the door behind him.

I closed my eyes and skimmed the wireless signals flying through the air. Pain blossomed in my temples. I pulled back and tried again, with an even lighter touch. I'd been practicing this technique for months, teaching my brain to feel the differences in the signals without fully decrypting them.

The hope was that one day my brain and the implant would be able to automatically distinguish important messages from the garbage and only spend energy decrypting the valuable messages. Ideally, I would be able to shut off all signal processing like flipping a switch, but without Gregory's genius, I had to take baby steps to get there.

None of the messages I checked were worth the headache of actively looking at them. I mentally let go and sank into a light meditation. Gregory had taught me patience, if nothing else.

I don't know how long I sat there, drifting in and out of sleep in a sea of mental calm, before the cell door opened again, but it was long enough that my legs had fallen asleep. When Rob didn't say anything, I cracked open one eye.

The other popped open in amazement.

Ian Bishop stood just inside my cell, dressed in dark combat fatigues and scowling violently. "What happened to your face?" he asked, his voice low and harsh.

"I don't know," I said, startled into honesty. How had he gotten here so quickly? And what was he wearing? I'd never seen Ian in anything other than a suit or tuxedo, but I had to admit the change was a good one. The shirt clung to his broad chest and flat abs, while the pants accentuated his lean waist and strong legs. "Are you real?" I blurted out.

Anger morphed into concern in an instant. "What is wrong with you?" he asked.

I'd thought myself crazy after Gregory had first injected me. He hadn't warned me about what he was doing, of course. I'd just woken up one day after being incredibly sick and had started hearing other people in my head. I hadn't known that I was unconsciously decrypting wireless communication signals. And since then, I'd had a secret fear that perhaps I wasn't as sane as I liked to believe.

"Nothing," I said. "I'm just surprised to see you."

"Get up, we're leaving."

"No."

Now the familiar scowl was back. "I don't have time for your games. Brava isn't safe. We need to go *now*."

I sighed and fought to control my temper. Ian could punch through my calm faster than anyone else I knew. "I *can't*. My legs are asleep." He moved toward me and I held up a hand. "Just give me a minute, Ian. You can certainly do that, since it's your fault I'm here anyway."

A muscle flexed along his jaw and his eyes narrowed. Oh, he wanted to argue with me but he knew we were being watched. I smiled at him and watched the pulse thrum in his neck.

I scooted to the edge of the bench and hissed as my legs lit up with pins and needles. Ian offered me a hand up. His hand was cool against my palm, his strength effortless. He pulled me up but my legs weren't quite ready to support me, so I over-balanced and collapsed against his chest. He froze and then started to set me away.

"Stop. Don't move," I said. I slid one hand up and wrapped it over his shoulder so he couldn't push me away. My other hand was at his waist and it took all my willpower not to trace the muscles I could feel under my fingertips. I mentally shook myself and continued, "My legs feel like they're on fire. Give me a second for the circulation to catch up."

A gentle touch traced over my bruised cheek. "What happened to your face?" he asked again, his voice quieter but no less fierce.

"They stunned me. I blacked out. So I really don't know. I probably hit it when I fell."

His muscles firmed under my hands, and his arm locked

around my back, his entire body going tense and still. "You were unconscious?"

"For a little while." I tried to push back to see his face, but I'd have better luck moving a brick wall.

"Did anything else happen?"

I shrugged. "They took my stuff, so they must've searched me."

"Your things will be returned to you," Ian said, as much to whoever was on the other end of the room's surveillance as to me. He gripped my shoulders and stepped away from me. When he was sure I was stable, he let me go.

I didn't make the mistake of thinking everything was cool between us. Banked anger still burned in his eyes, but he had rightly decided that this was not the place to get into it. I inclined my head in agreement.

Ian stalked from the room without another word, leaving me to trail along behind him like an obedient puppy. I bit my tongue and did just that. I could be reasonable when the situation demanded it.

We walked by two more cells, both empty, before we passed through a heavy door and out into the main area of the mercenaries' warehouse. The space was lined with gear cabinets. Two large electronic conference tables dominated the center of the room. The tabletop displays were covered in satellite maps, bounty information, and notes. My picture and bounty notice were prominently displayed on the closer of the two tables.

The far table was surrounded by six armed men who were trying hard to pretend they weren't watching us closely. Rob, the only mercenary whose name I knew, approached Ian.

"Where are Lady von Hasenberg's things?" Ian demanded, his voice ice cold.

Rob waved and a young boy appeared carrying a small bag and my cloak. "Give them to the lady," Rob directed.

Ian intercepted the boy, took the bag, and looked inside. The boy held out the cloak. I took it and shrugged it on. Ian handed me the bag with the rest of my stuff.

The bag held everything I'd been carrying, including the correct number of credit chips, but it remained to be seen if they still held their credits. I took out my main com and unlocked it with my identity chip and a quietly whispered phrase. I held the first credit chip up to the com and waited for the chip reader to register it.

Rob started to look nervous. I raised an eyebrow at him when the credit chip had fewer than half of the credits that were on it when I was captured. The other chips were the same, leaving me almost ten thousand credits short. "Did you not believe me?" I asked.

"I hoped you were bluffing," he said with a sigh. "What does a House daughter care about a few credits?"

"I will have them returned nonetheless. Do you need me to give you the total?"

"You are not what I expected, Lady von Hasenberg," he said. He produced a credit chip from his pocket and held it out. "I checked the total myself."

I moved across the room and plucked the chip from his fingers. I didn't need to look at Ian to know he was scowling at me again, I could practically feel the heat of it. I checked the chip and found the total matched exactly what was missing. "Thank you," I said.

"Are you sure you don't want to stay, now that your House knows you're safe?" Rob asked with a charming grin. "I could use someone good with numbers. Especially someone as pretty—and rich—as you."

I'd been deflecting empty compliments since I could walk, but Rob's pleasant sincerity was a refreshing change of pace.

"Lady von Hasenberg will be returning to the safety of House von Hasenberg," Ian growled.

I would be returning to the House but not quite yet. Still, I had to fight one battle at a time. "I would say it's been fun, Rob, but that would be a lie. Spend the bounty wisely."

# CHAPTER 10

Ian clasped my elbow and led me outside to a waiting transport. When I stopped before stepping inside, Ian demanded, "Get in."

"I will, on one condition," I said.

"No."

I planted my feet and drew myself up to my full height. These boots weren't as tall as I would have preferred and Ian towered over me. "Do you think I came to Brava on a whim?" I asked. "Stupid Lady Bianca, wandering into danger for no good reason?"

"I've never said you were stupid," he gritted out.

"You didn't need to," I said quietly. "Actions speak louder than words, and your actions tell me exactly what you think of me."

Something stark flashed across Ian's face before he smoothed his expression.

"I came here because my best chance of finding Ferdinand is here," I whispered fiercely, aware we were still in public. But the wind and rain would muffle my voice, and I was not leaving without a fight. "Tell me you've found him and I will return home without a peep. Tell me you have a solid lead—and what it is—and I will get in the transport. But if you can't do that, then promise me that you'll accompany me to my hotel to pick up the rest of my things and then you'll hear me out."

"You're staying in a hotel," Ian ground out, "in Brava. Are you insane?"

"It's in the flower district," I protested. "And don't try to change the subject."

"It's in *Brava*," he snarled.

"Do you have a lead on my brother or not? Because *I do*."

"Get in the transport."

"Your word, first."

"I will accompany you to your hotel to gather your things," Ian said.

I'd pushed him as far as he was willing to go for now, so I climbed into the transport without protest. I set the destination before Ian could change his mind. I pulled out my secondary com and prayed for a message from Guskov.

My prayers went unanswered.

It was midevening. There were still plenty of hours left in the day, so I didn't give up hope yet, but Ian would be far less likely to care about the possibility of a meeting than an actual meeting.

"What were you thinking?" Ian asked.

His tone, a combination of incredulity, impatience, and anger, immediately put me on the defensive. I took a deep breath instead of responding. If I didn't have myself under control, then once I started, I wasn't sure I could stop before I said something I would regret.

"I have explained myself. Repeatedly. But I will tell you again: my singular focus is finding my brother."

Ian ran a hand down his face as if he, too, searched for patience. "Have I ever given you a reason to doubt my loyalty to House von Hasenberg?" When I shook my head, he continued, "Then why do you think I won't do my job and find your brother?"

I blinked in surprise. "I don't think that at all. You're one of the best trackers I know."

"Then why do you keep insisting on throwing yourself into trouble and splitting my attention?"

I let the spike of anger at his phrasing roll over me like a wave, leaving behind calmer waters. "Just because you are good doesn't mean you wouldn't benefit from some help. All of my siblings are searching for Ferdinand in their own way, despite the fact that I'm the best at finding information. I don't begrudge them the help; I'm happy to have assistance. I told you to let me run. It was your decision to get involved."

"Unfortunately for you, you are not in charge of House von Hasenberg and therefore are not my boss. When Albrecht tells me to retrieve you, I have to listen, even if it takes me away from my search for Ferdinand."

"I refuse to be returned to a pretty cage," I said flatly. "Try it and next time I will do more than sneak out quietly."

"I've already patched the security hole you used to get access to the cameras. There will be no more sneaking out."

My smile was sharp enough to cut. "You just found the *one* hole, then? Not *holes,* plural?"

"Enough, Bianca!"

I stared out at the dark city flowing past the transport's window. If I couldn't win Ian to my side, I wasn't sure what my next move would be. I could shoot him. Rob had returned the blaster with the rest of my gear, but I didn't have a stun pistol, so I would be inflicting true, lasting damage. Did I want to become that kind of person?

"Silva has Ferdinand," I said quietly to the rain outside.

Ian cursed under his breath.

"I haven't quite figured out how or why, but I know there is no time to lose or they will break him beyond hope. Even a von Hasenberg will shatter eventually." I hoped Ian wouldn't notice the bitter bite in my voice.

The universe was clearly not in a giving mood today because he asked, softly, "Did you?"

I closed my eyes against the warm flood of tears. Von Hasenbergs didn't break and we certainly didn't cry. We picked ourselves up, put the broken pieces back together as best we could, and carried on as if everything were okay.

So I did just that, blinking away the tears and continuing. "I've heard rumors that the Syndicate is throwing one of their parties soon. If anyone knows when or where it is, Guskov will, but he only meets with contacts in person, here, in Brava. I didn't come here because I was stupid. I came here because I was desperate."

IAN SILENTLY FOLLOWED ME UP TO MY HOTEL ROOM. I'D fled the transport before he could respond and now he seemed to be biding his time. It made me jumpy as hell because I knew the attack was coming, I just didn't know when.

As soon as the door clicked closed behind him, he exploded on me. "Guskov? Your contact on this godforsaken planet is *Peter Guskov?*" He looked like he'd like to pace, but the room was too small.

"You know Guskov?"

"Of course I fucking know Guskov! I'm the director of security for a High House. It's *my job* to know people like Guskov. It's also my job to keep that murderous bastard far, far away from you."

"Can you get a meeting set up with him without jumping

through his hoops?" I asked hopefully. That would speed this process up considerably.

When he didn't respond, I tried again. "Ian, can you—"

"No," he bit out.

"I've already been to his shop. I'm waiting on the follow-up," I said. "That seems like our best option."

"No," he said again. "You are not meeting with Guskov."

"I am."

"You're returning home to House von Hasenberg."

"I'm not."

Ian looked prepared to argue, so I threw all of my hopes into the basket of one "murderous bastard." "If I am wrong and Guskov doesn't have any relevant information, I will return to Earth with you without any further protest."

"What makes you think I need your cooperation?"

I flinched then cursed myself for showing it. I straightened my spine and pulled my public persona tighter. I clenched my fists until my nails dug into my palms under the cover of my cloak. "Perhaps you don't. Perhaps you planned to drag me home sedated and compliant all along. But your job still involves finding my brother and I have a solid lead on his location. Are you going to ignore that just to punish me?"

Ian ran a frustrated hand through his damp hair. "Dammit, Bianca, I'm not trying to punish you. I'm trying to keep you safe."

"I've dealt with Guskov before. Alone. And I was fine. I'm not some defenseless hothouse flower with no sense; I'm the daughter of a High House. I take risks, but they are carefully calculated. If you stopped treating me like an 'empty-headed princess' and started treating me like an equal, perhaps you would see that."

Ian stood like stone, staring at me with an unblinking gaze. I could see the wheels turning in his head as he weighed his options. Finally, he said, "Suppose Guskov does have information on a Syndicate party. What is your plan then? Crash it?"

"Telling you my plan before I secure your cooperation would be foolish," I said drily. "But nice try."

"How sure are you that he has information?"

"Sure enough to stake my freedom on it," I said with far more confidence than I actually felt. Guskov was a wild shot in the dark. But I only agreed to return to Earth; I didn't agree to stay there. If I failed here, I would try again elsewhere.

"If I agree to let you meet with Guskov, you will promise to immediately return to Earth and stay there, without complaint, until your father releases you from house arrest."

The sneaky, underhanded bastard. I shook my head. "If Guskov knows where the Silva party is, you need me. You won't get within ten light-years of the place before they sniff you out and kill Ferdinand just to avoid you. I've dealt with them before. They will meet with me because I've proven that I am trustworthy. And that I have exceedingly deep pockets."

Ian raised his eyebrows. "You plan to buy your brother back?"

I shrugged. "Agree to my terms and I'll tell you. We go meet Guskov together. If he has information about the party, you agree to accompany me to it. If he doesn't have any information, I will return to Earth without a peep of complaint."

"And stay there until your father releases you," Ian added.

If I made the vow I'd be trapped by my own honor, something I took seriously. Ian had neatly boxed me in. Decline and he'd know I wasn't as confident as I seemed in Guskov's information; accept and potentially lock myself in a cage of my own making. But the other option was Ian dragging me home anyway, so I had to take the risk. "And stay there until Father releases me," I agreed.

Ian's smile looked a lot like victory.

I RETRIEVED MY HIDDEN CREDIT CHIPS WHILE IAN watched with an increasingly incredulous expression. I gathered up the rest of my things and then sat on the bed before popping back up and pacing in the tiny room, too agitated to sit still.

Ian leaned against the wall and stared at his com. He thought he'd won already, so I felt zero guilt at reading all of the messages he was sending and receiving. I pulled out my own com and pretended to use it while I focused on his messages. Concentrating on one signal was easier than trying to sort through all of them, but it still gave me a headache.

My persistence was rewarded, however, when I pieced together what Ian was doing—he was working on a side deal with Guskov, despite the fact that the man didn't usually deal in electronic form. He wanted Guskov to tell me that he didn't have any information on the Syndicate party, whether or not it was the truth.

Hurt warred with fury. Fury won. I held it close and let it burn away the pain. I carefully built my public facade, walling myself off from everything except cold determination.

It was nearly midnight by the time Guskov contacted me. I glanced at the message. "Guskov wants to meet in half an hour," I said. "Does that work for you?"

"Yes, the sooner, the better," Ian said.

"Very well," I said. "He is sending a transport. It will be here in five minutes." I stood and gathered my things.

I moved past Ian toward the door, but he stopped me with a hand on my arm. "Are you okay?" he asked.

Fury tried to rise but it was buried under a mountain of ice. "Of course," I said with a cool smile. "Why wouldn't I be?"

"You don't have to go to this meeting," he tried again. "He'll meet with me as your representative."

Oh, I just bet he would. And he would miraculously not have any information. I would be carted back to Earth while Ferdinand continued to suffer. The weight of the ice surrounding me was a comforting buffer against the pain. "I am prepared for the meeting. We should be going."

Ian released my arm with a frown. "Let me go first."

I swept a hand toward the door without a word. He paused for a long moment, then led the way downstairs. The rain had stopped, but the wind still whistled through the streets and tugged at my cloak as we stepped outside.

A sleek black transport waited for us, perhaps a bit nicer than most in Brava but otherwise indistinguishable from the exterior. The interior was a different matter. The space was luxurious and came with a small, built-in synthesizer for custom cocktails. But look past that and you would find the transport didn't have any windows or the ability to input a destination. Climb in and you were at the mercy of whoever had sent it.

I entered and sat on the right. Ian sat across from me. The transport door closed and the wireless signals in the air died. Interesting. Whether by design or as a consequence of the lack of windows, the transport acted like an isolation room.

The ride took twenty minutes, long enough that if we'd flown in a straight line, we'd no longer be in Brava. The transport door opened to reveal a small, unadorned hangar. A burly guard in a black suit indicated we should enter the door next to him.

Ian stepped out of the transport then offered me a hand. As much as I'd have liked to decline, we were being observed. I took Ian's hand and allowed him to assist me from the vehicle.

The guard said, "All weapons must be left with me. They will be returned when you leave."

I removed my blaster and knife and handed them over. Ian produced a remarkably large pile of weapons, including a pair of blasters, three knives, and a stunstick. Where had he been hiding it all?

The guard held up a scanner and ran it over both of us. He nodded at me. "Mr. Guskov is waiting for you, Lady von Hasenberg," he said.

"Thank you."

We were ushered through the door and into the room beyond. It was as lavish as the hangar was sparse, with real wood floors, thick silk rugs, and delicate antique furniture far nicer than anything in his shop. This was not his house—Peter Guskov was no idiot—but it was one of his finer meeting sites. He was playing nice.

The man in question stood at a sideboard, pouring himself a drink. He was a bear of a man, nearly two meters tall and barrel chested. He wore a dark blue suit with a white shirt and silver tie. He had a full, dark beard, neatly trimmed, and his black hair was cut stylishly long, brushing over his ears.

He wasn't handsome, not in the traditional sense, but he was arresting, like a viper wearing a shiny bow. Gold rings glinted from the fingers he'd wrapped around the heavy crystal tumbler. He raised the glass in salute. "Lady Bianca, I am delighted you could join me. Would you care for a drink?"

"Mr. Guskov, thank you for agreeing to see me on such short notice," I said. "I would love a glass of wine, if you have a bottle open," I said.

"For you, my lady, I would open a cask," he said with a charming smile. A servant stepped out of a hidden door carrying two bottles. He approached and showed me the labels.

Guskov had selected two bottles of wine from a winery I owned through a shell company. I laughed and inclined my head. Point to him. "The white, please," I said to the servant. He bowed and retreated to the sideboard to open the bottle.

"And for your guard?" Guskov asked, as if Ian Bishop were a normal bodyguard and not the director of House security.

"Nothing for me," Ian said. Guskov kept looking at me, ignoring Ian. Interesting.

"Nothing for him."

The servant handed me a glass of white wine. I raised my glass in a silent toast to our host, then took an appreciative sip. This vintage had turned out to be lovely.

"Come, sit," Guskov said, indicating a pair of leather chairs. He waited for me to sit, then sat beside me, leaving Ian to hover at my side. The move had to be intentional, but I didn't know what game he was playing.

"What can I do for you, Lady Bianca?"

"I am looking for information on the next Syndicate party," I said, cutting directly to the heart of the matter. "I have reason to believe it's soon. I need to know when and where."

"And you think I have this information?" Guskov asked.

"I think if anyone does, you do," I said with a smile.

Guskov sat without speaking for a few seconds, then said, "You're right. If the Silvas were having a party soon, I would know." He paused again, his dark eyes sharp. "The Syndicate is not having a party. Your information is wrong."

I hummed quietly, not quite in agreement, not quite in disagreement. I had to give it to Guskov, he made lies sound like truth.

"How sure are you?" I asked.

"Absolutely," he said.

"Then swear it's true on Svetlana Guskova's life." Rumor

had it that Peter Guskov would throw every member of his family under an oncoming freighter with one exception: his paternal grandmother, Svetlana Guskova. She was one of the only living members of his extended family, thanks in part to those pesky oncoming freighters.

He didn't flinch, but he watched me carefully. "You don't trust my word?"

"You told me you were absolutely sure about your information, so I don't see any reason for you to hesitate now. Unless, of course, you are *not* absolutely sure, and you know that I would take a vow on your grandmother's life literally. I do not suffer betrayal lightly."

He kept his expression perfectly blank. "If you don't trust my word, then I believe we are done here. Do not come to me again." He stood.

I remained sitting. "I always liked you, Peter Guskov, because I always thought you dealt true. And yet we've come to this."

Ian tensed beside me, a tiny shift that I caught out of the corner of my eye. Whether it was because he knew I was on to him or because he thought Guskov might attack was anyone's guess.

Realization dawned in Guskov's expression and he dropped back into his seat. "You *know*." He looked from me to Ian and back again, then anger reddened his cheekbones. "You were testing me?" A blaster appeared in his hand, pointing lazily at my chest. Ian moved closer to me. "I do not care to be tested."

"No," I said, the word sharp. "I am being betrayed from multiple directions tonight. I am just dealing with you first."

I'd caught both men off guard. Ian was better at hiding the surprise, but I'd bet my fortune that he was furiously trying to figure out how I'd intercepted his messages.

Begrudging respect glowed in Guskov's eyes, and he inclined his head. The blaster disappeared as quickly as it had appeared. Point to me.

"Forgive me this error, Lady Bianca, and I will tell you what you want to know. But I keep the money already offered," he said.

Ian started to object, but I spoke over him. "I am a very forgiving person—*once*," I said. "The money is yours."

Ian's fists clenched, but he remained silent.

"The next Syndicate party is tomorrow," Guskov said. He paused for a second to think, then continued, "Well, since it's after midnight, I suppose it's technically today. It's being held in Matavara on Chi Cassiopeiae Dwarf Six."

I raised an eyebrow. "Are you sure you're not just trying to get me killed?"

Matavara had a well-earned reputation for being one of the most dangerous cities in the 'verse. It made Brava look like a pastoral resort town. Matavara had no good districts; it only had bad districts and worse districts.

"Silva is providing their own security, so the event will be safe enough. I can't get you an invite, though, and I doubt gate crashers are going to be welcomed."

"Depends on the gate. And the crasher."

# CHAPTER 11

Ian seethed in silence as the transport returned us to Brava, which suited me fine. The transport dropped us at the Jade hotel, where this ill-fated evening had begun. Ian wrapped his hand around my upper arm, his grip almost painfully tight.

"If you want to bruise me, there are easier ways," I said.

He released me like I was on fire. "Do. Not. Move," he ordered, biting off each word. "I have a transport on the way."

"I must return to *Aurora* and prep it to meet us in Matavara. Or were you lying about that as well?"

Ian rounded on me so quickly that I couldn't suppress my flinch. Fury suffused his face before he took a deep breath and hid it beneath a mask nearly as perfect as my own.

"*Aurora* isn't going anywhere near Matavara," he said.

"You're breaking your word?" Disappointment, hot and heavy, pressed on my chest. I'd trusted him and he'd lied to me. Twice. Fool me once and all that, and I was indeed a fool.

The more I thought about the betrayal, the deeper the hurt stabbed, until my public facade was in danger of cracking. I shoved the feelings deep and locked the door.

I was done with people who lied to me. I turned on my heel and walked away.

But nothing was ever that easy when Ian was involved. He fell into step beside me. "I said *Aurora* wasn't going near Matavara, not you, Lady Bianca. I know you want to paint me as the villain in your little drama, but if you would stop jumping to conclusions, you would realize we were on the same side."

I stopped and spun to face him, anger blazing bright enough to shatter the ice surrounding me. "Oh, so we were on the same side when you were working a deal with Guskov that would send me home trapped in a prison of my own honor? Is that when we were on the same side? Or maybe it was when you were putting a bounty on me? We are many things, Ian Bishop, but we are *not* on the same side."

"Are you finished?"

Anger spiked into rage, but I wrenched my emotions under control, until my voice came out cool and cutting. "With you? Yes, I am quite finished." I started walking again, not sure where I was going except far away from him.

Ian did not follow me. Instead, he called after me, "We have an agreement. Now who is breaking their word?"

I kept walking. "I learned from you that I only have to honor agreements when it suits me," I said over my shoulder. "And today it does not suit."

"I can get us an invite to the party," he said.

"So can I," I called back.

"I have a ship that's ready to jump," he said. He was following me now, keeping me in speaking distance but not coming closer.

"I can catch a starliner."

"I can stop negotiating and return you to your father."

I whirled around and stalked back toward him. I stepped into his personal space, nearly chest to chest. I glared up at him, cursing my height as much as him. "Do it, then," I taunted. "I dare you. Lock me in my suite in House von Hasenberg. I'll be out before the end of the day and on my way to the party before you realize I'm missing."

"Keeping pushing me, Bianca, and I *will* lock you in your suite, even if I have to carry you there myself and then sit outside the door."

The thought of Ian carrying me to my bedroom was not as repugnant as he probably meant it to be. In fact, in the right circumstances, it would be *delicious*. I banished that thought before it had time to grow roots and make itself at home.

"Are you ready to be reasonable yet?" he asked.

I closed my eyes and counted to five. If I kept staring at his handsome, infuriating face, then I would do something unwise.

"Why did you betray me?" The question slipped out, tinted with sadness and pain.

I opened my eyes in time to catch the flicker in his expression. His mask slipped a tiny bit, revealing a kaleidoscope of feelings, before smoothing over once again. "My job is to keep you safe," he said. "I don't want to see you hurt."

"And it didn't occur to you that your betrayal would hurt me?"

I'd surprised him. He said, "I thought you would be furious."

"I am," I assured him, "but I'm also hurt. Despite rumors to the contrary, I am not a robot. When I trust someone and they break that trust, it stings."

"You trust me?"

"I did. Why would you doubt that? You're the director of House security and I've known you for nearly seven years. You may infuriate me on occasion, but you've never lied to me before."

His expression flickered again. Holy hell, he *had* lied to me before, and I'd not caught it. I shook my head at my own stupidity.

A transport settled next to us. Ian clasped my elbow with extreme gentleness, as if I were made of glass. He'd taken my dig about bruising to heart. "Please come with me, Lady Bianca," he said.

I shook my head. "I am not setting foot on your ship," I said. "You are no longer trusted. If you wish to accompany me, you may. We will go to *Aurora* to get supplies, then hop a starliner to Andromeda Prime. I need a dress."

"*Aurora* is already on its way to your sister on APD Zero."

My mouth popped open in surprise. "What?"

"Your ship is no longer here," he said. "It's in orbit, waiting to jump to APD Zero."

All ships were capable of autonomously navigating between locations without an active crew, but I'd never used the feature with *Aurora*. I liked my ship and stayed on my ship, and if I had to leave it, I came back for it. Although I knew it was perfectly capable of making the trip, anxiety fueled my anger.

"The guards just let you waltz away with my ship?" I demanded.

"The guards were well compensated to look the other way. If you didn't want me to steal your ship, you really should've changed the override codes."

Yes, I really should've. I could blame the oversight on weariness and adrenaline, but it was a critical failure on my part. I hadn't expected Ian to catch up with me so quickly and now I had to deal with the consequences.

"Why send the ship to Ada?" I worked through it. "You didn't want it on Earth where I could use it to escape again. You *bastard*."

He didn't reply.

"Were you ever planning to let me go to the Syndicate party or was this a ruse from the beginning?" When he remained silent, I closed my eyes. Of course. "I'm surprised you let me meet with Guskov at all. Why?" I paused. "Ah. You wanted me to be bound by my word to return to Earth. Well played, Director Bishop."

I'd been manipulated from the beginning. If not for my ability to read messages from thin air, I'd be on my way back to Earth right now. I tried to summon the protective fury I'd found earlier, but I just felt sad and tired. I don't know why I'd expected Ian to be different from everyone else, but I had, and the letdown hurt.

After Gregory's overnight switch from devoted fiancé to demanding husband, I thought I'd learned not to get my hopes up, but the lesson refused to stick. Maybe that's why it had been so easy for Gregory to manipulate me, too.

Looking back, it was easy to see that he had spent the first year of our marriage tearing me down so I'd be more compliant. He moved me away from all of my friends and peers, isolating me in Daln, a tiny city on a tiny dustball planet that no one ever visited unless they wanted to consult Gregory about his research.

Gregory was never pleased by anything I did, so I tried harder. I was a von Hasenberg. We didn't fail, we persevered, and I had desperately wanted a good marriage.

But that confidence that I could fix anything was ultimately my downfall. I was so busy trying to fix things that I couldn't actually see what was happening. By the time Gregory gave me the brain implant and modified my nanos, I was nearly broken and the resulting illness and weakness kept me that way.

Early on, in my darkest moments, when I'd been sick and

in pain, I'd begged him to help me. Gregory had laughed and told me that he *was* helping.

I had believed him, for a little while.

After Gregory's death, I had vowed not to make the same mistake twice. I wouldn't be so easily manipulated again. I jerked my elbow out of Ian's grip and stepped away.

Ian murmured something that sounded like, "Forgive me." While I was trying to puzzle that out, he *moved*. He wrapped me up in my cloak like swaddling, then picked me up before my brain realized what was happening.

"Let me go!" I shouted, trying to break free.

He bundled me into the transport and sat with me across his lap, held close enough that I couldn't escape.

It didn't stop me from trying.

"Stop squirming," he said tightly. His arms were like velvet-padded iron around me; they were gentle, but they had no give.

"You are a dead man, Ian Bishop," I threatened.

"It wouldn't be the first time, love," he said, his clipped accent more pronounced than usual.

The endearment kicked me in the chest and I froze. I knew it didn't mean anything, it was just a filler word like darling or sweetheart, but it hit on one of my secret longings.

I stared straight ahead and pretended my heart didn't ache.

IAN CARRIED ME INTO *PERSISTENCE,* ONE OF THE SMALLER House ships that could be used by anyone in the House. He didn't set me down until the cargo door had closed and locked behind us.

He kept hold of me and asked, "If I let you keep your weapons, do you promise not to use them on me?"

I stared through him. He sighed and rifled through my bag

and pockets, removing the weapons. I didn't bother fighting him. I would lose, and I didn't plan to shoot him anyway, no matter how tempted I might be.

"Are you planning to ignore me all night?"

Yes, yes I was. My emotions were all over the board. Silence was safest.

When I didn't respond, he said, "I've updated all of the override codes, so don't bother. There are spare quarters in the middle level. We will be departing immediately if you would like to join me on the flight deck."

I turned for the stairs without a word. My eyes caught on a familiar pile of cargo. He'd moved my supplies from *Aurora* to *Persistence*. I hesitated and Ian pounced.

"Curious?"

I was, desperately, but I refused to give him the satisfaction.

"I told you not to jump to conclusions, but you didn't listen. Would you like to listen now or do you want to continue to live in the imaginary world you've constructed?"

"By all means, tell me some more lies," I said bitterly, unable to maintain my silence.

"I wanted your oath because I wanted the *option* of sending you to safety. I used Guskov because I also needed confirmation of the party time and location. I'd heard rumors the party was on Matavara, so I sent your ship to your sister so you had a place to retreat to safely. I also sent a message letting her and Loch know where you will be and to find you if anything happens to me."

I heard truth in the words, as much as I didn't want to.

"I needed it to look like we were fighting, or your father would suspect I was working with you when I didn't return immediately. Unlike you, I can't just float around the 'verse on Daddy's money. I actually need this job to survive."

I smiled without humor. If Ian had the faintest clue as to what I'd had to endure to earn "Daddy's money" then he wouldn't be so glib about it. And while Father certainly had started my fortune and given me a vast advantage, I'd grown my accounts by an order of magnitude all on my own.

I couldn't keep the sarcasm out of my voice. "Let me see if I understand. You betrayed me, but it was for my own good, so I shouldn't be angry about it? Is that about right?"

"Bianca," he growled, "I didn't betray you. I'm letting you help, against my better judgment. Would you rather I send you to Earth?"

We could argue semantics all night, but my head throbbed and weariness pulled at my bones. "Ian, I trusted you and you lied to me. I know you think you were in the right, but I disagree. The next time I need to trust you, I'll waver. If we're going to work together, I need you to promise that you'll be honest with me, and I need you to keep that promise."

"And will you make the same vow?"

I kept a tight rein on my emotions, lest Ian see the terror that bolted through my system. I relied on secrets to stay safe. A crushing mountain of secrets where any one could bring down the whole lot. "I will not lie to you," I said at last, "but I won't subject myself to an interrogation, either. Just because you ask a question doesn't mean I have to answer it."

"Fair enough, I'll agree to the same: I won't lie to you, but I don't have to answer questions."

I had a feeling that we were both going to abuse the hell out of the question exception. After all, silence wasn't a lie, despite what people might think.

I crossed the room and held out my hand for a handshake. "We agree that we're working together to save Ferdinand and that we won't lie to each other."

"I accept. Do you trust me to keep my word?" he asked as he clasped my hand.

"Right now? No. I expect you to lie to me at the first opportunity. If you want my trust, you'll have to earn it back. You can start by telling me where we're going."

"Andromeda Prime. You said you needed a dress."

He'd surprised me once again. I hadn't thought he was paying attention. "I don't know if you had a city in mind, but Honorius has the best selection." Andromeda Prime was one of the oldest occupied planets outside of the Milky Way. The capital, Honorius, was known for its fashion designers.

"Honorius is fine. *Persistence*'s FTL drive is ready, so we can jump as soon as we clear the atmosphere. Depending on the gate delay, we'll be on the ground in an hour or so."

Honorius's time closely mirrored Universal, so it was also the middle of the night there. Shops would open for me no matter the hour, but my time tonight would be better spent sleeping. I'd napped earlier, but I needed deep sleep, preferably with a silencer running.

"After we jump, I need at least six hours of sleep. The last couple of days haven't been the most restful."

"The ship's compensators are good enough that you could sleep now."

"Thanks, but I'll wait. I want to wake up in Honorius and not Serenity, if you don't mind. And, really, even if you do."

Ian looked irritated, but he didn't contradict me. He led the way up to the flight deck. *Persistence* was a fairly modern ship with House internals capable of jumping up to two thousand light-years on its own. The FTL cooldown was a little slower than *Aurora*'s, but I couldn't remember by quite how much.

Ian took the captain's chair, so I slid into the navigator's chair and clipped in. Ian directed the ship with obvious skill and familiarity. Our route was duplicated on my screen. We were headed for Andromeda Prime and we were about twenty minutes deep in the gate queue. *Persistence* lifted off with a rumble.

"How did you intercept my messages to Guskov?" Ian asked.

"Skill."

When I didn't say anything else, Ian laughed and tilted his head. "Touché."

"Why did you decide to accept my help?"

"I've told you all along that I will do everything in my power to get Lord Ferdinand back, and it will be easier for you to infiltrate the party with me playing bodyguard than it would be for me to show up alone. If you've dealt with Silva before, they'll be more likely to hear you out."

"Does the House have a spare ship on Andromeda Prime? I'd rather not take a starliner to CCD Six if we can avoid it."

"I've arranged for a fresh House ship. The starliner route shut down a couple of years ago—too many losses and not enough profit. A few mercenary squads based on CCD Six offer passage on their ships, but the timing is irregular."

"So once we're there, we leave on our own ship or we're stuck for however long it takes for a merc crew to leave?"

"Yes. I've called in a security team to keep an eye on the ship while we're on-planet."

"Is that wise? Won't word get back to Father that you're conspiring with the enemy?"

"I trust my people," Ian said.

I filed that tidbit away. It was good that the director of security engendered trust, right up until that trust became loyalty to him instead of to House von Hasenberg.

The signals weren't as bad here, so I monitored the messages being sent from the ship. I sucked in a breath as pain stabbed through my head. I pulled back and tried again.

"Are you okay?" Ian asked.

"Just a headache," I murmured. Ian was sending a flurry of messages. I did my best to keep up with them. Some went to contacts I didn't know, setting details for the meet in Honorius.

I caught a message to Father and read it with trepidation. Ian admitted to capturing me, but before my rage could ignite, he also said I had time-sensitive information about Ferdinand that must be followed up immediately. And since he didn't think I would make my own way home, he was taking me with him. He told Albrecht not to expect an update for a week, as we would be in deep cover.

I'm sure Father would be apoplectic when he received that message, and I smiled in spite of myself. I would've preferred that Father didn't know how easily I'd been caught, but Ian had probably already told him that he was on the way to pick me up.

The rest of the messages were innocuous, so I stopped focusing and let them become background noise. I was getting better at tuning them out, but I still had a long way to go, as my throbbing head demonstrated.

While we waited for the jump, I used my com to open an encrypted connection to a secure server. I had no doubt Ian was monitoring all of the traffic that passed through the ship. The secure tunnel would slow him down, but it wasn't foolproof. I'd need a few more layers of protection that would take some additional time before I could safely connect to HIVE or check my digital drop boxes. I added it to the mental list of things to do before I slept.

I posted a message in our sibling channel, outlining in oblique terms what had happened in the last day and what I knew so far. Ada had reported that she and the others were still digging, but had not made any real progress. Hopefully, with a little more direction, they'd have better luck.

With that in mind, I sent a separate message to Ada, Rhys, and Veronica, asking them to look into the Syndicate party in Matavara, especially anyone who might have an inside line on an invitation. I hadn't been entirely lying when I told Ian I could get an invite—I knew of a few possibilities. But I'd take a sure thing over possibilities any day.

We made it to the front of the gate queue and smoothly jumped to Andromeda Prime. The planet glowed a distinctive red and blue on the forward video screens—it definitely was not Earth. Still . . .

"Open the shutters, please," I said.

Ian glanced at me in confusion, then his mouth tightened in anger. "The video isn't doctored."

"Then it shouldn't be a problem for me to see the planet for myself, should it?"

"Are you going to be this ridiculous the entire time?"

"Are you going to be a stubborn ass the entire time? In the time it's taken you to argue, you could've already opened the shutters."

He grumbled something under his breath, but he opened the shutters, revealing that the view of Andromeda Prime hadn't been a video trick. The planet was even prettier through the windows than it had been on the vid screens.

"Thank you," I said.

"You're welcome." He retracted the shutters as *Persistence* prepared to land in Honorius.

Even the fastest von Hasenberg ships wouldn't be able to jump again in less than six hours, and that's if Ian hadn't jumped the ship on the way to DTD Four, which he must've.

Therefore, I had at least six hours where I could sleep in relative safety without worrying that the ship would deliver me to Earth while I was out. I would take advantage of that while I could. I unclipped and stood. "I'm going to grab a bunk."

"I collected some of your clothes from *Aurora*. I put the bag in the first bunk, but you're welcome to choose whichever quarters you prefer."

The thought of Ian going through my undergarments caused a little frisson of heat to lick through me, half embarrassment, half desire. I bit my tongue before I asked him if he saw anything he liked. "Thank you," I said. My voice came out husky and I cleared my throat before continuing, "Wake me if anything changes. Otherwise, I'll see you in six hours."

"Sleep well."

"You, too." I left the flight deck, then skipped the stairs and slid down the ladder to the middle level. I grabbed a glass of water from the mess hall, then went in search of a bed.

# CHAPTER 12

**M**y purse and a large, unfamiliar pack sat in the middle of the bed of the first bunk on the left. There were a half dozen crew quarters on this level with a shared bath at the end of the hall. Ian would be in the captain's suite upstairs, which meant I wouldn't be tempted to find out how he looked without a shirt. He might be frustrating and infuriating, but damn if he didn't cut a fine figure.

And desire could be a useful weapon, but one best wielded carefully.

I went through my bedtime routine, then sat cross-legged on the bed in my makeshift sleepwear. Ian hadn't grabbed any loungewear, so I'd scrounged up an oversized shirt from the wardrobe that at least covered my underwear.

A scan for trackers and bugs in the room came back clean. Ian hadn't picked this room because he'd bugged it. Huh. Trying to figure out his reasoning made my head ache worse, so I chalked it up to a fluke and moved on.

I carefully set up my most secure network connection. Once I verified it was secure and my traffic was being obfuscated, I logged in to my Fenix account in HIVE with my smart glasses. I had a message from Nadia. She said she had the information I requested and that it was extremely time sensitive. The message included a link to a secure repository that would only unlock once the fee had been paid.

She wanted twenty thousand credits. I laughed at her audacity. The woman knew how to drive a hard bargain, but her information had always been worth it.

I paid the fee.

The unlocked message confirmed that the Syndicate party was happening tonight in Matavara and that Riccardo Silva would be in attendance. He was one of the younger sons of the main branch of the Silva family. I had not dealt with him before, but rumors indicated he was hotheaded, impulsive, and cruel. He wasn't the *last* Silva I'd want to deal with, but he was pretty far down the list.

The message also had a line on a contact in Matavara who might be able to procure an invitation with the right incentive. I copied down the info and sent a note of thanks to Nadia.

I had HIVE transport me to my safe house and went through the entry ritual. The cozy library living room appeared, now with a warm fire and darkness outside. The time here mirrored Universal.

Lili Hu sat curled up in one of the overstuffed armchairs by the window. Petite, with straight dark hair, her avatar looked exactly like she did in real life. She had decided to stay in her position, now that she had a support network and the option to leave. It turned out that her husband wasn't abusive, just neglectful. It was still painful, but not dangerous.

She smiled at me. "I was hoping to see you," she said. "I left you a note, but wanted to chat in person, too."

"Lili, how are you?"

"I am content," she said. "But I am sure you are in a hurry, so we will skip the pleasantries. You need to know about Silva, correct?"

I moved and sat in the chair across from her. "Yes, specifically Riccardo, if you know anything."

Her lip curled. "Do you have another option?"

"No."

"Too bad." She closed her eyes and gathered her thoughts. "Riccardo thinks he is the smartest person in the room, and the worst part is that he is often correct. It's made him overconfident. He *hates* to be proven wrong."

I didn't ask her how she knew. Lili was part of a lower house that allied with us, but they had shady dealings just like everyone else in the 'verse.

"Do you have any specific information on him that I can use for leverage?"

"No. I've only met him once. He can be very charming, but watch him. He's like a cat, waiting to pounce. And he likes to play with his prey." She shivered at some remembered horror. "Be careful." Her expression went distant. "I must go, but leave another note if you need more info."

"Thank you, Lili. Stay safe."

"You, too." She faded from the room.

I checked the board while I pondered her words. She hadn't told me much more than I already knew, but perhaps I could make it work. I had a few notes, but no one had any better information than I'd gotten from Lili.

I logged off, shut down all of my secure connections, and tossed my com on the nightstand. I removed my glasses and rubbed my eyes. It felt like I'd been awake forever. A peek into my purse revealed Ian had left the silencer. For once, something was going my way.

I double-checked that the manual lock on the door was set,

then I climbed into bed and turned on the silencer. I would be able to hear physical noises from outside the silence field, but right now, blissful, perfect silence echoed in my mind. I sighed in relief. Six hours of silence sounded like the best thing ever.

I closed my eyes and dropped into an exhausted slumber.

**A KNOCK ON MY DOOR DRAGGED ME FROM SLEEP. I FUM-**bled for my com and checked the time. I'd been asleep for less than thirty minutes. I dropped the com back on the nightstand.

"This shit has got to stop," I muttered to myself. I needed rest, dammit. Louder, I called, "What do you want, Ian?"

He knocked again and I remembered I was in a silence field—he couldn't hear me. I rolled out of bed and crossed the room. "What do you want?" I asked through the door.

"Are you okay?" he asked.

"Yes?" It came out a question because why wouldn't I be okay? "Is something wrong?"

There was a long pause.

I unlocked the manual lock and opened the door. "What?"

Two things occurred to me as Ian's eyes slid down my body: he wasn't wearing a shirt and I wasn't wearing any pants. Ian Bishop was *built*—defined chest, six-pack abs, and sculpted arms. He was muscled more like an athlete than a bodybuilder and the effect was devastating. All of that exposed, slightly sweaty, tanned skin conspired to short-circuit my brain.

I wasn't wearing heels and the top of my head just barely came up to his chin. I could step into his arms and curl up against his chest and have someone hold me for a second. The temptation was so strong that I swayed toward him before I got myself under control.

He smelled of sweat and warm skin, and I could feel the heat radiating off him. He had on a pair of workout shorts and running shoes. I blinked at his chest as I tried to figure out what was going on. "Ian," I said slowly, "why are you knocking on my door half naked?"

My brain was all too happy to provide some suggested reasons and associated activities. I curled my fingers to stop myself from reaching out to see if his chest was as firm as it looked.

Ian's eyes remained glued to my bare thighs. He shook his head, a barely there movement that made me smile. I wasn't the only one affected. He dragged his gaze up to meet mine. "You didn't see the news?"

I blanched, all thoughts of sexy time forgotten. "Ferdinand?"

He ran a hand through his hair. "No, sorry, I wasn't thinking. I haven't heard anything about Ferdinand."

I left the door open, retrieved my com, and shut off the silencer. Once the com connected to the network, it rang with an emergency message from Benedict.

"Is Benedict okay?" I asked while the message loaded.

"Yes," Ian said, but there was the slightest hesitation in his voice.

The message from Benedict was short and blunt: *Father is sending me to NAD Seven to oversee building a forward base. I know you'll blame yourself, but don't. We all knew it was only a matter of time. I wanted to you to hear it from me first; I'll post on the group channel tomorrow. I leave in three days. I will message you when I can. I hope you find Ferdinand.*

Fury boiled through me and I clenched my fists to prevent myself from doing something cathartic but unwise. Nu Antliae Dwarf Seven was the sole von Hasenberg planet in the disputed Antlia sector. Father was sending Benedict to the front lines of the war with House Rockhurst.

I closed my eyes against the furious, helpless tears that

threatened and inhaled deeply through my nose. Benedict would be fine. He *would*. He knew how to take care of himself, and he had a battle cruiser full of von Hasenberg soldiers who were fanatically loyal to him. As much as Father wanted to punish me, he wouldn't risk Benedict's ship unnecessarily. He would send a battle fleet with him.

It was a pretty lie, but the front lines were lethal, and a House son was a very tempting target, battle fleet or no. Nothing broke morale faster than killing off a leader. I'd already missed so many years thanks to Gregory, and now Benedict might be lost to me forever.

A sob lodged in my throat at the thought of never seeing my twin again.

Benedict and I didn't always see eye to eye, but we *always* had each other's backs. Father had tried to break our twin bond when we were young. He had failed, in part thanks to Ferdinand's subtle interference.

And now I missed both of my brothers. Grief cut like a knife, slicing through my armor to pierce my heart. I tried to hold myself together, but the heartbreak was too big, the anguish too strong.

My brother, my twin, could *die* and there wasn't a damn thing I could do about it except stand here and try not to bawl like a child.

"Are you okay?" Ian asked again.

"No," I said because I'd promised him honesty. And because he'd known the news would upset me and he'd come to check on me. Warmth sparked, a tiny flame in a sea of sorrow.

"Can I do anything?"

I barked out a bitter, watery laugh. "Do you know how to stop a war between High Houses?"

"No," he said after a short pause.

"Then there's nothing you can do." I sighed. I felt like I'd aged five years in the last five minutes. "I knew one of us was going to have to go, and Benedict makes the most sense tactically, now that Father banished Ada. I'm just glad it's not Catarina, though she's probably next on the list."

We were all on the list when it came down to it. Ferdinand was the safest, as the heir, and while he was missing, Hannah would be relatively safe, despite her resolve not to inherit the role. But Father would fling the rest of us at the front until we won or no one was left to send.

I sent Benedict a quick reply, letting him know that I expected him to stay in one piece. There was so much more that I wanted to say, so many things we needed to talk about, but I sent him only the most important: *I love you, baby brother.*

The fragile grip I had on my emotions wavered. My breath hitched. I was approximately thirty seconds from a meltdown. "Thank you for letting me know," I said to Ian. I backed into the room and gripped the door.

"Are you sure there's nothing I can do?"

I desperately wanted to ask him to come in, to find comfort in touch, but our relationship wasn't like that and I still had to work with him in the morning. It would cause more problems than it would solve, so I shook my head and gently closed the door.

The tears came and a sob worked its way past my control. I muffled it with my hand and retreated to the bed. I curled up facing away from the door and buried my head in a pillow. Only then did I let the sorrow spill out.

The door opened.

I held my breath and pretended I was invisible.

Footsteps approached. If he sniped at me right now, I would kill him dead. Sorrow could flash into fury at the slightest provocation and I would welcome the fight.

"I know you don't like me," Ian said quietly, "but I'm the only one available and I don't think you should be alone. Tell me to go and I will."

I didn't trust my voice, and now that he was here, I didn't want him to leave. I said nothing.

Ian moved quietly as he sat on the floor and leaned back against the bed. The room was pitch-dark, so I could track him only via sound. Once he stopped moving, he disappeared from my mental map. Having my back to a threat made me twitchy, so I rolled over onto my right side, facing him. I trusted the darkness to hide my tears.

I had learned long ago how to cry silently, but it had been over a year since I'd needed to and I was out of practice. I sucked in a quiet breath through my mouth and let the tears stream down my face into the pillow.

"When I was a boy, I lived in a group home," Ian murmured. His voice was unexpectedly close, but facing away from the bed.

"I was a scrawny kid," he continued. "Smaller than the other boys my age and underfed. I was picked on by the bigger, meaner boys, so I learned to fight well enough that they stopped bothering me."

Cocooned in darkness, with Ian telling me a story from his childhood, I could almost believe this was a dream. That Benedict wasn't really being sent to the front lines and that Ferdinand wasn't really missing.

"One day, I came across three older boys who had cornered a younger girl. I would've left them to it," he said, shame coloring his voice, "but she looked at me with these huge brown eyes full of terror and I just couldn't walk away. I could fight, but I was badly outnumbered and outmuscled. The three of them kicked my ass. I was laid up in bed for two weeks. The girl escaped.

"Every day for those two weeks, she would sneak into medical and sleep curled up next to me. I think it made both of us feel better."

"What happened to her?" I whispered.

"I don't know. She disappeared after I was released from medical. I looked for her, but she had vanished."

I reached out, intending to touch his shoulder, but I found the back of his head first, resting against the bed. The smooth strands of his hair slid through my fingers like water, a temptation I didn't need. I shifted until my fingers just brushed his shoulder. His skin was warm and solid and real.

"When I was eight, Father decided it was time I learned to fight compromised," I said. My voice was thick with tears and I stopped to clear my throat. "My self-defense tutor recommended against it, but Father was not swayed. Ferdinand and Hannah had learned at eight and so would I. He had the doctors inject me with a weaponized virus designed to defeat the nanobots in my blood. It worked far better than anyone expected. I could barely move."

I'd never been sick before and it had been terrifying. I swallowed the remembered horror and continued, "Benedict was injected at the same time, but he responded normally with a relatively mild illness. He sailed through his trials while I struggled to barely finish. He helped me where he could, but tests were individual except for the final one.

"For the final test, we had to fight each other. Benedict threw the match, despite me begging him not to. Father punished failure, but he punished insubordination more. Benedict disappeared for a month. When he came back, he was colder, harder. But whatever happened had honed his resolve and he threw every match after that, until Father finally stopped pitting us against each other."

"Then Benedict won in the end," Ian said.

"He did, but he paid a dear price. He never spoke of what happened whenever he was taken away, but he always came back colder and sharper." And having had my own share of "reeducation" time, I could well imagine what he'd gone through.

"Benedict would tell you that the result was worth the price."

"He would and he has." I sighed. "Ferdinand did the same thing, as did Hannah. Then we all did it for Ada and Catarina. The result *is* worth the price, but that doesn't remove the guilt. Benedict gave up little pieces of himself to save me."

"Do you begrudge Ada and Catarina for the pieces of yourself you gave?"

"No, of course not."

"Then believe that Benedict doesn't begrudge you, either."

"Easier said than done," I murmured.

"I know."

We lapsed into silence. I'd learned more about Ian in the last ten minutes than I had in the eighteen months he'd been my bodyguard. He'd shared a story from his childhood to make me feel better and to distract me from my worries.

"Thank you, Ian," I whispered.

"You're welcome."

I drifted off to sleep, still bound by the fragile connection of my fingers on his shoulder.

WHEN I AWOKE, IAN WAS GONE. LAST NIGHT WAS A HAZY memory, as ephemeral as a dream. Had he really come into my room to make me feel better or had I imagined the whole thing?

I checked my com and the message from Benedict was all too real. Ian could've used Benedict's deployment as an excuse to send me home, but instead he'd come to check on me and offer comfort. The man was a walking contradiction.

I showered and dug through the bag of clothes Ian had packed for me. As expected, he'd only packed what was in my closet, which was entirely utilitarian. These clothes would be perfect for fitting in on Matavara, but not so good for dress shopping on High Street.

Unfortunately, I didn't have any other option because from what I'd seen, Ada's supplies in the cargo bay included more of the same—she had outfitted me for combat, not shopping. I dressed in sturdy black pants, a short-sleeved gray shirt, and heavy boots. Any shop that turned me away didn't deserve my business in the first place.

The mess hall was a medium-sized room on the middle level, just down from the crew quarters. A food synthesizer and recycler were set into the back wall and the rest of the space was filled with two white plastech tables surrounded by chairs.

Ian sat at the near table, wearing a near match to my outfit. It was still disconcerting to see him in something other than a suit—it made him more human. He had a plate of what appeared to be eggs and bacon in front of him, along with a cup of coffee.

I nodded at him, wary, but he just nodded back and continued to eat his breakfast. Some of my tension drained away. Perhaps he wasn't going to mention my meltdown.

I crossed to the food synthesizer, a small rectangular box that ran off the ship's power. It converted energy into matter and could make nearly any food in the 'verse, assuming you'd bought the recipe. The Consortium strictly controlled both the recipes and the technology because synthesizers were one of the core technologies that made life easier, and the Consortium wanted everyone to know exactly who had provided that benefit.

And who could take it away.

I hadn't eaten since lunch yesterday, so I needed to try to force something down. After falling asleep without restarting the silencer, my head ached. I could feel the signals of Honorius pressing against my skull.

I settled on a cranberry scone with jam and a cup of sweet, milky tea. I preferred coffee, but sometimes my stomach reacted better to tea. Having been raised on freshly prepared meals, I thought synth food tasted slightly weird because the recipe in the system didn't match what our chefs had prepared. The difference was less obvious with simple foods.

The synth dinged when my food was ready. I opened the door and pulled out a plate with one perfect scone and a steaming cup of tea. I carried my breakfast to the small table Ian occupied.

"Good morning," I said. "Are we in Honorius?"

"Yes, we landed last night. We berthed next to our new ship. The security team will transfer the supplies once we leave. Do you know where you want to go shopping?"

"High Street. The boutiques there should have what I need, though we may have to try a few before one lets me in." At Ian's raised brow, I waved a hand at my clothes. "I don't exactly scream Consortium royalty in this getup and High Street boutiques are notoriously elitist. You don't need to go with me."

"But I will," he said, iron in his tone.

"Suit yourself."

I broke off a piece of the scone and slathered it in jam. I needed the calories however I could get them. The smell turned my stomach, but I forged ahead. Sometimes the nausea was a false alarm. I ate a second bite and my stomach rolled. I sighed and sipped my tea, hoping the warm liquid would settle the queasiness. It did not. I pushed the plate away, aware of Ian's sharp gaze following the movement.

"Is that all you're going to eat?" he asked.

"I haven't decided," I said.

"Did you eat dinner last night?"

I'd promised him honesty, but answering the question would just lead to more questions. "Did you?"

"Yes, I had a protein shake. Now stop trying to avoid the question."

"I did not eat dinner. I wasn't hungry." Not a lie.

"You need to eat more."

*No shit, detective.* I barely stopped myself from saying the words out loud. "I eat what I can. My stomach has been weak lately."

"Since when?"

*Since my husband injected me with experimental nanobots and fucked up my life.* "It is not your concern. It doesn't affect my ability to do my job or find Ferdinand."

"Your safety *is* my concern. If you pass out from hunger—"

"Give me some credit, Director Bishop," I said, my voice cold. "I've never passed out from hunger, nor have I come close. If it becomes a concern, I will let you know. Until then, I would appreciate it if you would leave it alone."

His jaw flexed, but he held his silence.

I finished my tea, forced down one more bite of scone, then dumped my dirty dishes in the recycler. It would break them down into energy that could be used by the ship or the synthesizer in the future.

"I'm ready when you are," I said.

Ian drained the last of the coffee from his cup and put his dishes in the recycler. "Lead the way."

# CHAPTER 13

People expected High Street to be a riot of color and fashion, but it was a quiet little street with wide sidewalks and old brick shops with frosted-glass windows and understated black signage. These boutiques didn't need to attract window-shoppers.

The first boutique worker took one look at my clothes and announced they were closed, despite the three other customers in the store. Ian bristled, but I just smiled and moved on. I was about to spend a mountain of credits—if they didn't want my business, that was their loss.

The girl working the front counter at the third shop couldn't have been more than eighteen, with freckled ivory skin and natural red hair. She wore a simple A-line dress that was the uniform of the boutique, but hers was in emerald green, which perfectly matched her wide eyes. She looked at me rather than my clothes. "Lady von Hasenberg," she stammered, "welcome to Boutique Blanchard. How may we assist you?"

"I need a dress and everything that goes with it."

"Right this way, my lady," she said. She led me to a richly

appointed sitting room, and gestured for me to have a seat on the upholstered sofa. "Madame Blanchard will be with you shortly. May I bring you some tea or coffee?"

"Tea with milk and two sugars, please," I said. "And black coffee for my guard." Ian glanced up in surprise, though I didn't know if it was because I knew how he took his coffee or because I'd remembered him in the first place.

The girl bobbed a curtsy and disappeared behind a curtain. A few minutes later, an older woman glided into the room. Her graying hair was pulled back into a sleek chignon. She was impeccably dressed in slim trousers and a tailored jacket in a soft shade of blue that complemented her deep brown skin.

"Lady von Hasenberg, I apologize for your wait," she said with a pleasant lilting accent. "I am Madame Blanchard, the owner. It is my pleasure to assist you. You need a new dress?"

"Yes," I said. "At least one." Her eyes lit up. "But time is of the essence. It must be ready today, preferably by the time I leave."

She inclined her head. "What sort of dress are you looking for?"

"Devastating," I said simply.

"Stand, if you please," she said.

I stood and spun in a slow circle. This wasn't my first time in a boutique, and making her circle me would just waste time.

"You are tiny," Madame Blanchard murmured to herself. "The dress must not overpower you. But perhaps if others underestimated you, that would not be so bad, no? A dress is a weapon. I have just the thing." She disappeared with a brusque command to strip.

Ian moved closer to the room's entrance and turned away from where I stood without a word. I stripped out of my clothes with brisk efficiency. The girl returned with my tea and I sipped it for warmth while I waited. My stomach was still uneasy, but the tea didn't make it worse. Perhaps I would be able to eat lunch.

Madame bustled back into the room, followed by another fair young woman in yellow carefully hauling an armful of dresses. The young woman hung the dresses on the rack and waited for direction.

"The silver, first, I think," Madame Blanchard said. She looked at my bare feet. "Do you normally wear heels?"

"Yes. I'll need a new pair."

"Very good." She murmured to her assistant and the girl disappeared, only to return a minute later with a box of heels in various heights, all my size. "Pick your preferred height and we will figure out the exact shoe later."

I picked the height that I was most comfortable in. It wasn't the tallest option, but I could move faster in these shoes. I'd give up the extra couple of centimeters of height for the ability to run.

Once I had the shoes on, Madame Blanchard's assistant helped me into the silver gown. It was gossamer-thin and flowed over my body like water. Before the young woman had even zipped me into it, Madame Blanchard shook her head. "Take it off."

Two more dresses suffered the same fate before we tried a dress in deep teal. It had heft from the intricately beaded bodice. The neckline plunged deep and a slit up the side rose from the floor to almost the top of my leg. The color made my skin look alabaster.

As I walked toward the mirror on the wall, my thigh flashed with every step. The dress enhanced my modest bust and made my figure look amazing.

"Stunning," Madame breathed.

I turned in the mirror, checking the back, what little there was. The dress was open from my shoulder blades to the small of my back. If dresses were weapons, this dress was a grenade—designed for maximum damage and impossible to ignore.

I stalked toward Ian, swinging my hips. He glanced at me and froze. His gaze slid down my body like a caress before returning to my face. Desire heated his expression before he remembered to hide it.

"I will take it," I said, turning to Madame Blanchard. I heard Ian suck in air as he caught sight of the back.

I also bought a more conservative dress in a dark gold that complemented my hair, slacks and a matching blouse, two full sets of undergarments, two beautiful half-face masks, and two pairs of shoes, which had to be sourced from another store. I added a generous tip to the total and directed that each young woman who helped should get 15 percent. Madame inclined her head in agreement.

The dresses were carefully folded and packaged while Ian went to wait for the transport. When I joined him by the door, he took the package from me. "Do you have everything you need?"

"I'm set for clothes. We won't be allowed to take weapons into the party, but walking around Matavara unarmed is just asking for trouble. I have a few weapons in the supplies you pulled from *Aurora*."

"Party invites include a berth in a secured spaceport adjacent to the venue. Guests are encouraged to remain within the confines of the property."

"Do you have an invite?"

"Not yet. Do you?"

"No. My contact is in Matavara."

"Absolutely not," Ian growled.

I shrugged in indifference. "I'd rather not venture out into the city if we don't have to but time is running out. We'll barely have time to recon the party location."

"You're not going to be reconning anything," Ian said.

Correcting him would just give him more time to argue, so I let the comment go. Our transport appeared outside and Ian ushered me out to meet it.

We returned to the spaceport, but rather than boarding *Persistence,* we boarded its mirror image, *Fortuitous.* All three High Houses had ships like these scattered across the universe to facilitate high-priority travel.

Two people, a man and a woman, stood in the cargo hold, blast rifles casually in hand. Both were tall and fit. The man had light brown skin and dark brown hair, longer on top than the sides. He was more heavily muscled than Ian, stopping just short of bulky. The woman had ivory skin and strawberry blond hair pulled up in a ponytail that reached past her shoulders. She was lithe, with the kind of supple strength that was easy to underestimate.

Ian clapped both of them on the back with a smile. "Thanks for coming," he said quietly.

"Of course," the woman said. The man nodded.

Ian turned to me. "Bianca, meet Alexander and Aoife." He pronounced the woman's name *EE-fa,* and he did it carefully enough that I knew it wasn't a mispronunciation of Eva.

"It's a pleasure to meet you," I said. Neither of them echoed the greeting, and they both stared coldly at me. Okay, then.

Clearly these two were not House von Hasenberg employees, which begged the question of where Ian had dug them up. I made a mental note to look into it, though Ian had been careful not to include their surnames.

Ian shot the two a warning look. A wealth of silent communication passed between the three of them as they all ignored me. I told myself it didn't matter, but being excluded still stung, just a little.

I sank into my public persona as I looked around the cargo hold and pretended indifference. The cargo had been moved from *Persistence,* and an additional crate of supplies had been added. I moved toward the new supplies, but Ian cut me off. "We need to get in the air," he said.

"I'm not stopping you," I said.

"You should be clipped in on the flight deck in case we run into trouble after we jump to CCD Six."

"You think someone will attack a registered House ship?"

"It's a possibility. We don't know what kind of defense the Syndicate has set up."

"Ian, what's in the crate?"

"Supplies."

"So you won't mind if I take a look?"

The muscle in his jaw flexed, but he ground out, "Not if you think it's worth the delay."

"You do realize it would be far faster if you just told me?"

Aoife and Alexander watched us with sharp eyes. They didn't have the body language to indicate they were a couple, but they were comfortable with each other. They'd worked together for a long time.

"Oh for fuck's sake," Aoife said. "It's a crate full of von Hasenberg prototype technology. Combat armor, weapons, et cetera."

I raised an eyebrow at Ian. "There, was that so hard?"

"Aoife, get us in the air," Ian growled.

She gave him an insolent salute and turned for the stairs. Alexander cast a suspicious look my way before following her, leaving me alone with Ian in the cargo bay.

"Nice crew," I said.

"They'll keep the ship safe and their mouths shut. And if things go poorly in Matavara, they'll get us out."

"Fair enough. Are the supplies for them, then? Because you know the Syndicate won't let you within two kilometers of the party with prototype weapons and armor."

Ian started up the stairs and I followed. "We don't know where Ferdinand is being held or what condition he is in. If you fail to purchase him, we'll have to break him out. That's why Alex and Aoife are really here."

"You think you can infiltrate a Syndicate compound with four people?"

"*Three,*" Ian said sharply.

Anger flared through the ice of my facade. "Oh, so you can defeat Silva security? Maybe Alexander or Aoife is a secret security specialist? No? Because *I am.* I'm one of the best systems crackers in the universe. That's why I run circles around your security protocols and why House von Hasenberg has never been hacked."

It was also one of the reasons Father was desperate to have me back, but Ian didn't need any more reasons to send me home.

Ian spun around to face me. He was a step higher, so he towered over me, an advantage he used to great effect. "Can your precious security protocols prevent you from taking a blaster bolt to the brain? Taking you on a rescue mission into Silva's compound would be like leading a lamb to slaughter. If it comes to that, you stay on the ship."

Bright, furious rage turned the world red. "When you get caught, and you *will* get caught, I am going to make you beg on your knees before I get you out."

"Dream whatever fantasy you want, love. I will protect you even from yourself, so stay out of my way and let me do my job."

I'd never before been so tempted to punch a man in the balls as I was right now. I uncurled my fist, one finger at a time, and tucked the rage away, until I was outwardly as still and calm as a windless lake.

The floor picked up a subtle vibration as the main engine started. I stepped around Ian without a word and continued to the flight deck. The door slid open to reveal Aoife in the captain's chair and Alexander in the navigator's station. I took the tactical station and clipped in, leaving Ian to sit along the wall.

*Fortuitous* was a lightly armed and armored ship, designed to be able to defend against most pirates, but it was not a war machine by any stretch. We wouldn't scratch a battle cruiser before they blew us out of existence.

The ship had already requested and received a jump point from the gate, so once we cleared the atmosphere, we could immediately jump to CCD Six. In half an hour, give or take, we'd be on the ground in one of the deadliest cities in the universe.

*FORTUITOUS* LANDED WITH A GENTLE BUMP, AND AOIFE immediately engaged the ground defense system. On the outside camera, the ship's shield turned red and a red projection on the ground warned of the danger. At night, the whole area would glow red. It was subtler during the daylight, but still visible.

If someone ignored the warning and ventured into range of the ship, an audible alert would sound. Fail to clear the area and the ship would open fire. Using the system in a regular spaceport was a dick move; using the system in Matavara was basic common sense.

Any crew members who wanted to leave would have to carry a beacon to identity them as friendlies. So of course they were targeted as soon as they were out of the ship's range.

I caught movement in my peripheral vision as Ian stood. "Aoife, you have the ship and Lady von Hasenberg. Alex, you're with me."

Ian left the flight deck without a glance at me. Of all the high-handed, arrogant . . . I clamped my lips together when I realized I was grumbling under my breath.

I stood and Aoife shadowed me. She was on bodyguard duty. "*Fortuitous,* where is Ian Bishop?"

"Request denied. You are not authorized," the ship replied.

Well, I'd have to fix that, but first, I needed to find Ian. I turned to Aoife. "Do you know where they went?"

She shrugged.

Of course she did. I headed for the cargo bay, silent shadow in tow. If Ian wasn't there already, he would be before he left. It would also give me time to look through the supplies that Ada had sent for me.

When I got to the cargo bay, Ian and Alexander were donning powered combat armor with the brisk efficiency that came only after doing it a thousand times before. I crossed to stand beside Ian. "Care to let me know what your plan is?"

He put on his helmet but at least had the consideration to leave the face guard open so I could see his hard expression. "Alex and I are going to secure an invitation to the party tonight. You and Aoife are going to stay here."

"So you're just going to leave the womenfolk behind while the big, strong men go off into danger?" I asked sweetly.

Ian's fingers twitched as if he'd like to throttle me. Good, then the feeling was mutual. "No," he said, "I'm leaving the most important asset behind with the best fighter after myself. I'm trying to protect you."

"I don't need your protection."

"The hell you don't!" he exploded. He gestured to the barely visible bruise on my cheek, hidden under my makeup. "I couldn't protect you from that, but I'll damn sure protect you from setting foot in Matavara any more than absolutely necessary. We don't need your expertise for this and the trip will go faster with the two of us than if we took you along."

By his tone, I knew Ian wasn't trying to be intentionally cruel, not like Gregory's snide little comments had been, but the verbal dagger slid home anyway, laced with poisonous truth. I sucked in a quiet breath and closed my eyes for a heartbeat.

Gregory had taken so much from me that now I was considered a liability rather than an asset. Even after his death, the bastard still haunted me. Would I never be free of him?

I retreated from the hurt and pulled on my public persona, the icy shell as protective as the combat armor Ian wore. This time I vowed I'd make it stick.

"If you do not return before the start of the party," I said coolly, "I will assume you have fallen. I will go to the party without you and without an invitation. Good hunting, Director Bishop."

A range of emotions flashed across his face before settling on suspicion. "You're going to stay here? Voluntarily?"

"Yes. Until the start of the party. Then I am going to leave, even if I have to go through Aoife to do it." I shot the woman an apologetic look, but she just tilted her head with a smile, the first I'd seen from her. "I suggest you move quickly."

Ian nodded and closed the face guard of his helmet. In the gray-and-black combat armor he looked massive. He had a blast rifle in hand, another strapped to his back, and two pistols in thigh holsters.

Alexander was outfitted with the same gear and impossibly huge. He moved lightly, though, the combat armor aiding rather than hindering. He and Ian visually checked each other to ensure the armor had sealed without gaps.

I mentally caught the signal from their internal com. I moved to the crate of supplies brought from *Aurora* while I shamelessly eavesdropped.

*Ready?* Ian asked.

Alexander agreed, then said, *You should apologize to the woman.*

Ian froze for a second. *Why?*

*She's hard to read when she goes all icy, but I think you hurt her. How would you feel if someone told you that you were a liability?*

I paused at Alexander's uncanny insight. I would be wise not to underestimate him just because he was big and quiet.

*I never said that,* Ian protested. *Focus on the mission, not Lady Bianca.* He turned on his external speaker. "Aoife, you're on the door. Lock it as soon as we're clear. If we're not back in three hours, take the ship into orbit and await instructions."

He'd just given me a deadline for overriding control of the ship.

As if he'd heard my thoughts, he turned his helmeted head in my direction. "Stay on the ship."

He did not apologize.

"Until you return or the party starts," I agreed.

The cargo door lifted and the two men jumped out, deciding not to lower the ramp. They landed with a muffled *thud,* but they were off and running a split second after they hit the ground.

The spaceport was littered with debris. Ian and Alexander hit the edge of our shield and a person popped up from behind one of the piles, leading with a blaster. The bolt deflected off Alexander's armor. Ian shot the shooter before he could fire again.

Now that they were clear of the ship's shield, individual shields shimmered around them. The shields were effective against energy weapons but wouldn't stop projectile weapons. The physical armor protected against both, even after the shield's energy was drained. The cargo door slid closed and Aoife holstered her blast pistol.

"Are you really better than Alexander?" I asked.

"Light-years better," she agreed easily. "Alex is smart, strong, and inexhaustible. If you need someone to haul fifty kilos over mountainous terrain all day, Alex is your man. But I'm lighter and faster. As long as he doesn't get close, I'll dance circles around him. And I'm also a better shot, so he wouldn't get close."

"Are you two together?"

She laughed, a deep belly laugh that rang pleasantly through the cargo hold. "Alex is my brother," she said.

I stared at her as I tried—and failed—to see the resemblance. She caught the look and clarified, "Adopted."

Heat climbed my cheeks. "I apologize," I said. "That was rude."

She waved off my concern, then her gaze turned shrewd. "Are you and Ian . . . ?" She moved her hands together.

"No."

"But you'd like to be." She stated it as fact and I wondered at how broken my mask must be that a stranger could see through me in under an hour.

"I did, once, but he made his feelings—his *lack* of feelings—very clear."

She made a little disbelieving sound under her breath but didn't say anything else.

I turned back to the cargo crates. Ada had not been joking when she said she'd packed a little bit of everything. The combat armor took up a third of the crate. The other two-thirds were packed with weapons, clothes, and technology. On top of everything was the wrapped package of coffee and chocolate.

I opened the chocolate and broke off a piece. Synth chocolate never tasted right to me, no matter which recipe I tried. But real chocolate . . . real chocolate was a little piece of heaven. The square melted on my tongue like a delicious, sugary blanket.

After a moment's hesitation, caused entirely by selfish greed, I held the bar out to Aoife. "Care for a piece of chocolate?"

"Real chocolate?"

I nodded and she took the bar from me as if it were made of gold. It might as well have been, based on the price. She broke off a square before handing it back. She nibbled a tiny bite.

"This is only the second time I've had real chocolate," she said with a delighted sigh. "It's better than sex."

I hummed my agreement. It was better than bad sex, definitely. Good sex . . . well, I hadn't had any of that in a long, long time, so chocolate had the edge, if only thanks to recent history. My mind flashed to Ian. I bet he'd beat chocolate. Too bad I'd never know.

I carefully wrapped up the chocolate and put it back in the crate. I couldn't be trusted with it in my quarters, not if I wanted it to last more than a day. I left everything else, too. I had enough clothes already, and if I needed to be armed or armored, I could grab whatever I needed on the way out.

For now, rather than sitting on my hands, I was going to do some digital digging. Being on-planet would give me greater access to the local systems.

"I'll be in my quarters if you need me," I told Aoife.

She moved to the cargo bay control panel and brought up the outside video. "I'm going to keep an eye on the perimeter," she said.

"Call me if you need backup. I've been trained with most weapons. I'm rusty, but I can shoot."

"Let's hope it doesn't come to that," she said, but not unkindly.

I silently agreed. If I was the only thing standing between raiders and *Fortuitous,* then we truly would be in deep trouble.

# CHAPTER 14

I n my quarters, I turned on the control panel built into the wall. I was locked into basic functionality—local and Universal time, a map of the ship, current location. I pulled up a hidden diagnostic screen and entered the default von Hasenberg override codes. I tried a dozen options, spanning twice as many years. They all failed. Ian had changed the codes on this ship, too.

I could crack the code, given enough time, but unless I got incredibly lucky, it would be too slow to be useful right now. I'd helped harden our shipboard system against attack. I had not left myself any *remote* back doors because that's how other people compromised your system.

But that's not to say I hadn't left myself *any* back doors.

I pried the control panel out of the wall far enough to access the wiring panel behind it. I rearranged a couple of cables, tapped a seemingly nonsense pattern on the screen, changed another cable, entered another nonsense code, and then put everything back the way it had been.

A new screen appeared on the control panel, just a blank box with a numeric input. I used the authenticator in my com to generate a twenty-five-digit code that included a hash of a secret shared key and the ship name. I entered the code on the panel. I was in.

I set myself up as an administrative captain. Ian wouldn't be able to remove me from the system using his own status, and my status would not show up in a simple query. While I might not need the ability to direct the ship, I believed in being prepared. I also changed the override codes. Even with them, Ian couldn't remove me from the system, but there was no sense in leaving them the same, either. I didn't want to make it too easy for him.

One problem down, now on to the next. I put on my smart glasses and set up a lightly secured connection to check my House accounts. Benedict had announced his impending departure on our sibling channel and the channel was rife with impotent rage. Ada was only half joking about plotting a coup.

Veronica had sent me an encrypted message while I'd been dress shopping. She'd found one of her contacts in Matavara who might be able to secure an invitation to tonight's party. I laughed when I saw the details. It was the same woman Nadia had charged me twenty thousand credits to reveal.

Veronica had forwarded my information as well as a letter of introduction to the woman, though, so I wouldn't have to figure out how to meet her without compromising the identity of my online avatar. Nadia would no doubt check on who came through the shop because information was money. If I had time to throw her off my scent I would send a decoy after I'd been there.

I sent Veronica a note of thanks, then disconnected. I set up a new connection, using the highest level of security. I didn't want anyone on the ship to be able to eavesdrop on this information because I was going to check my digital drop boxes.

Thanks to my semipublic call for information, I had received a flood of messages. I deleted most of them and flagged a few for later follow-up. The latest messages were from the last few hours, so information was still trickling in; I just had to be patient.

I worked my way through my various accounts, reconnecting each time. In the account most relevant to House news, I'd received replies to the two messages I'd followed up on before.

The first message related to Ferdinand's dinner with Evelyn. There was a picture of Evelyn alone in the restaurant and a short note that the photographer, presumably, had been tipped off by a member of House von Hasenberg staff about the meeting. He was trying to get a shot of the two of them alone together, but Ferdinand had never showed.

We screened our staff, but everyone was human. It didn't surprise me too much that someone had sold Ferdinand out, but the proof gave us a place to start. The informant might've told the Syndicate where to find Ferdinand on the night he was taken.

I asked Catarina to look into who had access to Ferdinand's schedule that day. My baby sister was desperate to help. This should be relatively safe for her, while also allowing her to meaningfully contribute.

The second message had claimed to have information about the shooter. I hadn't expected much, even from a regular contact when I'd paid the good-faith money, but he or she—and I tended to think she based on the writing—had delivered a treasure trove of information.

I'd have to confirm the authenticity, but based on a quick look, it seemed legit. The Syndicate had put a hit on me. Oh, I wasn't positive it was the Syndicate, because they weren't stupid enough to advertise the contract under any of their official accounts. But if it wasn't them, then it was the most coincidental timing in the history of the universe.

The picture became a little clearer. The Syndicate had hired a patsy to cause a distraction by shooting at me and maybe even killing me. I doubted the best and brightest would take a job on Earth, but maybe I was wrong and someone would see it as a challenge—of course, my continued existence sort of defeated that argument.

I wasn't sure why I'd been targeted, but as the information specialist, it would make the Syndicate's abduction of Ferdinand easier if I wasn't digging for answers. Or it could be that they thought I would be the least protected. Or they could've heard that I was in poor health.

Not only did my contact include a copy of the contract, she'd also included a short list of people suspected of accepting it. This person either had excellent sources or was high up in either the Syndicate or the Consortium. No one on the list was familiar, which meant it wasn't the top 1 percent jumping for a chance to off me. Not that they wouldn't, they just wouldn't do it on Earth.

Thank goodness for small favors, I guess.

I closed the connection and reconnected to a different set of secure servers. I would keep digging until Ian returned or it was time to prepare for the party. I set a timer, set the ship to alert me when the cargo door opened, and dove into the Net.

NEARLY TWO HOURS AFTER THEY'D LEFT, IAN AND ALEXander returned, their armor scratched in multiple places. Both moved easily, though, so nothing serious had made it through the tough composite and into their flesh.

Aoife handed them each a bottle of water and a protein bar. Alexander stripped off his helmet and chest armor, revealing sweaty hair plastered to his head. Ian took off his helmet, but left his chest armor. He frowned at the floor, not exactly the look of a man victorious.

I made my way down to the cargo hold. Alexander, Ian, and Aoife were arguing fiercely about something I couldn't quite hear but the three of them went silent when I appeared.

"Well, that's not suspicious at all," I said.

"What are you doing?" Ian asked.

"Deciding if I need to start getting ready for a party or for a foray into Matavara. Did you secure an invitation?"

"No."

The word was so unexpected it took me a few seconds to process it. "No? Did you go to Yuko?" I asked, naming Veronica's contact.

"Yes," he said wearily.

"Did you tell her it was for me?"

"No, but she knew. She said you had to come yourself. It's a trap, of course."

"Veronica vouches for her and sent me a letter of introduction. It's not a trap."

"You're not going." The words rang with a finality that made me want to gnash my teeth.

"Director Bishop, I am going to Yuko's shop or I am crashing a Syndicate party. Which would you prefer?"

"Matavara is even worse than I remember. I'm not letting you out of this ship."

That wasn't really his decision, but I let him think that it was. "Then we're crashing the party. Any idea how to get past security without getting caught? I hate going in blind."

"You and I are not crashing the party. I'm sending you home. Alex and I will infiltrate the party. *Fortuitous*—"

"*Fortuitous,* remove authorization for all personnel other

than myself," I said. I had hoped to save this ability as a surprise for later, but I wasn't going to let Ian ship me off the planet.

"Yes, Captain von Hasenberg," the ship acknowledged. "Authorization removed."

"I changed the override codes," Ian ground out.

"Yes, you did."

"How did you get in?"

My smile was sweet enough to cause cavities. "I *told* you that I'm one of the best systems crackers in the universe. That was not hubris." True, but in this case, it happened to be more helpful that I was a von Hasenberg on one of our own ships. I kept that bit to myself.

I continued, "So, with the understanding that I *will* do one of the following with or without you, would you prefer to go get an invitation or crash the party?"

"Aoife, armor up," Ian said. "Alex, you have the ship." Ian's furious gaze flashed to me. "You'll have to give him access to the doors and defensive systems."

I used the cargo bay's control panel to give Alexander limited tactician authority. He wouldn't be able to take off, but he could access the other systems required to keep the ship safe on the ground. I gave Aoife the same access, and after a brief pause, Ian, too.

"Do you know how to wear that combat armor in your crate?" Ian asked. It didn't surprise me that he'd gone through my stuff when he'd transferred it over.

"I've had the training," I allowed. I *hated* combat armor. I found it incredibly claustrophobic, and I wasn't usually prone to claustrophobia. But Matavara was hostile to outsiders and going out without armor would be incredibly stupid. Locals had some degree of protection from whichever gang claimed their territory, but outsiders stood out like red flags.

"Get it on," Ian said. "We need to make this quick."

On the protection spectrum, combat armor fell somewhere between simple ballistic armor and fully mechanized armor suits. It was made of a lightweight composite, but a full suit still weighed more than half as much as I did. Combat armor was powered and had some built-in movement assistance, but nothing like a fully mechanized suit that would let a user lift a transport.

Ada had procured a suit sized to my height—a feat in and of itself. I'd worn armor that was too big before, and it just made the whole experience worse.

I pulled the armor out of the crate, inspecting each piece. It was all pristine. I stepped into the lower body section and it clamped around my body from the waist down. I squatted down and the armor moved with me. So far, so good.

The chest piece went on over my head, like a bulky, over-sized tank top. The front and back clamped together. It wasn't tight but I had to fight the feeling of suffocation.

Each arm was designed as a single sleeve that clamped into the chest piece at the shoulder. My hands were covered by a stretchy, reinforced glove with light armor on the backs of my fingers. Blasters for use with combat armor had to have over-sized trigger guards.

I swung my arms and hopped in place, testing my move-ment. I was slightly slower and heavier than usual, but it didn't feel as if I was wearing an additional thirty-five kilograms of weight.

The helmet was my least favorite part of this whole ensem-ble. I pulled it over my head, but left the face guard open. I consciously kept my breathing slow and even.

Ian finished checking Aoife's armor and turned to me. "Do you feel any air gaps?"

I shook my head.

He circled me, stopping to press on my left side. Once satis-fied, he handed me a pistol blaster from the crate. "Yuko's shop is close to two kilometers away. It's ten blocks and the territory changes ownership around block six. We're going to run the entire way. Can you do it?"

Back when I was in shape, a two-kilometer run in armor wouldn't even be a warm-up. Today I would feel each meter. "I can do it."

"Don't stop for anything. Aoife or I may fall back to defend. Don't wait for us. I will send the address to your suit." He pulled his face guard closed.

I took a deep breath and held it as I closed my own face guard. It was made of a thick, transparent plastech. As soon as the helmet clicked closed, the heads-up display came on. Screens provided additional peripheral vision from helmet-mounted cameras and even the transparent face guard was overlaid with information streaming from the suit's systems.

I released the breath I'd been holding. The suit filtered out-side air and could even be completely self-contained for an hour or two, but I always felt like I was breathing stale air. It was entirely mental, but that didn't make it feel less real.

While I was fighting panic, a request popped up to join Ian's squad. He would be able to monitor my vitals, which meant I had to get my heart rate under control ASAP. Another breath and I approved the request. An address popped up, along with a faint green route marker stretching out in front of me.

"Ready?" Ian asked.

"Yes," Aoife said.

I echoed her. Time to make good on my promise.

Ian took point and Aoife took the rear guard, leaving me in

the most protected middle position. As soon as the cargo door was high enough, Ian jumped to the ground. I followed him, landing with a slight stumble. I caught my balance at the last second, saving myself from a mortifying face plant.

Ian had already put two meters between us, so I dashed into a run. Oh yeah, this was going to suck.

As soon as we cleared the ship's shield, a blaster bolt glanced off my arm. I returned fire on instinct without breaking stride. I missed, but the shooter went to ground.

When he popped back up, Aoife didn't miss.

"Shields up!" Ian barked.

I activated the suit's shield and kept an eye on the distance between us. Overlapping shields might do nothing, or it might cause one or both shields to catastrophically fail.

We cleared the spaceport and moved into the city. Very few transports operated in Matavara. Most people moved around on foot or on personal vehicles, predominantly hover bikes.

The buildings were short and square. Most had started as plastech but the constant fighting meant they were patched with whatever was handy, giving the city a hodgepodge appearance under the brilliant blue sky and harsh yellow sun.

Ian ran straight down the middle of the street. The few pedestrians braving the sidewalks hugged the buildings or darted into alleys until we passed. Most of them were just normal people, trying to go about their day. They wanted no part of the trouble we would bring.

Others, however, saw us as prey. A block ahead of us, three heavies in older mechanized armor spread across the street. They were trying to herd us into an alley half a block away, but Ian wasn't having it.

"I've got left and center," he called over our coms. "Bianca, straight through, right of center, don't slow down. Aoife, right and cover."

Ian wouldn't risk us unnecessarily, so I didn't question his orders. I might poke at him normally, but he knew what he was doing when it came to combat and security. He rested his blast rifle in the crook of his right arm and drew the electropulse pistol strapped to his left hip.

Designed to disrupt communication, electropulse pistols also worked well against older unshielded mechanized armor. It wouldn't penetrate to the person underneath, but it would shut down their system.

Electropulse pistols weren't super accurate at a distance, but Ian managed to hit his two targets and Aoife's shots from over my shoulder hit the target on the right.

The two outer suits froze, but the person in the center brought up an ancient projectile gun and opened fire. Bullets went straight through Ian's shield and glanced off his armor with metallic hisses. Ian holstered his pistol and pulled up his blast rifle.

"Bianca, stay behind me. Aoife, hit him if you can."

"On it," she said.

She moved two meters to my right and brought her blast rifle up, still running. The mech decided she was the biggest threat and changed to shooting at her.

Aoife didn't even break stride, she just consistently put shot groupings right in the mech's face guard, until, on the fifth grouping, he stopped firing. She had repeatedly hit a moving target fifteen centimeters wide from over a hundred meters away. At a dead run.

Note to self: do not challenge her to a shooting competition.

We dashed past the disabled mechs. Breath sawed through

my chest and my head pounded. My main focus became putting one foot in front of another. Ian shot at an unseen target, but they didn't shoot back.

It felt like a century later when Ian finally turned down a side street. We circled around so we didn't lead any pursuers straight to Yuko's shop, but time was of the essence, so Ian didn't bother with an elaborate deception.

Ian led us through a large, unmarked door. By unspoken agreement we all deactivated our shields. "Aoife, you have the door," Ian said. She murmured her agreement.

This shop didn't pretend to be anything other than what it was—an information exchange. A woman in her forties or fifties with straight, graying black hair and dark eyes stood behind a faux wooden counter. "Lady Bianca von Hasenberg, I presume?" she asked, her voice softly accented.

I opened my face guard over Ian's growled protest. "I am. And you are?"

"Yuko Ponseti, at your service. Veronica spoke highly of you."

"Of you, too." I paused, then dived right in. Some brokers preferred to chat before getting down to business, but the longer we lingered, the more time the local crime bosses had to set up an ambush for us. "She said you could get me an invite to the Syndicate party tonight."

"I can. In return for a favor."

"What favor?"

"Unspecified."

"I don't deal in future favors."

"I know, which is why it is so valuable."

I would do about anything for my brother, but open-ended favors were dangerous for both me and the House. "No."

Yuko stared at me for a long moment. "You're serious."

"Yes. I do not trade in future favors. Not even for this."

"Why not agree and then renege? You'd still get what you want," she said.

"Promises are important to me. I don't make them with the intent to break them."

Yuko smiled, a barely-there tilt at the corner of her lips. "Despite the rumors, I would not have believed it possible if I didn't see it with my own eyes. A member of a High House who believes in honor."

"I believe in keeping my promises," I said. "But if I don't secure an invitation, I'm going to sneak into the party even if I have to go through a whole host of guards to do it, and most would argue that's not entirely honorable."

"Promises are what I care about," Yuko replied. "My daughter is imprisoned on Pluto. She's been there for over a year, and for the last three months, my Pluto contacts have failed to check in. If you promise to do everything you can to get her out, I will give you the invitation you need."

Pluto was one of the oldest prison planets in existence and was now used almost exclusively for political prisoners the Consortium wanted buried. Pardons were difficult to obtain. "Does she have to get out legally?" I clarified.

"Legally would be better, but no. I just want her home."

"Very well. You get me a valid invitation to the Syndicate party tonight and I will do everything in my power to get your daughter out of prison, though it may end up being less than legal. The Consortium rarely gives up political prisoners, even to the daughter of a High House. Also, my brother's rescue comes first. As soon as he's safe—" I paused, but didn't want to think about any other outcomes. "Your daughter will be my priority after my brother."

She held out her hand. "Deal."

I carefully took her hand in my gloved one and shook it. "Deal. Send me whatever information you have on her, no matter how small."

Yuko nodded, then bent to open a small, biometrically locked safe. She pulled out a square envelope made of thick, expensive paper. "This is the invitation everyone received. There are no names, so you don't have to worry about faking an ID. Inside are the ship codes needed to land in their spaceport. The invitation itself is chipped and will be needed for entrance. The rules are explained inside, but weapons are strictly forbidden. It won't stop anyone, but you'll have to be sneaky."

She handed the envelope to me, and I carefully stored it in the compartment under my chest armor. If a shot got to it, it would get to me, so it was as safe as I could make it without stripping out of the armor.

"We're about to have company," Aoife called over our internal com.

"I hate to bargain and run, but my guard says we're about to be attacked."

"They will not attack the shop," Yuko said with quiet confidence. "And, despite appearances, my shop has many entrances. Go through the door and down the stairs. In the tunnel, go straight, straight, left, and then straight until the tunnel ends. Climb the stairs and you'll be out near your spaceport. Expect trouble at the end, but they'll be spread thinner than here."

I closed my face guard and used my suit's com to send her one of my private addresses. "Send me everything on your daughter. I will not forget this."

She inclined her head. "Safe travels, Lady Bianca."

# CHAPTER 15

We made it back to the ship in one piece. Barely. There had been heavy resistance between the tunnel exit and the ship, but Ian and Aoife had cleared a path. I'd done what I could to help, but honestly, they'd done the heavy lifting.

Now out of my combat armor, I trembled from head to toe, partially leftover adrenaline, partially overextended muscles. Sweat had drenched my clothes. I needed a shower and a nap, but I'd settle for just the shower.

Maybe a shower with the silencer running to give my brain a break.

Aoife crouched down next to where I was sitting on the edge of my supply crate. "You did well," she said quietly. "I've had trained soldiers perform worse under pressure."

"I am trained, too, it's just been a while."

She stood and slapped a friendly hand against my shoulder, then offered me help up. "Come on, Shaky, I'll follow you up to your quarters to make sure you don't trip on the stairs and break your neck."

"You're too kind," I said drily. But I smiled at her. I'd somehow proven myself in the last few hours and she was no longer cold and distant. But I couldn't say the same for either Ian or Alexander.

"We should return to orbit until the party," Ian said as I headed for the stairs. They were the first words he'd spoken to me since we returned.

"*Fortuitous,* take us into orbit," I said.

The ship chimed an acceptance and the engines came to life. It was a tiny bit irresponsible to launch without being on the flight deck, but this was a top-of-the-line ship with the best control system money could buy. It was designed to handle any number of issues, faster and more competently than a human pilot. It was only in case of catastrophic failure, where the captain would need to take control with the manual controls, that being on the flight deck might save the ship.

Ian growled something under his breath, but didn't question my decision.

To be on the safe side, I climbed the stairs to the flight deck and waited until we were safely parked in a geostationary orbit. There were a few other ships in orbit, but they were far enough away not to be a concern. Even older ships were good at avoiding each other in orbit. I told the ship to alert me on any changes, then headed down to my quarters for a well-deserved shower.

IT TOOK ME OVER AN HOUR TO GET READY BECAUSE I kept changing my mind about my makeup. Then I realized it was going to be mostly hidden behind my half mask anyway, so I changed it again.

Scarlet lips and smoky eyes would be too much without the mask but worked perfectly with the mask. My hair was piled on top of my head and held in place with two long pins that could double as stabbing weapons if needed.

Overall, I looked pretty, delicate, and mysterious. And the dress *killed*.

I kept my shielding bracelet, but I didn't have too many options for weapons. My hair pins would only be useful as a last resort. I'd love to have a blaster or two, but guests would be screened and I hadn't brought anything advanced enough to trick a scanner. Maybe Ian had something I could use.

I found him in the mess hall with Alexander and Aoife. A bottle of expensive bourbon was on the table and they each had an empty glass in front of them. Ian had changed into a black tuxedo and his golden hair was still damp from his shower. He looked amazing and my heart twisted, just a bit, at missed opportunities.

At some unseen signal, Alexander and Aoife stood and left the room, but not before both of them shot Ian a stern glance.

"Please have a seat, Lady Bianca," Ian said. I couldn't read his expression, but his eyes lingered on my dress. "Bourbon?"

"Yes, please." I perched gingerly on the edge of a chair. Sitting in a dress like this without flashing anyone required delicate movement.

Ian picked up the fourth glass and poured me a generous serving. He splashed a bit more in his glass, then raised the glass in toast. "To success."

I echoed him and touched my glass to his. The first sip blazed delicious warm fire down my throat, but I didn't think the heat in my belly was entirely due to alcohol.

Ian also took a sip, then he met my eyes. "I apologize for earlier," he said. "You are not a liability, as you've proven time and again, and I did not mean to imply otherwise. I meant it when I said you were our most important asset. The thought of you out in Matavara . . ." He trailed off and shook his head. "Please accept my apology."

"Are you truly sorry or are you trying to make nice so that

I'll listen to you tonight?" I asked. "And remember, you promised me the truth."

"I'm truly sorry. I should've apologized as soon as I realized how my words could be taken, but I have my own stubborn streak. You may have noticed." His grin was tinted with self-deprecation. "But I also don't want to go into a dangerous situation while we're fighting."

"Ian, I've said this all along, we don't have to fight. If we worked together, we'd be unstoppable. But you have to trust me to be able to do what I say I can. I don't boast without cause and I know my limits. If I can't do something, I'll tell you. If I suggest something, it's because I think I can do it."

"I know," he said. "I'm not used to people who are so self-aware. One of your brothers would insist he could scale a building barehanded and with one leg missing."

"I see you've met Benedict," I said with a grin. I loved him to pieces, but Benedict was not one for modesty, false or otherwise.

Ian smiled, then turned serious. "Do you have a plan?"

I took another sip of bourbon before answering. I wouldn't be able to finish the glass, but I let the liquid courage warm me. "Based on my contacts, Riccardo Silva is the representative attending tonight." Ian winced. "I see you've heard the same rumors I have. Have you worked with him before?"

"No, and I had hoped to keep that streak going. You'll have to charm him. Try to get him alone, or as alone as you can with the various bodyguards in attendance. He won't deal in public because he has an image to maintain, and he might try to double-cross you."

"He will definitely try to double-cross me," I said. "Do you have any weapons that will pass a scanner?"

"A blaster and a few knives, nothing major."

"I'll take what I can get. So we find Riccardo, get him

alone, and negotiate for Ferdinand. They won't have him here, so where would you like to do the swap?"

"Sedition," Ian said at once. "Your sister's contacts will help, the Consortium doesn't have a military presence to put the Syndicate off, and it's public enough that they will be less likely to cause a bloodbath."

I didn't miss that he said "less likely" rather than unlikely. Good thing we were all optimists here.

THE CODES IN THE INVITATION HAD BEEN ACCEPTED BY the spaceport ground control. *Fortuitous* settled on a narrow temporary landing pad next to a half dozen other such pads.

The ship wouldn't be allowed to stay on the ground, so I'd given Aoife and Alexander piloting privileges. Aoife had argued for five minutes that she should come with us, but the invitation was good for only two guests. If we ran into trouble, we'd be on our own. It would take ten to fifteen minutes for the ship to land to pick us up.

I stopped by my quarters to check my appearance one last time. The mask obscured the upper half of my face, making my darkly lined, golden-hazel eyes stand out. I had a short, thin dagger tucked down the front of my dress and another strapped high on my left thigh. Ian had assured me that they wouldn't show up on a scanner. He was carrying our only blaster because a tuxedo was far more concealing than this dress.

The silver shielding cuff circled my left wrist and my right was unadorned. Compared to the current fashion, I was practically plain. I hoped I would fade into the edges of the crowd.

I met Ian in the cargo bay. He had added a thin black mask that made him look more like a bandit than a security guard. It was a good look.

The cargo bay door was open and the ramp was lowered. "You ready?" he asked.

I took a deep breath and sank into my cool public persona. I would have to maintain the facade for hours tonight. "I'm ready."

Ian stepped close enough that I had to tilt my head back to hold his gaze. "You look amazing," he said quietly. "You'll have the room at your feet."

There was only one person I wanted anywhere near me and I wanted him higher than at my feet. "Thank you," I whispered. Nerves threatened my icy facade, and I added, "Please stay close."

"I will," he promised. He offered me an elbow and escorted me down the ramp. Aoife and Alexander were supposed to delay taking off until we'd successfully entered the party. If Yuko's invitation was bad, we'd need a quick exit.

The landing pad had a temporary plastech path leading to the door of a large three-story building. A soaring, triangular glass atrium carved a line through an otherwise boring building. It could've been an office building in any number of cities, but in Matavara, it stood out. I wondered how many of those glass panels they'd had to replace before the party.

Inside, a wide, faux marble staircase led up to the second floor. Soft music drifted from the open doors. Directly in front of us, a half dozen security guards manned a body scanner. At least six more guards were stationed around the edges of the room and I saw the tip of a blast rifle barrel sticking out of the third-floor balcony.

The Syndicate was taking no chances with security.

A security guard in a form-fitting tuxedo stepped in front of me. "Invitation, please," he rumbled.

Ian produced the invitation and the guard scanned it with his com. My heart stumbled when the guard stared at his device for what felt like forever. Finally, he waved us forward with a smile. "Enjoy the party. Remember the rules."

We walked through the body scanner one at a time and von Hasenberg tech proved its worth as we made it through without setting off the alarms. Of course, if we passed the scanners with weapons, then others had, too, so it was more about leveling the field than having a firm advantage.

A guard looked through my clutch, which held nothing more than a makeup kit and my com, then handed it to me with a nod.

Ian fell back behind my right shoulder. I climbed the stairs slowly, with measured steps—shoulders back, chin up, public persona firmly in place. This world belonged to me and others were merely allowed to live in it.

That really should be the House von Hasenberg motto. Or House Rockhurst or House Yamado. In fact, every High House thought it owned the universe.

The ballroom's walls were draped in soft fabric, and glittering crystal chandeliers illuminated a crowd of nearly two hundred. Most of the guests and their guards were masked, but a few brave souls were showing their faces for all to see. I recognized a few people both from the lower houses and from outside the Consortium entirely.

"Keep an eye out for Riccardo," I murmured to Ian. We were both miked and wearing tiny, hidden earpieces. The number of signals flying through the air was enough to give me an immediate headache. People chatted politely in small groups, but behind the scenes, their coms were working overtime, transmitting recordings and looking up data.

Around the edges of the room, curtained alcoves offered glimpses of the evening's more adventurous entertainments. Naked bodies writhed under—or over—mostly clothed guests; a gorgeous, naked brunette was being lovingly tied with silken rope by a masked woman; and two men fought with bloody knuckles and bleeding noses while a crowd cheered and bet.

I mingled throughout the room, avoiding the fringes and gracefully moving from group to group with the ease of long practice. Rumors about the attack on House von Hasenberg and the war between us and House Rockhurst were rampant. No one had any real information, but everyone wanted to talk about it.

My face ached from holding both my tongue and my polite smile. The next person who lamented that Bianca von Hasenberg hadn't been shot was liable to get a hair pin in the eye.

"You're glowering," Ian murmured. He grazed a featherlight touch across the exposed skin of my lower back to direct me around a drunken guest.

I shivered, but refused to be so easily distracted. "I'm about to do more than glare," I growled back. So far, Riccardo Silva had been decidedly absent. If we went to all this trouble and he failed to make an appearance, I didn't know what I would do, but I vowed it would be properly dramatic. I'd get his attention one way or another.

An older gentleman in a white tuxedo with graying hair, deeply tanned skin, and a slim build approached. A mask covered the upper part of his face, but his smile was warm. "Your dress is a work of art," he said by way of greeting.

"Thank you," I said. "I happen to agree."

"Would you care to dance?" he asked. When Ian stepped closer, he clarified, "In full view of your guard, of course."

"No, thank you. I appreciate the offer, but I don't dance."

"Then please allow me to escort you around the room. That dress is meant to be in motion."

I accepted his offered arm and let him lead me on a circuit

of the room. "So, are you a fashion designer or just a connoisseur of women's dresses?"

He laughed, a deep, pleasant sound. "Ten seconds and you already have me figured out. I'm a designer. And I'm betting your dress came from High Street."

"You have a good eye."

"When you've been in this business as long as I have, you learn to recognize the competition."

"So what's a fashion designer doing at a Syndicate party?"

"Hoping to negotiate for cheaper, better materials. The Consortium is killing my business."

It wasn't the first time I'd heard the complaint. Consortium taxes could be outrageously high, depending on how much pressure they wanted to put on a certain business or sector.

"And what do you do, my lady of good fashion sense?"

"I deal in information," I said.

He paused and turned to me. "I don't suppose *you* could find me a new line on materials?"

I laughed lightly. "You're single-minded, I'll give you that. But no, I don't deal in that kind of information. I could do it, but my fee is so high you'd lose any benefit the information would give you."

He started walking again, until we returned to where we'd started. He bowed over my hand and offered me a card. "The next time you're in Honorius and need a new dress, come see me. I may not be on High Street, but my dresses are no less beautiful. Even the High Houses will be envious by the time I'm finished with you."

"Thank you. I look forward to it," I said. I tucked the card into my clutch and bobbed a shallow curtsy.

The ballroom was nearing capacity as more and more guests arrived. The heat was stifling and I regretted not bringing a personal cooling field. On the far end of the room, wide glass doors were thrown open to an outside balcony. I headed that way. I just needed a few minutes of fresh air away from the din.

Small groups of people mingled on the balcony. I moved away from them, to a secluded corner. No breeze moved the air, but it was still nearly ten degrees cooler out here than in the ballroom.

"Are you okay?" Ian asked.

"Yes, just hot and frustrated."

"Perhaps I can help with one of those," a masculine voice interrupted. His accent was lilting, nearly musical. "I've been watching you all evening and I must say, that dress is my new favorite thing. But it would look even better on my floor."

I turned to face the newcomer and it was only through years of practice that I didn't roll my eyes at the terrible line or show my surprise when I came face-to-face with Riccardo Silva and his two bodyguards.

Riccardo was a handsome man, with blue-green eyes and warm olive skin. He wore a black tuxedo, perfectly tailored. Dark, curly hair gave him a tousled, touchable look. He was taller than me in my heels, but only just.

"Oh," I murmured, letting my voice go husky, "is your floor particularly attractive? Because I find it hard to believe that anyone could wear this dress as well as I do."

"Perhaps you should come with me and find out."

It *couldn't* be this easy. Ian must've thought the same, because he stepped closer.

"I don't even know your name, Mister . . ." I trailed off meaningfully.

"Riccardo Silva, at your service," he said. He bowed over my hand, pressing a lingering kiss, complete with tongue, to the back of it.

It took every ounce of willpower I had not to knock him senseless. Instead, I let my eyes go wide. "*The* Riccardo Silva?" I asked, breathless.

"The one and only. This is my party. All of these people are here to see me."

"I see you," I whispered. It sounded like a threat, so I hurried to add, "You're gorgeous." And he was. But his eyes gave him away—they were entirely predatory, not a hint of warmth.

"So, shall we take this conversation somewhere a little more private?" he asked.

"I can't leave my guard," I said with a little moue of distress.

Riccardo leered at Ian. "He can watch. I don't mind. These two do it all the time." He hooked a thumb over his shoulder at his guards.

Ian was practically plastered to my back, he was so close. I felt him tense and subtly elbowed him. It was almost certainly a trap, but that didn't mean we couldn't use it to our advantage. Lili had said that Riccardo thought he was smarter than everyone else and liked to play with his prey.

*So let's play.*

"Where did you have in mind?" I asked.

"I have a room upstairs that overlooks the ballroom. I could have you against the window and no one would know."

"Hopefully *I* would know," I said with a flirtatious smile.

"Why don't you find out?"

"Maybe I'm not that kind of woman," I hedged. Without being able to talk to Ian, I'd have to make up a plan as I went and hope he figured it out before we were both killed.

"In that dress? Please," Riccardo scoffed.

I made a mental note to knee him in the balls at the first opportunity. I forced my mouth into a coy smile and hoped the murder in my eyes was masked. "You're right," I managed to get out without choking. *Barely.* "Let's see this room of yours."

He held out his left elbow, forcing me to hold it with my right hand. With the clutch in my left hand, I appeared far more harmless than I was. I wasn't as strong left-handed, but I could still drop the clutch and stab him somewhere that would hurt, given the opportunity.

I flashed Ian a meaningful look. We had to act before we made it wherever Riccardo was leading us or we were toast. He nodded slightly in acknowledgment.

Riccardo placed his hand over mine, trapping my right arm. One of his guards followed directly behind us, then Ian, then the second guard.

I focused on the signals immediately surrounding us, and pain burrowed into my head. One of the nearby guards sent a message: *Target acquired. On the move.* Oh yeah, they were on to us.

Riccardo led me back into the ballroom, but stuck close to the wall. He held his arm over the chip reader of a side door and we slipped through into a service hallway. A pair of guards flanked the door. One of them fell in behind us. We were now outnumbered by four to two, not counting the other guards spaced throughout the hallway.

Riccardo's bodyguards weren't visibly armored, but their suits fit so poorly it was a good bet that the material was reinforced, which might be enough to stop my little dagger. If Riccardo's suit was reinforced, I couldn't tell.

We stopped at the elevator and one of the guards pressed the button. The elevator would have to be it. Fighting in such an enclosed space would work against us, but it would work against them, too. Presumably they didn't want to kill Riccardo, so it would be nonlethal close combat. They'd try to subdue us, because if Riccardo wanted us dead without talking to us, he wouldn't have gone to all this trouble.

The elevator dinged and the door slid open. Empty. I silently thanked the universe for small miracles. Riccardo and I stepped inside. The three guards paused at the door, drew blasters, and turned on Ian, preventing him from entering. He lunged for the closing elevator doors, but one of the guards tackled him, stopping him just short.

Ian's furious eyes met mine just before he disappeared under another guard. "I will come for you," he vowed. "Wait for—" The earpiece emitted a sharp whine then went silent. His mike had failed.

The doors slid closed and the elevator started upward.

"Well played," I murmured, burying both my worries and the flutter Ian's promise had elicited.

"We meet at last, Bianca von Hasenberg. Did you really think I wouldn't know who you were?"

"Do you actually use any of those terrible lines on women?"

He laughed. "No. I wanted to see if you'd break cover. Your restraint was admirable."

"You came close to physical harm."

"No, I didn't," he said with careless confidence.

I could use that confidence against him, just as Gregory had once used my own confidence against me. Confidence was great right up until the point that it became *over*confidence and blinded you to danger. I just had to wait for the perfect opportunity because I would get only one.

# CHAPTER 16

The elevator opened, revealing a basic office furnished with inexpensive faux wood furniture. Power cables criss-crossed the floor, leading to a pair of temporary desks loaded with multiple displays. Riccardo jerked his head and the man and woman behind the desks scurried from the room.

On our left, a wall of tinted windows overlooked the ball-room. I moved to the glass and Riccardo followed. Below, the colorful crowd mingled, unaware of our vantage point.

I turned back to him. "I expect my guard to be returned to me unharmed when I leave."

"So sure you will be leaving?"

I let some of Mother's icy hauteur slip into my tone. "Yes."

Riccardo laughed. "My sister said you were a cool one. Per-haps I should crack that ice you wear like armor."

"Are you sure you're ready to face what you would find? Per-haps this shell isn't for my protection, but yours."

Riccardo's eyebrows climbed his forehead. I'd set him off balance. Good. I needed to keep him there. "I've come for my brother, as I'm sure you know. I'm prepared to pay handsomely for his rescue and care."

A wrinkle appeared in Riccardo's forehead as he frowned down at me. "Rescue?"

"My brother lives, does he not? As far as I'm concerned, that's rescue enough. I will pay you, you will return him, and we will all forget this unfortunate incident ever happened."

"And if I refuse?"

I might not be able to effectively wield Mother's imperious stare, but I had Father's icy, murderous glower down pat. "Do not refuse."

Riccardo's right eye flickered, the tiniest sign of his unease. I'd backed him into a corner. He would attack soon, unable to stand not being in control. I had to turn that attack back on him before he realized what I'd done.

"Your brother is dead. Your guard is dead. And here you are, all alone with me. Perhaps I'll keep you until I tire of you. Then you will become my party's most prized entertainment."

I let the words bounce off me, betraying nothing. I gave him a deadly smile. "Are you sure it wouldn't be more accurate to say that *you're* all alone with *me*? Give me my brother and I will not only let you live, I'll pay a royal ransom."

His confident smirk telegraphed his intentions as clearly as words. It had been a long time since I'd had a self-defense tutor, but I'd trained for *years*. Muscle memory kicked in as he lunged for me.

I wasn't as graceful as I had been before Gregory, but I managed. I dropped the clutch and stepped into him instead of away. He wasn't expecting the move and didn't have time to counter as I drove my knee sharply into his balls. I stepped back as he gasped out a curse and crumpled.

I drew the tiny dagger from my bodice and grabbed Riccardo by the hair, wrenching him up to his knees. I pressed the sharp blade into his throat deeply enough to draw blood.

"Move and die," I said.

"You need me to save your brother," he sneered.

"There are more Silvas. You are not essential. Where is my guard?"

"I told you, he's dead. You're next. Then I'll make sure your fucking brother suffers before he dies."

*Ferdinand was alive!* I kept my emotions under a tight rein.

A commotion in the room next door drew my attention. Riccardo tried to break away, but he misjudged the hold I had on his hair. However, his struggles meant I didn't have time to swing him around as a shield, and without a free hand, I couldn't activate my cuff. I pressed the knife deeper. "Tell them not to shoot."

The door burst open and I tightened my grip, but no one entered.

"Get this crazy bitch off of me!" Riccardo demanded.

I jerked his head back and slid the knife deep enough that the tip disappeared into a well of red blood. "You're only alive because you *might* be useful. Call off your dogs."

I watched the door, tensed to dive behind the meager cover Riccardo provided. A familiar profile flashed into view for a second as the person on the other side of the door assessed the situation, then Ian appeared, missing his coat and mask and covered in blood.

Ian's lip was split, his nose was bleeding, and blood dripped sluggishly off of his left hand. On his torso, red stains stood out vividly against his white shirt. As I watched, the largest one spread. If all of that blood was his, then we were in deep, deep trouble.

"Impossible," Riccardo breathed. He tried to jerk away, but I tightened my hold and dug the dagger in a little deeper. More blood slid down the front of his neck and he swallowed, then held still.

Relief crashed into me. Ian was injured, but he wasn't dead.

"Where is Lord Ferdinand?" Ian asked in a deceptively soft voice. He favored his right side, but he still moved with most of his usual predatory grace.

"How did you get past the guards?" Riccardo whimpered.

"I killed them," Ian said without inflection. "You will be next unless you cooperate."

As Ian neared, Riccardo leaned back into my legs, trying to escape.

"Let him go," Ian said.

"I didn't search him," I warned.

"He's not going to try anything because he knows I'll kill him," Ian said. His voice was still too flat, much like his expression.

"I don't think he's that smart."

Ian took the decision out of my hands. He transferred his blaster to his left hand and wrapped his right around Riccardo's neck and pulled him up. He drove him back against the wall, holding him high enough that Riccardo was on tiptoe just to breathe.

"He is definitely not that smart," Ian growled. He held out the blaster. "Trade me and watch the door."

I took the blaster and gave him the short knife. "Ferdinand is alive," I said. "Find out where. You have House permission to do whatever it takes."

For a brief moment, Ian's expression morphed into familiar exasperation. It was a welcome change from the blankness he'd been sporting. Of course I knew he didn't need my permission, but perhaps Riccardo did not.

"We don't have Ferdinand," Riccardo whined.

"Then I suppose you are no longer required," Ian said. His knuckles whitened as he tightened his grip on Riccardo's neck.

"Wait," Riccardo gasped. "We don't have him *anymore*. But

I know where he is." When Ian didn't loosen his grip, Riccardo continued, "We sold him!"

"You *sold* my brother?" I questioned, my voice soft with menace. "To whom?"

Riccardo rolled desperate eyes to me. Whatever he saw in my expression made him flinch. "Swear to me that you'll let me go if I tell you."

I stared at him, trying to master my rage. "I will let you go if you tell me everything you know. Quickly." After all, if I'd found him once, I could do it again.

"We were paid an enormous amount of money to snatch Ferdinand from Earth. We were supposed to deliver him to our contact, but they never showed."

"Leaving you with a huge liability," Ian said. "Why sell him? Why not kill him?"

"Because we assumed our contact wanted him dead but didn't want any paper trails leading back to them. And while the Consortium might eventually overlook a kidnapping, murdering an heir is something else altogether. Plus, we don't work for free and the second half of our payment didn't go through."

"Who ordered the grab?"

"I don't know," Riccardo whined. "It was all done anonymously." Ian tightened his grip and Riccardo rushed to add, "We think it was someone high up in the Consortium, but we don't know."

"Who has my brother?" I bit out.

Riccardo wavered. "Remember your vow," he said. He swallowed. "We needed to get rid of him quickly and quietly. To put him somewhere he could be retrieved if needed, but otherwise wouldn't be found. Ever. And we needed someone who wouldn't ask too many questions during the transfer. That's harder than you might think."

If he was rambling this much, then it must be bad. "Who is it?" I demanded.

He glanced away and whispered, "We sold Ferdinand to Mine-Corp."

Fury blazed bright. "You sold my brother, the heir to House von Hasenberg, to a group of *slavers?*"

"They prefer indentured—" Riccardo stopped speaking with a strangled wheeze, and I didn't bother to stop Ian. MineCorp mined some of the most dangerous sectors in the universe, largely with a force of slave labor masquerading as "indentured servants."

Some people, like my brother, were sold to them under false pretenses, but some signed up voluntarily, lured by the company's slick spiel. When you had less than nothing, the promise of food and shelter was tempting, especially to those who didn't fully understand the contract. Thus it became a complex legal tangle, one the Consortium had no particular desire to untangle—not when profits were so high.

"Where did they send Ferdinand?" I demanded. "I'm assuming you disabled his identity chip?"

Riccardo gasped something unintelligible.

"Let him breathe," I told Ian.

Ian loosened his fingers and Riccardo sucked in air. "I don't know where Ferdinand is. We didn't *want* to know. We sold him through a series of intermediaries. His chip was removed and replaced." When Ian's fingers tightened again, Riccardo whined, "His new name is Nando Black. That's all I know, I swear. Now keep your promise."

Ian shot me a questioning look. Technically, I had already let Riccardo go, so my vow was met. However, I understood the true meaning behind the vow and promises were important to me. Just because a loophole gave me an out didn't mean it would be honorable to use it.

But honor and desire didn't always match up. "Don't kill him," I forced out with a grimace.

"Letting him live is a mistake," Ian growled. Riccardo began to struggle as his throat closed off completely. Ian kept him pinned to the wall with effortless strength. It would be so easy to forget the spreading blood on the front of his shirt.

"It is not a mistake because he will not cause us any trouble. If he does, I will personally ensure House von Hasenberg takes a much more active role in eradicating the Silva family one ship at a time."

Riccardo tried to nod, but I knew it was a lie. He wouldn't let this insult go. I would have to deal with him sooner or later. But a promise was a promise. I sighed. "Knock him out and we'll tie him up. Someone is bound to wander up here eventually, unless you killed *all* of the guards?"

I meant it as a joke, but Ian grimaced and didn't clarify one way or the other. My eyes widened. Surely not . . .

Riccardo's struggles slowed and stopped. Ian kept him pinned for another thirty seconds, then lowered him to the ground. "Do you have ties?" he asked, his voice rough.

"No."

He stripped off Riccardo's jacket and suspenders. He rolled Riccardo onto his stomach and wrenched his arms behind him. Ian used the suspenders to tie him hand and foot with quick efficiency.

"Are you okay?" I asked.

"I'm fine."

So, in universally understood language, he was *not* fine. "Did you call the ship back?"

"Yes, but Riccardo revoked our authorization. Alex is landing nearby and Aoife is going to meet us at the perimeter for an escort back." Ian staggered to his feet and I rushed to brace my shoulder under his arm.

"How many guards are between here and there?" I asked.

"Fewer than there were," Ian said. A glance at his face revealed a grim smile.

"How many did you disable?"

"We'll take the stairs," he said, changing the subject. "We'll be able to hear anyone coming up."

Warm blood had soaked through my dress, so I decided now was not the time to argue. "I don't suppose you saw a medkit on your way up? You're bleeding badly."

"Tie his jacket around my waist," Ian instructed as he took the blaster from me. "It'll work until we make it to the ship." He was starting to look gray, but the determined set of his mouth was familiar.

I picked up Riccardo's jacket and folded it to make a pad out of the front and back, then tied the arms tightly around Ian's waist. He grunted but didn't complain.

I found my clutch and tucked my com down the front of my dress, then I activated the cuff on my left wrist by swiping my right hand over the smooth surface from inside to outside and back again. I kept my hand in place for two seconds until the cuff vibrated. It had enough power to repel up to eight shots. If Ian stayed close, he would be partially protected, but if he went down, we were sunk.

"Let's go," I whispered, concern eating at me. Perhaps at the peak of my fitness I might've been able to carry Ian, but today I would be lucky if I could drag him on a smooth surface. We needed to get to Aoife as soon as possible.

Ian set off with an unsteady gait. In the room next door, two guards and two techs lay unmoving. The techs had been shot in the head, while one guard had a hole through his chest and the other had been shot at close range with what appeared to be his own blaster.

I closed my eyes at the destruction. I knew it had to happen, and I was no stranger to death, but so much carnage turned my stomach. Holding my breath, I stopped and collected the extra blaster. Ian's stance wobbled and his eyes were going glassy.

"Stay with me, Ian," I murmured. "I'm not leaving you and I can't do this alone."

"If I go down, leave me."

"I won't," I said calmly. "So you better not go down."

Determination lit his gaze, but by the time we'd descended the stairs, Ian had taken to leaning heavily against me. I paused to give him a chance to catch his breath. Everywhere I looked, dead guards stared back with unblinking eyes. Ian had single-handedly taken out at least a dozen armed guards after being outnumbered three to one in close quarters.

Speculation turned into suspicion. He *was* about the right age. And he knew Loch, though he tried to hide it. My eyes narrowed as the pieces snapped together. This entire time a member of the Genesis Project had been hiding directly under the Consortium's collective noses.

The Consortium had hunted Loch to the ends of the universe to cover up their little experiment and the fact that they had treated the project members as expendable and less than human. Ian had a good reason to hate everything about the Consortium. Was this his payback? Did *he* have something to do with Ferdinand's disappearance?

I spun around and planted my blaster in Ian's chest. His eyes widened, but he didn't move. "Did you betray Ferdinand?" I asked in a furious whisper. "Was this your doing from the beginning? Did you put a hit on *me*?"

He blinked and some of the fuzziness cleared from his eyes. "No," he said softly. "I did not betray you or your brother."

"But you must hate the Consortium."

His expression shuttered. "I don't know what you're talking about."

"Don't play dumb with me."

He sighed and the sound rattled dangerously, letting me know time was short. "Look around. If I wanted you dead, do you think I would need these imbeciles to do the job for me? I did not betray you, Bianca."

He moved surprisingly fast, knocking my blaster up toward the ceiling and spinning me around. His arms wrapped around me, trapping me with my back to his chest, the blaster pointing harmlessly away from us. I struggled, but I would have better luck breaking out of triple-max prison restraints.

"I did not betray you and I will not hurt you," Ian said. "But I will not let you expose me with your wild theories, either. Promise me that you'll keep any knowledge about me to yourself."

"I could lie."

"You could, but you won't. Promise me, Bianca."

"And if I don't?" I pressed.

"Bianca," he growled and gave me a little shake. "We're not leaving until you promise. Do you want to kill me?"

"Maybe I do," I bluffed.

"I don't believe you," he whispered into my ear. I shivered. "Promise me, Bianca."

"I will, if you'll promise me something in return."

I felt him tense against me, then curse under his breath. "What is it?"

"Promise me you'll let me help until Ferdinand is found. And *not* from Serenity or wherever else you plan to dump me. I go where you go and we find him together."

He sighed again, but I could tell his resistance was wavering.

"You owe me this much, at least," I said.

"Very well, if you promise to keep anything you may know

about me to yourself *forever,* I'll let you come with me to track down Ferdinand."

I could argue about who was coming with whom, but I decided to take what I could get. "I promise I won't ever use any of your secrets against you," I said quietly. It was a broader promise than he'd asked for, but trust was built slowly, one brick at a time.

I didn't have a good history with trust, but I would try, one more time. The thought of making another mistake terrified me down to my bones, and I didn't know if I could recover again, not if Ian was the one who betrayed me. I swallowed nervously as I waited for his answer.

"Okay," he agreed, letting me go. He staggered, then caught himself against the wall before he toppled. "I should've asked Aoife to bring me a dose of foxy."

Foxy was the street name for amphoxy, a mix of stimulants and painkillers. Soldiers used it to get wounded teammates back to safety or to complete an impossible mission. It tended to be a last resort because it overrode the pain receptors and made the user feel invincible, usually causing the soldier to end up *more* injured.

"Where is she meeting us?" I asked.

"North gate. We need to get moving." The *while I still can* was unspoken, but I heard it nonetheless.

For all of Ian's injuries, he was still an impressive shot. In the next hallway, he shot a guard before I'd even realized someone was there. When another guard rounded the corner directly in front of us, Ian felled him with a single swift punch. I swallowed as I realized just how gently he'd treated me.

# CHAPTER 17

We were almost outside when I stumbled and nearly went down as a wave of wireless signals drove a spike into my brain. I swallowed the urge to vomit. Either Riccardo had been found or something else big was happening. I tried to catch one of the messages but the effort made the nausea worse.

"What's wrong?" Ian whispered.

"Nothing. But we need to move fast to the gate. Can you do it?"

White lines of pain bracketed Ian's mouth, but he just straightened and said, "Yes."

"Keep leaning on me. It'll look like we're out for a drunken stroll. The cuff will protect us for a little while."

We stepped out into chaos. The evening had deepened into night, but floodlights lit up the area. Fire flickered from our left, the direction of the spaceport, and armed guards ran to provide backup. No one paid any attention to us as Ian leaned deeper and deeper into my shoulder. By the time we made the gate, I was half carrying him.

"Aoife?" I called.

She stepped out from behind the gate column, clad in her

combat armor. She slid open her helmet and I caught her frown. "Why are your coms down?"

I touched my ear but the tiny earpiece was gone. "Things didn't exactly go according to plan," I said. "You'll have to carry him."

Ian growled something under his breath, but he was far too pale. Aoife pulled the gate open, setting off a screeching alarm. She took in my heels with a glance. "Can you keep up?"

I could run in these heels, but not for long. "How far is the ship?"

"Over a kilometer. The dark will help, but we need to move." She assessed Ian with another probing glance. "I can't put him over my shoulder with a stomach wound like that, so I won't be able to shoot. It's up to you."

I took off the half mask I still wore. I needed to see as well as possible. I tried to take Ian's blast pistol but he clung to it tenaciously. "I'm not that helpless," he grumbled.

Aoife took off and within three steps I knew I wouldn't be able to keep up with my shoes on. I kicked the heels off and took flight barefoot. The pockmarked pavement was littered with debris that stabbed the tender soles of my feet.

The world narrowed to running and pain. The cuff pulsed as it repelled three quick shots. Ian shot over my head and a distant scream indicated a hit. My feet were on fire, sending lightning bolts of pain up my legs, but I blocked it out as best I could.

I hit one target but didn't have time to celebrate as another pulse vibrated up my arm. Was that six or seven? Somewhere I'd lost count, but either way, the cuff was nearly out of power.

Fatigue dragged at me and the air burned through my lungs. A side stitch felt like someone had stabbed me between the ribs and still we ran. When the ship came into view, the relief nearly put me on the ground.

Unfortunately, we weren't the only ones interested in the ship. A hail of blaster bolts greeted our approach and the cuff vibrated once, twice, then died. Pain, bright and familiar, tore through my right leg.

I stumbled, my body numb, but a hulking figure in combat armor scooped me up and ran for the ship. I clung to consciousness by the merest thread. I had to know if Ian was okay.

The bright lights of the cargo bay blinded me and I blinked the stars out of my eyes.

"*Fortuitous,* take us into orbit," Aoife demanded. The ship chimed an acknowledgment. "Alex, drop her in the medbay then go to the flight deck and get us hidden."

"Ian first," I mumbled as Alexander slid me onto the medbay diagnostic table. "I'll be okay for a while." My nanobots might be a huge pain in my ass 99 percent of the time, but even working slower than most, they wouldn't let me bleed to death from a blaster wound. Probably.

I grabbed weakly at Alexander's armored arm before he could move away. "Thank you," I said.

He inclined his helmeted head and disappeared. I blinked and Aoife's face appeared above mine. She'd stripped out of at least the top half of her combat armor. She reached for the diagnostic console.

"Ian first," I repeated.

"Funny, he said the same thing about you. But since there are *two* diagnostic tables on this ship, neither of you gets to make a noble sacrifice."

"He's been bleeding for far longer. Patch him up first," I whispered.

Something softened in Aoife's expression and she nodded wordlessly.

I drifted in a haze of pain, listening to Ian's grumbles and

Aoife's gruff bedside manner. I hurt from head to toe—literally—and did my best to lie completely still.

"Your turn, princess," Aoife said. She pressed an injector to my arm and pulled the trigger. "That'll take a while to hit, but your nanos have already started on your feet, so the diagnostic recommends digging out the debris as soon as possible. Can you stand it?"

I could've told her that my nanos wouldn't make much progress in five minutes, but that would just lead to more questions, so I took a deep breath and nodded. Pain and I were well acquainted.

She grabbed my left ankle and began poking and prodding the bottom of my foot. I locked my knee straight and gritted my teeth. Agony flared in waves as she removed tiny pieces of glass and metal. After a few minutes, I couldn't stop the tears, so I stared at the ceiling and let them roll silently into my hair.

The cool sting of an antiseptic wash was nearly a relief. Aoife slathered the sole of my foot in regeneration gel, though the wounds weren't deep enough to really need it, and wrapped my whole foot in bandages. "One down, one to go," she said. "You okay?"

I didn't trust myself to speak, so I merely nodded again. Her sympathetic face appeared in my view. "You're doing well," she said. "The painkiller should kick in any minute."

This leg was far worse because every time she moved my foot, the wound on my thigh sent slivers of pain straight up my spine. I kept still only through long practice and held breaths. When she hit a particularly deep piece of something, a tiny whimper broke through my control. I froze for a second before I remembered where I was.

"Stay down," Aoife commanded and I frowned at the ceiling because I hadn't moved.

Ian groaned and I rolled my head toward the sound, only to find him sitting on the edge of the second diagnostic table. His shirt was missing and his torso was wrapped in white bandages. "What are you doing?" I demanded. "Lie down before you hurt yourself worse!"

His eyes met mine. "I'm fine. Aoife patched me up."

Of all the stubborn men in the world, I had to get stuck with this one. "Ian Bishop, if you do not lie back down on that table, I'm going to come over there and make you. And I still have glass in my feet and a hole in my thigh."

He didn't move, so I sat up with a groan. The edges of my vision darkened, but I fought through it.

Aoife kept a hand clamped around my ankle. She grumbled something under her breath that caused Ian to flash a look at me, but all I could hear was the blood rushing through my ears. I was dangerously close to passing out.

I decided that consciousness was the better part of valor, so I wilted back to the table. I was so busy *not* passing out that I barely noticed Aoife bandaging my foot.

"The only other thing the diagnostic tagged was your thigh. Is that right? Are you hurt anywhere else?" she asked.

"Just my thigh."

"Looks like the bolt went through clean, so I just need to irrigate it and coat it in gel and you'll be good as new in no time."

My left foot was already starting to burn as the regeneration gel did its thing. My thigh would be far worse. I briefly considered asking for stronger pain meds, but without whatever specialized blend Gregory used to use, it wouldn't do much. Somehow, he'd tweaked my nanos to counteract painkillers. If I was a less charitable person, I'd say he did it on purpose because he was a sadistic bastard.

Wait, I *was* a less charitable person.

"Is it okay if I cut your dress?" Aoife asked.

The dress was soaked in Ian's blood. I wouldn't be wearing it again, no matter how much I liked it. When I nodded, she slit the fabric up to my waist.

"This may sting," she warned. The antiseptic wash did sting, but it was so mild when compared to my feet that it practically felt good. She probed the wound, checked the diagnostic scan, and then grimaced at me. "The gel needs to fill the wound, so brace yourself."

With that she pressed a thick syringe of regeneration gel to the wound opening on the front of my thigh and depressed the plunger. Now *that* stung. I blinked away tears as she wrapped a snug, waterproof bandage around my leg.

Both feet now felt like I'd propped them far too close to an open flame. Little tingles of pain shot up my nerves, making it difficult to hold still. But the second I moved, the pain tripled. In another minute or two, my thigh wound would burn like the sun.

I tried to speak but my voice came out in a pained hiss. I cleared my throat and tried again. "Would you mind asking Alexander if he could carry me to my quarters? I hate to bother him, but I don't think I can walk."

"You're not going anywhere," Ian said. "Not until you're healed."

"Lie *down,*" Aoife said, her tone half exasperation, half command.

"Do not remove Lady Bianca from the medbay until she is healed," he demanded.

"Please, Aoife," I begged softly. I was going to break under the pain and I didn't want an audience.

"Ian's right," she said at last. "You should stay here in case there are complications. But I'll move you behind a privacy screen."

Hysterical laughter tried to rise, but I shoved it down. Without a silencer to hide behind, I would just have to endure the agony. The next few hours would feel like an interminable hell.

With a button press, the diagnostic table rose a couple of centimeters and Aoife slid it into the little private nook along the wall. She drew the curtain and draped a blanket over me. The blanket's pressure on my feet sent sparks of pain lancing up my legs, but I just clenched my jaw and ignored it.

She paused and peered at my face. "You're still in pain. The painkiller should've kicked in by now."

"I'm slightly resistant, but I'm fine," I said.

"Do you want me to try something else?"

"No," I bit out. I closed my eyes. That was rude, but the pain in my thigh had begun to climb. "Thank you for your help. I am fine. Please leave."

I winced again because that hadn't exactly been polite, either, but it was all I could do to lie still and not scream.

"The table will keep an eye on your vitals, but call me if you need anything," she said.

"Thank you."

She nodded and blessedly disappeared behind the curtain. I heard her murmuring to Ian, but I couldn't make out the words.

Seconds trudged into minutes and sweat broke out along my forehead as my lower body was engulfed in fiery pain. I counted the ceiling tiles, the eyelets on the curtain, and finally, when the pain became overwhelming, the breaths drawn through clenched teeth.

The curtain's sudden disappearance distracted me and another mortifying whimper slipped past my control.

Ian stood hunched next to me, his eyes silently scanning

me from head to toe. I had little hope that he'd missed my clenched fists, sweating brow, and taut frame. He proved me right by asking, "What's wrong?"

I unclamped my jaw. "You should not be walking around," I whispered, avoiding the question.

"You shouldn't be in pain," he countered. "Didn't Aoife give you an anesthetic?"

"She did. I'm resistant. Please leave." The words were gritted out between breaths. Focusing on the conversation meant I had less focus dedicated to ignoring the pain and it bloomed around me in cascading waves.

"Your feet will heal quickly, but the hole in your thigh will take at least half a day. You can't stay in pain that long. Do you know of any painkillers that work?"

"Some do, but I don't know which," I said, wishing he would go away so I could suffer in peace.

"Do you trust me?"

I glanced at him. "In what way?"

He grimaced, and I realized that question had likely been answer enough. "I don't need pain meds often," he said, "but when I do, I use a special blend." His lifted eyebrow asked if I caught the meaning. I nodded. He wasn't going to admit to being a member of the Genesis Project outright, but he was strongly hinting in that direction. "It might work for you. I could give you a quarter dose and see."

I tried to weigh the pros and cons, but the pain made thinking difficult. "Try it," I conceded at last. Anything had to be better than this.

Ian disappeared for so long that I figured he wouldn't return. I decided I'd had enough. I wasn't going to stay here like a bug under a microscope. My brother had been sold to MineCorp and I needed to find him before the job killed him. If I could make it back to the privacy of my quarters, I could start searching for information.

Sitting up took an age and jostled my leg enough that I thought I'd pass out, but I made it. I waved away the diagnostic table's alarm and hoped Aoife hadn't been paying attention.

Moving a centimeter at a time, I slid my legs over the side of the table. Now for the tricky bit. I needed to slowly slide off the table so I didn't land too hard on my injured feet. Unfortunately, my arms trembled as much as the rest of my body.

Before I'd worked up the courage for the drop, the medbay door slid open and Ian staggered inside, followed carefully by Aoife. She didn't look at all surprised to see me trying to slip off the table. "You two are going to be the death of me," she griped. "This one takes a walk with a hole in his gut and you decide to stand with a hole through your leg. You are *perfect* for each other."

"I told you, I'm fine," Ian said. "I've had worse than this." He crossed the room and pressed an injector into my hand. "It's set for a quarter dose," he said quietly.

"Thank you," I whispered. I pressed the injector against my exposed thigh and pulled the trigger.

"Yes," Aoife said, still arguing, "but you seem to forget that you're not in some godforsaken hellhole where you have to keep going or die. *Fortuitous* has an excellent medbay that would get you up and going faster, if you would just stay put." She jabbed a finger at me. "And you, what's your excuse?"

"I'm going to my quarters."

She huffed out an irritated breath. "And how are you going to get there? Crawl?"

"If I have to," I said calmly.

Her eyes widened, then narrowed. "Think you can?"

"If I have to," I repeated.

She threw her hands up. "You're as bad as Ian, but I've got news for you both: you're staying here until you're healed. If you want out faster, I'll put you in the tank."

That caught my attention. "*Fortuitous* has a regeneration tank? Why didn't you start with it?" I'd thought the ship too small for a regen tank, but the double diagnostic tables should've been a giveaway that this ship didn't have the standard medbay configuration.

"Most people avoid the tank if they can," she said. "Your wounds weren't bad enough to require it, though Ian was close."

Regeneration gel healed even deep wounds and had the added benefit of mobility while healing. It burned like a bitch, but most people could dose up on painkillers and be fine. Regeneration tanks were reserved for critical wounds that needed intense healing. The tanks were faster than gel, but kept the patient tied to one location. They also fucking hurt and even good meds couldn't block all the pain.

"Put me in the tank for an hour. Unless Ian has opened his wound and needs it more."

"You could share," Aoife suggested with a smirk. "Then I wouldn't have to worry about chasing either of you all over the ship."

Sharing wasn't unheard of, but it was usually reserved for emergencies. Depending on the size, tanks could accommodate one to four people because someone had done the math and figured that it became inefficient after four. Large military ships had dozens of tanks.

Sharing a tank could be considered intimate because of the lack of clothes, but I'd lost my modesty years ago. And with the hole in my leg, I'd be in too much pain for anything fun, anyway.

"I don't mind if he doesn't," I finally said.

Ian's head snapped toward me, his expression unreadable. I shrugged at him. "Up to you."

"An hour," he allowed. "And I want a full report on MineCorp ready when I get out. If you need to jump before then, jump us back to Andromeda Prime."

Aoife hummed something under her breath, but she went to the control panel on the far wall and tapped the screen.

"I don't want full immersion," I clarified. "I'll sit." Depending on the injury, the patient could sit or float in the tank. Floating required a breathing mask, so I avoided it when I could.

"You sure about this?" Ian asked.

"Could you be more specific?"

"Sharing."

I grinned at him. "Are you worried for your virtue? I promise I won't take advantage."

His expression heated and the corner of his mouth tipped up. "I was less concerned about my virtue than yours."

"Oh, are you planning to ravish me in the regen tank while your gut wound heals? You *are* an overachiever, Ian Bishop," I teased. "But sadly for you, now that I know about your plan, I can take preventive measures."

A pleasant, warm numbness had dulled the sharp edge of my pain and I sighed in relief. It might not block the tank pain, but even a moment's relief was paradise right now.

"Is it working?" Ian asked. He watched my face closely.

"Yes . . . is something wrong?"

Ian shook his head. He really was unbelievably handsome. Had I thought his eyes icy? Today they were the warm blue of a cloudless morning sky. I touched his cheek, running gentle fingers over the bruise forming on his jaw before my gaze snagged on his mouth. I slid my fingers to the back of his head, into the soft waves of his hair and pulled him toward me.

He resisted and clarity briefly reasserted itself. I jerked my hand back. "Ian, did you give me a shot of foxy?"

"Foxy is included in the mix, yes," he said. "That's why I gave you such a low dose. I didn't expect it to affect you so strongly."

While foxy generally helped with focus and pain tolerance, it also had a well-known side effect as an aphrodisiac. Something about lowered inhibitions and feeling invincible made people excited. It's one of the reasons it was so popular as a street drug.

I'd used foxy before–*professionally.* The first time I'd needed it was during one of my very first solo missions. Things did *not* go according to plan. I'd barely dragged myself out for backup to find me. I'd used it a few times since then and I had never reacted to it like this. Of course, I hadn't used it in the past four years. This was yet another thing that Gregory's tinkering had broken.

Still, the warmth floating through my veins was nice. "Perhaps you should be worried for your virtue after all, Director Bishop," I said, using his title to remind myself of why that would be a bad, bad idea.

"I trust you, Lady Bianca," he said gravely, but his eyes laughed at me.

Perhaps he'd dosed himself as well.

And I needed to stop that line of thought before it began.

A panel opened in the smooth wall at the back of the medbay, revealing a closet-sized room with a straight-sided, hip-high rectangular tank large enough for a tall man to lie down in.

My stomach twisted with remembered pain. This was going to be unpleasant.

I pulled my com out of my bodice and dropped it on the diagnostic table. I needed to get in the tank before the pain meds completely wore off because the first few minutes were always the worst.

I slid off the table with barely a twinge of pain. Now that I knew what to look for, I recognized the feeling of invincibility. I moved carefully, aware that I still had a hole in my leg, even if I couldn't feel it.

"I've set the cycle for an hour. If you need out before then, hit the emergency release," Aoife said. "Remember, everything off, including bandages, before you get in."

I crossed to the open door and murmured, "Thank you, Aoife."

She smiled in sympathy and handed me a pair of bandage shears. "Good luck."

# CHAPTER 18

T he regen room was dim and tiny, just big enough to walk along the front of the tank. The healing liquid glowed a brilliant aquamarine under the special lights. It was beautiful, but that wouldn't make up for the fact that the next hour was going to suck.

I unwrapped the bandages from my feet and thigh. My bodice was secured with a row of tiny hooks behind my neck. I huffed out an irritated breath as I tried to remember which side was the hook and which was the loop because neither way seemed to work.

"Need help?" Ian asked from far too close. I froze in surprise before nodding silently. His warm fingers glided along the back of my neck as he worked his way down the short row of hooks. I shivered in pleasure.

He let go of the fabric to trace a finger down my spine. But with nothing to hold it up, the dress slipped down my body, over my hips, and to the floor, leaving me clad in only my underwear. Ian sucked in a startled breath.

I peeked at him over my shoulder. Mistake. His eyes blazed with heat and his expression was filled with what could only be described as *yearning*. A blink later, it was gone and the polite mask he usually wore was back in place. I frowned. Had I seen what I wanted to and not what was actually there?

I cleared my throat. "Do you need help with your bandages?" I offered.

"No, thank you," he said, turning away. "You can go ahead and get in."

The rejection was not unexpected, but it still smarted. I stripped off my last piece of clothing and climbed into the tank. The liquid was tepid, a few degrees cooler than body temperature and somewhat opaque, softening the clean lines of my limbs into hazy, shadowy blobs. Maybe this wouldn't be too awkward after all.

I tipped my head back against the end of the tank and closed my eyes. I could offer Ian that bit of privacy, at least. A tiny ripple announced his entrance, then his feet slid against mine as he sat. The tank was big enough that we only overlapped up to our knees.

I peeked at him from under my lashes. His mask was firmly in place, but his hands were tight on the sides of the tank. My own hands clenched as the first pulse hit. It felt a bit like a static shock, except it hit everywhere at once. The pulse passed and my feet and thigh tingled, a sure sign that pain was just around the corner.

"I forgot how much this hurt," Ian murmured. Gut wounds were notoriously painful.

"You want Aoife to knock you out? I'll keep an eye on you."

"No, it's not unbearable, just unpleasant." His smile proved he knew just what an understatement he was making. "Tell me a story."

Another pulse hit and I tensed as the tingle flared into a

burn. I decided to share one of my happiest memories. "When I was six, I convinced Benedict to run away from home with me. We waited for Mother and Father to be out of town, then we raided the kitchen for bread and jam, packed up our favorite things, and set out into the garden."

"How far did you make it?"

"The park in Sector Three. We set up camp—a tarp over a shrub—and gorged on jam sandwiches. We thought we were so clever."

"And how many guards were hidden around the park?" Ian asked with a smile.

I grinned at him. "Many. And Ferdinand and Hannah were in on it, too, of course. The next morning, like magic, a pot of soup showed up. We thought it was fairies."

"How long did you stay?"

"Two days. Until it rained and we realized camping wasn't fun when you were soaking wet. We snuck back in only to have Ferdinand and Hannah shower us with affection because we weren't dead and we came back. I didn't find out until I was an adult that they knew we were fine the entire time."

Another pulse hit and Ian hissed. "Can I do anything?" I asked.

"Tell me about MineCorp."

"They are a private company, but each of the High Houses owns a stake. They mine rare minerals from dangerous places. Their main workforce is made up of indentured servants. They employ guards to prevent worker escape as much as to prevent outside attack. Their turnover rate is high and they don't ask too many questions when people are brought to them."

Ian nodded, so I continued, "I haven't had any reason to look into them, so I don't know much more than what's public.

But as soon as—" Another pulse stole my breath. I closed my eyes against the pain and took a deep breath. "As soon as I'm out of here, I plan to rectify that."

"What will they do if they find out they have Ferdinand?"

I stared into the middle distance as I thought through the possible scenarios. "They'll kill him," I said flatly. "They don't want to give the Consortium a reason to poke into their business, and explaining how they came to be in possession of the heir of House von Hasenberg would be a pretty damn big reason."

Another pulse hit and agony flared. I blinked away tears and sucked in a breath. This was important. "It's also possible that if we go sniffing after his new identity in the official channels, they will dump him as fast as they can, then claim ignorance, for the same reason. Even if they don't know who he is, just the fact that we're interested will be enough to set off their alarms."

"Can you hack them? Find the information that way?"

A dangerous smile pulled at the edges of my mouth. "It would be my pleasure."

Then another pulse hit, and I lost myself to the pain for a few seconds. When I came back, Ian's voice rumbled nearby. I frowned. Was he closer than he had been? I refused to open my eyes and find out. I didn't need any more sensory input right now.

"Deep breath," he murmured. "When the pain hits, you freeze, but you have to breathe through it. In. Out."

I let my breathing fall into the cadence of his words, slow and deep. When the next pulse hit, I clung to his instructions. The pulses were getting worse, but I didn't black out.

His hand slipped into mine. "Good," he said, his voice rougher as his own pain intensified. "Now focus on your goal. What are you going to do?"

"I'm going to save my brother."

"Set your intention. Hold it close and let it burn away everything else."

I was going to save my brother and neither my father nor Silva nor MineCorp nor this painful fucking tank were going to stop me. A pulse hit and my grip on Ian's hand tightened.

*Breathe. Save my brother. Breathe. Save my brother.* I breathed and silently repeated the mantra over and over until the pulse passed.

"That's it," Ian murmured. His thumb glided over the back of my hand. "Remember to breathe. Remember your intention. And remember I am right here with you."

He was intent on helping me, even when his own pain had to be astronomical. Gratitude and affection swirled into a pleasant warmth that blunted the razor edge of pain. I squeezed his fingers. "Thank you for helping me, Ian," I whispered.

"I will always help you," he vowed softly.

Then another pulse hit and the time for talking was over.

MY WOUNDS WERE HEALED WITHOUT SO MUCH AS A scar. Well, without a physical scar at any rate. It would be a while before I could forget the pain of the regen tank. Ian also came out completely healed, which shouldn't have been possible unless his wound was way less serious than it had seemed. I chalked it up as another mystery that pointed at his enhanced physiology.

Showered and dressed in my own clothes, I felt almost normal again. Low-level anxiety still gripped me as my body waited for another wave of pain. I breathed through it as Ian had taught me. The anxiety would go away in an hour or two.

I put on my smart glasses and set up my most secure connection. I needed to log into HIVE because I needed information on MineCorp and my network was the best place to start.

I transferred to my safe house location and went through the verification process. It was late and the fire was burning low in the grate. I'd detailed everything about this space, from the fire to the fabric on the furniture, and it had taken me weeks to get it exactly right.

Tonight, two people sat by the fire, a woman with shimmering red hair that rivaled my avatar's and a man with bright blue hair. Neither of them looked anything like they did in real life. It was late in Universal Time, and Marcel, the blue-haired man, was on Earth. Alayna, the redhead, was on an out-of-the-way planet that didn't adhere to Universal, so I wasn't sure what her local time was.

"Is everything okay?" I asked quietly.

Marcel was happily married to his husband on Earth and was well on his way to running House Plitt, one of the midlevel lower houses, due to his mother's ill health. He had been pulled into my network because he'd helped me save his niece from an unwanted marriage. Since then, he'd been an invaluable source of information.

Alayna was his niece. She was a doctor and seemed perfectly happy to practice medicine in the middle of nowhere. The settlement she'd decided on had desperately needed a doctor, so it worked out for everyone. With a nearby gate, she was able to use HIVE to stay in touch.

They both smiled. "Everything is fine," Marcel said. His avatar's voice had a pleasant lilt while Marcel himself spoke without an accent. "We are just catching up on gossip. Is everything okay with you? Have you found your brother?"

"Not yet. I'm looking for information on MineCorp."

"Tori is your best bet," Alayna said.

I nodded. I'd helped Tori Waugh escape before she was pressured into marriage to a man who was nice enough but wasn't who she wanted. Now she worked at MineCorp. I wouldn't ask her to risk her job or her identity, but I hoped that she would have some idea on how I could get into their network.

I couldn't message her directly without potentially exposing her—even secure messages weren't *guaranteed* not to be intercepted and I wouldn't chance it—so I could only hope that she would check the messages soon. Most of the people with access to the HIVE safe house tried to check in every day or two, so my hope wasn't too misplaced.

"If you see her, tell her I'm looking for info, would you?"

They both agreed and I excused myself from their conversation. I checked the note board and found a few responses to my request for info on Silva. I didn't learn anything groundbreaking, but two more people had warned me that Riccardo Silva was an ass. Good to know we were all on the same page.

I took down my current note and changed it to a request for information on MineCorp. I changed the exclamation point to bright pink so people would know the note was new.

I responded to a couple of the other messages, then logged out. I'd done what I could.

My stomach rumbled and I tried to remember the last time I'd eaten. Healing took energy and I hoped that meant I would be able to keep something down.

In the galley, Ian was working his way through an enormous steak. He glanced up at me, then pointedly glanced at the synthesizer.

"That's what I'm here for," I said.

I put in an order for a light seafood and pasta dish. As hungry as I was, I might've been able to get away with something heavier and more flavorful, but I didn't want to risk it with an audience. I added a bowl of creamy raspberry mousse for dessert and a cup of apple juice.

Ian watched me out of the corner of his eye as I set my tray down and dug in. I ate slowly, savoring the food and the lack of nausea. Sometimes I would have a week or more of good eating days and sometimes I would have to sip meal replacement shakes just to get any calories down.

When I pushed away the half-eaten plate of food, Ian scowled. "Don't start," I warned, heading him off. "I know my body better than you. If I want to eat dessert, and I do, I can't finish this."

"Eat both."

"I would if I could." I sighed. I loved cooking and I used to love eating. Before Gregory, I'd been curvy. I missed my curves.

I dipped my spoon in the smooth mousse and took a bite. Sweet, slightly tart raspberry flavor exploded on my tongue and I closed my eyes in delight. Maybe I would get another portion of this.

"What did that bastard do to you?" Ian asked.

I blinked out of my mousse-induced haze. I had to tread carefully here because I'd promised him honesty. "Which bastard?"

"Your husband."

The mousse soured in my stomach. "He did many things, none of which I will discuss."

Ian's eyes flashed. "Did you kill him?"

I froze at the unexpected question. Of course Ian would've heard the rumors. Everyone in Serenity had heard the rumors, but no one had been brave enough to question me to my face. So I gave him the truth rather than a deflection.

"No," I said softly, "but I didn't save him, either."

"Wha–"

"What did Aoife learn about MineCorp while we were in the tank?" I interrupted.

Ian let me change the subject, but not without a look that

meant we'd be revisiting this conversation at some point. As far as I was concerned, it would be long after hell froze over.

"Nothing much more than what you already told me. They pick up new 'employees' all over the 'verse. There was an accident recently in the Triangulam sector, but the company shut down access before the full extent of the damage could be reported."

"Any chance Ferdinand was there?"

"No, it happened just before the kidnapping. But it might be a point of leverage we could use."

Aoife's voice came over the speaker. "A half dozen Syndicate ships just jumped in, and I'm assuming they're here for us since they're not heading toward the planet. They haven't spotted us yet, but it's only a matter of time. Where is our next destination?"

"APD Zero," I said before Ian could give her other orders. "I'll get us a landing bay in Sedition after we jump. Are you sure the Syndicate ships are searching for us?"

"I'm sure," she said grimly.

I hadn't expected Riccardo to keep his promise, but I also hadn't expected him to try to attack this quickly. "Did they bring in Riccardo's battle cruiser?"

"No, these are smaller fighters," she said.

I frowned at Ian. "Why would he assume we were still here? If not for the time we spent in the tank, we'd be long gone already. Jumping ships here is a waste of resources."

"We falsified our arrival time," Ian said. "He thinks we can't jump for another few hours. Jumping in just prior to the party was one of the requirements. Aoife, let us know if anything changes, otherwise we'll be on the flight deck in a few."

"Will do," Aoife agreed, then the speaker clicked off.

"Why APD Zero?" Ian asked.

"MineCorp has a large corporate office there. Their headquarters are on Earth, but that's too risky even for me, so Sedition was the next best option." And I could run my suspicions about Ian past my sister in person.

"You can't hack them remotely?"

"I won't know until I try. But they are a huge corporation with a lot of dirt to hide and plenty of people who would like to dig it up. I'm sure they have an entire division dedicated to plugging security holes. Physical access will likely be required."

"And you think you can just waltz in and they'll let you into their systems?"

"In a word, yes."

**THE SYNDICATE FIGHTERS HADN'T FOUND US, BUT WE'D** had a couple of near misses while waiting for a jump point from the gate. Imagining Riccardo's face when he realized we'd escaped brought me a great deal of malicious joy, but now I'd have to watch my back until I could deal with him. The trade-off wasn't worth it.

"We need a landing location," Aoife reminded me.

I may or may not have been dozing in the navigator's chair. It was after midnight Universal Time and today hadn't exactly been easy. Local time in Sedition was the opposite of Universal, so it was just after noon. At least I wouldn't have to wake Ada up this time.

I called her com, connecting voice-only.

"You have a lot of explaining to do," Ada said without preamble.

"Hello, Ada, I missed you, too. I need a hangar for a small House ship. Hidden if you have it. I'm in *Fortuitous*. And Ian is with me."

"Do you want me to get rid of him?"

"No, we've come to an understanding," I said. "We've made

some progress and our path led us to Sedition. I'll fill you in on the ground."

"Are you running on Universal? Would you rather sleep on the ship or here at Rhys's?"

"If Rhys has room and doesn't mind, I'll do that. We can chat on the way because I'll need your help while I grab some sleep."

"And Ian?"

"Hold on." I pulled the com away from my ear. "Ian, do you want to stay on the ship or join me at Rhys's?"

"I go where you go," he said. "These two"—he waved at Alexander and Aoife—"can keep an eye on things here."

"He's coming with me," I told Ada.

"I'll see if we have room for him," she said, her tone suspiciously mild.

"Ada . . ."

"Fine, fine. I'll send you the landing coordinates and meet you there. The hangar is enclosed so you'll need the access codes to land. Rhys owns the whole complex; you won't have to worry too much about prying eyes."

"Thanks, Ada."

"Of course, Bianca. You don't even need to ask."

Ridiculous tears pricked my eyes. I blinked them away. "See you soon."

She said farewell and disconnected the call. A few seconds later, she sent me the information I needed to land. I input it into the navigation system and *Fortuitous* chimed the atmospheric entry warning.

We landed in Rhys's hangar without any trouble. The building had space for four ships, but the other berths were empty except for one. I recognized *Jester*. Scarlett Hargrove must be waiting out her FTL cooldown on the ground. I hadn't forgotten

Ada's dislike, but Captain Hargrove had helped me escape Ian long enough to make him see reason. I needed to thank her if I saw her.

Wireless signals bombarded me. My first instinct was to tense up, to freeze, but I remembered Ian's rough voice in the regen tank. I kept my breathing slow and even. I focused on saving Ferdinand. I would do anything, endure any pain, in order to save my brother.

The pain in my head was still there, but it was manageable. Of course, we were on the edge of Sedition; it would be much worse when we moved into the heart of the city.

A hundred million people called Sedition home despite the fact that the island had a footprint of less than eight square kilometers. When the land ran out, buildings climbed upward. Now they towered in the clouds, a marvel of engineering.

Unlike most cities, where the rich wanted to live above the seething masses, in Sedition the elite sheltered on the ground. Staying low meant they were more protected from the penetrating heat of the sun thanks to shade from the surrounding buildings and a system of industrial thermoregulators.

It also meant that Sedition was one of the cleanest cities in the 'verse—littering of any kind was punished with a prison sentence, especially if you were stupid enough to drop something off one of the upper-level balconies. The rich didn't want to worry about dying from falling garbage.

I hadn't been to Sedition since Gregory had altered my nanos, and I wasn't entirely sure I would be able to stomach this trip. Even with Ian's pain management advice, I would have to take a silencer at the very least, or I'd be too sick to visit MineCorp.

Alexander and Aoife left the flight deck after a brief, quiet conversation with Ian. We would have to abandon *Fortuitous* because we didn't have time to wait the two days needed for the FTL cooldown.

Waiting for an FTL cooldown or taking a starliner had never bothered me before, because it was just the way it was, but now that I knew ships could jump in an hour, I understood House Rockhurst's logic. From their perspective, they *had* to go to war, especially if they knew alcubium was rare. The House that controlled the resource would control the universe.

It also meant stopping the war would be nearly impossible. And as soon as House Yamado found out what the war was really about, they would jump in, too. It would be a monumental disaster.

"Ready?" Ian asked, breaking me out of my depressing thoughts. "Your sister is waiting."

Sure enough, the outside video showed Ada and Loch standing at the bottom of the cargo ramp. "I need to stop by my quarters to grab a few things."

"I'll meet you outside."

I stood and tried to ignore the throbbing in my head. To distract myself, I made a mental list of the things I needed to pack. By the time I'd made it to my quarters, my list included pretty much everything I had.

After packing, I went to find Alexander and Aoife. I found Alexander first, in the mess hall. He glanced up when I entered, then raised an eyebrow when I approached.

"In case I don't see you again, I wanted to thank you for your help. You rescued me in Matavara, and without your help I wouldn't be here. Thank you. If you need any help in the future, please contact me."

I held out my hand for long enough that I figured he was going to leave me hanging. Just as I was about to retract it, he slid his palm into mine. His hands were large and calloused but he didn't try to dominate me with strength or go the other way and give me a fragile squeeze. His handshake was firm and solid.

"You're welcome," he said. He kept my hand as he peered closely at me. "Are you sure you're a von Hasenberg?"

My own eyebrows crept up my forehead. "Yes. I look just like my father."

"You don't act like one."

I smiled gently. "Of course I do. I just try not to."

The hint of a smile touched his mouth and he let go of my hand. "Maybe that's enough. Call me Alex."

I grinned and inclined my head in agreement before taking my leave.

I tracked Aoife to the engine maintenance area and only because I cheated and asked the ship where she was. She turned as I approached. She tried to avoid a handshake because her hands were dirty, but I firmly clasped her hand in mine. "Thank you for everything," I said. "We wouldn't have made it out of Matavara without you. I told Alex this as well, but let me know if I can do anything for you in the future."

I handed her the chocolate I'd snagged from the cargo bay. Once she realized what it was, she tried to hand it back. I waved her off. "It's a small gift. It's not enough, but I hope you like it."

"Ian hasn't told us to go, so I doubt this is good-bye, but you're welcome." She held the chocolate up to her nose and inhaled deeply with an appreciative sigh. "And thank you."

"You're welcome. Safe travels until I see you again."

"Safe travels," she echoed.

I exited the ship, running through my mental checklist. I thought I'd grabbed everything I needed. Ada, Loch, and Ian stood in strained silence at the bottom of the cargo ramp. Both men were tall and muscular, but Loch was bulkier than Ian. Looking at them together, I preferred Ian's more athletic build.

Ada smiled when she caught sight of me. "Finally!" she called. "I thought you weren't coming."

"Yeah, yeah, I had to pack." I smiled at Loch. "Hello, Marcus."

He inclined his head. "Hello, Bianca."

When I got close, Ada pulled me into a hug, then held me out at arm's length. "You look terrible," she said bluntly.

"It's been a day. I'll tell you about it, but not right now. Do you have a transport?"

She nodded and slid my bag off my shoulder. I started to protest, but she handed it to Loch and whispered, "You don't want him to feel useless, do you?"

Loch grinned at me over her shoulder and I chuckled. Marcus Loch was a Genesis Project supersoldier; he wouldn't feel useless because I didn't let him carry my bag. But Ada's comment had drawn me into laughter and she smiled, pleased.

# CHAPTER 19

Ada and Loch entered the transport first and sat next to each other, leaving Ian and me to sit across from them. Ian was stiff and quiet next to me. Ada swiped her identity chip over the reader and set our destination.

"So, what happened?" she asked.

I gave her a very brief recap of what I'd learned from Riccardo.

"The Silvas might be bastards but no one can say they're not smart bastards," Ada said. "When their deal went wrong, they made Ferdinand someone else's problem and got paid for doing it." She shook her head in grudging respect. "MineCorp will kill Ferdinand if they find out who he is. How do we get him back?"

Ada intuitively understood something it had taken me time to figure out. She'd always excelled at understanding tactics and motivation. Father had made a grave mistake when he'd banished her.

"I have requests for information out, but I'm probably going to need physical access to MineCorp's network," I said, "so I need you to set up a meeting for me later today. I was thinking we'd spin it as me doing preliminary research on companies to mine one of my planets."

She nodded slowly. "That might work. Are you sure you want to go in as yourself?"

"Yes, I'll need the power of our name to get deep enough to do any good. Set the meeting as late as possible. Claim my need for privacy or whatever else you have to do."

"I will be accompanying Lady Bianca," Ian said, his voice hard.

Ada raised an eyebrow and pointedly looked at me. I sighed. "Ian will be accompanying me, Ada. Play nice."

She didn't have to fake her incredulous expression. "You threatened to *geld* Marcus with a *rusty fork*. You have no room to talk about playing nice."

Ian launched into a fit of coughing that sounded suspiciously like muffled laughter.

"That was different," I said. I pointed at Marcus and mouthed, *I'll still do it, too.* His eyes crinkled at the corners as if he, too, was suppressing a smile.

So much for all of my supposed power. Not that I thought the threat was needed any longer. It was clear that Marcus Loch was ridiculously in love with my sister, and she with him.

Envy nipped at my heart. I acknowledged the emotion, then set it aside. I *did* want what she had, but I'd never begrudge Ada her happiness. She deserved every happiness in the world.

Ian finally got his "coughing" under control and asked, "Why don't we break in after hours? No one will know we're looking for Ferdinand and you don't have to betray your location to Riccardo."

"Does anyone know how good their security is? I *might* be able to override their surveillance system given a few hours, but it's not without risk."

"Ada and I will check it out while you two rest," Loch said. I started to protest, but he cut me off. "You're dead on your feet. Resting for a few hours will do far more for Ferdinand than if you keep going and make a stupid mistake because you're tired."

He was right, of course, but I hated to admit it. Ada grinned at my grumbling, but her eyes were serious. "You left me out before. This is something I can do without any unnecessary risk. Let me help," she said, her voice pleading. "He's my brother, too."

I closed my eyes against the tears and nodded. While I'd always see her as my baby sister, Ada was fully capable of assessing a building's security without my help. And with Loch glued to her side, she wouldn't be in any danger.

"Riccardo said the kidnapping contract was anonymous, which I believe," I said, "but he thought it came from someone high in the Consortium. Can you think of anyone in particular who would benefit from Ferdinand's disappearance?"

Ada thought about it for a minute, then shook her head. "No. It might weaken our House slightly, but Hannah would just step up and no one has gone after her."

I bit my tongue. Hannah had asked me not to share the fact that she *wouldn't* be replacing Ferdinand. Instead, I said, "Catarina is looking into a potential leak in the House. Perhaps they are related and it's just someone with a grudge."

Ian glanced sharply at me. "How do you know about the leak?"

"Someone tipped off a photographer about Ferdinand's schedule on the day he was taken. How do *you* know about the leak?"

"It's my job," Ian said. He ran a frustrated hand through his hair. "We've been tracking down a high-level leak for months, but whoever it is, he or she is being very, very careful."

"So we find the leaker, figure out who they leaked to, and find the culprit?" Ada asked.

I didn't think it would be as easy as that, especially if Ian hadn't already plugged the leak, but I nodded anyway. I'd update Catarina with the new information and see if she could make any more progress.

As we edged into the heart of Sedition, wireless signals flew fast and furious. Breathing helped, but not enough. I gritted my teeth and tried mentally pulling back, but it was like trying to escape a whirlpool in a rowboat. By the time the transport landed behind an impressive four-story stone house situated on a lot with a yard, my dinner was nearly ready to make another appearance.

The tiny portion of my brain not occupied with keeping the contents of my stomach where they belonged tried to calculate the vast amount of money each house represented. Every centimeter of Sedition was precious. Towers soared all around, but this street had seemingly been untouched by the ever-expanding climb upward.

Ian helped me from the transport, then lightly clasped my arm and let Ada and Loch precede us. "Are you okay?" he murmured into my ear.

I glanced up at him in surprise—he'd noticed something was wrong. I gave him an honest answer. "My stomach is upset."

"Can I do anything?"

Warmth bloomed, but I shook my head. Getting in a silencer would help more than anything else.

"Let me know if that changes," he said.

I inclined my head in agreement and he escorted me into the House.

Inside, the signal noise dropped a little, held back by the thick stone walls, similar to House von Hasenberg. From what I could see, the interior was as luxurious as a House worth more than some small planets should be. Ada led us up two flights of stairs, to a hallway with doors on both sides.

"Rhys and Veronica are out, but they should be back by the time you're up. Rhys said to make yourself at home. Marcus and I are here," she indicated a door on the right, "but the rest of the rooms are available. Help yourself. If you need anything, request it from the suite computer and someone will bring it up."

I stepped across the hallway and opened the first door. A pretty room in buttercup yellow greeted me and I shrugged. It had a bed, so good enough.

"I need six hours," I said. I really needed more like eight, but six would have to do. "If you decide we should go the meeting route instead of breaking in, set it up and call me so I get up in time. Otherwise I'll see you in the morning. Evening. Whatever." I was too tired to deal with time zones right now.

I moved back to Ada and hugged her close. "Thank you. Be careful."

"You're welcome and I will be."

Ada let go and Loch handed me my bag. "I'll keep her out of trouble," he promised.

Ian moved down the hall and opened the door next to mine. "See you all in six hours," he said. He looked at Loch. "Let me know if you need help."

Loch inclined his head in agreement. Satisfied, Ian disappeared into his room.

I waved to Ada and Loch, then entered my room for the night and closed the door. I crossed to the bed and dug through my bag until I found the silencer. I clicked it on and moaned in relief. I still felt shaky, but now that I didn't have to fight the signals for focus, my stomach started to settle.

I put the silencer next to the bed then moved away until the signals came back. I sent Catarina a quick message, then set my com on a dresser outside the silence field. If Ada called, she would be able to get through. That done, I explored the suite.

My room had its own bathroom—a giant, luxurious affair—and a huge walk-in closet. The third door opened upon a view of Ian in a pair of boxer briefs and nothing else.

My brain stuttered to a stop. Tan skin, taut muscles, and a face so handsome, it seemed sculpted. He glanced at me and raised one eyebrow. When he turned my way, I couldn't help watching the beautiful play of muscles as he moved.

Until I realized he was moving closer and I was staring.

I squeaked, my face flamed in embarrassment, and I slammed the door closed with a shouted, "Sorry!"

Then I promptly banged my head on the door and cursed under my breath for acting like a teenager instead of a grown woman. What was it about him that turned my brain into a pile of stupid?

The door had no lock, so when Ian tried to open it from his side, I silently held the handle and prayed he'd give up. I was not so lucky. "Bianca, let go of the door." The thick door muffled his voice, but I could still hear him.

"Let me die in peace," I moaned under my breath.

Somehow, he heard me, and his voice turned amused. "I don't think embarrassment is terminal."

"It might be in this case," I muttered, but I let go of the handle.

He swung the door open and there he was, in all of his near-naked glory. And it *was* glorious, even better up close than it had been from across the room. I jerked my gaze up to his chin and kept it there. Chins were safe.

I cleared my throat and pulled my tattered dignity around me. "Did you need something, Director Bishop?"

"I would ask you the same, Lady Bianca. What was so urgent that you needed to barge into my room unannounced?" Despite staring resolutely at his chin, I could see the grin hovering around his mouth.

"What makes you think I knew it was your room?" I asked breezily. "I was merely checking the exits."

He stretched and muscles flexed in my peripheral vision. The grin bloomed, warm and tempting. I wondered how it would feel against my mouth. Soft and gentle or hard and demanding? I shivered and my nipples tightened as desire licked through my belly—and lower.

"Are you satisfied or did you need another look?" he asked.

The teasing challenge brought my eyes up to his. I gave him a coy smile. "I don't think a look will satisfy. I prefer a more hands-on approach."

His eyes darkened and he stepped closer. "As the lady prefers."

I hummed in appreciation, then touched one finger to his chest. He froze. Now that I had his skin under my hands, slight though the contact was, I had to fight to stay on course. I wanted to run my hands across his chest, to see if the muscle was as firm everywhere as it was under my finger. Instead, I pressed him backward two steps.

Then, with fierce reluctance, I pulled my hand away from temptation. I turned and caressed the edge of the door and the handle. "Everything seems to be in order," I murmured. I winked at him and pulled the door closed while he stood stock-still.

Safely on my side, I blew out a slow, silent breath. Holy hell. A playful Ian was an irresistible Ian.

When a maid knocked on the door a few minutes later with a pot of sweet, milky tea that I hadn't ordered, I knew exactly who it came from. If I wasn't careful, Ian Bishop would steal my heart.

And I just might let him.

MY ALARM TRIED TO DRAG ME FROM SLEEP BUT I FOUGHT the pull. I'd slept hard, but I could use another hour or two. The heavy drapes were closed, leaving the room dim. Putting my com on the dresser had seemed like a good idea at the time, but it meant that now I had to drag myself from bed to turn off the cursed beeping.

A knock on the door added to the racket. I pulled a pillow over my head and willed everything to be quiet. A few seconds later, my alarm stopped. I blinked in surprise at the blessed silence, but didn't question my good luck. Now I could go back to sleep.

"Your alarm has been going off for fifteen minutes," Ian said. "And you didn't respond to my knocks."

I pulled the pillow off my head and glared in his direction. "I was sleeping."

Ian moved closer and I could tell when he entered the silencer's circle because his steps paused. "Why are you sleeping with a silencer?"

I peered at him in the faint light. I could just make out his outline near the end of the bed. "Ian, why are you in my room?"

"When you didn't turn off your alarm or answer the door, I thought something might've happened. Instead, I find you sleeping in a silence field where you couldn't call for help even if you needed it. Why?"

I sighed and gave him one of my truths. "Sometimes I have nightmares. This way I don't bother anyone."

"No more silencers. I can't protect you if I can't hear you."

"Not your decision. Now go away so I can sleep." But even

as I spoke, I felt the last vestiges of sleep slipping away. I wouldn't be able to sleep even if he left, which he showed no sign of doing. I sat up and glared grumpily at him. "Fine, I'm awake. Happy now?"

"No, I'll be happy when you agree about the silencer."

"Then I've got bad news for you, friend." I tossed the covers back and slid out of bed. I had on a T-shirt and underwear, so I was decent enough.

Ian moved closer. He was dressed in a dark shirt and dark pants. I was barefoot, and he towered over me by nearly twenty centimeters. Softly, he asked, "Why do you have to fight me on everything?"

"Why do you assume you know what's best for me?" I responded without missing a beat. "Look, I know it's a security risk. Of course I do. I weighed the risks and decided it was worth it. I don't know why you always assume I do things on a whim without a thought to the consequences. I *always* think about the consequences."

"And last night? Did you think about the consequences then?"

I glanced away. "I don't play with fire without realizing I could get burned."

"And did you want to burn?" His voice whispered around me, a temptation in itself.

*Yes. Yes, yes, yes, a million times yes.* I'd promised him honesty, so I said nothing at all.

He touched my jaw, turning my face up to his. I could just make out his handsome features, but the darkness washed the color from his eyes. "Tell me," he urged, his voice low and delicious.

If I admitted it, then I gave him the power to hurt me. He'd already hurt me once, long ago. And while I hadn't expected a love match with Gregory, I'd expected mutual respect and admiration. I'd gotten neither, only more pain. I wanted to trust

Ian, to trust that he wouldn't hurt me again, to trust that he wouldn't turn out like my late husband, but fear stole the words.

"What are you doing, Ian?" I asked instead, my voice quiet.

He ran a thumb across my bottom lip and chuckled. "I'm trying to convince myself to leave before I kiss you."

I made a mental list of why kissing Ian would be a bad idea, but, for once, I ignored it. I *wanted* him to kiss me, consequences be damned. I might not be ready to trust him with my heart quite yet, but I absolutely trusted him with my body. Ian would never physically hurt me, never take more than I offered. I knew it down to my bones.

"Kiss me," I breathed.

He slid his hand into my hair and angled my head. His lips covered mine, warm and firm and divine. I slid my hands up his chest, one to his shoulder, one to the back of his head, and pressed upward, desperate to get closer. He groaned low and sucked my bottom lip into his mouth.

I opened with a moan and slid my tongue against his. My nipples tightened and my pulse raced, pushed by the lust blazing through my system. Ian skillfully explored my mouth with seemingly infinite patience while I wanted to rip his clothes off and ride him to bliss.

I pulled back with a gasp, aware that I was teetering on a dangerous precipice. Ian nuzzled his way down my jaw, nibbling and kissing. I let my head fall back into his hand, enjoying the feeling. I drew a mental line in the sand: I would allow this, but no further. Kisses might complicate our relationship, but sex had the potential to destroy it.

Thoughts sorted, I used the hand buried in Ian's hair to pull his mouth back to mine. He came willingly, scorching a trail up my jaw. His hand slipped under my shirt and headed north. I stopped him before he reached his destination, though my breasts ached to be touched. But I held on to my resolve by the slenderest of threads—if he caressed me, I'd be lost.

Ian respected the line I'd drawn. His hands didn't stray, but his mouth tempted me with every firm stroke of his tongue. By the time he pulled away to rest his forehead against mine, I was lightly panting and nearly ready to combust.

"I should go," he said reluctantly, his voice a low growl. His breath came in uneven rasps. I wasn't the only one affected, then.

"You should," I agreed. I played with the soft hair at the back of his head, unwilling to let him go. Once we broke out of this quiet, hidden bubble, the real world would be all too eager to reassert itself, along with all of my doubts and fears.

He kissed the corner of my mouth and straightened. "Get ready and I'll meet you downstairs for breakfast. It doesn't make sense for us to switch to local time if we're only going to be here for a day." He pulled away slowly, then turned and disappeared through the door connecting our rooms, closing it gently behind him.

I stared at the door for a long moment, half hoping he'd come back and finish what he started. My body still hummed. It would take so little to push me over the edge. I'd never reacted so strongly to a kiss before.

I foresaw an icy cold shower in my very near future.

AFTER GETTING READY, I PUT ON MY SMART GLASSES, set up my connection safeguards, and logged in to my safe house in HIVE. Outside the window, golden early morning light hadn't quite burned off the fog, turning the forest into an enchanting wonderland.

The forest was part of this virtual location, so I often wandered through the trees, but today I didn't have time for a leisurely stroll. I had two replies on the note board and one of them was from Tori Waugh. Based on the time stamp, I had just missed her.

Both replies said essentially the same thing: MineCorp did not play when it came to network security. As expected, they had an entire department dedicated to locking down their systems. A remote hack was unlikely to succeed.

Tori's note went into further detail. She wasn't in the security department, but she knew her way around a network and had been doing a little snooping of her own. She said that a few old-timers preferred to use an older, less secure piece of software that left ports open on the systems. The sysadmins had been trying to crack down on it, but the people who used it were in upper management and they did as they pleased.

I murmured a little prayer of thanks for users who remained set in their ways. They made my job so much easier.

The ports weren't open from the outside, but if I could get physical access to the network, I could use a cracking script to get in. She even offered a few that might be useful. She warned that the sysadmins were good, so even if I got in, I wouldn't have much time before they caught me.

I saved the scripts, then wrote Tori an effusive note of thanks and attached enough credits to it that she and her wife could have a very nice dinner out. Unlike my other contacts, credits weren't required here, we just helped each other out when we could, but Tori had gone far above and beyond what I had expected.

I carefully left the safe house and logged out of HIVE. I rounded up a few more scripts that might get me into Mine-Corp's systems, then shut down my com and took off my smart glasses.

Now it was time to face Ian for the first time since our scorching kiss. Despite giving myself a stern pep talk about acting normal, my pulse fluttered as I made my way down to the dining room. The public areas of Rhys's house were opulent bordering on ostentatious. Rhys hadn't struck me as the type for conspicuous consumerism, so I wondered why his house was an altar to excess.

In the foyer, a stately gray-haired butler directed me to the formal dining room. An ornately carved table with seats for fourteen dominated the space. The glittering crystal chandelier fought for equal attention. I would've preferred a smaller breakfast room, but I suppose with local time being evening, that wasn't an option. I felt severely underdressed in my T-shirt and cargo pants.

Place settings for six were laid out in the middle of the table. Ian sat at the near end with a cup of coffee. He was dressed much the same as me, to my relief, but his expression was guarded.

"Is there tea?" I asked. I'd only been out of the silencer field for a few minutes, but I could already tell that the crush of signals would be a test. If I was lucky, I'd end the night functional but with a splitting headache.

Ian waved me to the chair on his left. While I sat, he poured me a cup of tea and added milk and sugar. After last night, it shouldn't have surprised me that he knew how I liked my tea, but the small kindness still warmed my heart.

He handed me the cup, and I took a fortifying sip. Desperate to break the awkward silence, I said, "Ada sent me a message to let me know she's on her way back. She and Loch should be here soon."

Ian nodded, still frustratingly silent. Finally, he said, "I apologize for earlier."

Humiliation heated my face. If he was about to give me a new version of the "empty-headed princess" speech, I didn't want to hear it. "There is nothing to apologize for. If you regret it, fine. We'll put it in the cabinet of things to never mention. But we were both consenting adults."

"I shouldn't have touched you," Ian said, his voice cool. "It won't happen again."

Pain squeezed my heart. He'd rejected me *again*. It seemed I would never learn where Ian was concerned. I tried to match his coolness, with only partial success. "Then why did you kiss me in the first place?"

He sighed and it sounded like it came from the bottom of his soul. "I was being selfish."

Hurt morphed into confusion. That wasn't the answer I'd expected. "What?"

"There's no future for us. I know that, but I couldn't resist. It's a lapse that won't happen again. I refuse to use you for selfish reasons."

There was an entire universe of things that needed unpacking there, but before I could attempt it, Ada called from the foyer, "Bianca, I'm home!"

"In the dining room!" I shouted back. Just because I'd had a decorum tutor didn't mean I had to follow her advice. I glanced at Ian. "This conversation isn't done," I whispered.

His mouth firmed into a straight line, but he nodded.

Ada entered wearing a sunny, colorful dress and a bright smile. Loch followed, dressed in his usual dark shirt and pants. "We found a way in, no meeting required," she said. She peered at me. "You look better; you've got some color in your cheeks, at least."

I very carefully did not look at Ian. "Sleep will do that," I murmured. "Tell me about the security."

"Let's wait for Rhys and Veronica. They're just a few minutes behind us and they may have suggestions. What's for dinner?"

I shrugged, but Ian said, "Prime rib. I think I mortally of-fended your chef when I requested that some breakfast items be added."

Ada winced. "Mrs. Willis takes her job seriously. She's prob-ably making a whole second meal. I'll see if I can head her off."

Ada dashed off and Loch slid into the open chair on my left. The air in the room changed, but neither Ian nor Loch gave away a hint of what they were thinking.

"Thank you for your help," I told Loch. "I know you did it for Ada, but I appreciate it, too."

He frowned and his eyes flickered my way. They caught the light and reflected silver for a fraction of a second. "Why do you think I wouldn't help you?" he asked, his voice low and gravelly. It's too bad he didn't talk much because I found his voice soothing.

"Ah, well." I scrambled for an explanation that didn't give everything away, just in case I was wrong about Ian. "I did threaten you with a rusty utensil."

"In defense of Ada, who you helped for years. You also helped me. Of course I will do the same for you." His gaze moved to Ian. "With *any* problems you're having." The threat was subtle but clear.

Ian bristled. "She doesn't need your help."

Loch grinned. "That's for the lady to decide."

I bumped my shoulder into Loch's. "Thank you," I said softly.

"You're welcome."

# CHAPTER 20

When Rhys and Veronica arrived, they hugged me like family and politely greeted Ian, making it clear whose side they were on. Veronica invited me to sit next to her, while Ada sat across from me with Loch next to her. It put Ian as far as possible from me, hemmed in by Loch beside him and Rhys across from him. It was some effortless, next-level hostessing, and I smiled into my tea.

Ada had not been joking about Mrs. Willis. The lady had outdone herself, serving up both breakfast and dinner. I wasn't particularly hungry, but after six hours in a silence field, I felt okay, so I filled my plate with fruit and yogurt and a tiny slice of prime rib. I knew I couldn't overdo it because I would feel worse and worse as the day went on.

"What did you find at MineCorp?" I asked Ada.

"Their office is on the ground floor, which is nice, but they're in a Rockhurst building, which isn't," she said.

Getting caught breaking into a Rockhurst building would make me a prisoner of war, never mind that I wasn't there for Rockhurst in the first place. Ada hadn't lost her art of understatement.

She continued, "Loch and I found a few potential entry points. The four of us should be able to slip in, no problem."

"Ada," I started.

She slashed her hand through the air. "No. If I didn't think we'd need your expertise for the system cracking, it would be done already. But if I can be patient, you can let us help."

"How is the building security?" Ian asked.

"Pretty standard for a nice office building: chipped doors, cameras, and at least one guard on patrol," Ada said. "Most of the surveillance is focused on the fancy glass front of the building. There's a maintenance entrance in the alley behind that's barely covered. Entrance through the ventilation system also seems doable, but a little more difficult."

I'd crawled through ventilation ducts before and I wasn't super eager to repeat the experience. A good codebreaker could get us through the door, but we still had to deal with the cameras. Without access to the system, physically disabling them would be easiest, but also the most suspicious.

"Thanks to Rhys, I got a copy of the building's blueprint. The servers are two stories underground, so that would be tricky. But if you just need access to a terminal, the executive vice president's office is on the corner of the third floor. Directly under a maintenance crawl space."

"Who owns the fourth floor?" Ian asked.

Ada grinned at him. "A hotel. And I've booked a fourth-floor suite for the night."

VERONICA HAD DISAPPEARED UPSTAIRS AFTER DINNER but Rhys had let us raid his warehouse for supplies. We'd loaded everything into suitcases and, to maintain the illusion, I'd donned the dark gold dress I'd bought in Honorius. Ada had loaned me a luxurious hooded cloak and a scarf to hide my face.

Now the obsequious hotel manager was showing us to our suite and trying to sneak peeks at Ada and me. Ian and Loch kept blocking him, but the man was persistent.

"Can I help you?" I asked in my frostiest tone.

"No, madam, I'm just so honored you have decided to stay at our hotel. I've personally ensured that the suite is prepared for your arrival."

"Then your assistance is no longer required," Ian interjected smoothly. The manager stammered out an excuse, but Ian was having none of it. Ian sent him packing and we made our way down the hallway on our own. Ada swiped us into the suite. We each took a room and scanned it for trackers and bugs.

Loch found three in the bedroom, I found one in the bathroom, and Ada and Ian each found two throughout the rest of the suite. In order to secure the suite she'd wanted, Ada had used her own name. The bugs could be innocuous or someone could be interested in Ada specifically. We wouldn't know until we examined them.

For now, though, we had a narrow window of time to get in position. The motion sensors in the MineCorp offices would be turned off while the cleaning crew worked. Working at the same time as the cleaning crew carried its own risk, but it meant I didn't have to spend time overriding the security system.

Ada and I commandeered one of the bedrooms to change into T-shirts, pants, and boots. "Are you sure I can't persuade you to wait here?" I asked.

She rolled her eyes and shot me an annoyed look. "I'm sure," she huffed.

I nudged her shoulder. "You're my little sister. I don't doubt your skills; I'm just trying to keep you safe."

She turned to me, her eyes solemn. "And who will keep *you* safe?" she asked softly.

I purposefully misunderstood. "I imagine Ian is going to be glued to my ass," I said. "You don't need to worry about me."

"So, you and Ian, huh?" she asked with an impish grin. "I thought you said he wasn't interested?"

I bit down on the instinctive denial. This morning's kiss hadn't felt uninterested, but then he'd gone and ruined it by apologizing. I didn't know where we stood, only that we needed to talk.

"He wasn't, but now I don't know. He kissed me this morning, then apologized and said it wouldn't happen again."

It was harder than I expected to open up to Ada. Before my marriage and her escape, she'd been my closest sibling. But I'd been keeping secrets for so long that I almost didn't remember how to share pieces of myself.

"He kissed you?" she hissed excitedly. "Why didn't you lead with that? How was it?"

Heat suffused my cheeks. She took one look at my face and dissolved into quiet laughter. "That good, huh?"

I also had forgotten the pure joy of laughing with my sister. Ada would always, *always* be on my side. So I gave her an honest answer because I could use her advice. "It was incredible. But then he ruined it by calling it 'a lapse' and apologizing."

"Are you *sure* he wasn't interested before?" she asked gently.

"When he first became my bodyguard, I expressed interest. He called me an 'empty-headed princess' and said in no uncertain terms that he wouldn't let me derail his career."

Ada winced then scowled toward the door. "Can I kick his ass now?"

Emotion overwhelmed me and I pulled her into a hug. She silently hugged me back. Ada had always been good at knowing what I needed, and after years of Gregory's callous disregard, I was starved for simple physical affection. When I let her go, she said, "I'm glad you're here, Bee. Now tell me why you won't let me kick his ass."

I smiled at her tenaciousness, but the smile died when I returned to the subject at hand. "I think he had a reason to dislike me."

When I didn't continue, Ada prompted, "Why do you think so?"

"I have no proof, but I think he's a member of the Genesis Project. You know how the Consortium treated them." It felt strange to say it out loud, even to my closest sister, the one I'd helped find data on the Genesis Project in the first place.

Ada didn't scoff. She tilted her head, considering. "Loch hasn't said anything," she said at last. "But I could see it. Have you asked him?"

"Not in so many words."

"Loch didn't tell me until we decided to give a relationship a shot. Give Ian time. It can't be an easy thing to reveal."

"I don't have the best track record with relationships."

"And you think I did, before I met Loch? Remember my first season?"

It seemed that all of the von Hasenberg women were destined to have disastrous first seasons. Ada had been lucky, in the end, but it had killed me to watch her heart break.

"When you're ready to talk about what happened while you were with Gregory, I'm here," she said.

I flinched and wavered. Ada could read me better than anyone else. Of course she'd noticed that something had happened. Would it be so bad to tell her?

Before I made up my mind, she continued, "But don't let Gregory's ghost ruin the rest of your life. I'm biased against Ian because of the last two years, but even I can see that he's a good man. I think you should give him a chance. Kick his ass for being an idiot if you need to, but give him a chance. You may not see how he watches you, but I do. You're not just a job for him. I saw it when we were in Serenity."

"He has a funny way of showing it," I complained.

"Let me guess, he's trying to protect you and you're making it difficult for him." She grinned at my incredulous expression. "Don't look at me like that, I'm not taking his side. I'm just pointing out that both of you could be looking at the same situation and seeing different things. Loch and I bang heads occasionally because we each want to protect the other."

Hope bloomed, as fragile as spun glass. I warned my heart against it, but it was no use. It had sprouted roots and clung tenaciously. Ian truly did have the power to hurt me now. I half hoped he never found out.

**LOCH AND IAN WERE STARING AT THE BLUEPRINT AND** speaking quietly when we joined them. "Changing the strategy?" I asked.

"No, just checking the exits," Ian said with a knowing grin.

My cheeks heated, but I refused to rise to the teasing. "So we're still going through the housekeeping closet?"

Ada had failed to mention that the hotel didn't have direct access to the maintenance areas. From the suite, we'd have to go through the floor, which would be difficult to hide. But the housekeeping closet next door backed to the metal sheeting surrounding the crawl space. It should be fairly easy to cut a hole, then tack the cut piece back in place after we were done. By the time it was discovered, we'd hopefully be long gone.

"Yes," Ian said. "Loch and Ada will cut the hole while you and I serve as lookouts and a distraction if needed. Once we're in the office, the roles will reverse. You'll have approximately twenty minutes to find what you're looking for."

I would need every one of those twenty minutes.

"In case things go wrong, the northwest stairs lead to the building's ground-floor service entrance. That's the primary means of quick escape, but the main stairs, maintenance crawl space, and elevators can be used if needed. Be prepared for resistance, but try not to kill anyone."

We nodded and geared up in silence. I had my main com, two secondary coms, various connection cables and transmitters, a small tool pouch, a pair of stun pistols, a codebreaker, and my smart glasses. I touched everything a second time to make sure I hadn't forgotten anything.

We all had transmitters and earpieces in addition to our smart glasses. We tested the communications before Ada and Loch left the room. Thirty seconds later Ada murmured, "We're in and the hallway is clear. No surveillance in here. Cameras are planted."

I used my smart glasses to pull up the video from the tiny cameras Ada had attached to either side of the housekeeping closet door. The first video showed the empty hallway. The second video showed Loch sprawled under a shelving unit, cutting a hole in the back panel with a portable plasma cutter. Various buckets and bottles of cleaning supplies had been pulled out to make room for him.

"I have eyes on you," I said.

It seemed to take forever but eventually Loch disappeared from view. "I'm through," he said. "There's a two-meter drop when you come through. Ladies, I'll lift you down, so don't try to stab me when I grab you."

Ada chuckled. "You deserved it, you jerk," she said without heat. I wondered at the story behind the gentle ribbing. Ada hadn't revealed much of what had happened when she and Loch first met, but I doubted it had been an easy meeting.

Ada quickly replaced the supplies under the shelf, pushing

everything to the sides. She crawled through the opening in the middle. She disappeared, then squeaked and laughed. "If you grab Bianca like that, I'm pretty sure Ian will remove your arms," she warned.

"I don't need Ian to fight my battles for me," I said drily. "I'm perfectly capable of removing Loch's arms on my own, so keep it appropriate, buddy." I checked the hallway video. "The hallway is clear. We're on our way."

Ian and I didn't encounter anyone on our way to the supply closet. "With the drop on the other side, I will go first," Ian said, "and hold you up while you reorganize the supplies."

Loch's quiet laughter rang through the earpiece but he didn't say anything.

Ian shimmied under the shelves. I heard the faintest ring of boots on metal as he landed. "Okay, Bianca, come through feetfirst on your belly," he said. "I'll grab your legs."

Loch had cut the panel at the floor so I didn't have to worry about a sharp edge digging into my skin, but easing my feet into a black hole while under a shelf wasn't exactly the most fun I'd ever had.

Strong hands gripped my ankles. "I've got you," Ian said. "Come back as far as you need."

I slid my lower body farther into darkness, trusting Ian to hold me up. Working quickly, I spread out the supplies so there wasn't an obvious empty space that someone might wonder about.

Movement in the hallway video caught my attention. "We've got potential incoming," I said. "Where is the panel?"

"It's folded up on this side. Get clear and I'll get it," Loch said.

I pushed myself backward into the hole and for a brief, dizzying moment, I thought Ian would drop me before one of his arms moved up and pulled me down to sit on his shoulder.

I gripped his head for balance, burying my fingers in his

hair. A blink later, my smart glasses adjusted to the dark and I could see Loch taping the panel into place.

He hopped down from the railing he'd been balanced on and started to say something.

"Quiet," I whispered as the supply-closet door opened. The hotel manager who had been bothering us earlier stepped inside and glanced around before moving to the wall on his right—the wall that was shared with our suite.

"You just *had* to sweep the suite, didn't you, you little bitch?" the man grumbled to himself. "Well, let's see if your fancy trackers can find this, hmm?"

He crouched down next to the shelves and peeled back a piece of tape that had been painted the same color as the wall. Whatever it was, it was just slightly out of frame, but when he pressed his face to the wall, I had a pretty good idea. The bastard had a spy hole into the primary bedroom. Ada and I had changed in that room.

He took something out of his pocket, aligned it just so, then carefully reapplied the tape. Unless you knew what to look for, you wouldn't notice anything wrong with the wall. Fifty credits said he'd just planted another camera or bug.

My fingers tightened in Ian's hair. If Ferdinand's life wasn't on the line, I'd climb back up there and give that asshole what he deserved—a solid ass-kicking.

"Hold on," Ian whispered. He moved down the walkway, his own smart glasses allowing him to see without light. Ada and Loch followed, silent as ghosts.

When the ceiling dropped, turning our walkway into a crawl space, Ian gripped me under my arms, lifted me off his shoulder, and then slowly lowered me to the ground. I tried not to think about exactly how much strength that move had required or I wouldn't be able to focus on the mission.

"Was that pervert trying to spy on us?" Ada asked in a furious whisper.

"Seems like it," I said.

Ian and Loch shared a glance that could only be called murderous. The manager was lucky we were busy or he might not have survived the night with all of his bones intact.

For once my height worked in my favor. The crawl space was just tall enough that I could walk crouched down, but Ada, Loch, and Ian actually had to crawl on their hands and knees.

Moving slowly and quietly, it took us a few minutes to reach the corner of the building. I took a deep breath and reached out for the messages swirling through the air. Pain spiked, but I didn't see anything from building security in my brief scan.

Ada flattened herself to the walkway and eased a tiny camera between the plastech ceiling tiles. The video came up on our smart glasses, and as one, we froze.

The overhead lights were off, but the office below us was not empty.

A blond woman lay half on the desk with her demure ivory skirt hiked up to her hips. Her legs were over the shoulders of a kneeling, dark-haired woman who had her face buried between the blonde's thighs. The blonde gave the brunette's hair a demanding yank and we could hear her groan straight through the ceiling tiles.

I barely dared breathe. The blonde was Carly Vignette, Mine-Corp's executive vice president on Sedition. I didn't know who the other woman was, but she clearly wasn't Mrs. Vignette's husband.

"Do we have any sedative?" I asked in the quietest whisper I could manage.

"No," Ian said, his voice equally soft. "Don't even think about it."

"With her access, I'll be done in five minutes."

"As soon as she signals distress, security will be here in two," he argued.

"So you'll have to keep her from doing that," I said.

"And then, as soon as we leave, she'll order Ferdinand killed."

He was right, dammit. We could probably stun her before she saw us, but the risk was too high when I could get into the system on my own. I cast one last, longing look at her arm. She was too far away to clone her identity chip, even if I had brought the appropriate equipment, which I hadn't.

I captured twenty seconds of video, just in case I needed leverage later, then turned to Ian. "Do you have a Plan B location in mind or do you want me to decide?"

From what I could recall of the blueprints, other than the vice president's office, this floor was almost entirely open. If we were lucky they had built freestanding cubicles, but based on how tonight was going, I wasn't counting on it.

Ian led us back the way we had come. Ada left the camera, allowing us to keep an eye on our after-hours complication. At least their presence meant the motion sensors were likely already disabled.

We worked our way back to the middle of the building. "Let's see what we're dealing with," Ian whispered.

"This is the last camera," Ada warned. She once again slipped the tiny device between the plastech ceiling tiles.

I groaned as the video appeared. A sea of open desks stretched from the vice president's office to the far wall. There wasn't a single handy cubicle in sight. As soon as I brought up one of those terminals, I'd be visible from the entire floor. The desks had half-height privacy panels underneath. I would be partially hidden if I stayed on the floor, but if anyone got down low enough, they'd spot me immediately.

The only good news was that the motion sensors were indeed turned off and I didn't see any obvious signs of video surveillance. It was technically doable, but I wasn't sure if it was actually less risky than breaking in on Mrs. Vignette and her lover.

"Do you think they're going to stay busy for the next twenty minutes?" I asked.

"Hard to say, but we'll have a little bit of warning before they appear. It should be enough for you to hide."

"Okay, let's go. Far corner. Ada and Loch, you two are on lookout. Let me know if anyone comes up the stairs or elevator, or if the ladies decide they're finished. I won't have enough brain power to watch the video while I'm working, so keep an eye on it for me."

Loch grinned and Ada smacked him playfully on the shoulder. "I've got the video," she said. "You watch the stairs."

"Ian, once I'm done, I'll need your help up," I said. There was a time when I could do pull-ups with the best of them, but that was long past. Once I dropped down into the office, I'd be stuck without help.

"I'm going with you," he said.

I didn't even try to argue. I wouldn't win and it would just waste time. "Can you get us closer to the corner before we drop down?"

Ian nodded and started down a new crawl space. I waved at Ada and Loch, then followed him. The path didn't make it all the way to the corner, but it got us to the far wall.

Ian said, "I'm dropping in."

Loch grunted his assent. "Stairway is clear."

"Ladies are still busy," Ada said.

Ian lay on his stomach and pulled up one of the square,

meter-wide plastech ceiling tiles from the wall side of the crawl space. He slid it over the tile next to it. The metal grating of the crawl space walkway hung over the opening by about a centimeter. Ian leaned down and peeked at the office. His head appeared on the video from Ada's camera.

He must've been happy with what he saw because he gripped the walkway and slid into the opening head first. Before I could ask him what in the world he was doing, his legs came up and he pulled his upper body parallel to the ceiling. In a ridiculous show of both arm and core strength, his legs dropped down as he lowered his hips, until he hung straight down from the walkway.

He dropped lightly to the ground and grinned up at me. "Your turn."

"Show-off," I grumbled.

My descent was far less impressive, but I made it to the ground without breaking anything. Ian pulled the ceiling tile back into place while I set a timer for twenty minutes. The time counted down in the corner of my smart glasses. I needed to make these minutes count.

I chose the desk in the corner. A hand wave brought up the display and the embedded keyboard in the desk lit up. I turned the display brightness all the way down, but it was still bright as hell in the dark office.

"Do you have to use that?" Ian asked.

"It'll be faster if I can get in."

Users logged in to these terminals with their identity chips but that didn't mean there weren't other ways in. Chip readers failed and system administrators couldn't always replace them immediately.

I brought up the admin log-in page and tried the most

common options. All failed. Of course this had to be the one company with competent sysadmins. Tori had warned me, but I'd held out hope that maybe she was wrong.

She wasn't.

I waved away the display and plugged one of my secondary coms into the diagnostic port underneath the desktop. Time to break out the big guns.

If the sysadmins were good, and I had every reason to believe they were, then trying to brute-force the admin password would set off all sorts of internal alarms. The terminal would automatically be quarantined and someone would alert security to physically check out what was happening.

But even well-run networks had to contend with users, and users didn't care about security, they just wanted their stuff to work. By using the diagnostic port, I could access the internal network from my com. And according to Tori, those same users would be my ticket in.

I kicked off two scripts. The first looked for vulnerable services that would give me access to a terminal. I didn't *need* a terminal to access my brother's information, but leaving myself a back door so I could check again later from outside the office was worth the search. The second script looked for servers with open ports.

The secondary com wasn't connected to my smart glasses, so I set it on the desk and used the projected keyboard to dive into the data. The world fell away as I finessed my way deeper into the network.

My first script found a trio of vulnerable terminals, so I kicked off a cracking script that would set up a remote back door in each of them. It was my own creation, designed to work around virus scanners.

I scoured fileservers and databases for any mention of

Nando Black, the name Ferdinand had been sold under. I'd made it more than halfway through the list before I finally got a hit. I copied the file to my com and opened it. It was a spreadsheet of transactions. It showed that Ferdinand had indeed been sold to MineCorp, but not where he ended up.

We were on the right track.

I pushed the smart glasses up my nose and kept going. You didn't run a huge company without a list of assets. Ferdinand's location was buried somewhere in this data, I just had to find it.

"Fuck, elevator incoming. Twenty seconds," Loch whispered.

I was so deep in the data that it took Ian shaking my shoulder for me to process the words. "You go, I have to stay," I whispered. I picked up the com and dove under the desk, being careful with the connection to the diagnostic port. I lowered the brightness on the screen until it barely emitted any light.

Ian cursed and followed me. The desk was two meters long by a meter wide, but we were both crammed as far back as we could get, which made the space feel smaller. The chair and half-height panels seemed very flimsy cover from this angle.

A man wearing an expensive suit and carrying flowers and a bottle of wine appeared on Ada's video. He walked with purpose and didn't so much as glance our way.

"Oh shit, that's the husband," Ada breathed. "Do you think he's invited?"

I checked the video from the office. The two women did not look like they were expecting company. The door eased open, and the man entered with a smile that promptly died. "What the fuck, Carly?" he roared. I had the video muted but he was loud enough that I heard him through the wall.

"Let me know if we're going to have to move. I'm close to finding Ferdinand," I said.

The cable wasn't long enough to reach from the plug under

the desk to the floor, so I couldn't set the com down and use the projected keyboard. Rather than use the on-screen keyboard, I connected the secondary com to my smart glasses. It pushed my primary com's display into the background, but with Ian next to me, that shouldn't be a problem.

I was well over my twenty-minute deadline by the time I found the information I was looking for. Three days ago, just a day after he was grabbed, Nando Black had been "acquired" on a space station in the sparsely populated Toucana Dwarf sector. He was listed as physically healthy but mentally unstable. He was also listed as mute. Dread curled into my stomach and made itself at home.

I scanned the files, looking for his location. He'd been tagged as a flight risk, which meant they would send him to the most dangerous, most isolated site they could find.

When I found the information, my heart stopped. I checked the file again, but the value hadn't changed. MineCorp had sent my brother, the von Hasenberg heir, to a Rockhurst planet in the disputed Antlia sector—while we were at war.

# CHAPTER 21

I quickly scanned the news feeds but I didn't see any notice about Ferdinand's capture. Would Rockhurst keep it silent if they'd found him? It could go either way, but it was more likely that they'd crow about it as a major victory.

The MineCorp records put him on Xi Antliae Dwarf Seven, the planet next door, cosmically speaking, to XAD Six where Ada had infiltrated the Rockhurst base and found they were actively mining and processing alcubium—right before Richard had captured her.

The XAD solar system was the heart of the Rockhurst stronghold in the sector. House von Hasenberg forces were concentrating around our planets, mostly in the Nu Antliae Dwarf system. Same sector, but they were so far apart it required a jump to move between them.

I pulled files to my com, taking more than I needed to hide my true intent. I also scooped up everything I could find about transport times and asset relocation.

"Something is happening," Ada whispered furiously. "The VP's com went off and she's looking your way as if she's trying to see through the wall. Time to move. Now!"

I kicked off a script to hide my tracks and unplugged the com. Ian pulled me out from under the desk and crouched down in front of me. "Climb on my back," he said.

I wrapped my arms around his shoulders and my legs around his waist. He stood and quickly moved beneath the ceiling panel we'd come down through. "Hold on," he warned.

I tightened my grip as he leapt straight up. He popped up the ceiling panel with his left hand while his right clamped on the metal grating of the maintenance walkway. We hung in place while he slid the panel out of the way, then he used both arms to pull us up into the crawl space.

He'd just done a pull-up while I was clinging to his back like dead weight and he'd made it look and feel effortless. He wasn't even breathing hard. I slid off him, pretty sure *I* was breathing harder than he was.

Ian quietly laid the panel back into place. I brought up my primary com's display in time to see Mrs. Vignette slam out of her office and march our way. The video from Ada's camera didn't give me a good enough angle to see if I'd left any evidence behind.

I held my breath when she stopped at the very desk I'd been using. Apparently their sysadmins were even better than I'd thought. She peeked underneath, then brought up the display. "There's nothing here," she said, her voice cold. "You interrupted me in the middle of an important meeting for no reason."

She listened silently for a few seconds before obviously speaking over whoever was on the other end of the call. "If you think someone is here, you're welcome to come in and check. In fact, I insist. Have a report on my desk by seven."

She ended the call, glanced around once more, then stalked back toward her office, where her husband and her lover were still arguing. I didn't move until the office door closed behind her.

Ian eased past me and motioned for me to follow him. We met Loch and Ada in the main part of the maintenance crawl space where we could all stand.

"Do they have him?" Ada asked softly. "Did you find him?"

"They have him, assuming Riccardo wasn't lying about his identity."

"Where is he?" she demanded.

"Let's discuss it once we're safe," I hedged. I didn't want to lie to her, but I didn't want to tell her the truth, either.

Her mouth flattened, but she nodded grudgingly.

We went out the way we'd come in. In the supply closet, Loch ripped the hotel manager's camera out of the wall and crushed it beneath his heel. He picked up the pieces and handed them to Ada. Her smile was malicious.

Ada opened our room door and by silent agreement, we didn't speak. We didn't know if more bugs had been planted while we were gone. Ada and I changed back into our fancy clothes—after quickly scanning the bedroom. We packed everything back into the suitcases, I covered my face, and we left.

"I'm going to rain holy hell on them about this," Ada said, holding up the camera Loch had smashed. "While I'm causing a scene, you two go ahead. We'll meet back at the House. It looked like MineCorp might've been on to you, so it'll be less suspicious if we're leaving because the room is bugged than if we left for no reason."

When we entered the lobby, Ada's expression transformed into an exact copy of Mother's when she was on the warpath. It was terrifying, and I wasn't the only one who thought so. Customers and employees tripped over themselves to get out of her way, especially with Loch's looming form following her like a scowling thundercloud.

Ian and I slipped through the lobby and out the front door

in the wake of hurricane Ada. We turned right, walking away from MineCorp. At the next transport pickup, we ducked into the waiting vehicle. I swiped my identity chip over the reader and directed the transport to circle Rhys's block.

Ian raised an eyebrow. "We're not going back?"

"I haven't decided," I said, smoothing a hand over the gold fabric of my dress.

"Exactly how bad is it?" he asked. I stared at him for long enough that he frowned and said, "We have a deal."

"I'm not sure our deal is going to survive," I told him honestly. "You're going to break your word and I will never forgive you."

Now it was Ian's turn to stare. "Fuck. He's in Antlia. Tell me I'm wrong."

I sighed and deflated against the seat. My head hurt, my heart hurt, and I was a breath away from betraying my sister in an effort to keep her safe. "He's in Antlia," I confirmed.

"Is he on XAD Six?"

"Are you going to leave me behind if I tell you?"

Ian leaned forward and met my eyes. "I will not break my word. But I will strongly discourage you from going. One von Hasenberg in Rockhurst territory is bad enough. Two is a disaster."

"You can discourage all you want. I'm going. You promised and you need my help." I trusted Ian, but I didn't trust him quite far enough to tell him about my modified nanos. I couldn't tell him that I would be invaluable if we were caught because I could listen in on the enemy.

Ian nodded, his face set in grim lines. "Your skills would be useful," he admitted. "But if you go, Ada *must* remain here. We can't give House Rockhurst the ability to knock out half of House von Hasenberg in one fell swoop."

"I agree. Ada can't go, as much as she's going to want to. If Ferdinand or I am caught, Father will likely negotiate for us. Ada was banished. Albrecht will write her off."

Father had started dropping hints that he would like me to find and disable Ada's death file—the documents that would automatically be released upon her untimely demise. She'd bought hers and Loch's freedom with a bluff about the amount of information she had on the Genesis Project. If Father knew exactly how thin the contents of those files really were, Ada would have an "accident" in her near future.

"Will she stay if you tell her to?"

I laughed. "Have you *met* Ada?"

The transport landed on Rhys's street and I changed the destination to his house. If nothing else, I needed to grab the silencer. It could come in handy in a variety of situations and I wasn't sure Ian had another one.

"Are we waiting for Loch and Ada or are we grabbing our stuff and getting out?" Ian asked.

I rubbed my eyes. Ada would forgive me. Eventually. Maybe. As long as I didn't die. "Pack fast," I said. I told the transport to wait for us.

The butler opened the door before I could knock. "Welcome back."

"Thank you, ah, sir," I said, drawing back the hood of my cloak. I'm pretty sure we'd been introduced at some point, but I couldn't remember his name. My memory was worse when I was tired.

A child's happy shriek drew my attention to the hallway that led to the family drawing room. The butler subtly moved in front of me. "If you would like to freshen up in your rooms, I will let Mr. Sebastian know you are here."

Well, that was about as subtle as a rogue freighter. Curiosity rose, but I shoved it aside. I had other things to worry about right now. "We will do that, thanks," I said.

Ian insisted on carrying my suitcase upstairs. I let him. He dropped it on my bed then crossed to the door to his room. "I'll be ready in three," he said.

I didn't take the time to change, I just shoved the few things I'd unpacked into the bag I'd brought with me from *Fortuitous*. I was ready by the time Ian reappeared carrying a small bag.

He picked up my suitcase. "Are you sure I can't change your mind?"

"I'm sure." I opened the door and came face-to-face with Rhys, who had his hand raised to knock.

"Going somewhere?" he asked mildly.

Ian stepped up behind me, but I held on to the door so he couldn't go around me. "Yes," I said.

Rhys didn't move. "Does Ada know?"

"No, and I'd like to keep it that way."

"Why?"

I tilted my head and studied Rhys. Ada trusted him, and he'd always treated me fairly, so I decided to give him the truth. "Because Ferdinand is in the Antlia sector and going there would be far more dangerous for Ada than for me."

Rhys grinned. "She's going to kill you when you get back." His grin faded. "Make sure you come back. Do you need a ship?"

*Fortuitous* couldn't jump for two days, and although *Aurora* should've arrived, it would be in cooldown, too. We needed a new ship. "I don't want to put you in an awkward spot with Ada," I hedged.

"I have a ship," Ian said. I glanced at him in surprise, but he didn't elaborate.

Rhys inclined his head and moved aside. "Should I tell Ada where you're going?"

"I will message her once we're in the air," I said. "When we have a solid plan, I'll send the details on a twelve-hour delay. Whatever happens, you can't let her come to Antlia. Find a merc crew or send one of your crews, I'll pay for whatever it costs, but Ada must stay safe."

Rhys drew me into a brotherly hug. "You know she loves you just as much as you love her, right? What would you do if Ada was imprisoned on a Rockhurst planet in the middle of a war?" He pulled back and grinned at me. "Don't let anything happen to you."

"I'll do my best," I said. "Thank you for the hospitality."

"Come back when things aren't so dire," he said. "Ada misses you."

Shame slid through my system. I hadn't visited because I wasn't sure I *could* visit without exposing how sick I became when the signals overloaded my brain. But my sister had been banished and I hadn't bothered to check on her in her new home. That was not the kind of person I wanted to be.

"Thank you, I will," I promised. Then I tacked on, "Assuming Father lets me out of the House after this."

IAN DIRECTED THE TRANSPORT TO A DIFFERENT LOCA-tion from where we'd left *Fortuitous*. The brightly lit city sparkled like a jewel under the dark sky. I was still on Universal Time, and I had trouble when the light didn't match my body clock. It was morning Universal, but it certainly didn't feel like it.

The wireless signals pressed against my skull. Tired and hurting, I took a deep breath and mentally pressed back.

For an instant, the pain lessened, until surprise broke my concentration.

It took me five minutes to replicate the result by focusing completely on building a mental shield. Even then, I could hold it for only a few seconds at a time. I didn't know if it was because I'd been able to better deal with the continuous exposure thanks to Ian's advice or if it was a benefit of the meditation training I'd been doing, but whatever it was, it was progress.

I might have a chance at normalcy.

The transport landed on one of the many small spaceports that adorned the tops of the various towers. This one had room for two ships, but only one landing pad was occupied.

The ship was smaller than *Aurora,* possibly only two levels, and painted matte black. It was a House Yamado design, a ship that could go either military or civilian, depending on the build-out.

"Is this a House von Hasenberg ship?" I asked Ian. I realized they were the first words we'd spoken since entering the transport.

"No," he said. "*Phantom* is my personal ship." He slanted a wry glance at me. "I'll thank you in advance for not locking me out of it."

My smile was sweet. "I won't have to if you don't give me a reason to."

He shook his head in exasperation, but a smile pulled at the corners of his mouth. "I contacted Alex and Aoife while we were at Rhys's. I briefed them and they agreed to join us again, but quarters are going to be tight. This ship was designed for a single person to be able to manage."

"I don't mind sleeping on the floor for a few days," I said. It wasn't my first choice, but I'd survived worse.

"You and Aoife can bunk together," he said.

*I'd rather bunk with you.* I bit my lip to keep the words from slipping free. One kiss did not make a relationship, and giving him a chance didn't mean hopping into bed with him at the first opportunity.

Before we boarded the ship, I scanned us both for trackers. We were clean. Ada had trusted me. Pain clutched at my heart and it felt heavy in my chest. I was going to break her trust, and even if she understood, we would both be changed for it.

I followed Ian into the ship's tiny cargo hold. Our supplies from *Fortuitous* took up more than half of the available floor space, leaving a narrow path through the hold.

At Ian's direction, I dropped my bag, suitcase, and cloak at the bottom of a short staircase. We climbed to the upper level, which had the captain's quarters, a mess hall, and the flight deck.

Much like *Aurora,* the captain's chair could control the entire ship, but Ian had also left the navigation and tactical stations. Aoife and Alex sat behind the two auxiliary consoles, hard-faced and intent. Aoife smiled briefly at me, but it didn't touch her eyes, and she didn't say anything. Ian said he had briefed them and she looked like she was readying to go to war.

It hit me then, the enormity of what I was doing. I was likely leading these two to their deaths, and Ian besides. I spun on my heel and marched back the way we'd come. I had to get out, to get away. Ian didn't know where Ferdinand was and he wouldn't go in blind. I could slip in, free my brother, and slip back out again. And if I was caught, at least I'd only be sending myself into death.

It was a ridiculous plan, and some part of me knew it, but I didn't stop, not even when Ian shouted my name.

He caught up to me in the middle of the tiny cargo hold. "Bianca, talk to me, what's going on?"

I stopped, but only because he'd wedged himself between me and the door control. "I won't be responsible for their deaths," I said. "Or yours."

He smiled at me, a true smile, and my breath caught at the beauty of it. "You may not have noticed," he said calmly, "but I'm hard to kill. Next concern."

"Alex and Aoife know they are going to die, and they're going anyway—I've seen that look before. They were kind to me and they helped me and I won't repay them with death."

Ian stepped closer, into my personal space. "Alex and Aoife are soldiers. They know what it is to prepare for battle. I didn't order them to come, they volunteered—after I'd warned them about the risks. They hope to be able to kick some Rockhurst ass, but they'll settle for MineCorp. Next concern."

"Ada will never forgive me."

Ian slowly and carefully slid his arms around me. When I didn't balk, he pulled me into a gentle hug. I rested my head against his shoulder and wrapped my arms around his waist.

"Your sister will forgive you," he said. His voice vibrated through his chest, a soothing rumble. "She understands sacrifice. Next concern."

Lulled by the comfort he offered, the truth slipped out. "I'm worried that if I let you, you'll break my heart."

I tensed. He froze. His breath caught, interrupting the even rise and fall of his chest. Finally, he said, very quietly, "Anyone lucky enough to be entrusted with your heart would be a fool to treat it carelessly."

"Are you a fool?" I ventured.

"I was, once. I try not to be anymore."

# CHAPTER 22

Ian coaxed me back to the flight deck. We did not speak of the final words whispered between us, but the sprig of hope nestled next to my heart burned brightly.

I responded to Ada's flurry of messages with just a single line: *I will bring him home.* I wrote another message with everything I knew about Ferdinand, MineCorp, and XAD Seven. I encrypted it with our shared key and set it on a twelve-hour timer. If anything happened to me, Ada would know where and why.

I briefly searched through the files I'd pulled from Mine-Corp. They had regular shipments of people headed to XAD Seven. Either Rockhurst was radically expanding mining operations, or workers were dying at an alarming rate. Maybe both.

Ian took us into orbit, then turned to me. "Where is Ferdinand?"

"XAD Seven."

"Fuck."

Well, that pretty succinctly covered my feelings, too. "Yeah. It's not quite as bad as if it was XAD Six, but it's not great. The only positive, if you can call it that, is that MineCorp keeps shipping in new people. We have a few options."

"Any idea how advanced their base is?" Aoife asked.

"No. Ada said XAD Six wasn't terraformed, so I don't expect Seven to be, either. They're mining, so they'll be underground. And based on the number of people they're shipping in, it's either a large operation or multiple sites."

"I will check to see if House von Hasenberg has any recent intelligence or surveillance," Ian said.

"As far as I can tell, we have three options." I ticked them off on my fingers. "One, we go in stealth and parachute in from a high altitude to avoid detection. Once we grab Ferdinand, *Phantom* will need to do a hot pickup then disappear."

Ian grimaced. It wasn't my first choice, either, but it was an option.

"Two," I continued, "I fake the registration on *Phantom* and we pretend to be a MineCorp special delivery or inspection. XAD Seven is far enough from a gate to buy us time while the verification goes through. Even if they've set up an FTL hub on XAD Six, we'd still have over two hours before the response comes back. But if they have their own hub, then we're screwed."

Direct FTL communication was tricky to set up and wildly expensive, so most messages were bounced through the gates on communication drones and passing ships. For distant planets far from a gate, messages could take days to be delivered.

I touched my third finger. "Or option three: we take over a real MineCorp shipment. Ian and I will sneak in and find Ferdinand while Alex and Aoife deliver the workers." My mouth curled in disgust at the word. We'd be delivering people to a hellhole they'd never escape—and we couldn't take them back out with us.

"Do you have a preference?" Ian asked.

"Option two probably has the fewest failure points," I said. "Especially if I can find an actual special delivery we can mimic. I grabbed a bunch of files but I haven't had a chance to look through them. What about you?"

"It would be better if no one knew we were there, but a ship entering the atmosphere is hard to hide. You're also hard to hide; you look like a von Hasenberg."

"People see what they expect," I said with a shrug. "No one would expect me to be on a Rockhurst planet in the middle of a war. Different hair, glasses, and a little bit of makeup will go a long way."

All three of them looked dubious. Aoife said, "Assuming that works, how do we get you out?"

"That depends on the capabilities of this ship and whether RCDF is enforcing the neutrality of the gate."

Attacking enemy ships within five light-minutes of a gate was technically against Consortium law, even during war. But controlling a gate gave one side control of the war, so it often happened when the RCDF wasn't around to stop it. Both Houses were likely rushing to set up temporary gates near their primary planets.

"RCDF has at least one ship at the gate, but I've also heard Rockhurst controls access. House von Hasenberg ships are being advised to use their emergency jump locations if they need to leave the area before the temporary gate is up," Ian said.

"Can you get us an emergency jump point for *Phantom*?" I asked.

Ian shook his head. Reserved for active military ships, emergency jump points were calculated in advance and deemed reasonably safe for a certain period of time, usually two months. Predicting clear space so far in advance carried an inherent risk. There had been a few accidents, so they really were meant for emergency use only.

"If the Antlia gate is not safe," I said, "then that complicates things. We'll have to jump to von Hasenberg territory. It's close enough we won't need a gate. Benedict's battle cruiser arrives tomorrow. He'll give us his emergency coordinates and protect us until we can jump again."

"I don't like having the three of you in one place," Ian growled. "It's a huge security risk."

"I'm open to suggestions," I said. "But unless we want to tip our hand by getting RCDF involved, I'm not sure what we can do."

"I'll see what I can find in our House intel. You look at the MineCorp files and figure out our cover. We'll stay here until we have a plan."

"Sounds good," I agreed.

Alex stood and gestured me to his console. I thanked him and slid into the seat. I plugged in my secondary com and started going through the files I'd grabbed. MineCorp was dumping a ton of people on both XAD Six and Seven. Ships were arriving twice a month with anywhere from five to twenty workers aboard.

I dug deeper, looking for patterns. Most of the laborers were unskilled indentured servants, as expected. The skilled workers included machinery operators, mechanics, supervisors, guards, and engineers. Occasionally, a new skilled employee would arrive separately to fix some immediate crisis.

I just had to invent an employee and a crisis, something urgent so they wouldn't look too closely at our identities.

I thought about it for a few minutes, discarding ideas as fast as I came up with them. It had to be scary and something the Rockhurst soldiers couldn't easily verify one way or another.

That left disease. Indentured servants didn't have money for nanobots. They were susceptible to all kinds of illnesses, but it needed to be a disease that made the soldiers want to stay away, too. A manufactured virus, sent as a weapon, designed to overpower nanos.

But before I could spread chaos on the ground, I had to make sure we'd actually get to the ground without Rockhurst shooting us out of the sky. The ship's registration would need to be bulletproof.

I checked the existing registration. *Phantom* was registered as a mercenary ship to a company I'd never heard of. A quick search didn't turn up anything, so it was either tiny or a shell company.

"Do I need to change the ship's registration?" I asked Ian. "Will it lead back to you?"

Ian glanced up from his console. "It won't lead back to me," he said, "but I'd prefer not to have to rename my ship after this, so at least update the name."

"Do you want to do it?" I asked. Just because I *could* didn't mean I *should*. I would be furious if someone messed with my ship's registration without permission.

Ian shook his head slightly. "I trust you," he said.

His tone was serious, not teasing, and the words arrowed straight into my chest. I ducked my head before the heat in my cheeks could give me away. "Okay, I'll save the existing registration so you can use it again when we get back. Do you have a name you'd like to use for the next couple of days?"

I peeked up at him and found his eyes were still on me. "How about *Opportunity*?" he asked.

I tried not to read anything into the name, but it was difficult when he kept looking at me, warmth and worry in his eyes. I cleared my throat. "It's a good name," I agreed. "I'll get to work on the registration change. I'm also going to buy, steal, or fake a MineCorp authorization seal."

"If you can, find out where their ships normally jump in. Our intelligence is showing a lot of activity in that area."

"I'm on it," I said.

I used my second spare com to set up a secure connection and bounced it through a few servers I didn't usually use. Then I carefully probed MineCorp's network, looking for the terminals I'd compromised. Two of them were down, but the third responded.

So had the sysadmins found my back doors and left this terminal as a honeypot, or had they merely overlooked it in their search?

Either way, I needed to move quickly and grab enough data to cover my true intent. I got to work.

**I LEANED BACK AND STRETCHED MY ARMS OVER MY HEAD.** I'd gotten closer and closer to the console over the last couple of hours as I raced to stay ahead of the sysadmins who were trying to keep me out. They'd been good, but I'd been better, and satisfaction filled me.

"You look pleased with yourself," Aoife said. She was sitting in the captain's chair and Ian was nowhere in sight. "Did you find what you were looking for?"

"I did." I'd carefully collected ship authorizations, employee rosters, and approved jump coordinates. It had taken so long because I'd had to dig through a bunch of data I didn't need to cover my tracks, but I had some interesting reading for later. Finally, I'd unleashed a destructive, fast-acting virus guaranteed to keep the sysadmins busy for a day or two.

I updated *Phantom*'s registration and added the MineCorp authorization seal I'd lifted from their servers. I was tempted to leave the internal name the same, but Ian needed to get used to the new name before we had to answer questions about the ship.

I turned on the ship-wide intercom and said, "The ship's temporary new name is *Opportunity*. Please use that name when making requests." I closed the intercom and followed my own advice. "*Opportunity,* where is Ian?"

"Captain Bishop is in his quarters," the ship responded.

Invading Ian's quarters felt a little too personal after our conversation earlier, but I needed to see what he'd found and let him know we could jump whenever he was ready. I also wanted to run my plan past him.

Aoife grinned at me when I stood. "Ian asked for you to come find him when you were done, but it seems you were ahead of him."

"I'm not sure that anyone is ever ahead of Ian Bishop," I said.

"Isn't that the truth," Aoife groused good-naturedly.

The door to Ian's quarters was closed. I knocked quietly. I heard a muffled voice from inside, then the door slid open. The room was small, with a double bed, a single chair next to a tiny table, and a door leading to either a closet or an en suite bathroom.

Ian sat in the chair, a tablet in his lap and a steaming cup on the table next to him. The room smelled like coffee. My stomach rumbled and I glanced down in surprise. I actually felt pretty good, despite the signals from Sedition. I would try to eat something before we arrived on XAD Seven.

"Come in, Bianca," Ian invited when I remained in the doorway.

I stepped into the room and the door closed behind me. I refused to let this be weird between us. I sat on the edge of the bed, facing him. "I got us MineCorp authorization and jump coordinates," I said just to break the silence.

"It's no wonder Albrecht is desperate to have you home," Ian said.

"I have my uses."

Ian grinned before he turned serious. "It's worse than I thought," he said. "Rockhurst is all over the sector. I had hoped to jump far enough out that we'd be ready to jump again as soon as we landed on XAD Seven, but I'm not sure we'll be able to. *Phantom* has an unmatched stealth system, but we can't avoid ships that are right on top of us."

"It looks like the usual jump coordinates are about an hour out. How long is the FTL cooldown?"

"Right at six hours," Ian said.

"It's better than eight, but there's no way we can drag it out that long. We can jump farther out if we come up with a believable excuse. Bad coordinates? Garbled message?"

"Maybe," Ian said. "It would help if we knew where Rockhurst was concentrating their forces, but so far our recon just shows them everywhere." He sighed and met my eyes. "I wish you would consider staying behind."

"I need to see this through," I said quietly.

He bowed his head in acknowledgment. "Did you find anything that could get us in?"

"I plan to claim a possible weaponized infection in one of the recent shipments of people. I'll be a MineCorp lackey sent to assess the situation and you'll be my mercenary guard. And of course MineCorp wants to keep it all hush-hush."

Ian mulled it over for a few minutes. "That could work," he finally said. "Let's talk it through. What if they want you to consult with their doctor first?"

I pursed my lips. "I'll have to do some research before we land. I'll find an appropriately horrible hemorrhagic fever and learn enough that I can wing it. But I'll attempt to talk my way out of the meeting if it comes to that."

"Are you going to have them bring the subjects to you?"

"No. I considered it, but really I want them to leave us alone as much as possible. I'll ask for access to their records and hopefully locate Ferdinand that way. It'll mean more work for us because we'll have to delve into the mine to grab him, but it'll also mean that we might be able to slip out unseen."

"And if they refuse to leave you alone?"

"We bring Ferdinand back for examination and then fight our way out. Did you find any intel on how big their base is?"

"Frustratingly little," Ian said. "They are focusing their forces on XAD Six but they don't want to give House von Hasenberg any chance to get a foothold in the solar system, so they're patrolling everything. We can't get drones close enough to do a ground survey."

"So we have no chance of being able to stealth in?" I asked.

Ian shook his head. If we wanted to retrieve Ferdinand, we had to go in as MineCorp. Five lives would depend on my ability to play a convincing role. I swallowed the anxiety that wanted to devour me whole.

Ian scooted his chair closer. After a brief hesitation, he reached out and squeezed my hand. "What are you thinking?"

"There are so many things that could go wrong. I could be leading us all to our deaths. But if we don't go, Ferdinand dies. It's impossible."

"You can do it," Ian said quietly. "Impossible isn't in your vocabulary. Look at what you've accomplished already. I would not be helping you if I thought you were going to fail."

I laughed. "I didn't give you much choice."

"Where your safety is concerned, there is always a choice," he disagreed. "And I chose to work with you."

Now I just had to live up to that trust. "When do you want to go?"

"The days are short on XAD Seven—around fourteen

hours," Ian said. "Today, midnight local time falls around six Universal. If we jump by four then coast in for two hours, our time on the ground will be in the dark. That gives us a little less than two hours of prep. Is that enough?"

"The less time I have to freak out, the better," I said. "Does the bathroom have cosmetics equipment? We both need to change our hair color. I have my handheld, but it'll take forever."

"This bathroom does," he said with a wave at the far door. "You're welcome to go first."

I hopped up, too anxious to sit still. "Thanks."

The attached bathroom was tiny but clean. I brought up the cosmetics settings and was happy to find the full suite of options. I watched the preview of the changes in the mirror as I swiped through the different hair colors.

My current color was light brown with blond and red highlights. It had taken me years to find the exact shades I liked and the profile was saved to my own cosmetics kit. Because of that, I'd been sporting nearly the same hair color for the entire time I'd been in the public eye.

I needed something that would blend in but also be completely different from my normal hair color. Black made my skin looked washed out and added several years to my age even before the makeup. I added strands of gray, aging me further. I turned my head, eyeing my reflection from multiple angles. This would work.

I removed the coloring wand from its dock and the mirror preview went translucent, so I could see my real hair color under the new color. I ran the wand over my hair from root to end, like I was brushing my hair. In the mirror, the section of hair under the wand turned black with gray strands, matching the preview.

I did my whole head, shaking my hair and repeating until

no brown remained. I waved away the preview and checked my true reflection for any missed strands.

I didn't look at all like myself, which was the point, but it was still weird. I put the coloring wand back where it belonged and tried not to stare at my reflection.

Next, I went through makeup options. I ended up with dull, sallow skin, dark circles under my eyes, and careful contouring that made my nose appear wider than it actually was. The woman staring out of the mirror looked overworked and at least a decade older than twenty-five.

I returned to the bedroom to get Ian's opinion. He glanced up when I entered the room, then did a quick double take. He squinted and tilted his head to the side, as if that would help him see the truth through the changes.

"That's impressive," he said at last. "I wouldn't have recognized you."

"Your turn. I'm going to go brush up on deadly diseases and figure out if I have any clothes that scream MineCorp peon."

"Good luck. I'll meet you on the flight deck in an hour."

# CHAPTER 23

**M**y only clothing option had been the pair of gray slacks and a white blouse I'd bought from Madame Blanchard in what felt like a lifetime ago. As expected, all of the clothes Ada had included were more practical than pretty. My shoe options had been the heels I'd worn with the gold dress or heavy combat boots. I'd opted for boots. It looked a little odd, but I didn't relish running in bare feet again anytime soon.

When I entered the flight deck, Aoife was in the captain's chair, and Alex and Ian were standing beside her. Ian had changed to dark brown hair, graying at the temples. He'd also given the stubble shadowing his jaw a salt-and-pepper coloring, giving him a more grizzled appearance.

Alex turned to glance at me. He pulled a blaster before frowning. "Bianca?"

"Yes. Did you think I was a stowaway?"

"The disguise is good," he said.

Aoife spun around. "You were not kidding about the hair and makeup making a difference," she agreed.

I moved closer to Ian, trying to get used to the new hair color. He'd also grown a paunch in the last hour. "Is that going to pass a scanner?" I asked with a glance at his newly enlarged belly.

"Of course," he said. He patted his stomach proudly. "Nothing but too much beer and good food in here. And a blaster, a knife, and a small amount of explosives."

It was my turn to frown. "Is that safe?"

"Safe enough," was his entirely unsatisfactory answer. "Are you ready?"

"Yes." It came out as more confident than I felt.

"Aoife is going to be the captain for this run. I'm the hired help and Alex is going to stay out of sight as our backup plan. We jump in, land, grab Ferdinand, and then make a break for the gate or the von Hasenberg system, depending on how things look."

"We should discuss contingency plans," I said. "What if we're discovered or one of us gets caught?"

"If we get caught before we find Ferdinand, we'll make a decision then as to whether we bail or keep looking. Afterward, our priority is to get both of you out. If Aoife has to leave before we're out, she'll try to go stealth and come back for us in twelve hours. Otherwise we're on our own."

"Let's hope it doesn't come to that," I murmured. I slid into the tactical station and double-checked the ship's registration. The MineCorp authorization was set to broadcast upon request. Everything was as ready as I could make it. "We're good to go."

"I've already requested a jump point from the gate," Aoife said. "We're jumping in to the most distant of the points you loaded into the system. We should have a little over an hour before we're on-planet."

"You have the ship," Ian said. "Jump when you are ready. Be prepared to talk to Rockhurst on the other side."

Aoife grinned and rolled her eyes. "Piece of cake."

Now that the time was here, fear and hope and terror churned in my stomach. The engine noise changed and the lights flickered as the FTL engaged. Everything went quiet. My stomach dropped as we jumped. I started a timer on the secondary com I'd be using for this trip. Six hours until we could escape.

The main engine had barely started back up before we were hailed. "Incoming communication," the ship intoned.

Aoife waved us away from her, then accepted the request on her console. It would prevent whoever was on the other end of the communication from seeing the entire flight deck.

"State your name and business," a male voice asked.

"This is Captain Glenda Starling of the *Opportunity*," Aoife said. Her accent had roughened around the edges. "I'm on a run for MineCorp to XAD Seven. Got one of their suits onboard. Must be urgent from what they're paying me."

"We don't have any MineCorp deliveries on the schedule," the man said.

"This isn't a delivery. This is a suit doing some sort of inspection. She was mumbling something about checking the last deliveries and wondering if we had any hazmat suits onboard. As if a merc ship carries hazmat suits." Aoife made a derisive noise. "Whatever it is, I'm glad it's her and not me."

"We'll clear you through to Seven. Do not deviate from the approved flight plan. Talk to ground control when you get there and they'll direct you. Good luck." The man sounded relieved that he wasn't dealing with whatever issue required hazmat suits.

He cut the connection and Aoife looked up. "How often has MineCorp shown up that it was that easy?"

"Often," I said.

"The flight plan they sent has us arriving in seventy-two minutes," Aoife said. "So if you have any last-minute prep, now is the time."

I couldn't stay here, where I could do nothing but watch and worry. "Come get me when we're ten minutes from entry," I said.

**THE SHIP WAS TOO SMALL FOR MUCH ESCAPE, BUT I** headed down to the lower level. It had a crew bunk and head, the medbay, and a tiny exercise room. I entered the exercise room and looked around. There was resistance equipment, a treadmill, and a small open space. The far wall was lined with mirrors.

I couldn't do much in my slacks and blouse, but all von Hasenberg children had been taught various martial arts forms. I moved to the open space and chose a gentle, flowing kata that would allow me to work out my excess energy while also sharpening my focus.

It had been a long time since I'd gone through this kata and my forms were shaky and weak. I closed my eyes so I wouldn't see my reflection and focused on the movement. Gradually, muscle memory returned and my movements softened and flowed properly.

By the time I finished the sequence, I felt better. Calmer and more confident. I opened my eyes and nearly jumped out of my skin when I caught unexpected movement in the mirror. I yelped and nearly tripped over my own feet in an attempt to leap away.

Ian's hand flashed out and he steadied me. I gulped in air, trying to get my heart rate under control. So much for my relaxed confidence.

"You scared me," I said, once I could breathe. "I didn't hear you come in, and you don't look like yourself."

"Sorry. I came to make sure you were okay, but then your movements were so mesmerizing, I kept watching. I apologize."

"It's okay. I don't mind an audience, but I had just calmed down and now I'm wound up again."

"If you go through it again, will you teach me?"

I glanced at him in surprise. "Sure, I can teach you. If you want to get the forms correct, we won't be able to do them all, but if you just want to get close, we can probably do the whole kata."

"Which do you recommend?"

"If you're going to do it, you should do it right," I said. He nodded in agreement. "The movements are intentionally slow and controlled. Keep your breathing even and your core engaged. Find your balance."

I moved through the first three forms, explaining as I went, then I turned to face him. "Follow along and I'll correct your form." At first, I gave him verbal corrections, but as he gained confidence in the movements and didn't need a guide, I touched him, adjusting the angle of his arms, shifting his center of balance.

I was achingly aware of him even as I fought to keep my touch professional. He had balance and strength and a natural grace that was beautiful to watch. It didn't help that he watched me with smoldering eyes.

We made it through a dozen forms before Aoife announced that we were fifteen minutes out. I bowed to Ian and he returned the gesture.

"Thank you," he said. "It's harder than it looks, but I can see how it would be meditative."

"You're welcome. I can teach you the rest later, if you're still interested." I sank enough emphasis into the phrase that he couldn't miss the fact that I wasn't just talking about martial arts lessons.

His expression heated deliciously before he remembered to wipe it clean. "I should go," he said.

I took a deep breath and decided to be brave. "Wait. Please. Why did you apologize for kissing me before?"

"I already explained."

"But I don't understand," I said softly. "I enjoyed the kiss. I didn't expect you to propose marriage afterward, if that's what you were worried about. The Consortium is weird, but we're not that weird. Hookups happen all the time."

He ran a frustrated hand through his hair. "I refuse to lead you on when nothing can come of it. You're so far out of my league, you're in another universe."

I laughed bitterly. I couldn't help it. "I'm damaged goods, a widow accused of killing her husband. *You're* out of *my* league."

He huffed at me. "You know what I mean."

I did. Even tainted, I was still a von Hasenberg and some would see that before they saw anything else. I tried a new tactic. "What if I *want* you to lead me on? Will you think less of me if I don't plan ten steps ahead and instead decide that I want this little piece of happiness for however long it lasts? Will you deny me that?"

"Bianca, you're killing me," he groaned.

"Walk away right now and I won't bother you again," I said. "I will respect your decision. We will be professional colleagues and nothing more. Or stay and see where it goes. With me."

Ian stood frozen and for an endless moment I thought he was going to turn and leave. I held my breath, waiting.

"I'm still here," he said a few seconds later. I'd expected him to leave, so it hadn't even registered that he'd stayed.

I edged closer. He stood his ground. I reached for him but stopped before I touched his chest. I met his eyes again, silently asking permission.

He wrapped his hand around mine and pressed it to his chest. "If we're going to do this, we're going to do it properly," he growled. "You can touch me." A devilish grin tilted the corners of his lips. "And I can return the favor."

I ran my hand over his firm chest before curling it around the back of his neck. I stepped close enough that his fake belly pressed against me. "If we're doing this properly, how about a kiss?" I asked. "For luck."

His arms slid around me gently as he gauged my reaction. When I tucked myself closer to him, his grip tightened. "How about a kiss because I've wanted to kiss you for the last hour?"

I leaned into him and pulled his lips down to mine. He buried a hand in my hair and plundered my mouth with lips and tongue. I moaned as goose bumps shivered over my skin, bringing my whole body to instant awareness.

I pressed closer still and slid my tongue into his mouth. He groaned low and the hand on my ass clenched tight. He lifted me and I wrapped my legs around his hips for balance. He took two steps, his muscles doing delicious things under my arms and legs, before I felt the cool metal of the wall at my back.

He pressed against me then growled in frustration at the lump of fake belly between us. I giggled, tried to stop, and only giggled harder. "Excuse me, sir, is that a blaster in your belly or are you just happy to see me?" I managed to gasp out between giggles.

He leaned back, his expression wicked. "You tell me, love," he said, his voice deep. He wrapped his hands around my hips and pulled my lower body closer, so the thick length of him pressed teasingly between my thighs, only separated by a few flimsy layers of cloth.

He pulled away then rocked back into me. My giggles died in a gasp. I squirmed and arched away from the wall, trying to get the right friction, but his hands held me immobile. I clenched my legs around him, digging my heels into his ass to pull him closer. He relented and captured my moan with his mouth.

He kissed me like we had all the time in the world, but all too soon, the one-minute atmospheric entry warning sounded. I reluctantly let him go. He stepped back and I leaned against the wall, needy and on edge.

His gaze was scorching, his eyes hot with desire. "We are not done," he said, his voice a low command. "We're going to go rescue your brother. We're going to win. And after we do, you and I are going to have a long talk. Without any interruptions."

I nodded mutely. I'd reached for something I wanted, and so far, it hadn't gone to shit. I just hoped that held true for the next twenty-four hours.

*OPPORTUNITY* SETTLED INTO XAD SEVEN'S MAIN HANGAR without any fanfare. From what we could tell on the way in, there was only the one main base. The planet had not been terraformed, so the hangar was one of the few surface buildings.

An atmospheric field shimmered across the hangar's open door, illuminated by the overhead light panels. We'd been advised the air in the building was breathable. However, hangar space was at a premium. Ships with extra crew were required to drop off passengers and move out into the unbreathable open, which ratcheted up my anxiety. Our quick getaway just became a lot more hazardous.

Ian and I had mikes and earpieces once again, and Aoife promised to monitor the transmissions. We had to assume Rockhurst would be listening in, even to our encrypted stream, so we set some predetermined codes to use in case of emergency.

I had my freshly recharged shielding cuff and a pair of hidden knives that would pass through a scanner, one at my waist and one near my ankle. Ian carried a range of weapons, some openly, some hidden. It would be weirder for a merc guard to be unarmed. We also wore air filtration masks we'd found in the emergency supplies. I had to sell this virus from the first minutes or we'd be toast.

I deactivated my main identity chip, activated the secondary chip, and touched my right thumb and ring finger together for five seconds. I stashed my main com in my crate of stuff. "Who am I?" I asked. The mask muffled my voice, an added benefit.

"Anna White, MineCorp middle manager who drew the short stick," Ian said.

"And you are Noah Peterson, flat-broke mercenary for hire. Glenda took you on because she owes her sister a favor."

"Ready?" Ian asked.

"Not even close," I muttered. "But I'm going anyway."

We both turned on our mikes and Ian lowered the ship's cargo ramp. We took a cautious breath. We didn't asphyxiate. Our first win.

A stern-looking older woman stood on the far side of the hangar. When she saw us, she waved an impatient arm. We moved to greet her, but she just turned her back with a sharp "This way."

She led us through a thick air-lock door and to an elevator next to a stairwell. She jabbed the elevator button then turned to look at me. "You are not our normal inspector."

They had already requested our identity information and the MineCorp authorization before we had been allowed to land. Still, I held up my secondary com and showed her the Mine-Corp badge I'd lifted while I was in their systems.

"No, I'm not," I said. "I'm Anna White. I'm here on a special, high-priority mission."

"What mission? What's so high priority that you couldn't wait until a decent hour to arrive?" She shot an irritated look at my mask. "The air here is perfectly breathable."

"I know it's breathable," I said, ignoring her questions,

"but I'm not sure it's *safe*." I pulled a penlight out of my pocket. "Would you mind letting me do a brief examination before we go any farther?"

"Examination for what?" she asked warily.

I smiled, even though she couldn't see it through my mask. "Are you the base commander?" I asked.

"I'm the interim commander. General Morius is away. I'm Lieutenant General Kora Imbor."

"May I call you Ms. Imbor?" I asked. "Lieutenant General is a mouthful." When she nodded, I continued, "Ms. Imbor, we have received a credible threat that one of our last two shipments was compromised. I was dispatched to verify the authenticity of such a threat."

I watched her connect the dots. "I have House Rockhurst nanos, as do all base personnel."

"It is merely a precaution," I soothed. "Have any of your workers experienced any recent illness or strange behavior? Aggression, fear, anxiety?"

She frowned. "A few of the miners attacked their guards yesterday morning," she said slowly. "The guard was bruised, but he recovered. The perpetrators have been dealt with."

Dread wrapped sharp claws around my heart. "Killed?" I asked.

"No, but they'll wish they had been by the time their punishment is over."

"I will need to examine them, too," I said firmly. "But first, if you wouldn't mind following the light with your eyes." I held the light up before she could protest and she tracked it. I quickly shined it in each of her eyes, then clicked it off. "I don't see any signs of illness," I said.

The elevator opened and Ms. Imbor breathed out a silent sigh of relief. She might be feeling better, but once Ian and I descended, we'd be trapped. I reached out for the signals flying through the air, but they were just typical base messages, nothing to indicate they were on to us.

We stepped into the elevator and Ms. Imbor pressed the only button. The ride took nearly twenty seconds. Just how deep underground were we? Ian—Noah, I reminded myself—was tense beside me.

The doors opened and I half expected a platoon of soldiers to be waiting for us. Instead, we were greeted by a wide stone and plastech corridor. Two meters in was a guard's station with a body scanner. It was protected behind thick metal bars. A wide metal door was set into the wall on our right.

Ms. Imbor strode forward toward the guard and waved her arm over the chip reader. The gate popped open. She held it and gestured to the chip reader. "Scan in, please," she said. I waved my right arm over the reader and Ian—*Noah*—scanned his left arm. The guard briefly looked at our IDs before he waved us through the scanner.

I passed through cleanly, but Ian wasn't so lucky. "Please hand over your weapons," Ms. Imbor said. "They'll be returned to you when you leave."

Ian grumbled under his breath, but removed two blasters and a long knife. When he went through the scanner again, it didn't go off. I didn't know how many weapons he had left, but the loss of two blasters hurt.

Ms. Imbor led us to her office. I made sure she caught me peering closely at the few people we passed. Her office was a small room, sparsely furnished, but nicer than most front-line bases. She settled behind her desk and waved me to the chair in front of her.

"You think I have a rogue virus spreading through my base," she said without preamble. "One that can overcome nanobots."

I held my hands up in a placating gesture. "No one is saying that," I said. My voice was still muffled by the filtration mask I hadn't removed, underscoring the inherent lie in my words.

"There *might* be a small issue with a few of the workers," I continued, "that *might* result in erratic behavior. MineCorp sent me to be their canary. I hired Noah here"—I hiked a thumb over my shoulder at *Noah*—"to protect me if there is a problem. And of course you will be compensated and the workers replaced. If needed."

"You expect me to shut down mine operations while you play doctor because of a rumor?" she asked, an impatient edge in her voice.

"No, of course not," I said immediately. "Give me the locations of the last two shipments of workers and I will go to them. And I wouldn't be here if the executives didn't think it was worth checking."

"Did your bosses tell you exactly how deep our miners are?" she asked with a skeptical frown.

"Err, no, not exactly," I said. "They decided expediency was preferable to in-depth knowledge."

"It's over an hour trek to get down to the working mine levels," she said. "Then anywhere from ten minutes to three hours to get to the active work sites."

"And the miners who attacked? Where are they being held? I should start with them."

"They are in the hole. On the mine level. I hope you're not claustrophobic, Ms. White."

# CHAPTER 24

**M**s. Imbor gave me a list of mine locations, but the list didn't include names—the MineCorp workers were just numbered. She also gave us each a canteen of water before directing a young, dark-haired corporal to take us down.

As she walked away, I caught the message she sent from her com. She asked about the status of my identity verification from MineCorp. The response said they were still waiting. If they had FTL communication on XAD Six, then we had less than two hours. We'd be buried even deeper in the ground when she found out I was a fake.

I set a ninety-minute timer on my com. Now two times ticked away in the corner of my smart glasses—one counting up the time until we could jump, one counting down the time until our ruse was revealed. The vast chasm between them heightened my anxiety.

The corporal led us back out the way we'd come, but instead of heading for the elevator to the hangar, he took us through the metal door. It did not escape me that an identity chip was required to open the door from either side.

The room beyond the door was rough-hewn stone with none

of the plastech niceties included for the rest of the base. A bank of six elevators, three per side, and another thick, metal door were the only options. The corporal swiped his chip over the elevator control, then pressed the button.

The first doors on our left opened, revealing a large, industrial elevator car, big enough to fit over forty people. The corporal ushered us inside. "I'm Rivers. Did the lieutenant general explain the descent?" he asked.

"No. Is there something we need to know?" Ian asked. It was the first time he'd spoken and his clipped accent was gone, replaced by a working-class brogue.

"It's a three-stage descent," Corporal Rivers said. "The reason it takes over an hour is because we have to move horizontally at each stage before we descend again. Every time they ran out of mineral, they just dug deeper."

"What if there's an emergency?" I asked. "Is this the only way up?"

Rivers nodded, then corrected himself. "There are stairs, but each descent is nearly a kilometer. There's nothing between the levels except occasional shelter rooms."

I drew a purposefully slow breath and told myself that the elevator walls were *not* closing in on me. I could climb three kilometers of stairs if I had to. I would do anything to save my brother.

*Breathe. Save my brother. Breathe.*

Five minutes later, the elevator reached the bottom. The hallway was three meters wide, cut out of the planet's stone. The light panels strung along the ceiling pushed the darkness to the edges of the hallway.

Still, doorways to rooms or tunnels—it was unclear which—lurked in the shadows, dark maws ready to gobble us up. I shivered as I followed the corporal. Ian touched my back, a gentle reassurance. I gave up on mentally calling him Noah. We were buried in the ground; I had larger concerns.

Along the way, we passed through three gates. They were as wide and tall as the tunnel, and folded flat against the wall to allow equipment to pass through. Each gate required a chip swipe to unlock. It took twenty minutes to reach the next elevator bank.

"It gets rougher from here," Rivers said. "Are you sure you want to keep going? The lieutenant general said I could bring you back up if you couldn't handle it."

"I can handle it," I assured him.

He shrugged and called the elevator. The trip took a little longer this time, closer to eight minutes. When the doors opened, the hallway was more roughly hewn and the light panels were farther apart.

We went through four locked gates. One of them required a swift kick to open properly. The trip took thirty minutes, in part because of the gate slowdown. The Rockhurst soldiers up above clearly did not want the workers escaping anytime soon.

The final set of elevators was noticeably smaller, with the exception of what appeared to be an equipment elevator. Our elevator made ominous noises as we descended. Even Corporal Rivers looked relieved when the doors opened and we could escape.

A wide foyer area was cut off from the main hallway by a guard's station and another heavy gate. The guard was on our side of the gate. She smiled at Rivers in greeting.

"They made it, I see," she said. "I'm five credits richer. I told Kelley that MineCorp wouldn't send someone who couldn't hack it." She looked at me. "No offense, ma'am."

"None taken," I said.

She looked like she wanted to question me about the face mask but the corporal shook his head at her. "Thank you, Private," he said. "Please let the hole know we're on our way. Tell them to hose it down."

We were too deep for wireless signals to reach, but Rockhurst had run down communication lines and put in signal repeaters. Based on the scarcity of messages, they weren't repeating everything topside. The private radioed a quick message and received a confirmation in response.

"They'll be ready for you, Corporal," she said. She stood back with her hand on her blaster while we went through the gate. After we were through, she checked that it had latched properly.

The hallway felt narrower on this level because pipes and wires were bolted to the ceiling and walls. The temperature was noticeably warm despite a cool breeze blowing from the direction of the elevators.

"Are we deep enough that heat is a problem?" I asked.

"Yes," Rivers said. He pointed at a thick pipe on the ceiling. "They pipe down a salt solution that they chill on the surface for the climate control system. It helps combat the heat in the main tunnels, but deeper in the shafts, the temperatures can hover over forty."

The light was better here, but only because the rooms carved into the rock on either side of the hallway were lit. We passed the typical military base facilities—barracks, medbay, and mess hall. I counted at least four off-duty guards milling around. Another guarded gate separated the soldiers' area from the miners' area.

The same rooms were duplicated on this side of the gate, bigger but more roughly cut. Guards stood at each doorway. In the mess hall, a few bedraggled men and women stared blindly at their plates.

I schooled my face into a cool expression and hardened my heart. I could not save them all. I had to save my brother, and

I potentially had less than thirty minutes until the lieutenant general knew that I was a fake.

We cleared the final gate, then Corporal Rivers led us through an increasingly complicated maze of tunnels that narrowed and heated as we went. Sweat plastered my blouse to my back. Just as I thought I'd be stuck in this rock hell forever, I heard the sound of laughter and spraying water.

We emerged into a small square room with open doors on both sides. A table with a half-finished card game and a pair of chairs stood off to the left. Three tall cabinets lined the right wall.

The air was blissfully cold. They must be using a cooling field because the change from hot to cold had been instantaneous between one step and the next. The laughter and water sounds were coming from the darkness beyond the far door.

"Looks like they're still cleaning up," Rivers said. He moved to the cabinet and retrieved a trio of light sticks, a flare, and a stunstick. He handed us each a light stick and kept the rest of the stuff for himself. "Are those smart glasses?" he asked with a nod to my face.

"Yes."

"Good, that will help. It's dark in the hole even with the light sticks." He glanced at Ian's face. "You and I are on our own."

He clicked on his light then led us through the far door. A short hallway led to a large circular room with a low ceiling. A waist-high railing surrounded a dark hole at least five meters wide. Two soldiers, a man and a woman, were using high-powered fire hoses to spray water into the hole.

"They use the same water used for the cooling system," Rivers said, "so it'll bring the temperature down for a few minutes while we're down there. Otherwise, it's stifling."

The soldiers shut off the water. "It's ready for you, Corporal," the man said. "We've washed out most of the shit, but watch your step."

"Thank you. I'll let you know if we need anything else," Rivers said. The two soldiers nodded and headed for the room we'd passed through.

I approached the railing with trepidation. What new horror lurked below? My glasses adjusted to the dark. The pit was approximately six meters deep. A deeper gutter lined with drains ran along the edge at the bottom of the pit. Five people were shackled by their ankles directly to the stone with less than half a meter between them. They were hunched in on themselves and none of them moved.

The only way down to the pit seemed to be a small lift cage dangling from a pair of chains attached to winches in the ceiling.

Rivers saw me eyeing the setup skeptically and laughed. "It's perfectly safe," he said. He ushered us inside and used the small space as an excuse to press up against me. Ian wrapped a possessive hand around my waist and neatly switched places with me. Rivers backed up fast with a nervous laugh.

The cage slowly lowered into the pit. The people huddled at the bottom didn't bother to look up, despite the fact that the winches and chains made a hellacious noise.

"How long have they been like this?" I asked.

Rivers glanced down at the captives. "No idea. But the hole breaks their spirit pretty quickly. They've been down here at least twenty-four hours, starving and dehydrating in the heat."

The cage settled onto the ground. Corporal Rivers was right; the darkness of the pit clung in dancing shadows every time our light sticks moved. My smart glasses fought to compensate, but it was a losing battle.

"Let me go first," Rivers said. "Just in case any of them are still feeling energetic."

"I need them alive," I said.

He unlatched the safety chain across the door and stepped out. The nearest captives curled more tightly as if to protect themselves from a blow. "Ms. White is with MineCorp. She's here to examine you. Give her any trouble and I'll stun you, then withhold water rations for the day," he said. "Get on your feet. Now," he shouted when none of them moved.

Three of them silently lumbered to their feet. The remaining two didn't move, not even when Rivers kicked them. All five of them had the same buzz-cut hair.

I held the light stick up and approached the first person. The light revealed it was a young woman with a bruised face. She kept her eyes glued to the floor.

I desperately wanted to move on, to see if Ferdinand was here, but my cover depended on this ruse, so I pulled out my penlight and asked her to track the motion. Her reactions were slow and her eyes were foggy. I wasn't a doctor, but that couldn't be a good sign.

I was examining the third captive, a middle-aged man, when I caught a flurry of wireless signals. Rivers touched his ear, frowned, and glanced at me.

My ninety-minute timer still had a few minutes left, but that didn't mean anything. The response had arrived from XAD Six. MineCorp had no record of me, and they had been hacked recently. They requested I be held for extraction tomorrow. The mercenaries were to be sent on their way after questioning. The ship would be kept under surveillance.

Rivers was ordered to subdue both of us because they figured my guard wouldn't take lightly to someone attacking me, even if he wasn't complicit in my plot. Rivers quietly acknowledged the order. I touched Ian's arm and tipped my head at Rivers. The corporal was very carefully not looking at us.

*He knows,* I mouthed to Ian.

Ian frowned. Out of the corner of my eye, I saw Rivers go white-knuckled around the stunstick. I couldn't let that touch me. Ian's eyes widened and he moved just as Rivers brought his arm up to hit me.

I scrambled out of reach as Ian caught Rivers's arm. I heard the crunch of bones, but by the time I turned around to see if Ian needed help, Rivers was unmoving on the floor and Ian had the stunstick.

"How did you know?" Ian asked. He riffled through Rivers's pockets, pulling out his blaster and com.

"I heard the messages," I said. I slashed a hand through the air when he would've questioned me further. "Leave it at that. MineCorp has outed me as a fraud and asked Rockhurst to hold me for questioning. You and the other 'mercenaries' are to be questioned and released if you weren't in on it. When Rivers doesn't report back, they'll send the base after us."

Ian pocketed the com and handed me Rivers's blaster. He sent Aoife one of our encoded messages, the one that meant we were fucked, then said, "Turn off your mike." We both went radio silent because Rockhurst could track us by our conversation if we didn't.

Ian looked around at the three captives staring at him with wide eyes. "If you want to live, stay quiet and don't harm her," he said, pointing at me. They all nodded.

Ian lifted his shirt and drew a blaster from the pouch strapped to his stomach. "Stay here," he said. "I'll take care of the guards up above and let you know when it's safe."

"They'll hear you," I whispered. "I can help."

"They won't hear me." He pointed at the two remaining captives. "Check them."

Ian didn't wait for me to agree. He tucked the stunstick

and blaster in his waistband, then climbed up the outside of the cage. He paused on the top for a second to assess his options. He gripped the chain closer to the pit wall and hauled himself up hand over hand with no apparent effort. It was only after he disappeared into the darkness above that I remembered he didn't have any smart glasses. At least the guard room was lit.

I edged around the three standing captives. Their eyes darted between me and the blaster in my hand. "Don't think about it," I murmured. "Even if you get it away from me before I shoot you, Ian will be back in two minutes. It's not worth it."

The last two people curled on the ground both had the right build. Hope warred with worry. The first person was a young man about the right age, but despite the massive bruising on his face, I knew it wasn't Ferdinand. The young man didn't respond to my touch at all, but a faint pulse beat in his neck.

I turned to the last person in the pit. "He's the instigator," the young woman I'd examined first said bitterly. "We wouldn't be here if it wasn't for him."

The man, if it was a man, was curled tightly with his arms protecting his head. I touched him, but he didn't move. Every centimeter of visible skin was mottled with fading bruises. I carefully pulled one of his arms away from his hidden face.

He lunged up at me, growling low in his chest. I stumbled back in shock, but I wasn't fast enough. The chain around his ankle brought him up short, but he took me down with him. Pain drove the breath from my lungs with a gasp as we landed on the uneven stone floor.

He'd tackled me around the waist, so the blaster remained out of his reach. He clawed for it, dragging me toward him a painful few centimeters at a time, while I tried to kick him off.

My smart glasses adjusted and I stared down into familiar brown and green hazel eyes. Shock stole my voice and he used my distraction against me. His hand closed over my upper arm, the grip bruising. I hissed out a curse, trying to stay quiet.

"Ferdinand!" I whispered harshly. "Stop! It's Bianca."

He pulled my arm down, reaching for the blaster. In desperation, I tossed it over my head. It slid off the edge of the raised floor and into the gutter. Ferdinand growled again and wrapped his hands around my neck.

I tried gently breaking his grip, but he was past reason. I pulled my air filtration mask down, revealing my face. "Listen to me! I'm your sister!" I hissed. I knew at least half a dozen ways to get out of this hold if I didn't mind doing serious injury to my attacker. I hesitated, even as my throat closed.

Strong arms pulled Ferdinand's hands away from my neck. *Ian.* I smiled in relief and took a grateful breath. Ferdinand tried to turn on Ian, but Ian refused to let go of his arms. "Stop!" Ian commanded, his voice quiet but forceful. He shook Ferdinand lightly. "You're attacking your allies. You hurt Bianca."

Ferdinand froze and blinked, squinting at me in the uneven light from the light stick I'd dropped. He looked so different with his shorn hair and bruised face. He made a noise, then grunted in frustration.

I climbed to my feet. My back ached, but I tried to keep the pain off my face because Ferdinand was still watching me. "What's wrong?" I asked.

He made more sounds, then finally opened his mouth and gestured. There was a void where his tongue should be. Shock and horror bloomed into furious, impotent rage. *Someone had cut out his tongue.* I clenched my fists against the need to move, to act, to somehow fix it.

"Did Silva do this?" I asked.

Ferdinand nodded. Ian let him go but kept a close eye on him.

I should've killed Riccardo when I had the chance, promises

be damned. Silva had mutilated my brother. "We will make them pay," I promised, "but first, we need to get out of here. Are you able to walk?"

Ferdinand grunted, then nodded. I handed him my canteen and he opened it with trembling hands. He drank the water so fast it ran down his face. Apparently the guard hadn't been joking about dehydration.

I turned and retrieved my blaster while Ian crouched and fiddled with Ferdinand's shackle. The metal opened with a screech. Ian turned to the remaining four people. "I am going to release you. Do not make me regret the decision."

The three who were responsive agreed instantly. "Take us with you," the young woman pleaded.

"We can't protect you," I said. "You'd be fodder."

"But you'll protect *him*?"

I tried to cut her some slack because she'd had a shitty few days at the very least, but her tone grated on me. "He's my brother, so yes, I'll protect him," I snapped.

Her eyes rounded and she clamped her mouth shut.

I caught a message meant for Rivers's com, asking about his status. "They're going to know the guard is down in about ten seconds," I told Ian. "We need to move."

He unshackled the remaining prisoners. The young woman and the middle-aged man shared a look. "Try it and I'll leave you down here," Ian said mildly.

They lunged for the lift.

Ian sighed and almost casually hit each of them with the stunstick. They went down with matching screams. The third person, a young man, stood frozen.

Ferdinand moved like someone in pain. He favored his left leg, but he didn't ask for help, he just hobbled to the lift. Ian gestured the remaining young man in with us. It was a tight fit, but the four of us made it to the top of the pit. After we exited the cage, Ian hesitated for a second, then sent the lift back down.

"Do you think they'll bring up the unconscious person?" I asked.

"It's on their conscience if they don't," he said. He turned to the unnamed young man with us. "Wait five minutes, then follow us. We'll make enough chaos that you might be able to slip out."

He shook his head. "I don't want out. There's nothing for me out there. I just want to go back to my usual work group. *They* never get in me trouble." He cast a bitter glance at Ferdinand.

I opened my mouth to argue, but then closed it without saying anything. If the kid came with us, he'd likely end up dead. Perhaps he was making the smarter choice.

"Five minutes," Ian reiterated. "Faster if the others come up before then, but I don't think they will."

"Wait," I said. "How do they get the ore out? They can't take it up the way we came down. Is there another way out?"

The young man shook his head. "Not unless you want to be liquefied first. They process it down here then pump it up in pipes. I don't know of any other exits."

Damn. It looked like we were going back up the way we'd come down.

Ian led us to the square room. The two guards were dead at the table, slumped over in their chairs. I couldn't see any blaster wounds, but their heads were at odd angles on their necks. I made myself look at the carnage, to acknowledge that these deaths were on *my* conscience.

I helped Ian search the cabinets on the far wall. We came up with three more blast pistols, a pair of stunsticks, and a few smaller light sticks. Ferdinand and I each got a blaster and a stunstick. I would've liked a long gun with a shotgun setting, but the universe didn't feel compelled to comply.

"Strip," Ian said to me. "The woman's clothes will be too big, but it's better than what you have now." He peeled off his outer shirt. Apparently we were both getting a wardrobe change.

I tried not to think too hard about what I was doing as I stripped a dead woman of her clothes and equipment. Revulsion welled, but I forced it down. I'd said I would do anything for my brother and it was still true. I didn't have to like it, I just had to do it.

I tucked the too long pants into my boots and cinched the belt tight around my waist, thanks to a new hole courtesy of the dead woman's knife. Deciding now was no time to be squeamish, I carefully removed her hair tie and pulled my own hair into a high ponytail. I dropped my air filtration mask next to her body. Gone was any trace of the MineCorp corporate drone who had come through earlier.

Ian looked the part in his Rockhurst uniform. The shirt was a little tight across his shoulders, but it was convincing enough from a distance. He'd also ditched his mask. With Ferdinand still in his mining clothes, Ian and I were just two soldiers escorting an injured mine worker, a common enough sight.

After we were properly clothed and equipped, Ian wrapped Ferdinand's arm over his shoulder and started into the complicated, twisting maze of tunnels between us and freedom.

# CHAPTER 25

F erdinand leaned heavily against Ian's side and grunted with every step. We had to take the elevators or Ferdinand was done. He couldn't climb three kilometers of stairs.

Ian stopped just before the main tunnel.

The wireless signals had been surprisingly quiet. Either that, or we'd been out of range. I had no idea what was going on ahead of us. Had they already created a blockade?

"Do you have a plan to get us through the checkpoints?" I asked Ian. Identity chips only worked if the person with the chip was alive, so we couldn't kill a soldier and chop off an arm. I didn't know how many explosives Ian had brought, but certainly it wasn't enough for the vast number of checkpoints we had to go through on the way back up.

"I've got a codebreaker," he said. "The bigger problems are the number of soldiers between us and the elevator and the lack of cover."

"I've got my shielding cuff. It's good for around eight deflections if they're using pistols. If they're using long guns, then the protection drops fast."

"I also have a von Hasenberg prototype shield. Ideally,

we'd save them until we reach the surface," Ian said. "Until then we'll have to rely on speed and shock."

I glanced at Ferdinand. He was barely standing. He was a few centimeters shorter than Ian, but he was solidly built. I *might* be able to carry him for a short distance if Ian helped me get him over my shoulders.

Ian caught the direction of my gaze. "I'll carry him," he said. Ferdinand made an indignant noise, but Ian overrode him. "You can barely walk and you expect me to believe you can run for several kilometers?" Ian asked. "Your sister's life is on the line. Swallow your pride and deal with it."

Ferdinand bowed his head and nodded.

"We run for the first checkpoint, shouting about a medical emergency," Ian said. "If they open the gate, we get through before we start shooting. If not, you apply the codebreaker while I shoot." He handed me the com-sized device he'd pulled from his belly pack. "After that, keep moving and keep shooting. I'm going to seal the gates behind us."

As far as plans went, it was pretty thin, but we were on a short time line and trapped in the ground with a military base above us. It would have to do.

Ian and Ferdinand tried various carry positions until Ian decided that a fireman's carry with Ferdinand over his shoulders gave him the best balance and mobility. It was less comfortable for Ferdinand, but he just clenched his jaw and held on.

As we neared the main tunnel, the wireless signals picked up. Apparently the tunnel to the pit hadn't been deemed a high enough priority for repeaters for the whole length.

I pulled Ian to a stop as I listened in. Pain spiked down my spine, but there were few enough signals that I could endure it. A four-person fire team was on the way down to retrieve us. They were still on the first level. Our level was on lockdown.

The soldiers supervising miners were told to stay in place and report any unusual movement.

"They're on lockdown," I said. "They won't believe a medical emergency."

Ian's mouth firmed into a grim line. "I'll activate my shield. We'll go in shooting." He pulled out a small silver disc about three centimeters tall and eight centimeters across. He clicked the button in the middle, then clipped it to his belt. "I'll provide cover and a distraction while you use the codebreaker. Can you stop their transmissions?"

"No." But right now, I wished I could.

"Then speed remains our first priority. Ready?"

Nerves and adrenaline made a toxic soup in my belly, but I nodded anyway.

Ian broke into an easy jog for the final meters of our tunnel, then we were in the main tunnel. He shot the soldier at the first checkpoint, a perfect head shot, before I realized he was shooting.

I snapped out of my shock and ran for the control panel. I attached the codebreaker and hit the override button. While the codebreaker worked, I popped up and looked for a target, but Ian shot them before I could aim.

An avalanche of wireless signals drove a pike through my skull. I looked at a few, but they were all calling for emergency backup while the people up above tried to figure out what was happening. They deployed a new squad to send down and told the fire team to haul ass.

The gate unlocked with a click. I pulled the codebreaker free, then provided covering fire while Ian opened the gate. He put a strip of insta-weld compound on the closing mechanism, then firmly pulled it closed behind us. Now we had to move forward or die here.

I shot a female soldier as she peeked out of one of the side rooms. She fell with a scream. Ian ducked into the guard station and slammed a hand into the emergency lockdown control. Doors banged closed and another burst of wireless signals flew through the air.

Ian grabbed a blaster from a downed soldier and tucked it into his waistband. The doors to the various side rooms remained closed as we advanced. They were solid metal, so I couldn't see inside, but I kept a wary eye on them.

I attached the codebreaker to the second control panel. The soldiers at the far end of the tunnel had finally organized. Blaster bolts sailed our way and Ian's shield took a number of hits. But without the ability to duck into the side rooms for cover, they had no escape from Ian. He methodically shot them down.

His face was a mask of icy calm and I worried about the price his soul was paying in order to help me. The gate clicked open, faster this time. The codebreaker had figured out the pattern.

We moved through the gate and into the soldiers' section of the level. Ian sealed the gate closed behind us. A door on my right opened and I shot the soldier before I could think about it. The man behind him clipped my left arm with a bolt before Ian put him on the ground. I flexed my left hand. Searing pain accompanied the movement, but my hand still worked. Good enough.

The soldiers could open the doors in this section from the inside, but I guess they didn't want to give the miners the ability to open the doors in their section during lockdown. It was hard to quell an uprising if those rising up could let themselves out.

I counted five soldiers down in this part of the hallway. At least two were down beyond the next gate. How many were left?

We dashed to the final checkpoint and I put the codebreaker to work. Ian watched our backs, but the hallway was eerily silent. The wireless signals were still flying fast and furious, but most of them were coming down from command. A few soldiers trapped deeper in the mine with the miners were requesting an override to the lockdown.

The gate clicked open and we were through to the elevators. The control panel was illuminated red and nothing happened when I pressed the call button.

"Don't bother," Ian said. "They won't work under lockdown and even the codebreaker won't be able to override it."

I stared at the stairwell door. We were three kilometers underground, which was likely over nine hundred floors. If a typical floor had fifteen steps, there were—I did some quick mental math—over *thirteen thousand* steps between me and the surface.

"I don't think I can do the stairs," I said. "I'll give it a shot, but I want you to promise to leave me behind if I can't keep up."

Ian grinned at me and some of his iciness melted. "I appreciate your honesty, but we're not taking the stairs quite yet. Hopefully. Help me get the elevator door open." He put Ferdinand down and leaned him against the wall. He handed him a blaster. "Shoot anything that moves in the hallway."

Ferdinand nodded shakily.

I wedged a combat knife in the sliver of space between the doors. Ian pulled them a few centimeters apart then ran into resistance. He strained, his arms flexing, and I heard metal snap. The door opened to reveal an empty space where the elevator car should be.

The elevator shaft was dark and silent and the air was calm. Still, Ian carefully glanced up, checking to make sure he wasn't about to be flattened by a descending car. "Stay here and keep the door open," he said. Before I could protest, he hopped down into the shaft. The top of his head was below the door level.

The elevator car to the right was also missing, but the car

to the left was in place. Ian slid between the left two tracks and scaled the elevator car with an ease that never ceased to amaze me. He disappeared from view and a few seconds later, the car moved upward.

"Ian!"

The car moved down far enough that I could see Ian standing on top of it. "I hope you're not afraid of heights," he said with a grin.

Heights didn't usually bother me but I had a feeling that standing on top of an elevator car in a shaft that was nearly a kilometer deep was going to test that truth before all was said and done.

"Let the door go and I'll open this one for you. Can you help Ferdinand over so I can grab him?"

I agreed and let the door go. It refused to close completely. By the time I'd helped Ferdinand hobble two doors over, Ian was waiting for us. The elevator car was half below the door, leaving a meter-long gap at the top. My brain gave me a vivid image of what would happen if the car moved upward while I was pulling myself through that gap.

Ian hauled Ferdinand up first while I kept a wary eye on the hallway. "Give me your hands," Ian said.

I tucked the blaster in my belt and raised my arms. Ian grabbed me around the wrists and lifted me easily. Sharp pain lanced up my left arm from the blaster graze, but the bleeding had already stopped thanks to my nanos doing their job.

The top of the elevator had a short safety rail around the three sides away from the wall and a control box with a few manual switches. Ferdinand sat next to the controls in the middle of the car.

"How did you know about this?" I asked.

"I had an adventurous childhood, remember?"

Perhaps, but I'd been trained to break into buildings and didn't remember anyone mentioning that elevators had manual controls on top. Or had they? I frowned as I searched my less than stellar memory.

Ian drew me closer to the center of the elevator car. "Stay away from the edges," he said. I nodded my agreement, still trying to remember if I'd ever learned about elevators.

Ian pressed and held a button on the control panel. We moved upward with stomach-dropping swiftness. The bottom of the shaft fell away with alarming speed. I crouched down, then when that didn't feel stable enough, sat on the roof of the elevator car, as close to the center as I could get.

Ian laughed. "It's disconcerting at first," he said, "but it'll get better once you're used to it."

I'd take his word for it. Thanks to the smart glasses I could see, but I wasn't sure that was actually a positive in this case. The frame holding the elevator tracks flashed by, punctuated every few seconds with an ominous creaking, grinding noise.

Ian glanced around, checked on Ferdinand, and looked up, waiting for the ceiling to come into view.

In a pitch-dark tunnel. Without smart glasses.

"You can see," I breathed.

Ian cut a glance at me, then Ferdinand, but my brother hadn't heard me. Yet Ian had. He nodded once, sharply.

I bit my lip to stem the tide of questions I wanted to ask.

We rode in silence for the rest of the trip. It took nearly fifteen minutes to reach the top. Ian stopped the car with our platform level with the bottom of the door. I'd lost signals during the trip, but now I could once again feel messages pressing against my skull.

"The soldiers are still on the first mine level," I said. "Command pulled the fire team back and now it sounds like they're planning an ambush. At least two teams, probably a fire team and a squad, so at least twelve soldiers. They are trying to capture us alive."

The three of us versus twelve of them in fortified positions was not good odds, even if they weren't shooting to kill. Ian must've decided the same thing because he was back to looking grim. He cracked open the door and surveyed the hallway beyond before opening it all the way.

"Hold this," he told me.

I stood and moved gingerly to the door. I purposefully did not look over the side of the elevator. I held the door open while Ian picked up Ferdinand again.

"We need to move fast," Ian said. "Before they have time to dig in further."

"You set the pace since you're carrying Ferdinand," I said. "I'll keep up."

Ian nodded and set off at a ground-eating lope that was a flat-out run for me. I gritted my teeth and kept pace, even when it felt like my lungs would explode from my body. I didn't get a break until we hit a gate, and even then, it was only the ten seconds it took for the codebreaker to unlock it.

By the time we made it far enough that we could see the elevators at the end of the tunnel, I was plastered in sweat and Ian was barely breathing hard, despite carrying another full-grown person. I would hate him if I had the energy to spare. Still, we'd covered the distance in ten minutes instead of the thirty it'd taken us going the other way.

Ian stepped into one of the side rooms and the lights came on. The room was a large rectangle, empty now. It could've been barracks or a mess hall. We checked all of the rooms clustered at the end of the tunnel, assuming that, like the level below, these used to be the soldiers' rooms.

They were all empty.

"They could've left us a few blasters at least," I grumbled. "Maybe some combat armor. A handful of grenades."

Ferdinand looked up from his position on Ian's shoulder and smiled at me, then rolled his eyes. My heart twisted at this small sign that my brother was still in there somewhere, maybe bruised and battered, but not broken.

I sobered. We were woefully underprepared to face a military unit in a fortified position. I'd hoped to be in and out before they realized I wasn't who I said I was. Even if Ian was some sort of Genesis Project supersoldier, he couldn't singlehandedly defeat a dozen soldiers and I was only of moderate help.

I needed to give us a chance. I used the codebreaker to unlock the final gate, then stepped through and asked Ian to hold it open. I wedged the tip of my knife into the edge of the gate's control panel. The face panel popped off, revealing the wiring underneath.

There was no handy diagnostic port this time. I cut the network cable then carefully separated the individual strands of optic cable. I forced myself to work slowly even as the seconds ticked by, each one reducing our chances.

I opened the cable port on the side of my secondary com and gently fed the correct cable into each slot. I'd taken this com to MineCorp in case I needed to use this same procedure, but I'd been lucky there. Now karma was swinging back around to punch me in the face. I didn't have time for this right now.

Once all the cables were in place, I set the com to fix the connections. Optical signals needed precise alignment and my just shoving the cable into the connector wasn't good enough. The com would minutely adjust each cable until the signal worked. It could take up to five minutes.

I set the com down on top of the control box. I could use it from that position and it wasn't at too much risk of falling.

"If you're done on that side, you can come through and let the gate close. I just didn't want it to lock you out if anything went wrong. This will take a few minutes, then I'll need a few more. I'm planning to unleash a virus on the base that will take out any connected systems. How long do you think it will take us to reach the upper floor by elevator?"

"You're taking out the power?" Ian asked with raised eyebrows. He came through the gate and set Ferdinand down next to the elevators.

"Ideally. Depends on how hardened their systems are."

"Fifteen minutes should be safe," he said.

I nodded. "Let's get ready."

Ian and I wedged open the nearest elevator doors but found a car instead of empty space. "Can you go through the roof?" I asked.

Ian grimaced. "I can, but it'll be easier if I don't have to."

We tried four more doors before we found an empty shaft. Ian hopped in and claimed the elevator to our right, where we'd already opened the door. He lowered the elevator until we could climb up through the gap.

When I checked the com, the connection was good. I poked around on the network for a second just to see if anything obvious came up, but I didn't see anything. It didn't matter. If there was the smallest opening, the virus would find it. It was designed to penetrate military-grade installations.

I set up a simple script that would release the virus then wipe the com. It would run after a fifteen-minute timer. I cut the connection to my smart glasses and triple-checked that everything was set up correctly directly on the com. I checked the current time then kicked off the script.

"We have fifteen minutes. We need to be upstairs by then, just in case."

Ian climbed onto the elevator, then waved off my attempt to help Ferdinand up. "You first," he said. Once I was on top of the elevator with him, he continued, "This is the control box." He pointed at the control panel. "This switch needs to be flipped to up, and the manual override set, like so. Then you must hold this button to ascend."

"Why are you showing me this?" I asked slowly.

"You're going up on your own," he said. "I'm taking Ferdinand up the stairs."

"No," I said flatly.

"Yes. If they ambush us on the landing, we'll be sitting ducks if we're both in the elevator. They won't expect me to take the stairs."

"You plan to climb over four thousand stairs carrying another person? You won't have to worry about me, I'll be in a cell long before you make it to the top."

"Want to bet?" Ian asked softly. He had a confident, arrogant tilt to his head that was wildly compelling. "What are you willing to lose?"

I huffed. "My life, apparently."

"Trust me, Bianca. You know I wouldn't put you in unnecessary danger. You go up in the elevator and provide a distraction. You don't even have to shoot at them. Give them some sort of sob story. Tell them I went crazy, but you escaped. Whatever, just keep them distracted. I'll follow and take care of it."

"I left my com behind. I won't be able to talk to you," I said, grasping at straws.

"But I can talk to you, right?" he asked, a speculative look in his eyes. He turned on his mike. "Testing."

I caught the signal, just as he'd intended, but I didn't give in. "Everyone else in the base can hear you, too."

He turned the mike off again. "I'll be careful with it. You can do this, love," he said. "You know you can."

Maybe I had known that, once, but that same confidence had also gotten me in a world of trouble.

He stepped closer and touched my jaw, a gentle press of fingers that tilted my head up so he could catch my gaze. "You are stronger than you know, Bianca."

Bitter laughter bubbled out and I couldn't stop it. "I'm sorry to disappoint–"

He pressed his finger against my lips, cutting off my words. "You do not disappoint me. Never. We are in a Rockhurst mine, rescuing your brother, because of *you*. Ferdinand is alive because of *you*. You can do anything you set your mind to. I would never, ever bet against you because that would be a sucker's bet."

His expression showed exactly how serious he was. He really did believe I could do anything. I stared at him in wonder, and then let his confidence buoy my own.

"Fine," I agreed. "Show me how to open the door."

He did, then he kissed me, a hard press of his lips against mine that I felt in every cell of my body. While I was still reeling, he climbed down and vanished through the elevator doors.

I touched my lips and firmed my resolve. I could do this.

I *would* do this.

# CHAPTER 26

Fourteen minutes had passed by the time the top of the elevator shaft appeared. I wasn't sure what would happen if the power died while I was on the elevator and I really didn't want to find out.

When the elevator platform came even with the bottom of the door, I hesitantly removed my thumb from the button. The elevator stopped and I breathed a silent sigh of relief. We hadn't plummeted to our death the last time, but then Ian had been at the controls. I still half expected to fall.

I unlatched the doors and pulled them open a few centimeters. The hallway beyond appeared empty. Ian's concern had been well-founded but unnecessary. I listened in on the signals I could hear, but the teams on this floor had gone silent.

I eased out into the tunnel. There were three gates between me and the next set of elevators. The tunnel wasn't perfectly straight, so I couldn't see any of the gates from here. Several dark doorways lined either side of the main passage, smaller tunnels that led into the maze of the mine. I couldn't possibly clear them all.

If I was setting up an ambush to capture rather than kill,

I'd position a few soldiers in the side tunnels to come in from behind and trap us against the main force of soldiers. It would also prevent us from retreating.

I set off slowly, keeping a mental ear on the wireless signals, searching for Ian's specific signature or for soldiers trying to flank me, but everything stayed quiet.

The codebreaker opened the first gate in less than ten seconds. I wondered if the stairwell had locked doors, and if so, how Ian planned to get through them. I really should've asked more questions instead of letting that kiss scramble my brain. I left the gate open.

A few meters farther down the tunnel, a flurry of messages spiked through my head. The virus had been loose for a little less than ten minutes. The cybersecurity team was trying to get ahead of it and not having a lot of success.

Thirty seconds and several messages later, the lights went out. My smart glasses adjusted, then adjusted again when the intermittent emergency lighting came on. Vast sections of the hallway were now bathed in shadow.

Coms went down and silence rang in my head. An emergency evacuation alarm went off, stopped, then went off again. I chuckled. I'd never seen this particular virus in use, but it was even better than advertised. I'd have to send my contact a bonus for a job well done.

I moved toward the next gate, keeping to the shadows as much as possible. Various alarms went off and were silenced, but the coms didn't come back up. The second gate appeared in the distance. As I approached, I caught the whisper of a com signal. Someone was transmitting nearby, but no one was responding.

I crept forward, trying to determine the location. Dark spots flashed in my vision. I was using my dubious gift too much and paying for the effort. Pain was my constant companion, but I needed every edge I could get.

I peeked into the next tunnel and found a soldier, com to his ear. I'm not sure who was more surprised, him or me, but I recovered faster and shot first. I'd been aiming for center mass, but I must've pulled it at the last second. The soldier fell dead, a perfect shot through the middle of his head.

Well, that was my allotment of luck for this century.

That proved true a second later when the soldier behind him shot me twice with a stun pistol before I even realized she was there. I went down with a scream of agony. I clung to consciousness by the tiniest of threads. Stun pistols packed less of a wallop than stunsticks, but my brain implant still did not appreciate the jolt.

"You stupid bitch! You killed Katz!" Her steel-toed boot to my stomach drove the breath from my lungs. She pulled back for another kick, but a third soldier stopped her. "Imbor wants her alive!" he said.

"Imbor can fuck off," she growled, struggling.

The male soldier shook her. "I'm going to pretend I didn't hear that, Private. Now help me cuff her before she regains muscle control."

The private rolled me over none too gently and drove a knee into my spine. I couldn't prevent my groan. She wrenched my arms around and secured them behind my back. My left arm throbbed with pain as the blaster wound reopened.

"You're a dead woman," she whispered into my ear.

She would have to get in line.

The male soldier searched me and took my blaster, smart glasses, and codebreaker. He left my inactive shielding cuff, thinking it jewelry. It dug into my arm above the restraints, but the pain meant I still had one form of protection if I needed it.

The man picked me up and tossed me over his shoulder. Blood rushed into my head and his shoulder dug into my bruised stomach. If I vomited on him he was totally going to deserve it.

He moved briskly down the tunnel. Without my glasses, I couldn't accurately judge time, but it felt like just a few minutes. If I remembered correctly, the second and third gates were fairly close together.

At least eight soldiers filled the hallway, standing in a pool of light. "Is that the woman?" a male voice asked. "Where are the man and the miner?"

"She was alone," the female who kicked me said.

I was unceremoniously dumped on the floor. I climbed to my feet and marched for the far elevators, the ones leading up to the base.

An older man grabbed my injured arm in a tight grip and spun me around. He sneered at me. "Where do you think you're going?"

*I think I'm getting you all to face away from the tunnel I just arrived through,* I thought to myself. Out loud, I said, "I am returning to the base to contact MineCorp. That crazy son of a bitch I hired shot me! Me! He'll never work again once my supervisors hear about this."

*Keep talking.* My brain caught the signal before I even realized who it was from. Ian was nearby.

"And you all can kiss your jobs good-bye, too," I said, my voice rising. "Who attacks a MineCorp representative? Don't you know who I am? That bitch who stunned and kicked me is first in line for firing. She should be happy that I don't demand her head. Release me this instant!"

The soldier holding my arm released me and everyone else laughed, but it had a tinge of uneasiness. Command might've said I was a fake, but my tone and accent said I was high class. I just needed to sow enough doubt to keep them distracted.

*Keep talking and don't move.*

I mentally rolled my eyes. Like I was going anywhere. I launched into another tirade. "I'm going to demand that Mine-Corp immediately revoke all House Rockhurst contracts. You clearly cannot be trusted—"

The heat of a blaster bolt seared my left side. The soldier who had grabbed me dropped to the ground. The other soldiers in the hallway soon followed. Only two had managed to get shots off.

"Time to go, princess," Ian said, stepping out of the shadows.

My whole body sagged in relief. "Can you find the key to the cuffs?"

"No need." Ian popped the plastech cuffs open with his bare hands, which should have been impossible. I was beginning to think the word didn't apply to Ian. But when he touched my wounded arm, his grip was gentle.

"Are you okay?" I asked. "Is Ferdinand? *Where* is Ferdinand?" I looked Ian over, checking for injuries. He didn't have any obvious wounds, but his shirt was soaked with sweat—what do you know, he was human after all.

"We're both fine. Ferdinand is a little way back. Thanks to your virus, we're going to have to go up the stairs. Can you do it?"

"Yes," I said. "Can you? How did you get up here so fast?"

His grin was sin and temptation. "Stamina."

A frisson of heat wove through me. "I see your ego didn't take any damage," I said with a laugh. "Go get my brother while I find my stuff."

I retrieved my stuff from the soldier who had searched me. Thanks to the smart glasses I could see the gate to the elevators in the distance. I kept an eye on it, but nothing moved. Based on the number of soldiers here, this was the sum total of everyone they'd sent down.

Ian returned with Ferdinand draped over his shoulders.

"Think they'll send a squad down the stairs?" I asked.

Ian shrugged. "Maybe. It seems like your virus is causing enough chaos that they'll try to deal with that first, though. Have you heard anything from Aoife?"

"No. Coms are down. I only heard you because you were close."

"Do you have a plan for once we reach the base level?"

"Keep climbing," I said. "If the ship is still there, we take that. If not, we steal something."

"Okay, let's go."

IAN SET A GRUELING PACE AND I KEPT UP OUT OF SHEER stubbornness. When I slowed, he took my hand and pulled me up a few floors until I recovered a little. He hadn't been joking—his stamina seemed inexhaustible.

When he stopped a floor below the top, I nearly collapsed in gratitude. My lungs burned, my stomach burned, my legs burned. *Everything* burned. Now that we'd stopped, my legs trembled uncontrollably.

"This is the base level," he said. "We'll have to change stairwells to climb to the surface."

I listened for signals, but the coms were still down. "I don't know what's happening up there," I said. "There could be a platoon of soldiers waiting for us for all I know."

"Your optimism knows no bounds," Ian said drily.

I shrugged. "I'm too tired for optimism."

"Activate your cuff," Ian said. "We'll run for the stairs, then run for the ship."

"What if they left already?"

"Then we'll improvise. Don't borrow trouble."

I nodded and activated my cuff. I promised myself that once this was done, I'd spend a week on the pink sandy beaches of GCD One doing nothing more difficult than sipping a fruity drink with a tiny umbrella in it.

We climbed the last floor to the base level. The codebreaker made short work of the door at the top of the stairwell and the door leading into the main part of the base.

"I'll cover you while you open the stairwell door to the surface," Ian said. "It's just past the elevator."

I nodded and we lunged into the main hallway. Ian shot the guard at the gate, but more soldiers milled in the hallway beyond. I attached the codebreaker while he laid down suppressing fire.

The door popped open. "Now!" I shouted. We dashed up the stairs. This stairwell was blissfully short compared to the one from the mine, but soldiers streamed in below us, shooting both bolts and stun rounds.

We surprised a quartet of soldiers in the hangar. I shot one and Ian shot three. Outside, *Opportunity* was in defense mode. Aoife stood on the cargo ramp in combat armor. At least four bodies in spacesuits littered the ground. An atmospheric barrier shimmered over the cargo bay door.

Ian put Ferdinand on his feet. "Bianca, help Ferdinand to the ship. I will be rear guard." He cut me off before I could protest. "I'll be right behind you. Remember, the air outside isn't breathable, so take a deep breath and get moving."

We didn't have time to argue, so I slung Ferdinand's left arm over my shoulder and pulled him into a slow jog that made him grunt with every step. "Deep breath," I said right before we hit the hangar's atmospheric barrier.

I sucked in air just as my cuff vibrated and blaster bolts sailed past. The ship was twenty meters out. Ferdinand dragged at me, but I pulled him inexorably forward. My lungs burned with the need to breathe. I gritted my teeth against the instinct.

My cuff vibrated again. I wanted to check on Ian, but if I stopped, I might not start again. Fire burned through my chest. The need to breathe became impossible to ignore. Ten meters.

We crossed into the ship's shield. Someone had turned off ground protection, so at least we weren't instantly incinerated.

Five meters.

I blew out some of my precious air, just so my body might think I was breathing and give me a fucking break.

It didn't work.

Ferdinand coughed and gasped next to me. Aoife stopped shooting long enough to come down the cargo ramp and drag us inside. I wanted to collapse into a coughing fit on the cargo bay floor, but I turned, looking for Ian.

He was still in the hangar, on the ground, surrounded by at least two squads of soldiers, half in helmeted spacesuits.

He'd promised to be right behind me. He'd lied and sacrificed himself. Irrational anger seared away all of my worry and fatigue.

Fuck that noise. He didn't get to die heroically for me. I was going to explain that to him in great detail using very small words, just as soon as I retrieved his captured ass.

I opened my crate of supplies, looking for my armor, but digging it out wasn't going to be fast enough. "Aoife, strip. I need your armor. Take Ferdinand and stick to the plan. I'm going after Ian."

"You can't," she said. She reached for the cargo door button.

"Touch that button and I'll fling myself out the door without a weapon *or* armor. I'm going, so start fucking helping."

I grabbed my primary com and a pair of long blasters from my crate. Aoife was half out of her armor, and as she took pieces off, I strapped them on. It would be too tall, but I'd make it work.

Ferdinand tried to stop me, but I batted his hands away. "I have to do this," I said. "If you keep slowing me down, it's going to be harder."

He backed away with a curt nod.

With Ian secure, the soldiers in spacesuits were approaching the ship. "Get Ferdinand to Benedict. I'm trusting you, Aoife," I said.

She nodded. "Good hunting. Don't die or Ian will resurrect himself just so he can kill me."

My feet weren't all the way in the boots and the face mask was a little higher than ideal, but I'd used oversized armor before. It clamped around me tightly enough that I could make it work. I put my com in the chest compartment and closed the face guard. I didn't have time for squeamishness.

I strapped one long gun to my back and held the other one with the muzzle pointing down. I activated the external speaker. "Go as soon as I'm on the ground," I said. "They must not catch you. I'm going to shift blame to Silva. If questioned, do the same."

"I'll make you a hole while the door closes. Make use of it. I hope you know what you're doing."

I hoped I did, too. If Ian was already dead, I'd personally revive him just so I could yell at him for being a lying bastard.

Aoife started picking off the soldiers. I bounded down the ramp, shooting as I went. I wasn't nearly as accurate as Aoife, but not too many of the soldiers wanted to take on an armored opponent. They scattered for cover.

I had an extremely narrow window of time where that

shock would carry the day. Then they'd armor up and over-whelm me. I had to be gone before that happened.

Once I was clear of the ship's shield, I brought the suit's shield up. Aoife's armor was top of the line and responded beau-tifully, even with the bad fit. I barreled toward the soldiers who were dragging Ian toward the elevator. If they got him inside, I was done for.

With Ian mostly on the ground, I had a clear line of fire on the soldiers around him. I did not waste the opportunity. After two of them went down, the rest dropped Ian and ran for cover.

Ian did not move.

Dread curled through my belly. Ian wouldn't give up; he would fight to the end. Was he truly dead?

I skidded to a stop next to him. The suit's heads-up display detected a faint heartbeat, thready and too fast. Not dead, but seriously injured. I carefully scooped him up in my left arm with the suit's help. His torso left a bright red smear on the hangar's floor. He hung limply from my grip.

I spun and checked my options one last time before I de-cided. *Opportunity* was gone and I breathed a sigh of relief. Even if my stupidity got me killed, at least Ferdinand had a shot.

A small Rockhurst planet hopper sat outside, covered in a layer of snow. Another small Rockhurst transport ship was parked in the hangar, but it hadn't been here when we'd ar-rived. That meant it had likely jumped in more recently than the hopper. Neither would have a sophisticated medbay or FTL drive.

There were no other options. Where in the hell did they keep their military ships?

I would have only one shot at this. If I chose wrong, we were captured at best, dead at worst.

Trusting my instincts, I ran for the ship outside. Ian was

inside my shield, but I shot at anything that moved, trying to keep them from returning fire. I couldn't tell Ian to hold his breath, so I'd have to give him CPR once we were inside. I silently prayed he would hang on.

The cargo ramp was down, and the door opened when I pressed the button. Alarms sounded as unbreathable air came in with us. The ship automatically began a purge as soon as I closed the door. I locked it behind us. It might buy us a few seconds.

Once the air was safe, I laid Ian on the floor and stripped off my gloves and helmet. He wasn't breathing. I started CPR, pressing his chest and filling his lungs with oxygen.

When he took a shallow breath on his own, I nearly cried. My hands came away red, but I had to get us in the air before I could do more for him.

I pulled out my com and searched for the Rockhurst override codes I'd recently found for Ada. In addition to the six standard codes spanning a dozen years, I had five newer specialized codes I could try.

I started with the standard codes because they were the most likely to work on a nonessential ship like this. The newest standard code didn't work, nor did the second newest. But the third code, the one from six years ago, gave me administrative access to the ship. How long had it been since they'd serviced this scrap heap?

I changed the override codes, wiped the existing crew, and set myself up as captain. I was conscious of each second that slipped past. I stripped off the rest of my borrowed armor and dropped it carelessly on the ground. I ran for the flight deck.

The ship had some technical name I couldn't remember. "Computer, plot a course to NAD Seven."

"Yes, Captain White," the ship responded. I'd used my secondary identity, just in case.

On the flight deck, I didn't bother to sit down. I leaned over the captain's console and checked the flight plan. It was both better and worse than I feared. The bad news was, we'd have to jump twice. The good news was, the FTL was ready to jump now. Any recent von Hasenberg ship could make the trip in a single jump, but this ship was designed with a cheap FTL for hops between relatively close planets.

I told the ship to follow the suggested flight plan, but a warning flashed on-screen. Rockhurst was refusing takeoff permission. Of course they were. I moved to the manual controls and clipped in.

I hadn't manually flown a ship in a dozen years. This would be fun.

I flipped the switches, overrode the warnings, and pulled back on the controls. The tiny ship shot into the air, far faster than I'd been planning. New warnings blared and I eased back on the controls. Once my stomach climbed out of my feet, I took a shaky breath.

I watched both the console and the forward vid screens, searching for other ships. They had to be out there, but I just needed to clear the atmosphere and then I'd be free to jump.

"Incoming communication," the ship intoned.

"Who is it?" I asked.

"Commander Rockhurst of the *Santa Celestia*."

I laughed without humor. Of course Richard Rockhurst would be here. Why wouldn't he be? The universe fucking hated me today. The *Santa Celestia* was a Rockhurst battle cruiser capable of blowing me out of the sky without even breaking out the big guns.

Had *Opportunity* escaped before he'd arrived? They had a little less than an hour before they could jump. If they could get enough distance, they could go dark and make themselves a harder target to hit, but hiding from a battle cruiser was a losing proposition.

"Accept voice-only," I said.

Richard's face appeared on-screen. With the trademark Rockhurst blond hair and blue eyes, he was gorgeous—or he had been. We were both twenty-five, but he looked like he'd aged a decade in the few months since I'd last seen him. "Stand down at once and return to XAD Seven," he demanded.

I adopted the rolling, lilting accent typical of the Silva family. "It is you who should stand down."

In three minutes, I'd clear the atmosphere. I just had to keep him talking. I pulled back on the controls a little more, pushing the ship to the edge of safety.

"Who are you?" he demanded.

"I am no one. A promise fulfilled," I said, "nothing more. But if you interfere, I will become an enormous problem."

"You're from the Syndicate?"

I said nothing. The silence stretched.

"What does the Syndicate want with one of our miners? We would've happily negotiated for his release."

I laughed low. "I know how you negotiate, Commander. MineCorp took something from us. We retrieved it. I regret that so many of your troops failed to stay out of our way, but such is life."

"Was the other ship the distraction or are you the distraction?" Richard asked.

"Perhaps we are both the distraction. Have your troops reached the mine depths yet, Commander?"

He gestured to someone off camera.

"What will the Syndicate give me for your safe return?"

"You should ask what they will do should I not return safely. That is the far more interesting question."

"If I let you go, you must do something for me in return."

"If you let both ships go, the Syndicate will honor one future request from you, free of charge."

"No, not them. You, personally."

I chuckled again. "I am no one. You are trading gold for dirt."

"It is my choice."

"What do you want?"

"I haven't decided," he said, "but can you put a price on two ships and multiple lives? My request will be worthy of that debt."

Did he know? Could he have possibly guessed who I was? I should promise him whatever he wanted and then break that promise, but even now, I couldn't quite bring myself to do it. Ian's lifeblood leaked in the cargo bay every second I delayed and even if we jumped, Aoife, Alex, and Ferdinand were trapped for another hour.

"Very well," I said. "If you look the other way while both of our ships exit your system, I will personally honor one future request from you that will take no longer than a week to complete and must not harm me or mine."

"How will I contact you?"

"Post a public request for information on a source of gold dragon scales. I will contact you."

"Very well, my lady. I accept. But if you go back on your word, I will destroy everything you love." He said it softly but steel laced his tone.

The blood froze in my veins. *He knew.* If not about Ferdinand, then about me at the very least.

"Why?" I whispered.

"Your family may yet prove useful to me," he said. Then with an arrogant little smirk, he cut the connection.

I didn't trust Richard in the least and expected a barrage of fighters from *Santa Celestia* at any moment, but the ship's sensors weren't picking up anything. I couldn't keep hesitating. I had to trust that Alex and Aoife could take care of Ferdinand.

I released the manual controls and let the ship take over. I checked our flight plan again then pressed the jump confirmation button. The engine noise changed and ramped up for an alarmingly long time before my stomach dropped and we jumped.

I checked our location, then put the ship in what passed for stealth. We would drift for four days before we could jump again.

Now I had to save Ian. I prayed I wasn't already too late.

# CHAPTER 27

I had to use the combat armor to carry Ian into the tiny medbay. The diagnostic table took up more than half of the room. I carefully maneuvered Ian onto the table and kicked off a scan before returning to the cargo bay to strip the armor off.

By the time I returned, the scan was done. The report listed his injuries from most to least severe, and it was a long list. The worst injury was internal bleeding from a blaster wound through his right side. That one needed immediate treatment. The report recommended time in a regeneration tank, but that wasn't an option—this ship had no tank.

The outlook for alternative treatment put his chance of survival at less than 50 percent and that was with his nanos. But if I could keep him alive for the next few days, the doctors on Benedict's ship could save him. I cut off his shirt, washed and disinfected my hands, and got to work.

I'd had some basic field medicine training years ago. I tried to remember what I had been taught as the diagnostic table walked me through a manual IV insertion. Usually an IV machine would start the IV for you, but this ship's medbay didn't have one, so I was on my own.

My hands shook so badly that I had to stop and take a deep breath. I could do this. It took three tries before I hit the vein. I hooked him up to a bag of synthetic blood replacement and moved on to his wound.

The blast had gone straight through. I rolled Ian onto his side, being careful with his IV. I irrigated both sides of the wound, and his blood ran like water. Luckily, the ship had a decent supply of regeneration gel. I pumped the wound full of gel. The regen gel congealed and sealed the hole, preventing him from bleeding out, but he might need another bag of synth blood.

I couldn't lift him to wrap bandages around his body, so I pressed thick pads of gauze against the wound on his back and taped it tightly in place, then repeated the procedure on his front.

I cut off his pants, then cleaned and bandaged the rest of his wounds. Most were shallow, but he'd lost a few decently sized chunks of flesh to blaster bolts. His heart rate began to slow as the synth blood replaced what he had lost.

With Ian as stabilized as I could make him, I cleaned and bandaged my own wounds. My arm wasn't bad enough to need regen gel, so I skipped it. I didn't have time for the pain and Ian might need more before we could jump again.

I turned on the audible heart monitoring on the diagnostic table and piped sounds from the medbay through the ship's speakers. I would hear if anything happened while I was exploring our refuge for the next four days.

The comforting sound of Ian's continued life followed me throughout the ship. The main area was a single level, with a half-height maintenance level underneath. Besides the flight deck, cargo bay, and medbay, there was a large passenger lounge filled with tables, chairs, and two synthesizers, a bathroom, and a tiny crew cabin with a narrow bed.

The ship was designed to ferry passengers between close planets in a system. Most trips wouldn't last more than an hour or two, so crew comfort wasn't exactly a priority. There also weren't any available communication drones, so I couldn't jump a message to Benedict.

I grabbed a meal replacement shake and bottle of water from the synthesizer. I wasn't hungry, but my head rang like a bell and I couldn't remember the last time I'd eaten. I briefly considered trying to get some broth into Ian, but decided that fluids via IV were less likely to choke him. He wouldn't starve in the four days before the real doctors could take over.

I stopped by the crew bunk and snagged a pillow and blanket, then returned to the medbay. I slid down the wall across from Ian and drank my shake without tasting it. I sipped at the water and listened to Ian's heartbeat.

Once I'd drained half the bottle, I leaned my head back against the wall and closed my eyes. Adrenaline gave way to exhaustion. It wasn't that late, but today had started early. I could hardly believe that we'd broken into MineCorp just this morning—it seemed like a lifetime ago.

The steady beeping of the heart monitor soothed me into a light sleep, so when Ian started thrashing, it took me a second to remember where I was and what was going on.

I sprang up and caught his arm before he could rip out the IV. His eyes were wide and glassy. I was no match for his strength, so he just pulled my body along with his arm. I climbed onto the table, being careful of his wound, and pinned his arms with my legs.

"Ian! You're safe. It's Bianca! I've got you. You're wounded and you're doing a good job of wrecking all of my work. Stay still!"

He stilled and blinked up at me, as if he couldn't quite make out my face. "Bianca?" he rasped.

"Yes, I'm here. We're safe. You have to stay still so you can heal."

"Don't leave," he demanded weakly.

"I won't. I'm sleeping on the floor. I'll be nearby."

"Sleep here."

I laughed. "This diagnostic table barely fits you. I'd roll over and be on the floor anyway, just with a few more bruises to show for it."

His breath sighed out. "Your laugh," he whispered, trailing off. His eyes closed and he relaxed under me. When I was sure he was out again, I carefully climbed off him.

The IV was still in place. The diagnostic table didn't flag any new injuries or worsening of his other wounds, so I returned to my place on the floor, wide awake.

It was going to be a long night.

I TENDED IAN FOR NEARLY FORTY-EIGHT HOURS BEFORE he decided, between one blink and the next, that he was awake and healed. I stared stupidly as he tried to get up. Finally, my tired brain lurched into action. "What are you doing?" I screeched at him, pressing him back against the table.

"I'm getting up." He looked at me like *I* was the crazy one here.

"I did not keep you alive for two days through sheer force of will just so you could randomly decide to get up and undo all of my work," I said. Then I did the worst possible thing: I burst into tears. I swiped at my cheeks. "These are angry tears," I growled at him, daring him to comment.

He sat up with a grunt and pulled me into a hug. I buried my head in his shoulder. His skin was warm and firm under my cheek. He was alive. I'd kept him alive. I let go of all the worry and sadness I'd been bottling up inside. He rubbed my back and petted my hair and made soft, soothing sounds.

"You lied to me," I whispered. "You promised not to lie to me."

Ian knew exactly what I meant. "It didn't start as a lie," he said. "I planned to be right behind you, but they had too many troops. If I'd kept my word, they would've gotten you, too. I couldn't let that happen."

"You nearly died. I'm still not sure how you're awake now."

"I told you I'm hard to kill," he said. "Tell me what happened after I went down. Where are we?"

Ian listened without commenting as I brought him up to speed. I hesitated when I got to Richard's involvement. After everything we'd been through, I trusted Ian, but he was going to be unhappy with my decision.

"What is it?" he asked.

"I owe Richard Rockhurst a favor."

He went perfectly still. "What happened?" I told him and he blew out a breath. "You had no choice," he said. "We'll deal with the consequences when they come. Do you know if the others made it?"

"No, I had no contact with them after they launched and this bucket of bolts doesn't have a com drone. We have two more days until we can jump again."

"Are you going to let me off this table?"

"No."

Ian mock-scowled at me. In the end, I relented. He needed food, and the diagnostic table proved him right—he was remarkably healed. He *had* to be a Genesis Project soldier. I wanted to ask him a million questions, but I also knew what it was to hold a secret close.

I removed his IV, then hovered as he slid off the table. He landed with a grimace, but he didn't need my assistance to stand. Still, I watched him out of the corner of my eye as we made our way to the lounge. And not only because he was wearing a pair of navy boxer briefs and nothing else.

I ordered a meal replacement shake and a cup of hot tea. I felt okay but exhaustion clawed at me. A shake was easier than trying to decide on real food. Ian did not have the same issue. He ordered enough food for a small army and tore through it with gusto.

When I finished my shake, Ian nudged a cup of raspberry mousse my way and finished his own dinner. I glanced up sharply. Did he remember it was one of my favorites or had it been a lucky guess?

His eyes were guarded. *He knew.*

I took it and the offered spoon with a murmur of gratitude. The first bite was bliss. I scooped up a bite and turned the spoon toward Ian. "Bite?" I offered.

He leaned over and I slid the spoon into his mouth. The room shrank until he was the only thing I saw. Warm blue eyes, straight nose, strong jaw. Ian Bishop was a gorgeous man. Two days of stubble gave him a rough, rugged look that only increased his appeal.

He took the spoon from my lax fingers and dipped it in the mousse, then fed me a bite. My eyes dropped closed and I hummed in appreciation. A second later, Ian's finger dabbed mousse on my lower lip.

I opened my eyes to find him centimeters away, his eyes glowing. "Allow me," he said. I nodded in agreement.

He leaned in and swept his tongue over my bottom lip. When he went to retreat, I buried my hand in the hair at the back of his head and pulled him to me. He wasn't going to get away that easily.

I slid my tongue into his mouth. He tasted of raspberry

mousse and desire. He let me lead. I kissed him slow and deep. I'd almost lost him. I poured my emotions into the kiss, everything I was too afraid to admit aloud.

Ian made a deep sound in his chest and pulled me closer. He took over, tipping my head back and plundering my mouth. I sighed in surrender. Lust blazed bright, accompanied by a softer emotion I refused to examine too closely. I shifted and squeezed my legs together. My breasts felt heavy.

I pulled back, panting. Ian was still recovering. I shouldn't be mauling him. Of course, he didn't look like he minded. His eyes glittered and his face was set in harsh lines of restraint. He lifted the spoon to my lips, another bite of mousse.

I closed my lips around it and tried very hard not to think about anything *else* I'd like to close my lips around.

Ian groaned. "I could watch you eat this all day," he growled. "Except I'm not sure I'd survive the experience. I'm already hard as a rock."

My mouth rounded in surprise. He hadn't just said that, had he? I peeked at him. An impressive erection tented the fabric of his boxers. He *had* said it.

He laughed, the sound rich and full. "You should see your face right now," he said. "Shocked you, have I? In that case . . ."

Before I could ask him what he meant, he lifted me from my chair and swung me into his lap, straddling him. When I stayed quiet, he froze and peered down at me. "Is this okay?" he asked quietly.

I found my voice. "Yes. Wait, no. You're injured."

"No because I'm injured or no because you're uncomfortable?" Ian clarified.

I was entirely comfortable. In fact, if I could slide forward a few centimeters, I'd be even more comfortable, because his hard length would press almost exactly where I wanted it. But even after our kisses and his obvious desire, he was confirming that I was still with him and that he wasn't taking more than I freely offered. My heart sighed and I knew I was a goner.

As if I wasn't already.

"The former," I whispered. "Don't hurt yourself." I met his gaze straight on and gave him a truth. "You scared me. I thought you were going to die."

He didn't shy away from my honesty. "I'm sorry I scared you. Dying wasn't my plan, but I knew it was a possibility. It was an acceptable risk to give you a chance."

I lightly smacked his shoulder. "It *wasn't* an acceptable risk! Promise me you won't do something so stupid again."

His jaw firmed, and his eyes lit with determination. "I won't lie to you, love. I would make the same choice a hundred times if it kept you safe." He sighed. "When I said I'm hard to kill, I meant it. As you've already guessed, I'm a member of the missing Genesis Project squad. We were engineered to be ruthless, indestructible bastards. It takes a lot to put us down permanently."

I smiled sadly. "No wonder you hated me when you arrived. I represented everything terrible that had happened to you."

Ian grimaced. "I was an asshole. I was overwhelmingly attracted to you and didn't want to be, so I pushed you away with sharp words and biting comments. I apologize. By the time I grew up enough to realize how stupid I was, you were married to that weasel. Then you came home but wanted nothing to do with me, which frustrated me into repeating the cycle." He shook his head. "Not my proudest moments."

I ran my fingers through the stubble on his jaw. "Would you like to know a secret?"

He nodded warily.

"I always wanted you, but you made me so tongue-tied that

I started intentionally making you angry enough to end our conversations early so I wouldn't look like an idiot. We're both assholes. I'm sorry."

He kissed my palm. "We're perfect for each other," he said.

Incandescent joy brought a smile to my face. It dimmed as I realized I had yet another secret to share. "Gregory was a brilliant man," I began.

"Bianca—" Ian started, but I pressed my fingers to his lips.

"I need to tell you," I said softly. "Gregory was obsessed with his research. It was one of the reasons Father pushed for our marriage—he wanted Gregory's discoveries to be House von Hasenberg discoveries."

I sighed and gave him the rest of the truth. "The other reason was that Gregory had gotten me pregnant. I didn't realize until later how carefully he'd planned everything, including our hasty wedding. I lost the baby two months later." My voice was flat, but I felt that wound still.

Ian wrapped his arms around me, offering silent support.

"The first year of our marriage, Gregory did everything possible to break me down and distance me from my support network, starting even before I lost our baby. All of my training and all of my intelligence and I couldn't see my own husband was manipulating me. I kept trying to *fix it,* but it wasn't something I could fix."

Even now, I wondered if I could've done something differently, and how fucked up was that? I *knew* he had manipulated me and still I wondered. I shook myself.

"The Consortium's regulatory agencies didn't move fast enough for Gregory. Human experiments require years of work before they're approved, so he decided to experiment on his own property, namely me. He wanted a piece of tech so irresistible that he could write his own rules."

"He experimented on you without your consent, didn't he?" Ian asked, his voice dark and dangerous.

I laughed without humor, the bitter sound dragged out of me by the thought of Gregory asking me for anything so trivial to him as consent. "He did not ask me," I confirmed. "He drugged me and inserted the implant in my brain. Afterward, he told me I had passed out and hit my head and he'd operated to relieve the swelling."

Ian swore viciously under his breath.

"The modified nanos came later. By the time I figured out what was happening, I was too sick to stop it. I almost died before he realized he needed to shield my bedroom from wireless signals. Then when I felt well enough to move from the bed, he threatened to do the same to my sisters if I told anyone or asked for help."

Now I could see that the threat was an empty one—my sisters were well protected in House von Hasenberg. But at the time, sick and in pain, I would've done anything to spare them the same fate.

Ian rubbed circles on my back. I wasn't sure if he even knew he was doing it, but it helped me to get the rest of the story out.

"I was too sick to go out in public, not that there was much to do in Daln anyway, and I'd cut ties with nearly everyone. My sisters still tried to visit occasionally. Gregory would put them off as long as possible, then have them visit me in a shielded sitting room while I was dosed with painkillers. He told me that if they found out I was sick, he'd kill me, so I let them think I was trying for a baby and it wasn't going well. They were so supportive—" My voice broke.

"Shhh," Ian whispered. He clutched me in a tight hug. I sucked in a few deep breaths before I felt like I could continue.

"Gregory knew the implant had the potential to decode

wireless transmissions, even encrypted ones, but he couldn't fully test it in the lab because it needed the connection to the human brain. And once implanted, it didn't have any diagnostic access, so he needed my cooperation."

It was a rare mistake. He must've thought he'd broken me enough that I would be docile and helpful. And no one would want an implant that could be hacked externally, so he must've implanted me with a prototype that was close to final. I often wondered who else he had experimented on and whether they'd survived, but despite my connections, I couldn't find a hint of them. Gregory had been paranoid about data security.

I continued, "When I failed to cooperate, he would lock me in the lab and bombard me with messages, encrypted and not, to try to get a reaction out of me. He put horrible things in them, threats and worse."

It had been a living nightmare and, even in the safety of Ian's embrace, I shivered in remembered horror.

"I never let him know how well his tech worked. No matter what he tried, and he tried *everything,* I had just enough stubborn determination to pretend his life's work was faulty. And no House or merc squad would risk their health for faulty tech. He died thinking he'd failed." It was my one point of pride, my one tiny rebellion. I hadn't been strong enough to fight him, but I'd clawed back just enough spark to stonewall him.

Ian's arms tightened around me. "That bastard is *lucky* he is dead."

"He died badly," I said. Satisfaction warred with pity. "We were in the lab. He was angry because I wasn't helping. I don't know how the fire started, but there were so many combustible materials it spread faster than anything I'd ever seen."

The roar of the flames, the heat searing my face. Gregory's

frantic screams for help as his coat caught. "He was trying to save his research files; he didn't believe in off-site backups, too risky. But the fire was too intense. I was right beside a fire extinguisher. I could've saved him. I didn't."

I shrugged as if the nightmares didn't still force me from sleep in a cold sweat. "I dragged myself out and the doctors treated me for smoke inhalation and a few minor burns. Once Gregory's family realized he'd died, they kicked me out of my own house because, of course, it wasn't mine, it was Gregory's. I had to ask Hannah to come get me."

"House marriages are fucked up," Ian growled.

I chuckled. "I agree. And now, thanks to my modified nanos and brain implant, I can 'hear' wireless signals without a com, including encrypted communications. In return, I get a splitting headache and constant nausea. The night I was shot at, I wasn't paying attention because I was trying to decrypt a tricky message."

"Who knows about your ability and what happened?"

"No one," I said immediately. "Father would order further testing. My siblings would blame themselves. It's better for everyone to think I'm grieving. In a way, I am."

"I wish *I'd* known," Ian said. "I'm so sorry, Bianca."

"I didn't tell you to earn your pity. I don't need it. I'm stronger than that now. But if we're going to explore this thing between us, I wanted you to know the whole truth from the beginning."

"We are *definitely* going to 'explore this thing between us,'" Ian growled. "You're not getting away from me again." He sealed his words with a kiss so tender it brought tears to my eyes. "Now I'm taking you to bed," he said.

Once again, he'd shocked me. He laughed and the vibrations rumbled from his chest to mine. "Get your mind out of the gutter, love. You're exhausted. I saw it as soon as I woke up. Now that you've eaten, you're going to sleep."

"Are you planning to be this bossy the entire time?" I demanded. "Because I think I've changed my mind."

He rubbed his nose against mine. "No, you haven't."

No, I hadn't, damn him.

I climbed off Ian's lap and led him to the tiny crew bunk. He eyed the narrow bed as if it had personally offended him. "You can have that one," I said. "I'll fold down the top bunk."

"Like hell you will." He climbed in and leaned against the wall behind him, leaving most of the bed free. "Hop in."

I thought about continuing to argue with the stubborn man just for the hell of it, but exhaustion dragged at me. He wanted me next to him and I wanted to be there.

I stripped off the boots and too big pants I'd been wearing for two days. I left the shirt and my underwear. I promised myself a shower once I woke. I slid in next to him, facing away and lying on my right side.

Ian wrapped an arm around me and shifted us until we were nestled together in the middle of the mattress, his chest pressed against my back. "Okay?" he asked.

"Perfect," I whispered.

# CHAPTER 28

I awoke to the heavy lethargy that meant I'd slept long and well. I was curled up against Ian's right side, my right arm and leg thrown across his body. He radiated heat like a furnace.

My eyes popped open. Did he have a fever? I moved my hand to his forehead but it didn't feel too hot.

The arm he'd wrapped around me flexed as he hauled me on top of him. "Ian, stop, you're injured! I'm going to hurt you."

"I'm not and you're not," he countered. "See for yourself."

I carefully pushed myself up, violently aware that I was straddling his hips and that he was hard under me. Several more things became obvious from my new vantage point. One, Ian was clean. He smelled like the light, crisp cleanser used in sonic showers. Two, he was entirely naked. Gone were the boxer briefs.

But the most amazing discovery was the complete lack of bandages anywhere on his body. I touched the right side of his abdomen. A jagged circle of pink skin was the only indication that anything had happened.

"How long was I asleep?" I asked.

"Ten hours."

"That's impossible. This looks a week old, at least."

"As impossible as being able to mentally decrypt com signals?"

I glanced up sharply, but he wasn't poking fun, he was seriously asking me to consider it.

"We're a hell of a pair, aren't we?" I finally conceded.

"You did say we'd be unstoppable if we worked together." He grinned. "You were right."

He shifted under me and I sucked in a breath. I rolled my hips and stars exploded behind my eyes. I climbed off him before I got distracted. His clean scent drove home exactly how badly I needed a shower.

"I'm going to get cleaned up," I said.

"Do you want the good news or the really good news?" Ian asked.

"Both."

"There's a shower. It's sonic, but it's not half bad. And there's not a stitch of extra clothing anywhere on this ship. So if you want to clean your current clothes, you won't have anything to wear while they dry."

I laughed. "I'm not sure I'd call that really good news," I said, but then my eyes snagged on him. He lounged in bed naked, with just a sheet slung low around his hips and all those glorious muscles on display. "Never mind," I murmured, "I see the appeal."

"If you want a shower now, you have five seconds to leave this room," he playfully growled at me. "Otherwise I'm dragging you back into bed."

I grabbed my pants and fled.

I RUSHED THROUGH THE SHOWER, NERVOUS ANTICIPA-tion fluttering in my belly. Once I was clean, I put my clothes in the circular shower stall and started a clothes cycle. Sonic showers used a light mist of cleaning fluid instead of gallons and gallons of water, so realistically, my clothes would be damp but wearable as soon as the cycle completed.

Fear gave me pause. Maybe I *should* wait for the cycle to complete. I stared in the mirror, trying to see myself from Ian's point of view. I was petite and too thin. I looked like what I was—someone who had been sick for a long time and who was just now starting to recover. I'd lost over fifteen kilograms and only in the last two months had I gained any back.

What if Ian saw only the sickness and not the strength?

I shook my head. Now I was just letting fear rule me. And procrastinating. I opened the door, determined.

Only to nearly run into Ian. His hot gaze made it to my breasts before he snapped his eyes closed and blew out a breath. He blindly held out a sheet. "I brought you this, in case you were uncomfortable. I should've sent it with you earlier. I wasn't thinking."

I stepped around the proffered sheet and ran my hands across his bare chest. "If you had taken that sheet off earlier, I never would've made it out of the room."

He looked down at me, doing an admirable job of keeping his eyes glued to my face. "Are you sure, Bianca? I don't want to rush you."

"I'm sure." I stepped close enough that his hardening length pressed against my belly and my breasts pressed against his chest. I ducked my head and gave him another truth. "It's been a while, and you're not small, so . . ." I trailed off.

Ian made a deep sound in his chest. "Are you going to fuss at me if I pick you up?"

"Are you truly healed?" I asked. He nodded. "Then I won't fuss. Not that I ever *fuss*."

He grinned and grabbed my ass. He lifted me easily. I

hooked my legs around his waist for balance. I shivered as his length pressed against my clit.

He slid me up a few centimeters, his eyes going heavy lidded. I glided easily against him. I wanted him enough that he could probably pull back and thrust home without any difficulty, despite my recent celibacy. I squirmed, angling for just that outcome, but Ian clamped his arm around my waist, pinning me in place.

"Now who's rushing?" he asked. He carried me to the bed and lowered me onto my back. He followed me down, his hips wedged between my legs. So close.

Then his lips were on mine and my thoughts scattered. I slid my tongue into his mouth only to pull back with a gasp when his fingers closed around my nipple. I arched into his touch. "Yes," I hissed.

He trailed kisses down to my other nipple before giving it a teasing lick. I buried a hand in his hair and pulled him closer. He groaned and drew the tight bud into his mouth.

I made a noise that was half moan, half whine. I arched again, trying to get him inside me. He chuckled against my skin and slid down farther. Now I did whine, until I caught the intent in his eyes. My breath hitched as he knelt beside the bed and angled my body toward him.

His first touch was tentative, reverent. A whisper-soft glide of one finger over my clit. My hips jerked, chasing the feeling. Ian smiled, a true, blinding expression of joy, before it gained a wicked edge. He pressed his other hand against my hip, holding me still.

Another touch, as light as the first. "Ian," I gasped, straining toward him, "you're killing me."

"It'll be a glorious death," he promised. Then he bent his head and fastened his mouth around my clit. His lips and tongue stroked me and it was indeed glorious. He pressed two fingers inside, a slow thrust that caused my whole body to clench in need.

I was so close.

When I pinched my own nipples, desperate to fall over the edge, Ian groaned against me and that was all it took. Pleasure exploded, bowing my back and stealing my breath.

After I recovered, Ian crawled up my body, his intent clear, but I decided he'd been in charge long enough. I flipped our positions—only because Ian allowed himself to be rolled. Now he was laid out below me like a feast.

I started with his luscious mouth and then moved south. I laved one flat nipple into a hard point with my tongue while I gently pinched the other. He made a low sound of pleasure that thrummed through me.

I continued down, kissing my way across his washboard abs. I stopped every so often to lick and nibble. His hands clenched. "Bianca," he said tightly, "please."

I bypassed the place he wanted me most and pressed a delicate kiss to his inner thigh. He made a deep sound of dissatisfaction. I took pity on him and wrapped my fingers around his length. His body went taut and he stopped breathing.

The first stroke was a light caress, designed to tease and tempt. He was almost too beautiful for me to believe this was real. All tanned skin and rippling muscles. Even his cock was perfection, long and thick. When he shot me a desperate look, I took pity on him.

I worked him with lips, tongue, and hands until his body vibrated with tension. He gasped my name. Then he pulled me up and kissed me deeply. His eyes were twilight blue, dark with desire. "There are no condoms," he said softly. "We both have nanos, but are you protected?"

Nanobots protected from disease, but they didn't protect from pregnancy. "I have an implant," I told him. "I'm protected."

"Thank fuck," he growled. He flipped us over and pressed against me. "Are you ready?"

"Yes, now," I demanded. I ached to be filled.

He nudged forward and we both hissed in pleasure. "Let me know if I need to slow down," he said tightly, the muscles in his neck standing out.

"You need to speed up!" I wrapped my legs around his hips and tried to pull him closer.

"Bianca," he growled. But still he resisted, barely moving. Why had I mentioned it'd been a while? I'd be dead before he decided I was ready.

Deciding to take matters into my own hands, I pulled myself up until my mouth was next to his ear. "Fuck me, Ian," I whispered. "Fill me with your cock."

He shuddered and his hips snapped forward, driving him a few centimeters deeper before he caught himself. My eyes crossed in pleasure. I skated on the edge of orgasm.

"I don't want to hurt you," he gritted out, all honor and anguish.

"You feel amazing. You're not hurting me, except by holding back. Let go, Ian."

He searched my eyes for several long moments before thrusting in to the hilt with a deep rumble of pleasure.

I sucked in a breath. He felt better than amazing. Nothing had ever felt this good. I teetered on the brink, wanting to fall over, wanting to draw it out. He pulled back, thrust again. And again. Wait, nothing had ever felt *this* good. It was only when he chuckled that I realized I'd said it out loud.

Ian sucked my nipple into his mouth and bit lightly. The

tiny, sweet pain seemed tied directly to my clit as pleasure zinged between the two. "Again!" I demanded. I felt his smile against my breast before he complied.

I sailed into orgasm groaning his name. His thrusts turned harder, more demanding, before becoming erratic as he, too, tipped into bliss. He collapsed beside me. We both panted like we'd run a marathon.

"That was . . ." I trailed off, trying to come up with an appropriate adjective. Glorious, amazing, and magnificent all fell short. "Mind-blowing," I decided.

"Yes, it was. You've killed me."

"Was it a glorious death?" I asked with a smile.

His answering smile was tender. "Very."

FOR TWO DAYS WE ATE, SLEPT, FUCKED, AND TRIED TO fill the hours of the day. I taught Ian the rest of the kata we'd started in his ship. He taught me more breathing and meditation exercises I could use for pain management. He built me up rather than tearing me down, and the contrast to my time with Gregory could not be clearer. I felt calmer, more centered, and more confident than I had in years.

Over food, we discussed a wide range of topics, but we were careful to not discuss the future. I didn't know why Ian didn't bring it up, but I avoided it because I'd half convinced myself that this was some sort of fever dream I'd wake from at any moment.

Even so, I was blissfully happy.

We were in the lounge, sipping after-dinner coffee and pretending we weren't watching the clock when the five-minute jump alert went off. "I need to get to the flight deck," I said. "If I don't start talking as soon as we jump, Benedict is likely to do something unfortunate." Like blow us up.

Ian stopped me before I would've dashed away. "Do you regret this?" he asked. He waved a hand between us, in case his question hadn't been clear. His expression was guarded.

"No!" I hesitated, then steeled my spine. "Do you?"

He shook his head. "You're the best thing that's ever happened to me. But you're a von Hasenberg and I'm an orphan from nowhere who's been genetically modified. You could do so much better. Once you return to Serenity, you'll see that."

This was an important conversation that needed more than five minutes. Still, I had to try or I'd lose him forever. "Ian, I let my husband burn to death. I'm a walking science experiment gone wrong. Being a von Hasenberg has more downsides than you might think. *You* can do far better than *me*. I'm terrified that you'll realize it at any minute and then leave me bereft."

He leaned his forehead against mine. "We're perfect for each other," he said, but it sounded like a question.

"We're perfect for each other," I said firmly, so there was no question. "I won't let you go without a fight, just so you know. And I fight dirty."

He rubbed his nose against mine. "I like you dirty."

"Good, because you're stuck with me," I said. "Now let's go prevent Benedict from shooting at us. I don't think this flying garbage bin can take it."

I slid into the captain's chair just as the engine noise changed. As before, it took longer than I expected before we jumped. I knew we'd made it when the ship intoned, "Incoming communication."

I accepted the communication on my console.

A young man appeared on screen in a von Hasenberg uniform. "This is *Transcendence*. State your—"

I interrupted him. "I'm Lady Bianca von Hasenberg, here to see my brother. Put Benedict on the line."

He blinked and squinted at me through the camera, then his eyes widened. "Right away, my lady." He gestured frantically at someone offscreen.

It took another thirty seconds before the video changed and Benedict appeared. "Bianca?" he asked. His light brown hair was rumpled, like he'd been running his hands through it, and he wasn't in his uniform jacket. It was half past nine, so he was likely off duty already.

"Yes. Did Ferdinand make it? And the others?" I wasn't sure what names they'd be using, so I didn't name them.

"Nice hair," he said. I touched my darkened locks. I forgot I didn't look like myself. He continued, "Yes, all three of them are here. What took you so long?"

"I'm in a planet hopper. Took two jumps."

Benedict grimaced in sympathy. "Park it in landing bay four until we can dispose of it. Port side, second bay."

I rolled my eyes at him. "I remember," I said. "And before I forget, I have Director Bishop onboard. He'll be bunking with me."

Benedict's eyebrows rose. He gave me a look that said we would definitely be revisiting this conversation later, but all he said was, "I'll meet you in the landing bay. Flight control will guide you in." He paused. "It's good to see you, Bianca."

"You, too, Benedict. You, too."

Benedict disconnected the call. I peeked at Ian to gauge his reaction to my declaration. We hadn't really talked about whether or not we were going public with our relationship, but I refused to hide him like a dirty secret. If that was going to be a problem, better to find out now. Benedict wouldn't rat me out. Well, he wouldn't rat me out to Father. The sibling gossip network was another matter entirely.

Ian met my eyes. "You told him." His neutral tone didn't give me any hint of what he was feeling.

"Yes. Should I not have?" Doubts crowded in. I wasn't ashamed of him, but maybe the opposite wasn't true. Perhaps he would've preferred to keep me a secret. I glanced away. "I can tell him to keep it to himself if you prefer."

Ian stood and closed the distance between us. He tipped my chin up. "What's going on in your head?"

I gave him the truth. I owed him that much. "I don't want you to be ashamed that people know we're together. If you're going to be, I can't do this. I just can't."

He knelt beside me, so we were eye to eye. "Bianca, you have no idea how fucking much I like and respect you. You are incredible. I am not ashamed of you and never will be. You just caught me off guard. We need to talk about what to do about Albrecht before he hears it from someone else, but I'm thrilled you claimed me to your brother."

I closed my eyes. Father was a concern I'd been trying to avoid thinking about. Ian was right, we needed a plan, or Albrecht would roll right over us and do precisely what worked best for him.

"We'll figure it out," I promised.

The ship chimed to indicate we'd received a flight plan from *Transcendence*. Once I checked and approved it, the autopilot took over. We'd been given priority, so ten minutes later our little planet hopper settled in the middle of landing bay four, next to Ian's ship. The area was suspiciously clear of soldiers. Had Benedict ordered them away?

By the time we lowered the cargo ramp, Benedict was waiting. I rushed to hug him. He squeezed me tight. My twin had stolen all the height I was missing, so when he hugged me and leaned back, my feet left the floor.

"You scared me to death," he murmured in my ear. "When Ferdinand arrived and I heard what happened, I feared the worst."

"I'm sorry I worried you. Have you told Father that Ferdinand is found?"

"No. I figured you had some grand plan."

I squeezed him tighter, this brother who knew me so well. "Thanks."

Benedict let me go and turned to Ian, his expression cold. "Director Bishop."

Ian inclined his head. "Lord Benedict."

I'd had to cut Ian's pants off while I was trying to save him. We'd managed to sew and tape them back into some semblance of decent, but his shirt had been a lost cause. If confronting my brother while underdressed made Ian uneasy, you'd never know it from his tone.

"What are your designs on my sister?"

I groaned and rolled my eyes. "Benedict, could you not?"

"She's mine," Ian said simply. "And I'm hers. I intend to cherish and protect her for as long as she'll let me."

"Seems like you'll have your work cut out for you," Benedict muttered. I elbowed him in the side. "Ow! You arrived in a Rockhurst ship after breaking into a Rockhurst military compound. While we are *at war*. You have no reason to elbow me!"

"Respect your elders," I said with a grin.

Benedict huffed out a breath. "Oh, right. I forgot that extra thirteen minutes makes you a paragon of wisdom."

"Of course it does." I sobered and changed the subject. "How is Ferdinand?"

Benedict's eyes darkened. "We healed what we could and got him fitted with a subvocal microphone and speaker so he can communicate audibly. The ship's doctors can't do anything for his tongue. They said it's possible a lab in Serenity could regrow it from stem cells and reattach it, but it would be a brutal surgery and recovery with a low chance of success."

"Fuck."

"Pretty much." Benedict sighed. "We're keeping his presence under wraps. Yours, too. I trust my troops, but we *are* at war and sitting within jump distance of Richard's battle cruiser. Ian's ship is ready to jump. I told Ferdinand and the others to meet me here in ten minutes if I didn't send them a message."

"So soon?" I asked, stunned.

"It's not safe, Bianca," he said gently. "You know that. I would've had them come with me, but I wasn't sure if you needed medical aid first. I have doctors waiting in the hall."

"How close are you to getting the temporary gate up?"

Benedict laughed. "Not close enough. It'll be another three weeks, at least. Ian's mercs explained that you planned to use my emergency jump point. Clever. Dangerous, but clever."

"So have we really lost the Antlia gate to Rockhurst?"

Benedict's jaw firmed. "For now. But Rockhurst doesn't have the firepower to hold it. We'll see how they like it when the tables are turned."

"Don't get in trouble with RCDF," I warned.

"If they would do their fucking job, I wouldn't have to waste ships to secure something that should be neutral."

"I'll make some inquiries when I get home. I'll jump a com drone to you and let you know what I find. Be careful."

The hatch between the landing bay and the rest of the ship opened, revealing Ferdinand, Alex, and Aoife. All three moved easily. Ferdinand showed no hint of the leg injury he'd sported. But he still looked strange with his shorn hair.

Alex and Aoife nodded at us and headed straight for the ship. When Ferdinand reached us, I tilted my head for a cheek kiss and he obliged. Ferdinand was the most reserved of all of my siblings—he hadn't had anyone to protect him from our parents.

"Thank you, Bianca," he said, his voice computer generated. "Remind me to yell at you later for being so stupid." His gaze flicked to Ian, ice cold and sharp enough to cut. "I will speak to you, too, Director Bishop."

"Leave Ian alone. He was trying to protect me, and you know it's an impossible task. Don't make me hug you, brother. I'll do it. You know I always get my way when I hug you—it's my superpower." My voice had picked up a wobble that I couldn't quite hide.

Some of the ice melted from Ferdinand's eyes and his expression softened. He opened his arms and I didn't wait for a second invitation. I locked my arms around him while he awkwardly patted my back.

"I was so worried," I confessed to his chest. "Then when we found you in that pit." I shook my head. "I should've killed Riccardo when I had the chance."

A shocked silence fell. Ferdinand held me out at arm's length. "Bianca," he said slowly, "please don't tell me you spoke to Riccardo Silva in person."

"Okay," I agreed. I stepped back and gave them my most innocent expression, all wide eyes and sweet smile. I must've overdone it because Benedict and Ferdinand shared a look and groaned in unison.

"She totally did," Benedict said. Ferdinand nodded in agreement. Benedict gave Ian a sympathetic look. "Good luck, buddy."

Ferdinand frowned but didn't comment.

Benedict pulled me into another hug. "Stay out of trouble. Send me a message when you get home so I won't worry. We have com drones running twice a day until we can get the gate up."

"I will. Be careful. Don't do anything stupid until we get this war stopped. I expect you to return in one piece."

He nodded and let me go. "Safe travels."

I prayed this wouldn't be the last time I saw my brother.

# CHAPTER 29

We jumped to *Trancendence*'s emergency location safely, without even a rogue asteroid to spice things up. Aoife put us on a course toward the nearby gate and away from the jump point. It was unlikely Benedict would need to immediately follow us, but better safe than sorry.

"Where do you want to go?" she asked Ian.

"APD Zero," I said. "I want to return Ferdinand to Earth in *Aurora*. The delay will be minimal, and the impact will be worth it."

Ian inclined his head in agreement. "Your father is going to be furious that I've been out of contact for nearly a week. I left Deputy Director Stevens in charge while I was gone. I am confident she's kept the ship afloat, but we'll see if she's been as successful in fending off Albrecht. I may be the universe's newest wanted man."

"You're too good at your job," I said. "Father won't let you go so easily. He'll rightly blame me."

"We have six hours until we jump," Aoife said. "I'm going to get some shut-eye since we have to be up early." She glanced at Ian. "How are we bunking?"

"Ferdinand and Alex in the crew bunk. You'll have to bed down in the exercise room."

She nodded and she and Alex left the flight deck.

"And where will Bianca sleep?" Ferdinand asked. The computer-generated voice might not have much emotional inflection, but Ferdinand's expression had no such trouble. He radiated hostility.

"I will sleep with Ian," I said. I met Ferdinand's glare head-on. I'd dealt with difficult men all my life, but I had an advantage here—Ferdinand wanted to see me happy. "You can support my decision or you can yell, but the outcome will remain the same," I said quietly, my voice edged in steel.

He looked away first. "I can't believe you have people convinced you're the timid one," he groused. "Everyone is wary of me, but they should be watching out for you."

That hadn't always been true, as evidenced by Gregory, but since his death, I'd done my damnedest to relearn how to stand up for myself. I smiled at Ferdinand, glad that he'd noticed. "A hidden dagger is far more effective."

"Father isn't going to like it."

"Father can bite me," I said. But I knew it was true. "I'm working on it. If I bring him you and the identity of your attackers as a fait accompli, he'll be more reasonable. I'm hoping Catarina made progress while I've been gone. Do you have any idea who might want you dead badly enough to hire the Syndicate? And I'm betting whoever it was also told them to take the hit out on me. So someone who knows I deal in information."

Ferdinand shook his head. "I don't have any big deals going. Nothing that someone might want to disrupt."

"Who benefits from your death? Any ex-lovers or other surprises in your will? What about Evelyn? Does her family know?"

Ferdinand's expression turned wary and his eyes flickered to Ian before returning to me. "What do you know about Evelyn?"

"I know about you and Evelyn," Ian said. "I'm the director of security; give me some credit."

I said, "You were supposed to meet her the night you were taken. I met with her the next day. She said you were together."

He blew out a breath. "We are. We're keeping it quiet because we know neither of our families would approve."

"She said House Rockhurst didn't order the attack, but if someone in the House was upset about your relationship they might think taking you out served two purposes."

"Maybe," he allowed. "But it wasn't Evelyn."

"I agree."

"Otherwise, all of my assets go to family. Hannah would be the one to gain the most by becoming heir, but we've talked. She doesn't want it because it would give her bastard husband more power. The rest of my personal assets are split among all of you."

"After you disappeared, Hannah told me she planned to abdicate." That put me next in line if anything happened to Ferdinand. "Please don't die," I told him seriously.

"I'm not planning on it." He gave Ian a hard stare. "You heard nothing about Hannah."

Ian nodded easily.

Ferdinand told us what he remembered of the capture and the captivity, but they'd kept him drugged and blindfolded, so it was precious little. He did tell us that they'd killed all of his bodyguards and jettisoned their bodies.

Poor Edward. The young man with the quick smile and easy laugh who'd been my bodyguard these last few months didn't deserve to die. And now his family would never have closure. I made a mental note to set up a fund for his sisters.

When Ferdinand started hinting he'd like some time alone, Ian and I retired to the captain's quarters. I couldn't shake the feeling that this wasn't a random hit. Someone had put thought, effort, and money into it. They had targeted me and Ferdinand but not Hannah, Benedict, or Catarina.

What was I missing?

I mulled it over as I got ready for bed. I used the cosmetics kit to return my hair to its usual light brown with blond and red highlights. I felt more like myself with my hair back to normal.

Ian reclined on the bed, clad in a pair of low-slung pajama pants and nothing else. He looked to be asleep, but when I paused to admire the view, one eye cracked open. "You changed your hair back."

"Yeah, I'm stuck on this attack problem so I thought I'd knock out another item on my to-do list while I thought about it."

Ian sighed and sat up. "We're missing something, and being out of contact for four days doesn't help."

I worked through the time line out loud. "I caught a tricky encrypted message of just the word 'Go.' I was attacked publicly and violently. Meanwhile, Ferdinand was snatched silently, without leaving a trace. The next morning, I met with Evelyn and then a few hours later, someone painted me as a traitor. Do we know who started that rumor?"

Ian shook his head. "I had people looking into where the traitor rumor came from, but I didn't follow up with them. Too much other stuff going on. You didn't tell me about the first message you'd caught."

"I didn't tell anyone."

I tapped my fingers against my lips and paced at the foot of the bed. Something about the original message had been important. I focused on how it had felt to unlock the encryption because my emotional memory tended to be more permanent than the thoughts themselves. Joy and pride and a fierce sense of accomplishment. Then confusion. I stopped midstride.

"The message that kicked off the attack was encrypted twice. The outer encryption I'd never seen before. But the inner encryption was standard von Hasenberg encryption."

Ian's gaze sharpened. "Someone connected to the House was involved. Why didn't you tell me this before?"

"At the time, there was no way to tell you without explaining how I knew. Then I had to run and it slipped my mind. The brain implant screws with my memory sometimes."

Ian spat out a low curse. "I failed to protect you, Bianca. I knew you were unhappy, but I never thought it was something like this." He met my eyes, expression solemn. "I am so fucking sorry."

I edged around the bed to where he was sitting and took his face in my hands. "It's not your fault. I don't blame you." He looked like he wanted to protest, so I bent my head and kissed him.

His mouth parted under mine with a groan. I licked into his mouth, and his hands clenched on my hips. He leaned back, pulling me with him, until he was flat on the bed and I was straddling him.

"You're wearing too many clothes," he growled.

"Trust me, I'm going to burn these clothes at the earliest opportunity." I was still wearing the too big fatigues I'd stolen from the mine guard. They'd gone a few cycles through the sonic wash, but I was happy to have my own clothes as an option again.

"So you won't mind if I do this?" He didn't wait for a response before he pulled the front of my shirt apart, sending buttons flying.

Lust warred with amusement. When he palmed my breasts, lust won.

**WHEN WE STARTED DOCKING AT THE SPACE STATION OR-** biting APD Zero, I called Ada. She didn't pick up, despite the fact that the early hour in Universal meant it was late afternoon in Sedition. I knew she'd be pissed that I'd left her behind, but I didn't expect her to dodge my calls. I hoped she was away rather than ignoring me.

I connected to the Net, brought up my usual security precautions, and checked my messages. I'd been offline for over four days, something that never happened. Ada had informed our siblings of what I was attempting in Antlia. Three days ago, Benedict had reported Ferdinand's arrival with a warning to keep it to themselves until I turned up.

After that, I'd received a series of increasingly worried messages from my siblings, until the final one from Ada yesterday morning that merely read: *ARE YOU DEAD?*

Benedict had sent a message late last night, assuring everyone I was alive and on my way home with Ferdinand. He told them to keep it quiet until I said otherwise. I posted the same and swore them all to secrecy about Ferdinand because I wanted to spring it on Father myself.

The messages from Catarina were the most interesting. She'd been digging into who had access to Ferdinand's schedule while I was "off having fun"—her words, not mine. Then she'd expanded her search into who had started the traitor rumor, with Deputy Director Stevens's help.

Three days ago, she'd found a suspect.

She wouldn't tell me who it was on an insecure connection, but yesterday they'd had enough to pull him in for questioning.

I tried to read between the lines, but she'd been careful and there were no hints. Was it someone on the security team? What would he gain? Revenge?

Ferdinand pulled me aside while Ian spoke to Aoife and Alex. "What aren't you telling me?"

"What do you mean?" I asked warily.

"I heard Aoife talking about how the Rockhurst battle cruiser was going to eat our lunch. There's only one Rockhurst in Antlia and he wouldn't let us get away for free. What did you do?"

"I said I was with the Syndicate and heavily implied that retaliation for my death would be swift and brutal."

"And Richard believed you?"

"He didn't shoot us down, did he?"

Ferdinand narrowed his eyes at me. "I taught you that trick, Bee. You won't distract me so easily. What did you do?"

I sighed. "I promised him a future favor."

"And of course he extracted it from the one person who will honor their word. *Fuck.*"

"I won't apologize for getting you out. I was prepared to do whatever it took. I will deal with the consequences when they arrive." Because I had no doubt that I would pay, it was just a matter of when and how much.

"Don't forget that you have support. You don't have to take on the world by yourself. The family will help you. And it seems like you're stuck with Director Bishop, too."

A soft smile pulled at my lips. I hoped I was stuck with Ian for a long time.

**THE TRANSFER TO** *AURORA* **WENT QUICKLY. WE LEFT** most of our gear behind. Aoife and Alex promised to keep an eye on *Phantom* until we could come back for it. I hugged both of them good-bye and made them promise to keep in touch.

I breathed out a sigh of relief to be back on my own ship. *Aurora* had made the trip from Brava without any trouble, but I had worried, like a mother worrying after a child left home for the first time.

The gate queue was fairly light, so the estimated wait time was only twenty minutes. I undocked from the station and moved away from trafficked space so we'd be ready to jump when we got the coordinates.

With *Aurora*'s von Hasenberg seal, we'd be able to jump in close to Earth. We'd be on the ground in about an hour. I started working on my game face. I had to play this just right or Father would ignore my wishes.

I sent Catarina a message, asking her to meet me in the primary hangar. I also asked her to bring new clothes for me and Ferdinand. I needed information before I made a move, and I needed to look like the daughter of a High House, not a merc.

Ian moved to my side and touched my shoulder. "We need to discuss how to deal with Albrecht," he said quietly. "Can we talk in your quarters?"

I nodded. "Ferdinand, keep an eye on things, please. I'll be back in a few."

"Take the time you need," he said. "I'll watch your ship."

I led Ian next door to my quarters. He smiled at the cyan walls in the sitting room. "It suits you," he said. I settled on the sofa and patted the spot next to me. He sat, then picked me up and tucked me sideways across his lap with his left arm providing a backrest. I rested my head on his shoulder and took a deep breath of the warm, clean scent of him.

"What will you tell Albrecht?" Ian asked.

"I will tell him we're together. I've done my duty for the House once. I won't do it again, which will likely derail his plans. Worst case, he'll disown me."

"That's a pretty fucking bad case," Ian said. "You can't—"

I shushed him. "I can do whatever I want. But I doubt it will come to that because Father knows how valuable my skills are. If he loses me, he loses my information. I would prefer to stay in the House because I need to keep an eye on Catarina, but I'm willing to give it up if it comes to that. You need to decide where the line is for you."

Ian thought about it for several long moments. I didn't rush him, though I dearly wanted to. He needed to decide what he was willing to risk to be with me because the last thing I wanted was for him to be unhappy.

"My job is important, not only to me, but to the rest of the squad," he said quietly. "As director of security, I have access to information that keeps them safe."

I fought hard not to tense up but I must not have been entirely successful because he ran a soothing hand down my side.

"That said, I think you could get most if not all of the information I rely on from your own network. If Albrecht bans you from the House, I will go with you."

"Ian, you don't have—"

"It's my choice," he said firmly. "I choose you. If it comes down to it, we'll go to APD Zero and annoy the hell out of Loch."

My smile had to be blinding, but I didn't care—*he chose me*. Hope and happiness blazed bright. Father didn't stand a chance against the two of us.

I pulled Ian's head down to mine and lost myself in a scorching kiss full of promises.

AFTER WE RETURNED TO THE FLIGHT DECK, THE TIME both flew and crawled. The three of us got our story straight with what we planned to tell Father. We decided to stick to the basics: Silva took Ferdinand. I had a contact with information who only dealt in person. Ian tracked me down, but then we had to stick together due to timing. We rescued Ferdinand after Silva sold him to MineCorp.

By the time we'd worked out all of the details and all of the things to avoid, *Aurora* was nearly on the ground. A few minutes later, we touched down in House von Hasenberg's primary hangar. The message was clear—I wasn't slinking home defeated, I was returning in a blaze of glory.

The cameras showed Catarina waiting in the wings with a large bag. So were a squad of House soldiers.

"I'll deal with them," Ian said quietly. "You change."

Ferdinand and I met Cat in the cargo bay and she ran to Ferdinand. She didn't wait for an invitation, she slammed into him and squeezed him tight. "I'm so happy you're okay!"

"I'm happy to see you, too, Cat," he said in his computer-generated voice.

She stepped back, shocked. "What happened?"

"Silva," he said.

Her eyes narrowed, but she didn't question him further. "I brought clothes."

We changed in the cargo bay. Cat had brought Ferdinand a charcoal suit with a white shirt. She'd brought me a deep sapphire sheath dress and strappy black heels. The dress was one of my mourning dresses, nearly black.

While we were getting dressed, Cat talked. "I've been working with Marta Stevens to track down a couple of leads. We didn't use the rest of the security team because she feared we had a high-level leak, but Marta is good. We did not expect both lines of inquiry to lead to the same person."

"Who was it?" Ferdinand and I asked at the same time.

"Pierre, Hannah's husband. He sang like a bird when Marta brought him in for questioning."

I froze in the middle of twisting my hair up. "What? He's a bastard, but he's married to a High House. Why would he risk it?"

"He's deep in gambling debt, like destroy-his-family's-House deep. He's burned through all of the money he got from the marriage and Hannah refuses to give him more. He had to take a loan from one of his mother's companies to hire Silva. It's unclear if she knew what the money was for. We're digging into it."

I pinned my hair in place, trying to understand his motivation. "What does he get if Ferdinand dies? Who holds his markers?"

"It's more what Hannah gets. She becomes heir, which puts her—and by extension, him—in charge of the vast resources of House von Hasenberg. House James has quietly been buying his markers through a series of shell companies. They have ties with Rockhurst, but they haven't declared war, and we haven't been able to find evidence that they're working together. Yet."

"What does House James want?" Ferdinand asked.

"Mineral rights in Antlia."

I snorted. "Good luck getting that one past Father. I'm sure he was just going to let Pierre sign away the very mineral we're going to war to claim."

Ferdinand shook his head. "Mineral rights agreements don't need Father's signature. As named heir, I can sign them. Hannah's husband could sign them and they would be legal if she were the named heir."

"Really?" I paused. "Wait, if I didn't know that, how did *he*?"

"Someone's feeding him information. Maybe House James,

maybe someone else. We haven't had time to track it down," Cat said.

I used the handheld cosmetics kit I had to apply light makeup. "Why attack me?" I finally asked.

"He knew you dealt in information and Silva needed cover. That dinner party that Hannah mentioned on the night of the attack? It was in the building across from House Chan. Pierre left a door unlocked for the shooter and sent the message when you appeared. We wouldn't have known any of that yet except he confessed. He thinks by cooperating and giving up his allies, he'll be exonerated."

Cat continued, "When the attack failed, Pierre seemingly panicked and tried to discredit you. That's ultimately how we found him. That and he was paying one of Ferdinand's bodyguards to send him Ferdinand's schedule."

I shook my head. Pierre had never been the brightest, but I'd thought he was smarter than this. "Is it possible he's a patsy?"

Catarina thought it over. "It's possible," she said at last. "He was definitely involved, but someone is manipulating him. House James was leaning on him, threatening all sorts of ruin. Perhaps someone was leaning on them. We don't know, yet."

"Where is Pierre now?"

"He's in 'protective custody.'" She made air quotes around the words. "He still seems to think he's going to walk. I managed to persuade Marta to wait for Director Bishop's return before going to Father."

"Does Hannah know?" I asked.

Catarina nodded. "I briefed her. We managed to snag Pierre quietly, but she deserved the truth. She certainly wasn't heartbroken, but she's beating herself up."

I knew exactly how she felt. Relief mixed with an equal

measure of guilt. Mine for letting Gregory die; hers for not seeing what Pierre was doing.

"How do you want to do this?" Ferdinand asked.

I closed my eyes, trying to process everything I'd just learned. We had enough to destroy Pierre, but we needed to know if his family was in on it, and if House James was in league with House Rockhurst. And if we had more leaks.

"We have to tell Father," I said. "He needs to know, and he's going to be furious with me, so giving him something else to focus on is a win. We need to see what else we can dig up on who was manipulating Pierre."

"Are you going to tell him I was in a Rockhurst mine?"

"Not if I can avoid it. I don't want to give him a reason to accelerate the conflict. I'm going to blame Silva and the Syndicate, with a hearty dash of MineCorp blame thrown in for good measure."

Ferdinand nodded. He looked grim and determined. The short hair made him look harder somehow, a stark contrast to the expensive suit.

"How do I look?" I asked.

"Fierce," Cat said.

I'd take fierce any day. Now it was time to live up to the description.

# CHAPTER 30

The soldiers had disappeared, but Ian was deep in conversation with a beautiful, statuesque woman. She had inky black hair and deep brown skin. I hadn't dealt with Deputy Director Marta Stevens much, but I got the impression that she was smart and driven.

Ian turned as we approached. "Did Lady Catarina bring you up to speed?" he asked.

I nodded and smiled in greeting at Marta. "It's nice to see you again, Deputy Director Stevens. Thank you for helping my sister."

She inclined her head. "I am glad you have safely returned, Lady Bianca. It was my pleasure to assist Lady Catarina." Her serious facade cracked into a grin. "You better keep an eye on her, though. She's too smart for her own good."

"She's too smart for all of our goods," I said and nudged Cat's shoulder. "I was hoping she wouldn't find out."

"Too late," Cat said. "That's what happens when you all run off on adventures and leave me behind to pick up the pieces."

Her tone was light, but there was a thread of seriousness underlying it. Marta's teasing comment could also be taken as a warning. I met the other woman's eyes and she nodded, very slightly.

I knew Catarina felt stifled on Earth. We'd tried to shelter her as much as possible from House business, which meant she hadn't had as many opportunities to get out and see the universe. I would need to change that or she would take matters into her own hands, for better or worse.

I turned my attention back to the upcoming meeting with my father. "Ferdinand and I are going to see Albrecht. I plan to recommend that we keep Pierre in custody and keep digging. Someone is manipulating him."

"I agree," Ian said. "I will go with you. He's demanded my presence as well. He's waiting in his study."

Of course he was. Very little got past Albrecht von Hasenberg. He hadn't ruled a High House for nearly twenty years by luck alone. He wasn't a figurehead; he *was* House von Hasenberg.

"Good luck," Cat said. "I'm definitely *not* going with you. But I'll find you later if you survive it." She kissed the air next to my cheek then disappeared with Marta.

Ferdinand, Ian, and I made the trek to Father's study. By now he must know that Ferdinand had returned, but still he let us come to him. I sank deeply into my public persona. Father wouldn't be won by emotion. Logic and facts would win the day.

The study door slid open as we approached. He was expecting us.

The room was ornately decorated with real wood paneling and heavy, carved furniture. It smelled faintly of cigar smoke and expensive alcohol. Father sat behind a massive wooden desk, watching us with a blank expression. Ian and Ferdinand bowed. I curtsied.

"Father," Ferdinand murmured.

At the sound of Ferdinand's voice, Albrecht's eyes narrowed. "Explain."

"The Syndicate removed my tongue."

"Can it be fixed?" Ferdinand didn't flinch at Father's cold tone, but I did.

"I don't know," Ferdinand said.

"Go see what the doctors can do for you," Albrecht said. "I will speak to you later."

Ferdinand bowed and left the room. Lucky man.

Albrecht moved his glare to Ian. "How did the Syndicate snatch my heir out from under your nose?"

"Ferdinand had three bodyguards with him. All three died defending him. The Syndicate had an inside spy. Pierre von Hasenberg fed them information. He seems to be working on behalf of House James. We have him in custody and he's confessed. We believe he is being manipulated, possibly by House James, possibly by someone else. We are still looking into it."

"I expect a full report on my desk by the end of the day. Dismissed."

Ian glanced at me and I inclined my head. His presence would likely make Father even more disagreeable than usual. He bowed and left.

Father and I stared at each other in silence. "My prodigal daughter returns," Albrecht said at last. "What do you have to say for yourself?"

"Did you really think I was a traitor?"

He scoffed. "Of course not. I've known about Ferdinand and Evelyn for months. I am not surprised you figured it out."

"Then why order me detained?"

He stared at me for long enough that I figured he wouldn't

answer, but I'd learned patience. I waited him out. "You needed a push."

I digested that nebulous statement. He could mean any number of things, but I decided to interpret it my own way. "It worked far better than you could've imagined," I said.

His eyebrows lifted, but I knew he wouldn't bother to ask, just as I wouldn't ask what he meant. We were two of a kind.

I let him wait for several long seconds before continuing, "Ian and I are dating."

Father laughed harshly. "No daughter of mine is going to date the help. Fuck him if you must, but be discreet."

"I'm going to marry him."

Red crept up Albrecht's cheeks as true anger kindled. "No, you will not. I already have a man for you."

"I've done my duty to the House. I will not marry for your pleasure again."

He slammed his hand on his desk. "You will do as you're told!"

"I will not," I said calmly. "You can disown me. Ian and I will move to APD Zero with Ada. You will lose your two best sources of intelligence. My siblings will revolt. You'll be fighting a war at home as well as in Antlia."

"Are you threatening me?" he asked, his voice a furious growl.

"No, Father. I am giving you a choice, something you never gave me. You *could* disown me, or you could give me, if not your blessing, then at least your acceptance. In return, you keep me here, working for the good of the House."

He leaned back in his chair, his gaze calculating.

"Lord Henderson will accept Catarina in your stead. She's the one he wanted in the first place, so he'll be pleased."

I kept my expression cool through sheer force of will. Lord Henderson was at least as old as Father and had a well-known penchant for young women. But House Henderson was one of the strongest lower houses, and he was careful to select women of legal age, so nothing came of it other than rumors and speculation.

"Do you care so little for your daughters?"

His face hardened. "We are at war. Alliances are few and far between. I will take what I can get. I ensured you can look out for yourselves. What more do you want?"

Love, care, decency. Any number of things, really, but I kept my mouth shut. Catarina would be getting her adventure sooner rather than later if Father continued down this path. I'd have to send her into hiding.

"If I agree to your little farce of a marriage, you will stay in Serenity for five years, working for House von Hasenberg. You will not interfere with Catarina's marriage. And if Director Bishop leaves you, I get to pick your next husband."

I wasn't sure if I should be insulted or amused. "No."

"No, what?"

"No to all of it. Don't insult me, Father. In return for leaving us alone, Ian and I will continue working for the House. I will come and go as I please, but I will spend the majority of my time in Serenity for the next year. If anything at all happens to Ian or his job, I will move to APD Zero before the news has hit the rumor mill. And I'll never again marry a man you choose, even if Ian publicly denounces me to the entire Consortium."

"Tread lightly, daughter. You are not irreplaceable. Three years," he said. When I inclined my head in agreement, he continued, "I'll have the contract drawn up."

"Save us both time and don't be a dick," I said.

Exasperation gleamed in his eyes for a brief second. "You are dismissed," he said.

I knew when to pick my battles, so I curtsied again and fled.

**WITH NOTHING ELSE THAT REQUIRED MY IMMEDIATE AT-** tention, I retreated to my suite. It wasn't until I was in the lightly shielded room that I realized the normal signal level in the House hadn't bothered me.

I stepped back into the hall. I could feel the signals, and if I concentrated, I could read them. That caused my head to ache. But when I stopped actively trying to listen in, the pain subsided. Had I used the ability so much that my body was adapting? Or, more worryingly, was I getting better at ignoring pain?

I returned to the suite and collapsed on the sofa. I would have liked to take a nap, but I needed to update my siblings. I sent a series of messages to our group channel. I laid out what we knew, what had happened, and how Father had reacted. I left out the information about Pierre until I could talk to Hannah directly.

I was staring at the ceiling, trying to decide if I'd forgotten anything when Catarina waltzed in, her nose in her com. "Well, you don't seem to be under house arrest, so that's good. I've scheduled breakfast with Hannah. She needs support and you need to be there."

I knew it was true, but I gave the sofa a longing glance before I allowed Catarina to pull me up.

**SOMEHOW, I MADE IT THROUGH THE DAY. HANNAH WAS** furious that she'd missed the signs of betrayal, but between us, Cat and I managed to persuade her that it wasn't her fault and murdering Pierre wasn't worth the prison sentence.

Breakfast was followed by lunch, then an afternoon tea, then dinner. Hannah and Cat both declared I needed to see and be seen with the full support of the House to squash any remaining rumors.

By the time I pleaded a headache, it wasn't even a lie. My head throbbed. It wasn't nearly as bad as it had been, but I wasn't miraculously cured. The improvement gave me hope, at least.

I'd messaged Ian a few times throughout the day, just to check in and ensure Father hadn't done something terrible, but after spending a week with him constantly around, the change jarred. I missed him.

When I arrived at my suite, I went straight for my bedroom. The bed sang a siren song of wireless protection and horizontal comfort.

It took me a few seconds to realize it was already occupied.

I had a blaster in hand before I recognized Ian. I huffed out a breath and ordered my heart back into my chest. "You could've warned me."

"Sorry, wasn't thinking," he murmured sleepily. "Your bed ambushed me."

I smiled at him. "It does that. Are you going to explain how you got into my suite?"

He propped his head up on his arm. His hair was back to its usual dark blond and he'd shaved. He'd left his suit jacket and tie draped over the chair in the corner. His crisp white shirt was open at the collar. He looked so delicious I almost missed his reply.

"Nope," he said.

"I'll figure it out," I warned.

"I have no doubt. You're going to force me to become sneakier."

I kicked off my heels and crawled into bed beside him. I closed the curtain behind me and blissful silence fell. I sighed in relief.

"The curtains block the signals?" Ian asked. He rolled me onto my stomach and massaged the tense muscles in my neck and upper back.

I hummed my agreement, then melted as his fingers worked their magic. I'd only give him a year or twelve to stop.

"I talked to Albrecht," Ian said, ruining all of the relaxation I'd achieved.

I rolled over to face him. "And?"

"He offered me a million credits to leave today and never contact you again."

It was a fortune several times over. With a million credits wisely invested, he could easily become a new lower house in the Consortium. I was actually kind of shocked that Father thought I was worth so much. "You declined?"

"I declined," he agreed.

"What did he do?"

"Yelled and threatened, mostly. Told me I'd never get my hands on any of House von Hasenberg's money, even if I married you. But it seems like I still have a job, for now. What about you, how did it go?"

"As well as can be expected. I'm not disowned, at least not yet. We'll see after I read the contract he's sending over."

He frowned. "What did you agree to?"

"I'm pretty sure I agreed not to start a civil war in the House." When he didn't smile, I told him about the negotiations.

"That seems suspiciously reasonable," Ian concluded. "He probably thought he could convince me to take the money and run."

"Yes, and now that you didn't, I'm assuming the contract will be a real piece of work."

"Are you sure I'm worth it?" he asked. "It would be so much—"

"I'm sure. Don't freak out, but the reason Father brought up marriage is because I told him that I'm marrying you. One day. If you'll have me. In the future, I mean. If you ask me."

Ian looked stunned. I clamped my mouth shut before I could make it worse. I closed my eyes. My cheeks burned. Perhaps I would die from embarrassment and save myself from having to live through the next few minutes.

"Yes."

I warily cracked one eye open. "Yes, what?"

Ian's face lit up. "Yes, I'll marry you."

Pure joy made me return his smile, even as I protested, "That wasn't a proposal! It was a warning!"

His smile morphed into a grin. "I accept your warning," he said solemnly.

I rolled him onto his back and straddled his hips. This dress was not designed for straddling people—the skirt rode indecently high, but Ian didn't seem to mind. His smoothed his hands down my back and over my butt before pulling me closer.

"Did I tell you that you look amazing in this dress?" he asked. "Because you look amazing."

"Flattery will get you everywhere," I murmured. I leaned down and pressed a kiss to the smooth skin of his jaw. He buried a hand in my hair and pulled my mouth to his.

I shivered as his tongue slid against mine. The kiss was a slow seduction, stoking desire until it threatened to burn us down. I pulled back with a gasp. "Take your clothes off," I ordered.

Ian's eyes laughed at me, but he unbuttoned his shirt. I helped by pressing kisses against the skin he exposed.

He sat up with a growl. "My turn."

He made short work of my clothes, though I did have to stand to get the dress off. While I was doing that, he removed his pants, so when I climbed back into bed, he was laid out like a feast before me.

When I took too long admiring him, he reached for me

and pulled me on top of him. His lips closed around my nipple. Pleasure slammed through me. I moaned low and arched into him, rubbing against his length. I wanted him, needed this connection.

I sat up and lifted my hips. He fisted his cock, rubbing it against me. Stars exploded behind my eyes when he hit my clit. He must've seen the expression on my face because he did it again before holding steady.

I had meant to take this slow, but desire drove me now. I moved his hand to my breast and slammed my hips down, taking him deep in one smooth movement. I hissed in pleasure. I would never get tired of the delicious stretch of him.

He sat up, changing the angle of penetration and rubbing against my clit. "Yes," I moaned. I kissed him, a battle of tongues and lips where we both came out victors.

Then I shifted, lifting and dropping along the delicious length of him. We found the rhythm and chased bliss. His thumb pressed against my clit just as he thrust home and I tipped over the edge. Pleasure exploded outward, sending my heart flying.

"Fuck," he groaned. "You feel incredible." He rolled us, pressing me into the bed. His thrusts gained a desperate edge that pushed me higher before he, too, fell over the edge.

He collapsed against me, a heavy weight that I wouldn't move for the world. In a moment of brilliant clarity, I knew I loved Ian Bishop to the bottom of my soul. The realization shook me, so I desperately latched on to anything to change the subject.

"How do you feel about a trip to Pluto?" I asked, then closed my eyes. *Of all the inane . . .*

"Bianca," Ian groaned, "we just survived one hellhole and you're ready to jump into another one?"

"I promised Yuko I'd rescue her daughter, and a promise is a promise," I said. "Plus, you know you love me."

I said it lightly, teasingly, a reminder to myself that I needed to back off, but he raised his head. His expression turned solemn. "I do love you," he said softly. "I've loved you for years. I know it's too soon, but I was serious earlier. I will marry you one day if you'll have me. You're the one for me."

Happy tears flooded my eyes. "Me, too," I whispered, working up the courage to say the words. "We're perfect for each other. I love you." I felt lighter and happier than I ever had before. All of the problems we still needed to tackle seemed insignificant in comparison. As long as Ian and I were together, we could do anything.

Ian kissed me, deep and slow, then spent the rest of the night showing me just how amazing our future was going to be.

ALEXANDER AND
CATARINA'S
INTREPID TALE
BRINGS THE
CONSORTIUM
REBELLION TRILOGY
TO A STUNNING
CONCLUSION
ARRIVING ON EARTH
MAY 2020

# ABOUT THE AUTHOR

Jessie Mihalik has a degree in computer science and a love of all things geeky. A software engineer by trade, Jessie now writes full time from her home in Texas. When she's not writing, she can be found playing co-op video games with her husband, trying out new board games, or reading books pulled from her overflowing bookshelves.